Crime Ink:
Iconic

An Anthology of Crime Fiction Inspired by Queer Icons

EDITED BY

JOHN COPENHAVER AND SALEM WEST

2025

Advance Praise for Crime Ink: Iconic

"*Crime Ink: Iconic* is a dazzling showcase of what happens when marginalized voices take center stage. Inspired by queer icons and spanning every corner of the genre, these emotionally rich, razor-sharp stories prove that LGBTQIA+ writers don't just belong in crime fiction—they're redefining it. A must-read for anyone hungry for fresh voices and fearless storytelling."

—Jess Lourey, Edgar-nominated author of *The Taken Ones*

"*Crime Ink: Iconic* isn't just a thrilling collection of crime fiction from some of the best writers working today, it's a necessary work of art that brings us closer to a world that still believes in hope."

—S.A. Cosby, bestselling author of *King of Ashes*

"The mystery genre has attracted queer writers for decades because its protagonists are outsiders, reviled by the respectable world, but embodying all the virtues that world pretends to value but seldom demonstrates, a situation that precisely describes the LGBTQ+ community. This landmark anthology presents some of the best contemporary queer crime fiction writers and shows the tradition is still going strong and is in better hands than ever."

—Michael Nava, seven-time Lambda Literary Award-winning author of the Henry Rios Mysteries

"The marvelous thing about an anthology is the variety of stories that promise to satisfy an equally diverse readership. And with the quality of stories this high, it's hard to imagine a more fitting tribute to the queer icons honored across the collection."

—Rob Osler, *USA Today* bestselling author of *The Case of the Missing Maid*

"An anthology filled with standouts both cutting and camp, *Crime Ink: Iconic* helps to popularize the world of crime fiction not just with more great stories, but more great stories about us."

—Lev AC Rosen, acclaimed author of the Evander Mills series

"*Crime Ink: Iconic* is a who's who of crime fiction and a snapshot of this moment, where LGBTQ+ crime fiction writers are receiving some (not nearly enough!) of their hard-fought due. An inspiring project and thrilling read."

—Lori Rader-Day, award-winning author of *Wreck Your Heart*

"An anthology of queer crime stories by queer crime writers is long overdue. Each author's creative approach to incorporating their icon has resulted in a collection as diverse as our community. *Crime Ink: Iconic* is a jewel-toned assortment of chocolates—delicious, delightful, and deadly. I devoured it."

—Joshua Moehling, *USA Today* bestselling author
of the Ben Packard series

"Vivid, wildly entertaining and pulsating with feeling, *Crime Ink: Iconic* is a treasure chest of stories by some of the brightest lights in the genre. An indispensable and long overdue contribution to the genre."

—Megan Abbott, award-winning author of *El Dorado Drive*

"Fast-paced fun! I devoured this anthology, eagerly flipping t hrough each captivating story. What a compelling short-story collection from a diverse group of voices, offering an exhilarating tribute to queer history."

—Lisa Gardner, #1 *New York Times* bestselling author
of *Kiss Her wGoodbye*

"From Marlene Dietrich to James Baldwin to Elton John, queer icons inspire and inform crime writers across a stunning array of storytelling shapes and styles—from witty whodunits to dark noir and through the diverse spectrum of modes and moods in between. The concept is fabulous, the stories themselves even better."

—Art Taylor, Edgar Award-winning author
of *The Adventure of the Castle Thief*

"It's a delight to report that *Crime Ink: Iconic* is a delicious serving of dark, bite-sized yarns, spun by some of today's most talented LGBTQ+ fiction writers. At this moment in history, the queer population is once again being cast as outlaws. So what genre could be more perfect than an anthology of crime stories written by the very group being targeted?"

—Allan Neuwirth, associate producer of *Call Me By Your Name*
and co-creator of the Lambda Literary Award-nominated
classic queer comic strip "Chelsea Boys"

TABLE OF CONTENTS

A NOTE FROM THE EDITORS
SALEM WEST AND JOHN COPENHAVER

In 2023, Jeffrey Marks conducted a study for Queer Crime Writers examining 517 stories across thirty crime fiction anthologies. Fewer than one percent of those stories was written by LGBTQ+ authors—a stark reminder of how underrepresented queer voices remain in the genre. The goal of this annual study is to push mainstream anthologies toward greater inclusivity. More broadly, Queer Crime Writers continues to advocate for expanding queer representation in traditional publishing—not confined to the LGBTQIA+ "ghetto," but reaching readers of all identities and backgrounds.

And change is happening. In 2024, four of the ten *New York Times* Best Crime Novels were written by queer authors—all of whom are featured in this anthology.

That's worth celebrating. But in a time of escalating political hostility, censorship, and rampant book bans aimed at erasing queer narratives, we felt an urgent need to carve out a space that showcases the richness, range, and sheer inventiveness of queer crime fiction.

From that need, *Crime Ink: Iconic* was born—the first in what we hope will become a series, each installment inspired by a different theme. For our debut, we chose queer icons. Why? Because queer icons often serve as sources of inspiration, solidarity, and creative fire for our writers. These figures—whether from history, pop culture, activism, or the arts—embody resistance, complexity, and unapologetic self-expression. They aren't always queer themselves, but they awaken something deep within us, energizing our storytelling and connecting us to the long, vibrant history of queerness in literature.

While queer icons unite this anthology, the stories within it reflect a stunning diversity—of voice, identity, experience, and subgenre. Our contributors include long-celebrated authors like Ann Aptaker, Katherine V. Forrest, Greg Herren, Ann McMan, Penny Mickelbury, J.M. Redmann, and Jeffrey Round, as well writers garnering national attention such as Christopher Bollen, Katrina Carrasco, Margot Douaihy, Christa Faust, Cheryl Head, Mia P. Manansala, and many notable others. Together, they offer a wide-ranging sampler of LGBTQIA+ crime fiction: hard-boiled, PI, amateur sleuth, noir, police procedural, legal thriller, psychological suspense, historical, cozy, domestic, puzzle mystery—even speculative crossovers.

Settings span time and space—from New Orleans to New York City, rural Maine to 1950s Los Angeles, 1920s London to deep space. Some stories lean into forensic precision; others are lyrical, metaphor-rich explorations of the criminal psyche.

And there are deeper threads, too. In a time marked by fear, uncertainty, and a rising tide of transphobia and misogyny, some stories are infused with righteous anger and despair. But just as many are rooted in hope, resilience, and quiet determination. Some narratives follow characters grappling with questions of agency; others simply center queer lives—solving crimes, navigating relationships, and existing unapologetically.

As you make your way through this collection, we hope the stories resonate—whether you identify as part of the LGBTQIA+ community or not. We hope you find insight, thrills, and catharsis. Above all, we hope you are entertained and moved by the power of queer crime writing. Because queerness is not a monolith—but it *is* singular. And from that singularity comes some of the most dynamic storytelling in the genre today.

FOREWORD

ELLEN HART

The saying, "May you live in interesting times" was once thought to be a Chinese blessing, of course, understood ironically. Turns out, it's a Western idea. But no matter who came up with it, there's no denying that we are living in "interesting" times.

When I started my career as a mystery author more than thirty years ago, it wasn't easy to get out and promote my books to audiences that would appear decidedly itchy if not overtly uncomfortable when I explained that my main character was a lesbian. In those early days for me, people would often come up after a talk or a panel discussion to offer a comment, and while we were talking, they would appear to have difficulty even touching the books I had for sale.

Happily, that changed significantly over the years. I believed we were making progress. But social mores, as we've all discovered, don't only move in a positive direction. Perhaps Martin Luther King was right. The arc of the moral universe does bend toward justice. But in my lifetime, at least at the moment, it looks as if it's moving in the opposite direction.

I've always felt that the mystery, as a genre, was perfectly positioned for queer writers. It's a familiar bridge over which readers of all stripes could move to a more nuanced understanding of our lives. I've received many letters thanking me for writing the kind of book that could be given to a parent or friend, something that wasn't scary or difficult, but that helped open up a dialogue. Mysteries are a perennially popular genre, second only to romance novels in sales. As long as the writer provides a compelling read, just about any subject can be explored. I'm sure my sleuth's sexuality put some people off, but I'm also sure that for those who gave the books a chance, an important understanding began to develop.

The famous British author, P.D. James, once pointed out that the crime novel was positioned squarely within the moral universe. That's one of the main reasons so many people are drawn to it. When you couple the exploration of moral and ethical dilemmas with mystery—the quality in any piece of fiction that drives us to read on to find out what happens, or simply what happens next—you have the key to the mystery's popularity. That's what makes LGBTQ+ mysteries so essentially and deliciously subversive.

Humans need stories. We eat them. We breathe them. We test ourselves against them. We find them in movies, on TV, in magazine articles, in everyday gossip, and in novels and short stories. Stories are essential. As much as we want to understand other people lives, their actions and motives, we also want to see our own lives reflected in literature. And yes, mysteries can be literature with a capital L. Genre status is an artificial hierarchy. You can find great books across the spectrum. To say that LGBTQ+ voices have been wildly underrepresented in published literature is to state the obvious. And that brings me to this anthology.

What you hold in your hands is the culmination of an important effort to redress that lack. The short pieces of fiction assembled herein are written by new voices as well as some our best, award-winning mystery authors. It's my hope that you will delight in these tales and that you will pass them on to family and friends as a way to build those vital, life-affirming bridges during a time when so many want nothing more than to blow them up.

CRIME INK:
ICONIC

HOLLYWOOD PROMETHEUS
CHRISTA FAUST

Los Angeles
1952

"Are you married, Mr. Cole?"

I was not married. I was also not Mr. Cole, but I'll get to that in a minute.

First, some relevant details about the questioner, a Mr. James Whale. A British man with a Hollywood tan. Early sixties. Six feet. Full head of white hair and dark, haunted eyes. Large hands with long expressive fingers toying restlessly with a French cigarette. Well-dressed, clean shoes. A once famous man, now less so, but still far more so than I.

My usual tactic when asked that particular question was to fall back on a self-deprecating comment about my profession. After all, the science of the dead holds little appeal for marriage-minded ladies. But when Whale asked me that question, he made it quite clear that he was asking an entirely different question. One that made my palms sweat and my heart race like a whipped horse. One that I could not possibly answer.

It was difficult not to flinch from the filmmaker's gaze as he analyzed the angles of my face and body, perceiving me relentlessly and without mercy. Placing me into a narrative context of his own creation just as he would have positioned an actor within the camera's frame.

His scrutiny made me want to abandon my quest and flee with all my monstrous secrets clutched tight to my chest.

I didn't. I simply responded to his question with a terse shake of my head and looked down at the business card I'd given him. The one he'd regarded with a wry, raised brow and then tossed onto the rococo coffee table between us. My boss's business card, Deputy Coroner Hayward P. Cole.

"Tell me about the boy," I said. "The boy in the purple jacket."

You want to know about the boy too, don't you?

He came in as a John Doe on the second day of one of my boss's increasingly frequent dipsomaniacal absences.

I'd started off as a janitor in the L.A. County morgue and through a combination of intelligence, ambition and a strong stomach, I'd risen up the ranks to become Ward Cole's assistant and indispensable right-hand man. I did nothing to discourage his drinking, because it made him increasingly dependent on me to cover for him and keep our department running smoothly. It also allowed me unfettered access to an endless supply of hobos and hopheads whose broken, unloved bodies taught me far more than the night school classes I'd been taking in my spare time.

So it was just me and the boy that day. The unexpected police sergeant who had come in with him was quite emphatic that this case needed a tight lid. That this one was rough, so rough that several uniforms lost their lunch on the scene.

"Brass needs this to stay out of the papers," the cop had said, his tone hushed, like whoever had done this to the boy might be listening and come back to do the same to him. "Minimal paperwork, COD unknown. Rubber-stamp it, file it as indigent and transfer the stiff over to Boyle Heights in the next batch of unclaimed remains."

"What do you want us to do with his clothes?" I asked. Unless they had been fused to the body, by extreme heat for example, personal effects were supposed to be either bagged and tagged or discarded before any cadaver arrived in our department.

"Make 'em disappear," the cop replied, pressing an envelope of cash into my hand. "Along with the rest of that kid."

He couldn't leave quickly enough.

The boy had been young. Maybe sixteen. Five foot five. Slight build. Pale complexion. Dark hair, freshly barbered in a sporty brush cut. Precise eye color difficult to determine upon initial examination due to corneal opacity and extensive conjunctival petechiae.

The clothing in question consisted of a flashy purple dinner jacket, a matching cummerbund, a starched white shirt and a black bow tie. No pants or shoes, just a single black sock.

Which brings me to the aspect of this case which needed to be kept out of the papers. Not the boy's death, because the death of one more juvie hustler was hardly newsworthy in a ruthless Hollywood ecosystem that ate pretty teenagers for breakfast every sunny, postcard-perfect day.

It was the manner of his death that needed to be kept hidden. Not the asphyxia that sped up his inevitable demise, but rather his more unusual pre-mortem injuries.

There is no gentle or pleasant way to say what I must say next, so I will simply state the facts in a straightforward and clinical manner. Both the genital and rectal areas exhibited extensive laceration consistent with a small but sharp object, such as a pocketknife, resulting in substantial tissue loss.

It was this grievous wounding that had been so unsettling to the patrolmen who had found the boy's discarded corpse in some scrubby underbrush near the Greek Theater. Far more so to me, who saw these wounds clearly and completely, illuminated by the harsh fluorescent light of science, and yet was still undone on such a fundamental level that I could barely breathe. Albeit for entirely different reasons.

At home that night in the modest courtyard apartment I shared with a clever tabby tomcat named Percy, I could not get the boy out of my mind. I could not eat my half of the tinned sardines I normally shared with the feline, so I shoved away the unopened sleeve of saltine crackers and scraped the remaining fish into his bowl.

Allow me to reiterate at this point that I am not a man who is easily disturbed by the indignities of the murdered dead. If I were, I would not have been fit for the job I'd worked so hard to hold. But I do suffer from a pathological loathing of excess flesh, one that leads me to limit my daily caloric intake in a rather strict fashion. You see, I had been quite fleshy in my youth and that fleshiness had attracted the attention of a certain man. A man who availed himself of my flesh and left me anguished and deeply confused by a slew of terrifying and contradictory emotions that shattered the very foundation of who I believed myself to be. Caustic shame. Existential dread. Horror and hunger and beneath it all, a perverse longing for the very debasement from which I so viscerally recoiled. From that point on, I vowed to whittle away the flesh that had betrayed me and assiduously avoid being touched by anyone ever again.

The boy in the purple jacket had touched me. Even in death, he had touched me in a dark, unspeakable place hidden deep inside my calcified heart, dredging up old terrors and bringing back that anguish and loathing with such intensity that I found myself driven out into the balmy Southern California night. I walked the streets of my sleeping neighborhood at a brisk, near panicked pace that bordered on a run, as if I could outrun the demons that the boy had awakened inside me.

I could not, of course.

I'm sure that by now you are beginning to sense the shape of deliberately omitted information lurking like monstrous shadows behind my carefully crafted recollections. I promise you I will eventually tell you everything. It's just that my secrets are shy creatures who cannot be forced from their hiding places. One must wait patiently for them to emerge.

In the days that followed, I found myself possessed by a burning desire to find out everything I could about the boy before his transfer to the crematorium.

My first stop was a small tailor's shop called Marcel's in Bunker Hill. I had been directed there by the label inside the purple jacket I'd carefully removed from the boy's cold body.

Marcel's was on Clay Street, which was barely more than an alleyway lurking beneath the tracks of Angel's Flight. The only indication that the little shop existed at all was a hand-painted sign in the dirty, opaque window featuring a dancing needle and thimble and an arrow pointing towards an otherwise unremarkable metal door.

Marcel himself proved to be a chatty Black man with conked hair and an unabashedly feminine demeanor. Five foot eight, thickly built in the lower body, wide-set dark eyes and a large mole on his left cheek.

He wore a gold pinkie ring and pinched the humble gray fabric of my Sears and Roebuck suit jacket with curious, hungry fingers.

"You came to the right place," he said, looking me up and down. "Because these lapels should've never come home from the war."

"I'm not here for clothing," I replied. "I'm here for information."

His eyes hardened, face locked up tight.

"You a cop?"

"No." I took the carefully folded purple jacket from my attaché case. "I'm looking for information about a . . ." I paused, forcing myself to push through my hesitation. "A young friend. He was last seen wearing this jacket."

Something unspoken seemed to pass between us, and his face softened.

"Where did you find it?" Marcel asked, taking the jacket and smoothing it out gently on a nearby table. "How'd it get cut up the back like this?"

"It was discarded in the brush near the Greek Theater," I said. I didn't tell him that the boy had been discarded with it. I also didn't tell him that it was I who had carefully excised the bloodstained sections as I cut it free from the boy's body. "That's all I know."

"I made five of these," Marcel said. "For a client named Jerry Tashman. Runs a chicken house and likes his boys to match for parties. I like the repeat business."

"Do you have any idea where he might have taken those boys two days ago?" I asked.

"Ain't my place to know Hollywood people's business," he said with a shrug. "And from the look of you, I'd say it ain't your business either."

"Where can I find this Tashman?" I asked.

"You don't listen, do you?" Marcel shook his head like a disappointed parent. "When he's not busy casting, you can usually find him holding court at the Shanghai Room. But you didn't hear it from me."

I let him sell me a silk tie that was entirely too luxurious for my line of work, which he knotted around my neck with a flourish. Then I headed west, into the Other Los Angeles.

The bus that ran west on Sunset Boulevard was always crowded with stoic domestics and gossiping waiters and hard-faced, bosomy b-girls stuffed into obscenely tight dresses. Denizens of my humble Los Angeles traveling into that glitzy, Klieg-lit dreamland of movie stars and hot spots and the perpetually illusive promise that you too might "make it."

I didn't look out the window. I wasn't interested in glitz or fame. Quite the opposite, in fact. My reading material, a lovingly worn copy of *Simpson's Forensic Medicine*, assured that I had no seatmate for the entire trip.

The Shanghai Room was just down the block from the Mocambo but it may as well have been on another planet. The sign was only slightly more obvious than Marcel's but the faded, faux-oriental interior was something out of a 1930s movie about opium smugglers. Threadbare red velvet and chipped gold flourishes and dusty Chinese lanterns that cast strange feverish shadows across the faces of the patrons. I wondered which one of them might be Tashman.

I ordered and paid for the signature Shanghai Mai Tai, which I did not touch, and observed the scene for several minutes. The patrons were mostly men, except for one older lady with a long cigarette holder who had not changed her style since the silent era. The woman was the only one who could have been described as holding court, surrounded as she was by her all-male entourage of admirers.

"Want to order something else?"

The bartender was a tall man with a slim build, slicked back salt and pepper hair, a pencil mustache and a distinctly smarmy demeanor. He was clearly not Chinese despite the vaguely Asian cut of his uniform jacket. He gestured at my untouched drink.

I looked at the drink, which was really quite attractive with its cheerful fruity garnish, but given the egregious amount of sugar contained therein, I would have sooner ingested rat poison.

"It's fine," I said anyway, sliding a folded ten-dollar bill across the bar's sticky surface. "I'm looking for Jerry Tashman."

The bartender quickly suppressed a bemused smirk.

"Really?" he said. "You don't strike me as a Bobby Driscoll fan. I'd have pegged you as more of a Muscle Beach enthusiast. Skinny, bookish types like you usually want to get tossed around."

How could he possibly know something so private about me? How could a complete stranger have intuited my most shameful secret so easily? Yet this man had just said out loud a thing that I had been unwilling to acknowledge even to myself.

Because I do, in fact, own a stack of Muscle Power magazines, each one purchased from a different newsstand in far-flung neighborhoods across Los Angeles. And I do, in fact, look at them in the lonely hours of the night with a combination of corrosive jealousy and helpless, primal arousal culminating in a humiliating paroxysm of involuntary physical response. Which I vow never to repeat yet inevitably do.

"I need to talk to Tashman," I forced myself to say.

"Well, you're out of luck," he replied. "Word is he skipped town just yesterday. Must have gotten caught with his hand in the wrong cookie jar."

"I'm looking for one of his boys," I said. "Five foot five, dark hair, slight build."

"You just described them all," he replied, his knowing smirk back in spades. "Tash definitely has a type."

"Where are they now?" I asked. "These boys?" He shrugged.

"Some got scooped up by other agents right away," he said. "Others went back to wherever they came from." He poked a thumb at a doorway marked PRIVATE. "I got one back there working stock and sleeping behind the empty kegs if you want to talk to him."

Needless to say, I did.

That boy was named Billy, and he was eerily similar to the boy on my slab. The only difference was a spray of charcoal freckles across his upturned nose. That, and the spark of life in his bright blue eyes, of course. When he saw the money in my hand, he flashed a sugary Shirley Temple smile.

"You want a suck job, mister?" he asked with the chipper enthusiasm of a newsboy hawking the morning paper.

I shook my head.

"I want information," I said. "About one of your friends who went missing yesterday."

A shadow of hesitation flickered across his face, but it was easily dispelled by a generous handful of the police sergeant's cash.

"Adam," he said, brows creased into a thoughtful frown. "He left the party early and that's the last anybody saw of him. We were supposed to meet up the next morning, but he never showed."

"Do you know Adam's last name?" I asked. "Or where he was from?"

Billy shook his head.

"We all go by Tashman," he said. "And most of us don't wanna remember where we're from."

"Where was this party?"

"Up in the hills near Griffith Park," he said. "At this big fancy estate owned by some old movie director. Great pool."

That was how I wound up talking to James Whale.

"Jerry Tashman?" Whale shook his head. "Doesn't ring a bell. Must be one of Pierre's friends."

He gestured with his chin towards a tan and semi-comatose young man lying on a chaise lounge out by the pool. He was quite hirsute and barely dressed in tiny white swimming trunks that did little to conceal the anatomy beneath.

"I hardly know anyone at my own parties these days," Whale said, dark eyes gone contemplative and melancholy.

"You're too young to remember," he continued. "But the time between the wars was nothing like today. So open and vibrant, filled with art and wit and beautiful young men who thought the party would never end. That all changed with the Second World War. Did you serve?"

"Four F," I said, my usual response. Given my eyeglasses and ninety-eight-pound weakling's physique, it was never challenged. I had, of course, avoided military service in an entirely different way.

Whale's gaze was already turned back inward, as if my response had barely registered.

"I fought in the Great War," he said.

He fell silent, accessing some profound emotion I could not fathom.

"For a time, it seemed as if we had won. Like we were finally free."

I could not begin to imagine that kind of freedom, now or ever.

"Now there's this air of paranoia beneath the revelry," Whale continued. "Moral panic. The Blacklist. 'Are you now or have you ever been a sexual deviant?'" He shook his head. "Every maudlin old man looks back upon his younger days with a biased eye, but believe me when I say that these are dark times for men like us, Mr. Cole."

I wanted to protest that I was nothing like him, that he didn't know anything about me, but he did, and I was. I also wanted him to keep talking, so I changed the subject instead.

"But you do remember the boy at the party," I said, trying to bring his focus back to my original question. "Don't you?"

"I remember a group of boys," he said. "Four or five, I think, all wearing the same jackets, though not for long. Everyone ends up naked in the pool eventually, but there was one boy who refused to disrobe. A quiet lad, a bit more reserved than the others. If I recall correctly, he wanted to be driven home, and eventually, someone agreed to take him."

"Try to remember who that could have been," I said.

"It wasn't Fredrick, it was someone older. Ah yes, I remember, it was Bruno. Bruno Sherry." Even I knew who Bruno Sherry was.

"He's married, you know." He spoke that word with an undisguised contempt. "Men like him can do as they please, so long as they maintain plausible deniability."

He paused, gaze drifting over to the young man by the pool. His expression was not one of fondness or desire but rather one of deep, brooding ennui.

"You must excuse me, Mr. Cole," he said, stubbing out his cigarette in an otherwise empty jade ashtray. "I seem to be feeling rather more unwell than I realized. My housekeeper will see you out."

He stood and walked away without another word.

If you were hoping for a Hollywood ending, you have not been paying attention. There is no version of this story in which I, like some rock-jawed matinee hero or relentlessly clever fictional criminologist, bring the murderer to justice. That's not the way things work in the Other Los Angeles.

This is not only because I am fundamentally a coward and terrified of calling attention to myself, although that certainly is a factor. It is also because Adam's ending had already been written by larger forces long before we ever met. Hollywood bigwigs like Bruno Sherry rarely face consequences for their actions. No one cares what happens to shadow-dwelling monsters like us. This is why we must take care of our own in whatever ways we can.

To that end, I made sure that Adam did not go to the crematorium where his unclaimed ashes would be poured into a mass grave with the rest of the forlorn and forgotten dead of Los Angeles. In death, I gave him dignity. I gave him what he could not have in life.

We may never know exactly what motivated Bruno Sherry to perpetrate such a gruesome and heinous mutilation, but I have my suspicions. And as much as I may loathe and fear this kind of frank disclosure, I simply cannot go on without finally acknowledging my most perverse and terrible secret. A secret I suspect you may have already discerned. Regardless, I will do my best to relate the truth to you in a clear and scientific manner.

I am in a unique position to grasp both the precise nature of Adam's injuries and the psychological complexities behind Bruno Sherry's possible reactions when confronted with the unexpected physiological features that the boy and I share.

You see, I intimately understood the nature of this anatomical dissonance even before I removed Adam's bloody shirt to reveal the tightly wrapped binder beneath. When I first examined the body, I knew that I was not looking at a void left behind by the removal of male genitalia, but rather a series of furiously jagged incised wounds to the external female genitalia, exposing the vaginal canal beneath.

For many years, I was certain I was a terrible and singular creature. A monstrous deviant so rare as to be undefined by standard medical textbooks on psychosexual disorders. Despite the fact that my conviction was not shared by those who raised me, I have always known myself to be unquestionably male since childhood. As such, I had always assumed that I would naturally develop an interest in the fairer sex. When the opposite occurred, I was plagued with crushing doubt and confusion. I was so desperate to be perceived as a normal man, but yet felt so fundamentally abnormal that I knew my only hope for survival was to forgo all sexual relations of any kind and devote myself solely to the pursuit of science.

Adam's arrival in my morgue and in my life was evidence that I was not alone. He gave me a strange and terrifying gift, and I wanted to give him something in return.

It was quite easy for me to repair his wounds and correct his anatomical defects. I was able to remove the excess tissue from his chest and give him what I so longed for and knew that I could never have, courtesy of a post-mortem donation from the well-endowed wino who would be headed to the crematorium in his place.

I buried Adam's surgically perfected body in a blue mohair suit made by Marcel, although I lied and told him it was for me. I was able to make it work for Adam with a few strategic pins. The flat granite headstone I picked out was simple and elegant and when they asked me for his surname, I didn't want to use Tashman, so I gave him my own instead.

You may laugh, but I chose my name when I was still quite young. The last name was admittedly more aspirational than descriptive, and my first name had been inspired by a handsome actor on whom I had an embarrassing fixation at the time. I swear that it was not inspired by the scientist in James Whale's most memorable film, although in retrospect that would not have been entirely inappropriate.

My name is Victor. The grave marker I had made for the boy reads:

Adam Strong, Beloved Brother

I visited Adam often, as he was my only family. I visited him five years later when I read about the lonely suicide of James Whale and shared with him the complex emotions that news evoked in me. I visited him when Bruno Sherry died a wealthy and successful man, surrounded by adoring grandchildren. Whenever the weight of my monstrous secrets became too much to bear, I found solace in the peaceful silence of Adam's grave.

Maybe that's not a Hollywood ending, but it's not an entirely unhappy ending either.

SWAN CLUB

ANNE LAUGHLIN

London
March 1929

The rain was falling steadily as I walked through the peaceful quiet of St. James Park to my club. Many famous gentlemen's clubs were found in the area—the Carleton, the Oxford and Cambridge—but the Swan Club was the only one that would accept me as a member, the only one I was interested in joining. My skirt was drenched by the time I got there, but I carried a change of clothes suitable for the club in a bag swinging at my side. I couldn't wait to get into them.

I was not allowed to enter the club by the front door in my feminine garb, so I climbed the metal stairs at the rear of the building. When I knocked on the door, an immaculately dressed man swung it open and stepped aside for me to enter. Stuart was new to the Swan Club, but he fit the role of valet as if born to it. He had a military posture and a voluptuous mustache that defied gravity.

"Hello, Stuart," I said, handing over the bag. "Do you have time for me now?"

"Certainly. If you'll follow me to dressing room two."

I followed his march down a long corridor, passing several closed doors along the way. I almost expected his heels to click when he stopped to open the door to number two. When I stepped through, a feeling of relief swept through my body. Now I could get out of my skirt and high heels and step into the clothes that made me feel wholly myself.

Stuart took charge of my carpetbag and set my clothes on a high table. He handed me some boxers, an undershirt, and a bandage roll and pointed to the bathroom. Before putting on my underwear, I wrapped my breasts tightly with the bandage until they were crushed against my chest. When I returned in my skivvies, he began layering on the fine clothes that transformed me into a gentleman. He paid no more attention to my body than he would a post box. First, my bright, white shirt, made of fine linen, followed by a waistcoat, cufflinks, garters and stockings, trousers and suit jacket. Then he wet my short wavy hair and combed it into a masculine style, using a scented oil to hold it in place. I looked at myself in the mirror. I could see how handsome I was. Georgia was gone and George had slipped into her place. I thanked Stuart with a generous tip and went to the top of the club's main staircase. The second floor held the dressing rooms and guest rooms where members slept when the nights grew too late. Downstairs was the heart of the club. I trotted down to the main level, where my friends waited.

The Swan Club was unique in its membership, which was made up of society women who dressed as gentlemen while in the club. Sometimes we went out of the club, escorting our ladies to events and dinners, but most of our time was spent inside where we could relax with like-minded people. Swan Club was fitted out the same as any gentlemen's club—wood-covered walls and ceilings, giant hearths in the bar and parlor, a billiards room, a library, a dining room, kitchens, guest rooms, and staff quarters. I went straight to the parlor for tea, just in time for the first pour. The whiskey would come later.

The parlor was a large, square room where members were scattered in small groups. A tea trolley was making its way around the room, depositing small towers of pastries and tiny sandwiches on each table. The walls were lined with paper sporting the insignia of the Dragoons, or some other military unit—no one cared which, just that it looked masculine. Most of the chairs were occupied, but in the corner by the hearth my friend, Archie, waved me over. He pointed me into a club chair.

"Archie, old man. You look positively ill," I said, taking Archie's hand in a firm shake. "What's the matter?"

"We just got word from Henry that there's been another murder of one of our members."

"No. How is that possible?"

"He saw the body himself. Ask him. He's on his way over."

I looked toward the opposite side of the room and saw a tall figure walking toward us. As Henry approached, I poured a third cup of tea and put it in front of an empty chair.

Henry was the alter ego of Vita Sackville-West, a notorious womanizer in both London and the landed countryside. Whether in male or female garb, Vita always had several lovers going, all women of good birth. As Henry, he often went cruising in the lower-class lesbian bars in London, but those conquests were good for one night only. His long-time lover, Violet, would accompany Henry on weekends away where he never got out of male attire and played the role of gentleman throughout their trip. No one ever suspected a thing. Now he joined Archie and me and immediately took out a cigarette.

"What's this I hear about another murder?" I noticed the other men in the parlor were leaving their seats to congregate and talk in the center of the room. Apparently, I was the last to know.

"It's horrible," Henry said, sprawled in his chair and signaling for the waiter. "Saw it myself when Violet and I were returning from the bar. A large crowd was huddled in a circle in St. James Square, with a couple of bobbies trying to push them back.

"Who was it?"

"Fergus. I got close enough to see his red hair and recognize his overcoat. When I asked a bobby if it was Fergus Donnelly, he said they'd just pulled out his wallet and identified him."

I felt my heart sink. "Not Fergus, please. He was such a kind soul. Why would anyone kill him?"

"It's a fucking outrage, is what it is. I'm more than ready to believe someone is after our club members. There was the John Winters murder earlier this year."

My brain started whirling. When not in the club or carrying out Georgia's duties as the heir to a great fortune, I worked for a small detective agency, specializing in marital infidelity. It wasn't the most high-minded work, but it ate up some of my idle hours. The stories I told were worth it alone. Everyone loved my stories. I felt professional curiosity stir. Who was after members of the club? How could I find out?

"Do you know what killed him?"

"Probably a knife wound like the John Winters murder. I saw a huge puddle of blood where Fergus lay. The bobbies were standing well away from it before the detectives and coroner arrived."

"Well, it's terrifying. Who could know that John and Fergus were cross-dressers?" Archie said.

"I hate that term," Henry said.

"Transvestites, then, if you want to get clinical."

A waiter approached and we ordered whiskey neat. Normally, drinking was done in the bar, but tea was not enough now. I needed to pace myself, though. I had a late-night rendezvous with Lady Mary Upshaw, one of a surprising number of titled ladies who welcomed the gentlemen from the Swan Club into their social lives and their beds. Hiding the liaisons from their indifferent husbands was easy and the reward great.

I lit a cigarette. Only the staff and members of the club knew the members cross-dressed, plus whichever women the members chose to tell when they were sleeping with them. That's a fair amount of people, but all were sworn to secrecy and, so far, had kept to that oath. Most of the lovers were married women who didn't want their infidelity known, let alone that they broke their vows with another woman.

The waiter handed us our whiskeys and Henry's was down the hatch at once. "Somebody who knew about Swan Club either committed the murders himself or gave the names to a third party, God knows why. It's not like John and Fergus ever stirred up any controversy."

"John was downright boring," Archie said. "I don't know if anyone's noticed he's gone."

"You're a terrible prick, Archie," I said. "How you get away with half of what you say confounds me."

Archie was not at all offended. "It's the charm, my dear George. Pour it on just thick enough and people forgive you anything."

Henry waved his hand impatiently. "I haven't told you yet what happened when the detectives and coroner arrived. The coroner undid Fergus's shirt buttons to check on something, and of course, he realized there was a woman underneath the suit. I could hear him say, 'Crikey' and the two detectives started laughing. Word began to spread through the crowd and they started pushing to the front to see. Half the crowd had joined the laughter, while the other half were disgusted."

"They're all cretins," I said.

"It's a good indication the police are not going to do anything to find the killer. Even if they put it together with John's murder a few months ago, they're unlikely to care," Henry said.

"I'm not sure that's a bad thing. Do we want the police in here? I know I don't. I couldn't take their abuse on my home turf," I said.

"Agreed," Archie said. He was searching for the waiter to order more whiskey.

Henry lay back in his spacious club chair, his long legs nervously moving up and down on the silent carpet. "You're a detective, George. Why don't you look into it? If this is coming from inside our own club, we must stop it before someone else gets killed."

I sat up straight in my chair. "I do infidelity cases, a good long way from solving murders."

"You have the instincts and perseverance of an investigator. You simply expand your thinking and follow your nose." Henry turned to Archie as if the matter were settled.

I thought about Henry's suggestion as I dressed for dinner in the upstairs dressing rooms, with Stuart assisting. I wasn't opposed to the idea of investigating, just intimidated. If a few members paid, I would have a bona fide client and could appeal to my boss for help. With a little direction from him, I was nearly sure I could pick up a trail and find the killer. God knows it was worth the effort. Not only were members' lives at stake, but the life of Swan Club was also. If another murder were to happen, members would start dropping out of the club. The club needed a certain minimum of members to make it solvent, and it already hovered around that number. The membership fee was high enough to discourage all but a certain class of person from joining. Applicant qualifications might need to be relaxed to keep the membership level up. I knew what my fellow members would think of that.

Early the next morning, I was dressed as Georgia and walked from my Mayfair townhouse to Oxford Street, where Arthur C. Nettles Investigations was found. I wore my most business-like outfit, a wool suit of jacket and pleated skirt, with a man-style shirt and short tie, frilly enough to be feminine but close enough to a suit to appeal to the George in me. I dodged pedestrians on the busy shopping street until I found the address and climbed two flights of stairs to the office. I walked straight in, knowing Arthur Nettles would already be at work.

Nettles was one of the few outside the club who knew of my two identities. The others were my household staff, who were used to seeing me take women upstairs to my bedroom. When I applied for the job at Nettles' agency, I was dressed as George, figuring a woman would have slim chance of being hired as a detective. When I realized Nettles was a fair-minded and liberal man, I told him the truth—that I was both male and female. He took it in stride and immediately put me to work as both a male and female detective. Whenever a husband or wife was under surveillance, Nettles sent George or Georgia, depending on who was being watched. Most often it was George following a wandering husband.

I knocked softly at the inner office, and Nettles raised his head from a ledger and smiled.

"Early bird, I see," he said. "Do you have something for me on the Hendersons?" He put his pen down and pointed me to one of the wooden swivel chairs in front of his desk.

"I'll have something for you tomorrow. Mr. Henderson is going to a 'business dinner' tonight, and we're pretty sure he'll go straight to his mistress. I'll be following him."

"As George?"

"Yes, as George."

"Very good. If we close out that case quickly, we'll have had an excellent month. You're a big part of that."

I shrugged. "I have something I hope you can help me with." I put my briefcase-like bag on the floor and leaned forward.

"Anything I can do, I'll do." I found Nettles friendlier and more approachable when I dressed as my female self. There wasn't the same warmth with George.

I told him about the murder the night before last and the one in the past few months. "That puts a dent in your membership," Nettles said. "Did you know these men?"

"Of course. Everyone knows everyone else at the Swan Club. There are only twenty-five of us. Well, twenty-three now."

"What I wouldn't give to see the inside of that place," Nettles mused. "That's not going to happen, so what can I do to help? Have you talked to the police?"

"I was hoping you could use your contacts at Scotland Yard to give us a look at both police reports as a starting point."

Nettles was a former police detective who left the life for something simpler, where he could control his work time. Wandering husbands and wives were nothing if not predictable and catching them was like plucking fish from an overstocked pond. Business was booming. Nettles promised to try to get the reports and I promised to have some evidence against Mr. Henderson by the morning.

As I strolled back to Mayfair, I tried to think of the meeting I had in the afternoon with the primary banker for the estate. There were always details to be gone over, most of them stultifying. My thoughts wandered back to the previous night spent with Lady Mary Upshaw in the Brown Hotel. It was the first time we made love, the first time I'd revealed my body to her. I survived the agonizing moment when she realized my body was female and would either look puzzled, laugh with delight, or scream in terror. Lady Mary laughed and said she wasn't the least bit surprised. I worried for a moment that I'd let a bit of Georgia slip into my George persona, but Mary took me in her arms, and all such concerns were forgotten. Our goodbyes early the next morning held promise of more nights to come, and I was unusually excited. Maybe there could be a real relationship with Mary, something more meaningful than my usual quick and intense encounters. The feeling of being accepted by her without judgment was almost too exquisite to bear.

My approach to finding evidence that Henderson was cheating on his wife was simple—follow him. His townhouse in Mayfair was near mine. I sat in a park across the street and waited for Henderson to emerge. Imposing townhomes lined the streets around the square, with gas lamps lighting up the buildings as well as the park. I wore my warmest topcoat as the air was cold and damp, lit a cigarette and leaned against a tree—just a gentleman stopping for a smoke in the tiny, fenced-off square.

Henderson was a wealthy man, as was everyone living there, and I could only hope he would walk this evening instead of using a driver. At seven-thirty, he emerged from his home and started up Half Moon Street to Piccadilly, towards The Ritz. At least, I guessed that's where he was going based on its reputation as a trysting place for the very rich. The streets were crowded with pedestrians, and it was easy to remain undetected. I followed him into the Ritz lobby—glittering, bright as full sunshine, swirling with the colorful dress of wealthy women and their escorts—and took a place near the door. I watched as Henderson checked in at the front desk and then sat on the other side of the lobby. Fifteen minutes later, Lady Penelope Burton entered the hotel. I knew her—or rather, Georgia knew her—as a society woman with no more on her mind than the latest fashions. It appeared Mr. Henderson had expanded her interests. Henderson popped up from his chair and went to her, making a slight bow and offering his arm. They proceeded to the lift and disappeared.

I figured they would be about an hour—Lady Penelope had a husband she couldn't long hide from. I popped into the bar for a drink. Customers were three deep at the bar, but I managed to get a pint and find a corner to lean against. I talked to no one. My suit was flawless in hiding my femininity, but my voice was a bit high. I kept most of my conversations to those with people I know or want to know. Back in the lobby, I waited only a few minutes before Lady Penelope emerged on her own and swept through the lobby to the exit. I thought I detected a flush on her face. Some minutes later, Henderson appeared and left the hotel, with me on his heels. I wanted to give our client a full report of his activities and thought he might be headed for his club, which was quite near the Swan Club.

He took a jog in the opposite direction to walk in Green Park toward St. James. The mass of pedestrians on the street melted away to a few people strolling down the path heading south. It was much harder to follow someone without being noticed, though if Henderson were to turn back and see me, he wouldn't know me from Adam. I felt confident he wouldn't twig onto the fact his wife was having him followed. He probably couldn't imagine her doing such a thing.

The park grew darker as a copse of trees swallowed up the light. There was no one now between Henderson and me, and I slowed my pace to keep well back. Suddenly, I heard a whoosh as someone ran up behind me and clobbered me behind the knees with a stick, sending me tumbling to the ground. I was so shocked I couldn't react. I had twisted onto my back as the man fell upon me and saw the glint of a knife come into his hand. Now, I started scrabbling with all my strength. The problem was that though I was dressed as a man, I didn't have the strength of a man. I couldn't break free of his hold on me, and I felt terror spread as the knife lowered, aimed at my throat.

I'd not had much call to fight in all my time as George, but London was a big and sometimes dangerous city. I carried a cosh in my left pocket, a telescoping stick with a brutal metal ball at the end. Collapsed, it was no more than a few inches long. As my assailant raised his right arm to strike, I pulled out the cosh and struck him hard in the nose. He wailed and fell over, and I scrambled to my feet. I couldn't tell who it was because his hands covered his face, blood streaming down his chin. Suddenly, he shot out a hand to grab my ankle, and I saw that it was Stuart, the valet, without his prominent mustache.

"You're a disgusting creature," he spat. "You all deserve to die."

I stomped on his hand with my other foot, and his grasp loosened. I should have killed him with one wicked cosh to the head, but killing didn't come to mind. Here was the murderer of John and Fergus, and all I could do was run as fast as I could toward the Swan Club, just two city blocks away. As I ran, I turned to look behind me, but no one was on my heels. I made it into the club using my key, not waiting for the butler to open the door as was preferred. I headed straight for the bar, where Archie and Henry lingered over a nightcap. Archie got up and led me by the elbow to an empty chair.

"What's happened?" he said. "Have you seen a ghost?"

"Good God, man. You do look a fright," Henry said.

I took Archie's whiskey out of his hand and drank it down. I could have used ten more. My hand shook as I put the empty glass down. I told them all that had happened.

"There's another valet down," Archie said. "Why do we have such a hard time keeping them?"

"Thanks for your concern, Archie. I was three inches away from dying. And by Stuart. Who would have guessed it of him? His eyes were murderous, savage. Gives me the chills."

"Sorry," Archie said. "I can be glib at the worst times. I'm sure you're still in shock."

I looked at both of my friends. "We have to call the police."

Henry shifted in his chair. "Certainly not. We'd have to reveal the secret of our identities, especially if we suggest Stuart killed both John and Fergus and was about to do the same with George. Otherwise, what would be the motive?"

"You weren't the one sprawled on the ground with a knife to your throat. He's likely to strike again." I ran my fingers through my hair, wanting to tear it out. "We must get them involved. None of us is safe until Stuart is caught, least of all me. The police would know what to do."

"I know what they'd do—nothing. And if they found they could be arsed to do anything, it would be to shut down the club. Get rid of the victims rather than the criminal. We can't allow that," Archie added.

The bartender brought over a tray of drinks, and we all reached for them at once.

"We can't let Stuart off without any consequence," I said, my voice loud enough to draw attention.

"We won't." Henry steepled his fingers, as if the problem was academic. "We'll find him."

Archie shook his head. "First of all—how? Secondly, what do we do with him when he's found?"

"You're not suggesting we kill him, are you?" I tried to picture myself as an accomplice and failed miserably.

Henry lit a cigarette and picked a flake of tobacco from his tongue. "I've no more interest in hanging than you do, George." I noted he was more appalled by the punishment than the crime. "We could muscle him out of town. Even better, out of the country. I know certain men who could do this for us, for a price."

I was struck by the brilliance of the idea, and relieved Henry didn't intend for us to be the muscle.

"The breadth of your acquaintances is truly amazing, Henry," Archie said.

"Let's do it," I said. "If the police won't protect us, we must do it ourselves." I finished my drink and stood, weary beyond measure. "Let me know the cost and I'll send my share over."

"Get some rest," Henry said. "I'll take care of everything."

"Stuart knows I can identify him. I'm a target, a vulnerable one, between now and whenever your mystery men do whatever to him."

Henry looked unconcerned. "So, stay at home. It won't take long to find him. These chaps are remarkably good hunters. They'll find Stuart straight away, and all this will be behind us."

"That's a laugh," I said. "This is just one example of how we're vilified and put in danger, of how our very lives are denied." What energy I had left drained away. I'd had enough for one night.

Archie and Henry watched silently as I picked up my coat and left the bar. I didn't bother to change back to Georgia. My staff wouldn't take any notice, not that I particularly cared at the moment. I was warm with resentment at having everything about George's existence belittled, dismissed, reviled. So much so that Stuart was trying to kill us off. Simple justice was beyond us.

I would feel better in the morning, when I had another evening with Lady Mary to look forward to. She, at least, made me feel wanted. I dreamed every day of acceptance for who I was, and Mary gave me that. I struggled to hold on to the feeling after being nearly killed by someone who saw me as my true self and wanted me dead. It was hard to feel anything but anger and not a little fear. All I could do was carry on, for George was a part of me. George was me. There was no getting rid of him.

FINDING JIMMY BALDWIN

CHERYL A. HEAD

June
1954

The bell over the door jingled. A thin, light-skinned woman, her gray hair pulled back in a net, pushed through the swinging gates of the kitchen, wiping her hands on a cotton apron decorated in a fruit-and-vegetables pattern.

"Hi, Miss Shirl."

"Hi, Baby. Go ahead and sit. I'll bring you your coffee."

Roy slid into Jimmy's booth. That's what regulars at Shirley's Cafe on 130 at Lenox called the seat at the far end of the front window. An homage to the neighborhood's favorite son.

"I'm running late. I thought he'd be here by now."

Shirl shook her head, placing two cups and a small container of milk on the table. "I got excited when I saw you. Thought maybe he was right behind you. He wasn't here yesterday either."

"No?"

Roy stared at the cockeyed cat clock on the paneled wall. Its swinging tail marking the seconds. It was 12:15. He and Jimmy had a standing lunch appointment at Shirley's. Noon on Tuesday. They'd picked up the routine a month ago when Jimmy returned from overseas, but it had begun a dozen years before that. Back when Roy and Jimmy were a couple of teens trying to figure out their space in the world.

At 12:30, Roy ordered the meatloaf plate and watched the front door. He was halfway through the mashed potatoes when they caught in his throat. A patrol car had pulled to the curb in front. Two cops exited the car, adjusting their duty belts as if they were about to do some real work. Roy recognized one of them. Everybody on 130th Street knew Sgt. Peterson.

Peterson reached up to silence the bell as he entered. He stood wide-legged in the open door, hands on his hips, like Columbus returning to Queen Isabella to report he'd discovered America.

"Can I help you, Sergeant?" Shirley asked from behind the counter. "You mind closing the door. I don't like to get no street dirt mixed up with my food."

Peterson signaled the junior officer to get the door as he sauntered to the counter. *You Send Me* wafted through the jukebox speaker—Sam Cooke and the whining ceiling fan making the only sound in the cafe. Peterson hooked his thumbs in his belt.

"Investigating a missing person's report. One James Arthur Baldwin. He might have been abducted, and his sister claims she hasn't seen him for a couple of days."

"Well, I haven't seen him myself since last week," Shirley responded with an involuntary look at the back booth. "We was just talking about that."

The policeman swiveled his head, and Shirley dipped hers in regret as she and Roy made quick eye contact. Peterson ambled to the rear of the cafe. Passing tables and booths, staring brazenly at those holding suspended forks and unswallowed food. He'd always loved using his power to intimidate Black folks. He'd been at it for two decades.

Peterson had more citizen complaints than any other officer in the 32nd precinct. He was known for accosting groups of loitering teens, driving them to Morningside Heights to walk home, putting one or two in the back of a patrol car for a beating, or worse being carried to the precinct. As a rookie cop Peterson had picked up Roy and Jimmy on their way home from a movie theater in the Village and drove to an alley near Colonial Park where he used a Billy club on them. Jimmy's mother walked to the precinct that same night, but was turned away without even the pretense of someone taking her citizen complaint. Then, and now, the police honchos hadn't seen fit to free central Harlem's residents of this brutal cop.

"Well, if it ain't Roy Willoughby. Haven't seen you since you got back from the Army."

"The Marines," Roy corrected.

Peterson squinted and sucked his teeth. "Heard you made Corporal. I was surprised. Didn't think you'd even have the discipline to do your full stint."

"I'm full of surprises, Peterson. Did I hear you say you talked to Jimmy's sister?"

"I'm asking the questions here. You seen him?"

"No."

"You two used to be thick as thieves. A couple of pansies in fairyland."

Roy stared at the policemen and tapped his thigh. Sometimes, the tapping stopped his head from doing its thing. The young officer's hand was on the butt of his revolver.

"I told you I don't know where he is," Roy said in an even tone.

"Don't think I believe you, Willoughby. I'm getting all kinds of grief about finding your girlfriend. If you ask me, it's a waste of time and money, but the Commissioner is busting our balls about that little ..."

Shirley's arrival stopped Peterson in mid-slur. She slipped her wiry body between the cops and began wiping the table. She handed Roy a paper bag. "Got you another meatloaf to take home. You better go on over and check on Gloria." Shirley gathered condiments, addressing the two interlopers without looking at them. "Like I said, Officers. Nobody's seen Jimmy. We've been wondering ourselves where he was off to."

Gloria lived in a six-room flat at 128th that had been purchased twenty-five years ago by the Baldwin patriarch—a Pentecostal minister. Even then, with three bedrooms, the apartment was barely large enough for Jimmy and his eight brothers and sisters. The other siblings had fled the crowded quarters and their violent father as soon as they were old enough, but Gloria stayed on to take care of her parents. Her faithfulness paid off when the flat was left to her in her father's will.

Roy climbed the stairs, stepping over discarded children's toys, trash, and a couple of needles. He didn't remember the hallway being this narrow, but he hadn't visited in years. Not since Jimmy had left the neighborhood to be part of that book crowd he desired so much.

Leaning his ear to the door first, Roy finally knocked. Children shouting "auntie" over and over changed the previous silence into a commotion of voices, scraping chairs and shuffling footsteps. Roy waited the two minutes it took Gloria to make it to the door, view him through the peephole, and fling it open. He hadn't seen her for several years and caught himself when he realized shock had widened his eyes. He tried to play it off with a smile, but Gloria winced before she met his gaze again.

"Gloria, baby," he recovered. "It's been too long."

"Well, I been here, Roy."

"I know. I know." Roy waggled his head, then removed his cap. "Work and everything keeps me kinda busy."

Gloria stepped aside. "I was hoping you'd come. You heard?"

Roy nodded somberly.

The flat was smothered in furniture and stale air. The framed family pictures hanging in the vestibule were as he remembered, and Roy would swear the plastic-covered sofa that centered the living room was the one he'd sat on twenty years ago. Now, it was surrounded by tables and chairs of all types and sizes. On the other side of the entryway was a dining room with French doors—he'd eaten hundreds of meals in that room. But now the door was closed and covered by heavy drapes.

He completed his scan of the living area. Only the dim light gave it grace.

Roy sat in a stuffed chair, avoiding the wire spring that protruded from the upholstery near his leg. Gloria sat on the couch joined by three kids—a boy and two girls. The boy appeared to be about ten. The girls younger. Their brown, sallow faces proved they were siblings. The boy sat between the two girls holding their hands and staring at their visitor.

"Those are Ruth's kids. I keep them for her sometimes when she's at work."

"I can see the resemblance. Gloria, what's happened with Baldy? That asshole Peterson came down to Shirley's this afternoon looking for him."

Gloria reached for a tissue in her robe pocket to stop the sudden tears streaking her cheeks and causing her nose to run. She was the youngest sister but looked twice as old as Jimmy. Her thinning hair reached in all directions, and the once caramel complexion was blotched with dark spots. Her crying had shifted the boys' stare to a menacing glare. Roy stuck his hands into his leather jacket to hide his finger taps.

"He's been staying in the dining room. I fixed it up nice with a sleeping cot, and he was using the table for his desk. We've had some good days together since he got back. The kids love him, and he's been helping me out with a few expenses." Gloria sniffed, wiped at her nose, and leaned forward. "He said you all had picked up just like old times."

"Today was our lunch meeting at Shirley's. I waited over an hour for him." Roy shifted in the chair, careful not to snag his pants on the sharp coil. "When was the last time you saw him?"

"Sunday morning. He got dressed. Said he was going to church, and he'd be back with supper. I talked to Reverend Wilkins. Jimmy never even made it to church."

Roy looked at the kids again, and then around the living room. He considered that the children and the space could use a good scrubbing. "Gloria, how are you doing with bills and things? You need anything?"

Gloria leaned back on the sofa and pulled herself together. She stood. Adjusted her robe. "I'm doing just fine, Roy. You don't need to concern yourself with me. It's Jimmy I'm worried about. I haven't seen or heard from him in two days. The police said he might be kidnapped. Who would want to do that?"

Roy didn't respond, and for a while, they kept their own thoughts.

"The police also think he just decided to go back to Europe, or to be with his friends downtown." Gloria shook her head. "But Jimmy told me he found himself a place on West 96th. All his stuff is in the dining room, and he left his typewriter. He wouldn't go nowhere without that typewriter."

Gloria began to cry again until she was sobbing. The little boy jumped from the couch and wrapped his arms around his aunt's thick legs. The two girls were also crying. "You know that, Roy. He'd never leave without his typewriter."

Roy inhaled a flood of air when he got outside. He scanned the street, a habit he'd picked up even before his military training, and pulled his cap down firmly. It was windy. Pieces of paper swirled under the parked cars, and around the legs of pedestrians and loiterers on both sidewalks. The corner store was busy this afternoon, and the women coming back from the sidewalk market held onto their canvas bags and purses with one hand, and their skirts with the other. Roy looked up when he heard piano music wafting from one of the open windows in the apartment building across the street. He unlocked the Ford Country Sedan and sunk into its upholstered seat—way better than Gloria's lumpy chair. He rolled down the window halfway to catch the breeze. According to Gloria, Baldy wasn't leaving. But, that's not what he'd said.

Roy merged in behind a delivery truck going up 7th. Traffic was light today. There was little he didn't know about cars or driving or the street addresses of Harlem—it was his business as the owner of a jitney cab. He'd been picking up passengers for eight years. First, driving for the Jewish man who owned the limousine company, then after starting his car service four years ago. He owned two cars now. The Pontiac and the six-passenger Ford station wagon. Sometimes, his regular clients required rides to and from church, and the big car was paying off.

Roy was a few blocks from home when he confirmed that he was being followed. Probably that dumbass Peterson or one of his squad. He didn't want to lead the cops to where he lived, so he headed to the garage where he kept a small office. It was risky. Gomez—his mechanic, second driver, and friend—would be there if things went badly, but Gomez wouldn't be happy about Roy delivering NYPD to his place of business.

Roy parked the station wagon in front of the open bay door, grabbed the bag Shirl had packed, and stepped into the shadows of the garage. He turned to see what the black Plymouth would do. It slowed, then moved down the street.

Gomez rolled out from under a red Chevy Deluxe. "Hey man. Whatcha, doing?"

"I thought maybe I was being followed."

"Were you?"

Roy shrugged. He and Gomez had been through some life-or-death situations in Iwo Jima, and a few times out of loneliness and need they'd serviced each other. It was common between young soldiers who counted every day as their last. All of that ended with Gomez when they got back to New York, but there was still no one he trusted more.

"I'm going up to the office for about an hour," Roy said. "But, I got a booking for tonight. I might want to take the Pontiac."

"Okay, I'll change out the cars. Then I'm gonna lock up early. I got something tonight with Ynez and the kids." Gomez sat up on the creeper and stared at Roy. "I hear your old buddy, the writer, is AWOL. The police say he's been abducted. They've been all up and down the Avenues, harassing people and asking questions. I guess 'cause he's famous or something."

"Yeah. I know," Roy said, heading up the backstairs to the office. He unlocked the door, stepped into the dim office, and relocked the door. He went straight to the closet, withdrawing the .38 from his waistband, and slowly opened the door. Jimmy's bulging eyes were staring up at him. Conscious now, but still gagged.

"Stop fighting," Roy said lifting Jimmy from the floor. "Don't you see I have a gun? I'll remove the gag, but you better not make any noise."

Roy undid the rag and restraints, led Jimmy to the bathroom, and watched him pee. When he pulled the seat down, Roy stepped out of the room, leaving the door open.

It had been an impulse to take Jimmy. But what else could he do?

They'd been having lunch at Shirley's last Tuesday when Jimmy told him about the actor he was in love with—a man five years his junior from a wealthy Parisian family. The boy had arrived in New York that morning to convince Jimmy to return to Europe. Roy had seen the ticket. Passage to Le Havre on the Île de France for the following Monday. They'd argued about it.

"Why do you want these white men, Baldy? To them you're just something exotic. A show pony. Don't go back with him. You belong here with your family, and the people who really love you."

Jimmy shook his head. "We're both more than we were— two misfits who didn't seem to belong, except to each other." Jimmy waved his hands as he talked. Cigarette smoke circling the table. "Two ghetto kids scurrying like roaches and rats looking for a refuge. You found yours in cars. Mine was in books and writing. You understood that. It's why I moved to the Village."

"But Greenwich Village isn't across the sea. You came back to help your people. You always did. You said yourself that

Gloria needs you."

They paused the quarrel to sullenly eat their food and smoke. Shirley came to the table to top off their coffee and gave them both a curious look before retreating. Roy broke the silence. "I've seen the stories about you in the magazines, Baldy. It's just like they used to say about you at school. You're some kind of genius. But does that mean you have to belong to white people?"

Jimmy stubbed his butt into the ashtray and immediately lit up again. He studied his friend. Roy had always been taller, more muscular, more masculine. And certainly, more handsome. They'd felt an attraction for each other even before they understood the words for it. Jimmy used his thumb to trace the scar on Roy's forehead.

"Gloria wrote to me when you joined the Marines. And again, when you were injured. You and I were always proud of each other, Roy. You never tried to make me feel guilty. I guess you've changed more then I realized."

"No more than you, Baldy," Roy mumbled stubbing out his cigarette. "Maybe you just hate us. Maybe you hate yourself."

"No." Jimmy slammed his hand on the table. "It's a simple equation. I love Black people. It's America that hates us. Our ancestors had no agency over their enslavement, and I have no agency over the systems that shackle my hopes and ambitions. I can't breathe here. In Paris at least I have the freedom to find myself. To understand where my blackness ends, and my manhood begins."

Roy lit a Camel and stared at his friend. There was never a time Jimmy wasn't like this. Talking about things none of the kids ever thought about. His nose in a book that hadn't even been assigned by the teacher. Weaving abstract images with his words—the school principal called it a 'silver tongue.' Roy loved him for it. But then he'd always loved Jimmy.

"It may not make sense to you, Roy. But ideas are erupting inside me," Jimmy splayed his slender fingers on his chest, "demanding their release because they're not mine to keep. They're meant for the world."

"And that means you're leaving again." Roy shoved the cruise ship ticket across the table. "Back to your white people."

After dropping off the Robinsons and their two kids at church, Roy saw the blue Ford pull up with Jimmy in the passenger seat. The white driver was talking and gesturing. The church doors had already closed when Jimmy tried to leave the sedan, but the man reached across and held the door. They seemed to be quarreling until the driver began to caress Jimmy's head and then his face. Their heads tilted together in a kiss.

As soon as Roy saw Jimmy in the car, he started the tapping. The VA psychiatrist said the technique might help ward off the headaches so he wouldn't have to take so many pills, but it wasn't working this time. He reached into his pocket for one of the yellow pills and swallowed it dry. For a few seconds, he could hardly breathe. And then the violent pain began crowding his brain. He clung to the steering wheel until the drug began doing its work. His vision cleared in time to see the Ford drive away from the church. Roy followed the pair.

They weren't careful. A mixed-race couple drew attention. Even in Harlem. Especially if they were in a flashy new Ford. Roy knew what they were up to as soon as the car entered the park and drove the long stretch of unpaved road leading to the river turnoff. Roy had been there himself. Many times. In passionate entanglements with delicious dark-skinned bad boys, he'd picked up at a bar or one of the private homes where his kind gathered. But never in broad daylight on a Sunday morning. Cops knew about this place, and there was always the risk a vice squad car, and a paddy wagon, would roll up the wooded road to arrest another group of homos. The joke was that half those conducting the raids and roundups were probably gay themselves.

Roy parked at the edge of the road only a few minutes before deciding. He reached into the glove compartment for the small dark bottle and a rag, then tucked the handgun into his waistband. Dipping in and out of the trees, he stopped when he reached the overlook. There was only the Ford parked near the twelve-foot, chain-link fence that separated the grand view of the river from the careless or suicidal. As Roy drew closer, he saw the white boy in the front seat. His head bobbing. Roy yanked open the passenger door and slugged the driver with the butt of his pistol. The man's face fell onto Jimmy's lap.

Stunned, Jimmy could only utter a momentary protest before

Roy leaned his weight to confine him and pressed the rag against his mouth and nose. Roy winced at the sweet smell of the chloroform and watched Jimmy's shocked and pleading eyes go dim and finally close. He lifted Jimmy's limp body over his shoulder and carried him into the woods.

Jimmy gulped water from the small sink then stumbled out of the bathroom, his legs still cramping from being holed up in that tiny closet. Jimmy resisted before finally allowing Roy to help him to the desk chair.

Roy placed the paper bag in front of Jimmy. "Here. Eat. It's from Shirley's." He sat on the edge of the desk. The gun on his lap.

Jimmy hadn't said a word to Roy. And he didn't speak now. He tore open the bag and consumed the meatloaf with his fingers. Still dressed in his church suit, he paused a second before wiping his fingers on his shirt.

"Aren't you going to say anything?" Roy asked.

"Why?" Jimmy's voice was hoarse.

"You can't break a person's heart over and over again," Roy said, sniffing at the tears trying to form. "You just can't, Baldy." Roy wiped at his face. "Is it true what Gloria told me? You're staying? You got a place?"

Jimmy had avoided Roy's eyes, but now looked at him. "I thought about what you said. Gloria *does* need me." Jimmy paused. "Is Philippe alright?"

"Who? Oh. The white boy. He must be. The police think you've been kidnapped, and he's the only one who could have told them."

Jimmy's anger spilled over. "Why the fuck did you do this? You're a goddamn animal."

Roy couldn't stop the tears this time. "I couldn't stand to lose you again." He covered his face with his sleeve. The tears continued, and he rushed to the bathroom, leaving the gun on the desk. Jimmy watched the gun as if it might have its own life but didn't touch it. Instead, he searched the desk for paper and a pencil. When Roy returned Jimmy was scribbling so frantically he didn't notice.

"Baldy. I'm sorry. I'm truly sorry. Do you hear me?"

"I'm desperate for a cigarette, Roy. Do you have one?" Jimmy asked still writing. "And I need a drink of water."

Roy lit a cigarette and put it in an ashtray on the desk. He found a glass and filled it with water. Then he paced. He heard the bay doors slam shut when Gomez locked up. Roy looked at his watch then stood near Jimmy who was hunched over the desk.

"Baldy. I need to get you out of here. I'm sorry I drugged you and hit that guy. I just lost it. I don't know how else to explain it. You have every right to turn me in if you want to."

The light from the half-boarded window was dimming, and Jimmy's face was all eyes and gap-toothed smile when he responded.

"We were two boys adrift, you and I. You were once my sanctuary. How could I turn you in?"

"Come on. I'm taking you back to Gloria's."

"Not yet. We'll need a story. The police will ask questions. So will the papers. I've been writing some notes. Our cover story. I'll tell them I wasn't kidnapped, that I needed to get away to think. That being back in this country after so many years away brought up all the old terrors I felt about being an American Negro."

"What about your boyfriend?" Roy asked dourly.

"I'll smooth things over with Phillipe. I'd already told him I was staying in New York a while longer." Jimmy's face went soft. "He's really a very sweet man, Roy. I think you'd like him."

Roy tapped his thigh.

Jimmy stood. His legs shaking. "I can call the *Times* and *Harper's*. I might even give the story to *Amsterdam News*," he said excitedly. He looked down at the condition of his clothes. "If they send someone to interview me tonight, I'll need to change."

"You really think they'll buy it? That you just wanted to disappear for a few days?"

"Agatha Christie did it. So why shouldn't I?"

Roy clutched Jimmy's elbow steadying him as they descended the backstairs into the garage. A blue Caddy was up on cinderblocks in the first bay. The red Chevy was ready for pickup in the second, and the station wagon was parked next to it. That meant the Pontiac was waiting for him outside.

Roy moved to the side door and turned off the overhead light. He helped Jimmy through the door and turned to lock it. Then he heard approaching footsteps.

"Be still. Both of you," Peterson warned. "No. Don't turn around until I tell you, Willoughby."

"You're the one who's been following me," Roy stated.

"That's right. You've been lying since you were fifteen years old, why would I start believing your sorry ass now? I thought I'd find you two girls together, eventually."

Peterson wasn't in uniform, and it was the Plymouth, not a patrol car, parked in the side lot. He angled a small-caliber pistol back and forth until it stopped at Jimmy. "Boy, you've caused me a whole lot of grief," Peterson snarled. "Maybe you and the others think you're important now, but to me, you're still a piece of shit." Peterson took a step toward Jimmy. "I'm taking your black ass to the precinct so all those bleeding hearts at city hall can take a breath. But, before you get there, you might suffer a fall and . . ."

"Like the ones we had when you used to knock us around in the precinct basement?" Roy challenged; his back still turned. He'd been tapping his thigh since he heard Peterson's voice, but now he was having difficulty getting air.

"Shut up. You're in enough trouble as it is. Kidnapping, obstruction…"

"Wait a minute," Jimmy interrupted. "There's been no wrongdoing. It was me. I left for a while to clear my head."

Roy suddenly tossed the keys onto the gravel. The clatter caused Peterson to turn and fire, but not before Roy's shot caught him square in the chest. Peterson was dead before he hit the ground.

Roy fell too, writhing and holding his head. "Where'd he hit you?" Jimmy shouted.

"I'm not shot. Call Gomez. His number's in my pocket."

Gomez was at the garage within twenty minutes. Before he arrived, Roy's headache subsided to a dull thud. That's when he insisted Jimmy leave the scene and drive the Pontiac to Gloria's to initiate the cover story.

Using gloves, Roy and Gomez carried Peterson to his own car and dropped the body into the trunk. While Gomez raked the gravel in the side lot, Roy dumped one pair of gloves, and the two guns, into a vat of motor oil. He donned the second pair to drive Peterson's Plymouth to the river overlook. Roy kept an eye on the rear mirror. Gomez, calm and armed, followed.

The only other vehicle at the overlook left even after Roy gave the signal. Lights off, then on, and then doused again. When Gomez drove away, Peterson was still in the Plymouth's trunk. The keys in the ignition.

It was almost nine o'clock when they drove past Gloria's building. Roy's Pontiac was parked at the curb, but so was a patrol car. From around the corner, Roy made his way to the back entrance. This time Gloria answered Roy's knock immediately. She smiled, looking ten years younger than earlier.

"He's home. He said you'd be coming."

Roy accepted the beer Gloria offered and was back in the menacing chair. Jimmy, on the sofa and dressed in fresh clothes, had his arm around the little boy who was sleeping.

"You called the newspapers?"

Jimmy nodded. "There might be something in the *Times* tomorrow. The police were here, too. They seemed relieved when they left."

"They're still parked outside. Maybe in case you get another notion to go off and find yourself."

The two old friends laughed. Roy finished his beer, and Jimmy lit a cigarette.

"Don't ever ask me any questions about tonight, Baldy."

"I won't. But I have something to say to you, Roy. There's a price this republic exacts on every Black man or woman walking. That's the real crime. And we paid that price long before tonight. Remember that."

THE PROPHET DANIEL

CHRISTOPHER BOLLEN

Loren made it clear that I would not be meeting Elton John in Venice. For the record, Loren is an art advisor. We live in London, but he has a growing roster of clients in Venice, mostly the idle and irrational who have flocked to the city post-Brexit and -pandemic and now find themselves desperate for contemporary art to spice up their *piano nobiles*.

We've come to Venice for two weeks in chilly January because of Sir Elton John. He's one of Loren's top clients, and therefore, when he requested a total refresh of the art in his Venice apartment at the last minute, Loren couldn't exactly say no. Look, I love Elton John. I grew up on his music. I listened to "Daniel" on repeat my sophomore year of high school when the boy I was in love with (who was straight and not named Daniel) moved away to Colorado. Yes, I did fantasize about Elton, his husband David, Loren, and I repairing to a canal-side taverna in the evening to drink Aperol spritzes (does Elton drink?), bonding over lost early loves and maybe even singing "Daniel" with the man himself (I still know all the words). But that's not going to happen, because Elton isn't even in town.

As a consolation prize, Loren took me to see the apartment on the day I arrived. Elton John is one of our finest songwriters, but he has seriously suspect taste in art—his collection is all shine and flash, Damien Hirst and Jeff Koons, gaudily vacant objects that leave me with a crushed soul and a light migraine. Elton's apartment is tucked inside a seventeenth-century palazzo, but we could have been in a Miami penthouse but for the fact that it sits on the tip of Giudecca, with windows staring out over the slate-blue lagoon at Piazza San Marco. If I owned it, I'd strip the walls bare and let the view do all the work. I'd hang a solitary painting of the Annunciation over the sofa and call it a day. But I'm not a rock star, and I don't have rock-star tastes.

There are one hundred and thirty-nine churches in Venice, and I've already visited half of them. Since Loren works all day, I have a lot of hours to fill. I don't know how Annunciation paintings became an infatuation. It's like a song that gets stuck in your head, an earworm for the eye. I lingered in front of one in a church in Cannaregio, and now I can't stop looking for Annunciations everywhere I go.

The Annunciation is the moment the Archangel Gabriel surprises Mary in her house, confronting her with the most preposterous story and asking that she believe it. I've been collecting Annunciations, taking photos of each one I find. I tried showing Loren—"Honey, come look at these paintings"—but he's grumpy after a day of work, and his specialty is contemporary art, to the point that he shows zilch interest in anything before Picasso.

Most Annunciations are too passive, the main characters too psychologically resigned. I realized this while visiting the Palazzo Ca' d'Oro, studying a fifteenth century Annunciation painted on wood by a forgotten Lombard master. In it, Gabriel's wings are colored a repulsive, sulphureous green. It dawned on me, *yes, that's exactly how Mary would have perceived this uninvited ethereal visitor*: a creature terrifying and alien, utterly monstrous, something to tremble at, not the way most Old Masters paint him, as a laid-back, cherubic twink with bright parakeet wings and a fistful of lilies. I started paying particular attention to Annunciation Marys and none of them conveyed any sense of shock or surprise. That is, until I stumbled on the Veronese Annunciation in the Accademia Museum. The teenage Mary has her hand to her chest, cowering in terror, a look of *oh god you can't be serious* on her face. If I had my way, I'd splice together the Ca' d'Oro Gabriel and the Veronese Mary, creating the ultimate Annunciation.

Our accommodations in Venice are humdrum. Loren rented a no-frills Airbnb just north of Campo San Cassian in the San Polo neighborhood. Our apartment is on the second floor, with one unit below us, accessible from the street by a precipitously steep set of stairs. *You will eventually break your neck on us*, the stairs seem to murmur every time I use them, *maybe not this morning, but soon.* On my third evening in Venice, I nearly died tripping up them, hurrying to change before dinner, having spent the afternoon on my Annunciation tour. Loren was due home any minute, and I was pulling on a turtleneck when the buzzer rang. I assumed it was Loren, who must have misplaced his keys. I opened the apartment door and peered down the stairs. A slim older man was standing on the first-floor landing, right in front of our neighbor's door.

I must have startled him, because he tossed up his hands as if spooked. "I'm sorry," he said in perfect, Italian-accented English. "I am the owner of this building."

"Okay," I said. I began to retreat into my apartment, but he waved his hands more frantically.

"Please," he begged. "Wait. I rang your bell because I am locked out. We had the doors fixed last week, and now they lock automatically when they close." He mimed a door shutting and then twisting the knob and his not being able to open it, as if the concept were impossible to grasp without a demonstration.

"Oh no," I groaned. I figured he lived on the ground floor and had come up the stairs hoping one of his renters was home.

"Yes, it is very bad," he said, shaking his head. "And my phone, it is in the apartment. My phone, my keys …"

"You want to use my phone?" I asked. "To call someone?"

"I have such a bad memory. Even my wife's number I do not remember." He eagerly began climbing the stairs toward me. He wore a maroon puffer jacket and faded blue jeans. He seemed about 60, with a shiny bald pate and white bristles on the sides. He increased his earnest smile, which emphasized the boniness of his face, and his teeth were the gray of dried glue. I got the impression that he wanted to come inside and wait for his wife to return. Since he technically owned the apartment, I wasn't sure I could refuse.

Loren would be back at any minute, tired and cranky, and he would regard the surprise visitor as yet another example of my tendency to get tangled up in the problems of strangers, too weak to say no. Loren is 37, one year older than I am, but he treats me like he's a decade wiser. I knew he'd be annoyed. But the owner stopped two steps before our door and made no indication of entering.

"How do you like your stay?" he asked. Before I could answer, he blurted out, "This building used to be much bigger, connected to the building next door." I nodded, feigning interest in the useless piece of trivia. "Do you see your door, it is strong. You can't break it open. They are made by a special locksmith in Mestre who keeps the codes to open them."

I knew that Mestre was the first town on the mainland. It was where most Venetians lived these days, ousted by the tourists. "Can you break open a window around back?" I suggested, and he reacted in horror to the idea of destroying his property.

"I'm sorry to ask such a favor," he said nervously. "But could I borrow some money, just enough to get me to Mestre to the locksmith? My wallet is also in the apartment . . ."

"Of course!" I was relieved. He wouldn't be waiting around in our living room when Loren came home. "Hold on." I let the door hang open—mine did not automatically swing shut and lock—to fetch my wallet. I returned, waving a ten-euro bill.

"God bless you," he exclaimed. "You are a lifesaver. I will return with the money and slip it under your door. You will have it back in two hours."

"Don't worry. It's just ten—"

"I shall need, oh, forty or fifty euros?" He must have noticed the confusion on my face. "You see, I need to take a boat, then a train, then a car to the locksmith who has the codes." The amount seemed high—couldn't he just walk to the train station?—but I pulled out two twenty-euro bills and handed them to him. "I hate to ask," he said shyly. "Can I borrow sixty? It will get me there faster."

I'm not stingy, but sixty passed a line of generosity that forty only toed. It was all the cash I had, but Loren and I were staying in this man's apartment for two weeks. How could I face him again, turning down his urgent appeal to reach his locksmith before they closed for the night?

I handed him another ten.

"I will slip it in an envelope under your door in two hours. Bless you." He began to hurry down the stairs, arms wide like a giddy child, and I smiled and waved. He stopped at the door to the first-floor unit. "I will fix this door."

"Wait, you live in the apartment right below ours?" Loren had told me that a long-term renter from Barcelona was staying there, an artist teaching a semester at the university. He'd met her on his first day. "Is Gemma your wife? The woman visiting from Barcelona?"

The owner looked pained. He grabbed the collar of his maroon puffer jacket as if to protect his neck from the cold.

"We moved her," he said. "She wanted more space, and we own a bigger apartment on the other side of the Rialto."

And yet I'd heard Spanish being spoken through the floorboards last night and smelled the reek of weed as I passed her door this morning. It seemed wildly unlikely they'd moved Gemma today and that he'd had time to reclaim the apartment as his residence. My eyes scanned his hands for the money I'd just given him, but it was already tucked in his pocket. I wanted to ask for it back. Or at least forty of it. Take 20 euros. That's more than enough to get you to Mestre. It was too late.

"God bless you," he said again. "I'm so glad you like the apartment." He stumbled down the rest of the steps and bolted out the door.

Loren returned ten minutes later. I was sulking on the couch, staring impassively at the beamed ceiling. "What's wrong?" he asked.

I wanted to tell him, "I think I've just been scammed," but I knew he'd jump on it as evidence of my innate gullibility, such a dupe, a born sucker, *why didn't you just hand him your credit cards and passport while you were at it?*, so instead I said, "Let's just go to dinner."

At the restaurant, I drank too much, almost an entire bottle of red, and when we climbed the steps three hours later, I held my breath as Loren unlocked the apartment door. There was no envelope.

I try to put it out of my mind. *It's only 60 euros,* I tell myself. I decide, no eating lunch for the next three days—that will cover the cost of your stupidity. I tell myself, you saw a person in need, you were charitable to a man so desperate he needed to concoct an outrageous lie to gather enough money to eat. You are a good person; that's your only mistake. But sixty euros! How could I have given so much away? I scold myself, first you were conned, now you're just being cheap. Let it go.

I spend my days walking around Venice on the hunt for him. Maroon puffer jacket. Bald head. Gray teeth. I try to continue the Annunciation tour, but my eyes no longer flock to the Gabriels and Marys. They're more interested in scanning the thin January crowds filling the museums and churches for the man who scammed me. My eyes and anger have joined forces, refusing to let me take in any of the pleasures of Venice. I simply can't let it go. For the next days, I move through the streets while Loren is at work, a hunter in search of his prey. We all know that Venice is a labyrinth. But it's also a finite city, a closed circuit, and eventually, if you keep walking, you visit the same corners and see the same inhabitants again and again. I follow a steady route, making two or three laps a day, oblivious to the gurgling canals or shimmering basilica domes or the ancient one-handed clocks. I go from the Rialto to San Marco over to Cannaregio, then swoop down into San Polo and through the student quarters of Dorsoduro. Maroon puffer jacket. Bald head.

I spot him standing in line for gelato on the Zattere. I catch a glimpse of him selling cuttlefish in the fish market. I watch him glide by on a vaporetto on the Grand Canal. All mis-IDs. I come home exhausted, my feet swollen, grumpier than Loren, who's been rearranging Elton's vomitous masterpieces. In bed, I refuse Loren's pelvis-grinding attempts to initiate sex. When he sleeps, I stay up, catching the mosquitos that helicopter over our bed, which I blame on the owner of this apartment for his shoddy window repairs, picturing my scam artist, even though he isn't the real owner.

On day six, I'm on the verge of giving up. The damp Venetian cold has a way of creeping under your clothes and settling in your joints. I'm passing through a campo in Castello when the miracle happens. It's so sudden and mundane it comes as a shock. He's loitering outside a tobacco shop, puffing on a cigarette, a beam of sunlight on his face. He's even wearing the maroon puffer. Elation rushes through me. I nearly run with my arms wide to hug him. *I've been looking for you for so long, I never thought we'd find each other again.* But then my rage returns, along with the memory of the money he stole from me, preying on my kindness, and now he's standing openly in a campo without the slightest hint of fear. He clearly counted on me staying only a few nights, figuring he was safe because tourists are here on a limited clock. How many others has he scammed this week?

I flip up my coat collar and put on my knit cap to prevent recognition. My scam artist finishes his cigarette, waves to a friend, and strolls past a church whose bells are tolling. I follow him down a long calle at a safe distance. He pops into a bar, slaps down a bill, knocks back a shot of liquor, and is out the door again, strutting down a narrow alley. In January many of the restaurants are shuttered, but mask stores do a brisk business thanks to the upcoming Carnevale, and I nearly lose my quarry twice, getting tangled in a knot of shoppers. I manage to extract myself and two minutes later watch as my scammer enters a small storefront. I approach cautiously, peering with one eye through the front window.

It's an antique glass shop, pink chandeliers with flowering arms, lopsided prism-bright vases, flamboyant animal-stemmed champagne flutes. "Tutto Autentico Vetro di Murano," a sign reads above the register. A young man stands behind the counter, and my scammer is berating him, his face a blunt instrument without its conning smile. The young man meekly attempts to defend himself but is shouted into silence. My scam artist opens a metal box, removes a bundle of cash, and heads for the door.

I hunch against the wall, pretending to be absorbed in my phone as he rushes past me. Like a golden retriever, my instinct is to follow at his feet, afraid to lose sight of him again. But what do I intend to do once I confront him? Grab him by the collar and demand my money? Drag him to the police station? Loren is right, I'm so hopelessly non-confrontational, such a pushover, a weakling. It's more likely he'd punch me in the stomach, leave me beaten in a doorway without my wallet, threaten to break my legs if I don't leave Venice immediately. All these days of searching and I never bothered to devise an intelligible revenge plot. All I have is this glass shop, his tether to a legitimate business.

"Greetings," I exclaim as I enter the shop. My voice startles the young man at the counter, who clutches his chest in fright. I remove my cap and offer a broad smile.

"Buongiorno," he says, trying for warmth. His skin is pale, with a pink blush splotching his cheeks, his dark hair·cut in the current mode of Italian youth—short except for tousled bangs that hang like a clump of ivy over his eyes. His right ear is pierced with a diamond stud, which no longer tells me anything about his sexuality. His upper body is a little chubby, but it might simply be leftover baby fat. He's an awkward cherub, not yet certain, wings already clipped.

"Are you the proprietor?" I ask. He wrinkles his forehead in confusion. "Are you the owner of this shop?"

"No, no," he says vehemently, as if I've accused him of a crime. "Is my father. But he just left for the day." He glances out at the front window and so do I, as if we both my see his alcoholic father floating by, waving the euros he stole from me.

"It's a shame I missed him. I'm very interested in this shop!" I make a show of looking around, admiring the enormous glass fish sculpture and the colorful abstract blobs. It's really not such a terrible inventory, just old, covered in a fine, customerless layer of dust. "You see, I'm a big collector of glass, and I've been marveling at your pieces through the windows. Superior quality! You must sell the best Murano artisans!" I have no idea where I'm going with this charade. It's all improvisation, me white knuckling any revenge I can eke out. I'm not even sure the young man is fluent enough in English to follow what I'm saying, but he brightens at my egregious shower of compliments, smiling with the most beautiful white teeth, the very opposite of his father's.

"We are proud," the young man says, moving around the counter. "So many shops in Venice, they only say Murano. They are made in factories in China. But this shop was opened by my father in 1997, a true Venetian. We only sell true Venetian glass!"

"He's got a great eye! I wish I could have met him. Maybe you could give me his home address? I could visit him tonight, ring his bell around dinnertime, and offer him more money than he's ever earned from a sale before?" The perfect revenge comes to me in a flash: showing up to his door, a rich, gullible American ready to throw bags of money at his feet, only for us to recognize each other and what he'd already pulled over on me.

The young man looks embarrassed. "We don't live in Venice right now. We moved to Mestre."

"That's unfortunate. You see, I *urgently* need to buy a large quantity of glass to fill my apartment!" I'm laying it on a little thick, but ridiculousness seems to get lost in translation, or ridiculousness is the lingua franca of rabid Murano glass collectors. Mostly, I'm feeding off the young man's excitement, his brown eyes widening, his teeth obscenely pretty, his skin so dewy and unwrinkled I can't help imagining putting my lips against it. "Carlo Scarpa. Martinuzzi. Really anything by Venini," I say, blowing my entire knowledge of Venetian glass in four seconds. "I'm obscenely wealthy. It's a shame your father isn't here. A good proprietor should stay in his shop, not run off drinking all day. Will you be sure to tell him he missed a huge sale with a rich customer? I was almost ready to come on board as an investor in this shop." Who talks like this? Apparently, I do in the role of manic billionaire benefactor. But is it any more outrageous than the story of woe and pity and covert locksmiths in Mestre that his father told me?

The young man swallows hard. "You are visiting from America?"

"No, I live here," I reply. "I bought a huge apartment on Giudecca. It's in a seventeenth century palazzo right next to the Hotel Cipriani." I'm thinking of Elton John's place. "I have so much contemporary art but no glass. And it's been a dream of mine to co-own a glass store in Venice. Anyway, it's a huge loss for your father. Unless, of course, he could meet me here at the shop later this afternoon? Tell him I'm ready to spend."

"Please," the boy whispers. "My father is not well. He's . . ." He stops, conflicted, worried about the information he's just let slip. "How about I arrange for him to meet you in an hour at a café across town? You can talk to him there about your plan? Would that work? Please?"

It isn't ideal. I'd rather embarrass him at his home in front of his wife, or even here in the shop with his son watching. But a public shaming does have its advantages.

It starts to rain in the hour that I wait to meet him. I'm nervous. I linger under store awnings, preparing for the role of ultimate dupe, someone the father could have taken for tens of thousands, not a mere sixty euros. Perhaps I'll even lead with something like, *Oh, it's you! Are you still on your way back from the locksmith in Mestre? Can I give you more money to slip later under my door?*

I'm five minutes late to the café. A jackpot machine is blinking bright red cherries, and next to it is an old-fashioned jukebox. I'm shaking, slightly terrified, but I'm also already excited by the idea of telling Loren the full story of how I didn't back down. The café is dark. There is only one table occupied.

It's not the con artist who's waiting for me. It's his son. He eyes me apologetically from his seat, his fingers wiping the rain off his cell phone, his curly bangs glistening with raindrops. The young man looks older and more serious now that he's free of the yoke of his father's store. He's changed into a white Oxford shirt, and I can see his doughy nipples through the wet fabric. He extends his hand, gesturing for me to sit opposite him.

"I thought I was meeting—" I start, but he speaks over me.

"I'm sorry I tricked you. All I ask is for a minute of your time. My name is Matteo Daniele. I am twenty-two, no boy, a very honest, trustworthy man." He drops his head, struggling to find the words of an honest, trustworthy man, and when his eyes resurface, they look daring and electric, as if he's about to ask me on a date. He shows off his lovely white teeth, and a waiter sets two espressos in front of us. "I order for you," he says, like we are on a date, then gets down to business.

He tells me his father has gambling debts and that for the past few years, he's been declining mentally. He tells me his dream of getting out from under his father's thumb and starting his own art-glass gallery, contemporary pieces; there are so many amazing glass artists working today in Venice. Do I know who Ritsue Mishima is? Ritsue spends half the year here, and Matteo would love to introduce me to her. All he needs is an investor, someone to give him the seed money to get started, someone who loves glass art as much as he does, a partnership, a friendship, an opportunity. When I came into the shop unexpectedly this afternoon and professed my passion for glass, it was like a miracle, a reason to have faith in the future again.

His eyes are shining with hope, and I realize that it's the son, not the father, who I'm punishing with this fabrication. Matteo licks his lips, his saliva streaked across them, very kissable, a handsome young man under his pelt of curly bangs. He blushes slightly, recalibrates his eyes, waits for my verdict.

I say nothing.

"Another thing," he adds, and I feel a hand pressing on my knee. "Something else about me that my father cannot accept. Another reason I need to be on my own. I think you understand?"

I gasp, reflexively moving my knee away, although I instantly wish I hadn't. "Yes, I understand . . . I think." I'm blushing and fumbling over my words, returning my knee to its previous position, hoping Matteo will resume fondling it. I'm thirty-six, hardly middle-aged, and yet I'm suddenly scared I'll never again be hit on by a twenty-two-year-old Italian.

"I need this money, need you to take a chance on me. It is only an investment of twenty, maybe thirty thousand to start. We will make three times that in a year. We work side by side. You and me. Together. Our love of glass . . ." His hand briefly flits across my knee, and I'm lost in a spell, one where Loren's plane is taking off to London, and I'm not on it.

Matteo flips his phone over on the table to check the time. "Will you promise to think about it?" he pleads. "You won't be sorry. Just think. Okay?"

"Yes. I'll consider it."

He smiles and excuses himself to the bathroom. As he passes he squeezes my shoulder.

Alone at the table, I see my future playing out in various ways. I see myself stealing Loren's key to Elton John's apartment and inviting

Matteo over when it's empty, having sex with him in several different positions on Sir Elton's bed. I see myself dumping all my savings into Matteo's glass store, spending half my year in Venice just like Ritsue Mishima does, working side by side with my young Italian boyfriend. I see Matteo's father standing broken on the other side of a canal, rending his maroon puffer jacket, yanking at his non-existent hair. *Give me back my son,* he cries. And I cry back, *Keep the sixty euros. Consider it a gift from me and Matteo Daniele.* I see a glass angel, a startled Mary, the promise of impossible things.

Matteo's phone vibrates with an incoming call. I pick it up to stop its juddering on the table. The phone is locked, but the name "Giulia" flashes across the screen, along with a photo of a skinny blonde girl kissing Matteo's smooth neck.

The phone case has a small leather pocket sewn onto its side. In it, Matteo keeps eighty euros, but I only take sixty, the amount owed to me.

As I pass the jukebox on my way out the door, I check to see if it has Elton John's Greatest Hits. I put on "Daniel" for Matteo before I leave. The song costs two euros, but it's worth it.

THESE TRUTHS

RENEE JAMES

She's so tense she could break out in hives. It's killing me. We seemed so compatible on the app, but she's been twitchy since we got in the car, and I don't have a clue about how to put her at ease. I had such high hopes for this date.

"Is there anything you want to know about me?" I ask. It's not like I want to talk about myself, but when I try to get her to talk about herself, she acts as if I'm invading her privacy.

She purses her lips and furrows her brows in thought. Something about her expression seems familiar. A movie character, maybe, or someone I kind of knew once. I have a good memory for people, and I should be able to recall who she reminds me of, but I'm coming up with blanks. She's pretty, in a kind of exotic, gothic way. Like an Italian version of the actress Laverne Cox—dark eyes, dark hair in a twist, fringes framing her face, a nice figure clad in tasteful clothes. And tall. All of six feet.

"Are you violent?" she asks. No smile, her hands clutched together on her lap. Her eyes stare straight ahead, over the hood of the car. The lights of the city flash by, but I don't think she notices them. I've never made anyone this nervous.

"No, I promise, you're safe," I say. I glance across the center console and flash a friendly smile.

She looks at me and tries to return the smile. It's gone in a trice. Silence fills the car while I negotiate traffic. "Have you had problems?" I ask.

She shrugs, a feminine gesture with thin arms and a serious face with the pursed lips and furrowed brow again. "Girls like me, we never know."

"Can I ask you about that?"

She shrugs again. "As long as you're not kinky about it. I'm open about who I am."

"When did you know?" I ask.

She takes her time answering. "I always knew, but I didn't really admit it to myself until high school."

"Is that when you transitioned?"

"No, college."

I ask where she went to school. "California," she answers. Another minimal response. They all are.

"Berkeley?"

"UC San Francisco." No elucidation, no details.

"Are you a native Californian, then?" She shakes her head, no.

I ask her where she grew up. I'm watching the road, but I can see her grimace and frown in my peripheral vision. "My bio's on the app," she says. "Can we skip the small talk?"

I start to point out that her bio is sketchy and doesn't include anything about where she grew up, but I stop myself. She's wound too tight for a challenge from me.

She takes a breath. Some of the tension leaves her body. She pivots to me. "I'm sorry. These situations are very difficult for me. Can we just do the weather and favorite songs kind of stuff for a while?"

I nod and do my best, but talking with her is exhausting.

Thankfully, we get to the art museum, an environment that doesn't demand conversation and offers many alternatives to talking about ourselves. She relaxes a little as we drift past the paintings and sculptures. We share short comments, mine, mostly attempts to be witty, hers, appreciative, insightful, informed. I ask if she was an art major at UCSF.

"No," she laughs. There's actual humor on her face and she shares a beautiful smile. "It's famous for its medical school and medical research. I went there to become a surgeon and to get my gender surgery."

"Wow." I'm properly impressed. "You're a surgeon?"

She nods. "Surgical resident at County Hospital." Before I can ask another question, she changes the subject. "What about you?"

I blink. It's a sudden transition. "I teach high school English. Literature, composition. I'm hoping to get a creative writing class, too."

She looks at me and we hold eye contact. It's just for a second, but something happens. Her eyes do something. Maybe widen just a fraction. I sense she had a moment of alarm, like realizing that the log you're sitting on is an alligator. She recovers and asks, "Was that what you always wanted to do?"

I'd rather dodge the question, but I feel compelled to be honest. If she can be upfront about being transgender, I can share my awkward truths. "No. When I was in high school, I wanted to go to West Point. In college, I started aiming for law school." I pause, trying to parse my words so I don't scare her.

"But?" She's terse, even with her questions.

"But I got in trouble in high school. I couldn't get into West Point, and it made a legal career iffy." If she wants the details, she'll ask.

Her head snaps forward again, eyes fixed on a painting. Her lips are taut, her jaw flexes. Looking at her in profile, standing next to me, I again get the feeling there's something familiar about her, like someone you saw every day in a terrible TV ad.

"I promise, you're not in danger," I say. "I really just want to . . ." My voice trails off. It sounds phony when I think it, but I go ahead and say it. "I'd just like to make a friend."

"Do you have a hard time making friends?" she asks, not looking at me.

"I don't have any close women friends." I don't know what to say next. Since my divorce, I've had a few short-term hook-ups. It's not a preference, just what's been available to me. But one-night stands remind me that I'm lonely and I suck at relationships, so the friendship thing is for real. It's a moot point. She still avoids looking at me. Something about me spooks her.

We drift through a few more rooms, exchanging a few words about the art, but nothing else. She's really distant. I sigh. It happens. I'm not ugly, but I'm no matinee idol, either. When I made this date, I was hoping it would be enough that I was a nice guy, that we could be friends who did things together, whether a romance bloomed or not. No such luck. The only thing we've established is that she'd like to cut this date short.

"I have a table reserved at a place near here," I say, "but if you'd rather go home, no hard feelings."

She finally looks at me. Her face has one of those expressions only women can make: *why would you think such a thing?*

"Dinner would be nice," she says. She holds my eyes as she says it. She has a lush, throaty voice, and she forms her words with intricate precision. She exudes elegance. I feel a tiny surge of hope even though I'm several rungs too low on the social order for a beautiful surgeon, and I know how this will end.

The restaurant is a small, dark, Italian place, maybe a dozen tables. I don't know how such a small place stays in business, but Tomaso's has been here forever. Some say Tommy, the owner, runs a back-room bookie operation, but all I've ever seen here is great food and an owner who treats every patron like royalty and remembers names forever. We enter to the aromas of garlic and seafood and things being cooked in butter. Tommy greets me by name, like I'm a famous billionaire, even though I'm just an occasional patron. I introduce Sydney. He kisses her hand. Her hand is long and graceful, large for a woman, but pretty, with plain gold rings on two fingers, and short nails painted in a light pink polish that blends with her skin tone. She beams that beautiful smile again. She loves his gesture, though if I had greeted her that way, I'm pretty sure she would have passed out.

We make small talk and order. When the waiter leaves, silence descends on us, even though the room is alive with chatter and din. We sip wine. She looks at me and smiles. I catch her eye, and she holds my gaze. Progress.

"Have we met before?" I ask.

"Like in a previous life?" She smiles. Humor.

I ask her biographical questions again. She doesn't seem to mind now. After college and med school in California, came here for residency a year ago. No time for dating or hobbies, just work, early morning runs, nighttime gym workouts a few times a week.

Our order comes. Conversation focuses on the food, which is superb. Thank goodness. She may not enjoy my company, but she likes this place. Maybe she'll come back here on her own and think fondly of me for a moment as she relishes her meal.

We finish and sip wine in lieu of dessert. "Why did you respond to my message?" The question reveals my self-doubts, not a good first-date strategy but, realistically, we have no future together anyway. Might as well fill in a few blanks before I never see her again.

She's surprised by the question and takes a moment to consider her answer. "You sounded like you'd be a gentleman." She says it like there's more, but she stops.

"Surely that's not a unique trait among people who respond," I say. "I mean, even an egomaniacal Alpha would keep it together long enough to write a civil note of introduction."

"You'd be surprised." She sips her wine. I wait for her to say more, but she doesn't.

"What kind of responses do you get?"

She pauses, thinks. She doesn't want to have this conversation. "A little of everything," she says. "Religious diatribes. Propositions for sex. Declarations of open-mindedness. A few nice letters—intelligent, polite. Like yours."

"Did anything differentiate me from others in the gentleman class?" I add a small smile to show the question is offered with humor, so she can ignore it if she wants to.

"Probably."

I cock my head in question.

"Well, you're the only one I went out with," she says.

This is like trying to catch a slippery fish with my hands. "That makes me more curious. Why me?"

Shrug. Small smile. Deep breath. "I think we knew each other once."

I stare at her. Surely, I would remember a woman like her. "In California?" I ask.

She seems to tense up. "No." Deep breath. "Before that."

"High school?" I try to place a tall, pretty girl in the hallways of my school. Nothing. "Where did you go to high school?"

Another deep breath. "Actually, in this area." She's being vague again, but before I can ask her, she volunteers, "Granville."

I can't stop staring at her. She takes a sip of wine to break the eye contact. "I went to Granville, too." Then it dawns on me, Sydney would have been a boy then.

"We knew each other?" I can barely say the words. We must have. And she might have known it from the start of this date. Her nerves.

Unwillingness to look at me. Did I do something horrible to her former self?

She glances into my eyes, looks away, then focuses on me again. "Yes." She smiles a little, nervous. "Simon. I was Simon Green. Same year."

I've always been good with names and faces. Simon pops into my mind like it was yesterday. Thin, nice-looking guy, Mediterranean skin, quiet. Honors student but never an asshole about it. We weren't pals, but we said hi when we passed each other in the halls between classes. He was an okay guy. I wouldn't have put Simon and Sydney together on my own, but now that I know the answer, yeah, I can see some similarities.

"Yes, I remember you." I smile. "You ran cross-country. National Honor Society. You were an artist. Your paintings hung on the walls."

She smiles self-consciously and looks down at the table. "My mom wanted me to be an artist. Well, an art teacher."

"How does she feel about the way things turned out?"

She laughs this time. "Surgeon made her 'okay' list. The daughter part came as a surprise, but we've bonded. Dad's doing his best."

"Was I . . ." I pause. How to phrase this. "We weren't friends, but was I okay to you? I had some issues in high school."

Smile. "You were always nice to me," she says.

I exhale. I realize I've been holding my breath. High school was a tough time for me, which might explain why I relate pretty well with high school kids today, especially the kids with issues. I'm still studying her. Something about her silence tells me there's more.

"You knew who I was when we made this date," I say. I let that statement hang in the air, a question.

She looks away, looks back at me, looks down at the table. Sips her wine. Looks at me. "I owe you an apology." She stops and looks away. Silence. She's straining to find the words.

"You kicked my dog?" Maybe a little humor will help.

Smile. Small laugh. "Did you have a dog?"

"Stole my car, then?"

She laughs. "Did you have a car?"

"Actually, I did." The image of my old rust bucket forms in my mind.

She smiles at me and holds my gaze. "I remember it," she says. "Red and black, and a bit rusty." I nod. Her face saddens, her dark eyes become morose. "I owe you an apology." Her lips seem to quiver just a little.

"I can't think of anything you need to apologize to me for," I say, trying to smile gently to put her at ease. "But if it's getting you down, you can take me to Disneyland or something." Dad humor, not that I am one. Not that my own dad was anything but a surly ogre of a man. But I've read a lot of Dad jokes, and I like them.

She forces a laugh. She appreciates my attempt at humor. She looks me in the eye. I'm letting myself admit how beautiful she is, how much I'd like to see her again. It hasn't been like this for me since the divorce. Before the divorce, if I'm honest. Years.

"Senior year. My friends and I tagged along with you and your friends one night," she says. "There were four cars. I was in the last one. Mostly just driving crazy fast and making a lot of noise. All of us following you and your friends in your beater."

I tense a little and scrutinize her again, trying to place Simon in that event.

"You don't remember me being there," she says. "No surprise. It was very out of character for me and my friends to be out raising hell like normal teenagers. We were library nerds, and I was"—she looks away, then back—"I knew I was queer and scared to death it showed. The nice part of that night was you and your friends just accepting us, letting us tag along. I felt like I was having my first real high school experience." Her voice trails off.

"And then?" The bitch of it is, I know where this goes, but I need to hear her version of it.

"Then we stopped in this subdivision, and you pulled something out of the trunk of your car, a big, heavy chain that was hard for you to carry, and we started walking across lawns. Quiet. Like cat burglars. I remember feeling excited, like I was on an adventure. The air was crisp. Our breath put out plumes of condensation. My friends and I straggled along in back, wondering what was going to happen. And then you walked up to a house and threw the chain through a picture window, and we all ran like crazy back to our cars and split. My friends and I were scared to death. We drove to the next town and sat for an hour in a McDonalds parking lot, wondering if we were going to get arrested, wondering how we would explain ourselves to our parents."

She stops and looks at me. I shrug and look back at her, puzzled.

"I heard about your arrest, and I read about the plea deal," she says, her voice tight. "I should have come forward." She stops.

"You didn't do anything," I say.

"I was there. You shouldn't have had to face the judge by yourself."

"I didn't. Joe and Rob were with me." Their images come into my mind. Joe, a tough, wiry kid. Chip on his shoulder worse than mine. Managed to get into the army after high school and got himself killed in one of our glorious wars. Rob, good-looking guy, gearhead. Not too smart, didn't say much. His family moved away after the plea deal, and we lost touch. Actually, I lost touch with everyone after that. No one wanted to associate with a felon.

She's crying, real tears. Her mascara runs. She dabs at her eyes with one hand, the other rests on the table. I reach for her hand out of sympathy. I try to be comforting. "There was nothing you could do," I say.

"I could have vouched for your character," she says. "I knew you weren't a bigot."

"How could you know that?" I ask. "That was the only time we ever hung out."

She sniffles. "I knew you chose that house at random. You didn't know who lived there."

My smile is forced. I'd like to change the subject. "Look at it this way," I say, stroking her hand with my fingers. "If you'd gotten me off, I would have gone to West Point and ended up killing people. I've bored kids to tears in English class, but I haven't bored anyone to death. You saved lives." I smile to show I'm offering this as humor.

She forces a return smile. "I didn't come forward. I was a coward. I prayed you and the others wouldn't tell the police we were there. I was scared to death. I could see my whole life going up in flames."

"They wouldn't have charged you," I say. "You didn't know I was going to do that."

She straightens. She's not crying anymore. She composes herself. "Why did you do it?"

I shake my head. It's automatic. Whenever that question comes up, I always start with a slow shake of the head. "I don't know, Sydney. I carried a lot of anger then. I guess it just came out that night, that way." As I say it, I try to quash the images of fists flying and angry curses in my bloody showdowns behind the gym, an unwelcome montage of my high school years.

She puts her hand on mine and brushes her fingers back and forth, a friendly massage, sympathy, not seduction. We've switched roles, I realize.

"Where did the anger come from?" Her voice is soft and supportive, which is why I answer. The only other time I answered that question was working with a shrink in college.

"Mainly, my father. He was a mean, angry man. A bully, a whiny coward who carped and complained about everything. He never hit me or my mother, but he criticized everything we ever did. He never once said anything positive to me. Never came to a soccer game or even asked how I did. Never any praise for my grades. The first time I made Honor Roll he figured I scammed the system somehow. He told me I was as dumb as my mother."

"He said that, really?" Sydney's eyes widen in surprise.

I nod. "Yeah. The last time, senior year, I hit him. I think more for my mom than me. There wasn't much left of her by then."

"You hit your father?"

I take a long look at Sydney. "I knocked him cold. I had a powerful right hook. He didn't know where he was for a while. I told him not to get up, that I'd just plant him again, that he needed to stop harassing me and Mom. He stayed down until I left the room. He left me alone after that, but he got even. He wouldn't give me money for a lawyer for the trial, and he never gave me a dime for college."

Sydney looks at me with the wide-eye thing again. She's impressed. "You did college on your own?"

"My great achievement." She draws me out on how I did it. The old-fashioned way: scholarships, loans, odd jobs for an elderly couple in return for a free room and board. Sydney shares that she had a lot of help from her parents. She says it like a confession. "Don't apologize to me," I say. "That's what I'm going to do for my kids. If I have kids."

"Is that in doubt?" She asks the question, but her body language tells me something else is going on in her head. I think she likes me. My tragic story. Jesus, I think she's crushing on me.

"Uh," I fumble for words. "Well, basically, I'm not having much success socially."

She flashes a teasing smile. "You can always adopt."

I shake my head. "I couldn't raise a child myself."

"I bet you'd be a great father," says Sydney. She's definitely crushing.

"I feel like I'd be pretty good, but not good enough to do it on my own."

"You won't have any trouble finding a wife," she says.

"Right now, I'd settle for a date." It's my turn to raise eyebrows.

"If you're asking me out, the answer is yes." Sydney flashes that full, beautiful smile again. My heart flips a little. I come back to earth. She's a good person. Not just hot and beautiful, warm-hearted and empathetic, too. She deserves to know the rest.

"The thing is, Sydney . . ." I pause. Do I really want to do this? I must. "The thing you need to know is, that house wasn't randomly selected. I didn't know the people who lived there, but I knew they were Jewish."

Her jaw drops in surprise. She blinks. She struggles to speak. "I'm Jewish."

"I know," I say. I shake my head, trying to communicate how ashamed I am.

"Are you antisemitic?" she asks. "Were you then?"

"No." I pause, shake my head, look for words. "I don't know why I did it. I don't know why I picked a Jewish neighborhood. I was so angry I thought I'd explode."

She's reappraising me, a tormented expression on her face. Her eyes pull away from me. She purses her lips and furrows her brows again. Her hands come together, and she starts to twist them as though she's trying to wring out all the angst in her body. She feels me watching and drops her hands to her lap, below the table. If she gets any more tense it seems like her body could shatter.

"I'm not sure I can see you again," she says.

The only surprise is that she can talk at all. "Of course," I say. I try not to think about another silent Sunday, doing laundry, cleaning, reviewing lesson plans. About summer break coming up, me teaching summer school just to have a social life.

We descend into a paralyzing silence that surrounds us like a prison, two people trapped together with nothing more to say to each other. I call for the bill and glance at Sydney. She's staring at the tabletop. I let my eyes pour over her; I let my mind appreciate her beauty and think about what it would have been like to embrace her, to make love with her, to feel her body against mine. To talk, laugh, hold hands.

I pay the bill, and we head for the exit. I hold the door for her and think of all the things we won't talk about on the endless ride home.

A LEOPARD'S SPOTS

KATHERINE V. FORREST

"I know these events are very upsetting . . ." The deputy sheriff's tone was steeped in sympathy; a line between her gray-green eyes distinctly deepened. "May I know your names, please?"

Distraught as she was, Ruth Whitman nevertheless was interested that a small, coastal California county would have a woman on its police force, and a bulky, middle-aged one at that.

A reedy voice came softly from beside her: "I'm Benjamin Dickinson. My friend here is Ruth Whitman."

"Dickinson and Whitman," the deputy repeated, writing in her notebook, her face still somber but the crease between her eyes lightening. "Like the poets."

"Last Halloween somebody did call me Emily," Dickinson offered. "But I was trying to be Eleanor Roosevelt."

Bannon cast a brief glance of amusement at him, then said, "Ms. Whitman, would you step outside with me? Mr. Dickinson, I'll be back in a few minutes."

"Everyone calls us by our last name," Whitman said. Catching Bannon's eye, she nodded meaningfully toward Dickinson.

This time Bannon's glance evaluated the grayish pallor in Benjamin Dickinson's face, the sag in his thin shoulders. She said to him, "On second thought, let's you and me have a brief chat."

Dickinson pulled his pea coat from the coat tree and donned it as he followed Bannon from the parlor of the Pinckney house out onto the porch.

Whitman sank heavily into the yielding depths of the brown corduroy sofa. Deferring to Dickinson as the first to be questioned had been an act of pure altruism. Grieved and heartsick over what had occurred here, she was anxious to tell what little she knew and leave this place; the superficial conversation with Bannon had in itself taxed her reserves of strength. But she owed Dickinson extra consideration; he had lost Roy to a heart attack less than a year ago, while her own loss of Margaret was in its eighth year—a bereavement she felt no less keenly, she was certain, than Dickinson suffered his more recent loss.

She leaned over to prop her elbows on her knees, rubbing her face with both hands. For months, death had hovered over this house, and had now struck twice, turning it into a place of horror . . . with more horror to come. Six friends had come here today, friends who were undergoing the same police questioning as herself and Dickinson. Which of the six was a murderer? And why?

Dickinson eased himself into the old-fashioned bench swing on the porch; Bannon sat opposite him, gingerly arranging her bulk in a flimsy canvas deck chair.

"I understand what's going on here." The swing creaked beneath him as he looked out at the powder blue squad car parked in the lane. "You've separated all of us because we're witnesses, and you police need to interview us individually."

Bannon contemplated the slight, elfin man, meeting his shrewd blue eyes as he turned back to her. She said equably, "Sir, what's your relationship with the victim?"

"She's—she was a friend. To all of us. A friend of long standing."

She nodded and wrote in her notebook. "What brought you and all the other people together here today?"

"The same activity that's always brought us together—except for the past few months, of course. Our weekly poker—I mean card game," he amended hastily.

Waving a hand, she said brusquely, "I don't care about any gambling in a poker game, only Grace Pinckney's death. You said the group hadn't met for the past few months. Why?"

"Ralph got a lot worse—"

"You're referring to Ralph Pinckney, the victim's deceased husband?"

"Yes. He had the upper hand on prostate cancer till he got a bad case of flu." Sighing, he sank back into the swing and crossed his arms to encourage more warmth from his jacket. "Fighting on one front is hard enough …"

"I saw the obit in *The Clarion*—just last week, wasn't it? Ran the Hearth Insurance Company, isn't that right?"

"Yes." He raised his gaze to a sky milky with fog. "Poor Dan and Gene came up from San Jose for their father's funeral, and now they have to come right back and bury their stepmother …"

"A tragedy indeed," Bannon murmured. She asked softly, "What happened here today, Mr. Dickinson?"

Dickinson massaged his eyes with his fingertips. He did not want to talk about it. He did not want to remember.

Bannon put aside her notebook. She said, "Just tell me what you saw."

Whitman helped herself to her plaid wool jacket on the coat tree, tucked herself into a corner of the sofa, and pulled the jacket around her. The parlor, cozy as it appeared with its gold curtains and oval hooked rug and corduroy sofa, had grown colder on this chilly October day. The log fire Grace and Chris had built in the living room fireplace had long since burned low; foggy sea air was permeating the house from doors opening and closing as the deputies and Doc Phillips went about their work.

She knew that the scenes of this day would remain imprinted on her mind like a series of engravings. Arriving here fifteen minutes late because of Dickinson's usual dithering—although she didn't blame him this time. Even though they'd all rallied around the Pinckneys as Ralph sank toward death, she herself had been reluctant to return to a house void of Ralph's presence, and Dickinson had too recently gone through his own tortures …

The round dining room table had been moved into the living room and set up for poker as usual, exactly the same as before, when a robustly alive Ralph presided over the game in jovial tyranny. The Andersons, Pete and Gladys, sat in their usual places at the table, Fernando across from them; Grace had set out cheese and crackers, tortilla chips and salsa, the wine glasses already in front of everyone, including Grace's special glass from the breakfront, which stood beside Chris's glass on the mantel. Chris coming in with the bottle of wine. Chris, so handsome in his blue turtleneck sweater and crisp jeans, had had the wine. And Chris had poured the wine.

Bannon was writing in her notebook. "So, no one ate or drank anything till Christopher Fontaine brought in the wine. Are you certain it was Mr. Fontaine?"

Dickinson sighed. "Yes, it was Chris."

"Had the bottle been opened?"

"It had. The cork was still in it, but it'd been pulled."

"And who poured the wine?"

He admitted, reluctantly, "Chris."

"You seem very unhappy with the statements you're making," Bannon observed.

He closed his eyes for a moment, against the image of the disbelieving horror in Chris's chalk-white face when Doc Phillips had pronounced Grace dead. "I haven't known Chris that long," he said candidly. "None of us has. But he's a good man, he was here for Ralph all hours of the day and night—"

"I understand he'd been Mr. Pinckney's private nurse."

Dickinson nodded. "Ralph couldn't manage to get himself out of bed at all some days, Grace couldn't really look after him, she needed someone—"

"My brother-in-law had cancer," Bannon murmured. "It's a terrible thing."

Roy at least hadn't suffered, Dickinson thought, and he quoted the ancient words of the Latin poet Martial that had brought him a degree of solace: "'Life's not just being alive but being well.'"

"Very true, Mr. Dickinson. So, Christopher Fontaine came in with the bottle of wine and poured glasses all around. What happened next?"

"We drank a ritual toast to our missing player. To Ralph."

Whitman was reliving the scene. All of them on their feet, awkwardly holding a long-stemmed glass of red wine, Fernando emotional as always, excusing the tears rolling down his cheeks by mumbling about his Latin heritage, Pete and Gladys holding hands, Gladys sniffling, the deep network of lines in Pete's face as he tried to conceal his own sentiment. An arm around Dickinson to give him physical as well as moral support to get through this moment, she and Dickinson had joined Grace and Chris who were standing at the mantel. All of them with their glasses raised. Grace in her white wool dress, looking younger and fresher than she had in months, saying: "To you, dear Ralph. I know you're watching, just like you promised . . ."

Grace taking a ceremonial sip of the Brown Brothers cabernet, then placing the wineglass on the table.

Everyone gathering at the poker table, and Grace drinking more of her wine; everyone knew she loved good red wine on the very rare occasions when she did take a drink. Then she had dealt the first hand . . .

Then Grace uttering, "I feel dreadful," and getting up and staggering toward an armchair and collapsing into it in stark confirmation of that fact. Seconds later, a faint reddish mottling rising in her face: "I can't breathe—" Fingers at her swelling throat: "Oh God, it's penicillin—get Doc Phillips. Quick!"

Chris looking on in frozen, open-mouthed horror, then running for the phone; Dickinson springing into motion, rushing to her aid . . .

Bannon asked Dickinson, "So at first you had the victim sit up?"

"I was trying to help her breathe. My partner got pneumonia twice. He tended to hyperventilate . . ." He paused, bitterly aware of the irony that Roy's death had released him from reticence about his relationship with the man he had loved in secret for thirty-two years. "Doc Phillips got here in fifteen minutes but . . . she was gone." He looked out toward the shrouded ocean and shuddered in agonized memory of Chris's screams of desperation, Chris seizing Grace's shoulders as if he would shake the breath back into her. "I tried everything. CPR, everything—" Coughing, he broke off.

"Mr. Dickinson—"

He turned back to her. "I'm all right. Bad enough we couldn't save Grace, now we have Doc Phillips going around demanding which one of us gave her the penicillin that killed her . . ."

Seeing Bannon's mouth tighten, he said, "Doc was upset. We were all upset. Hysterical, if you want to know the truth."

Bannon asked, "How did Grace come to know you, Mr. Dickinson?"

"Our profession. We're all ex-professors; we moved here to retire. Well, except for Ralph and Gladys and Fernando."

"So you're from out of town."

"Not very far. I taught at San Francisco State, so did Grace. Whitman was UCLA. Pete originally taught at Duke—"

"Beyond that, how would you characterize Grace's relationship with the other people here?"

An image of Whitman filled his mind, the fortitude in her slender, lined face, the wiry body that seemed possessed of a confident resilience, a tensile strength. How would he ever have managed this past year without that sturdiness to lean on? He decided that she could answer this deputy's question instead of him. He told Bannon, "As old Queen Bess once said, 'I would not open windows into men's souls.' I won't, either."

Bannon shook her head. "Sir, I'm not asking you to open windows. I'm just looking for a few facts."

He did not reply. Bannon regarded him for several moments, then tucked her notebook into her shirt pocket. "Why don't I have a deputy drive you home. We can take down your official statement later, when you feel better."

"I came with Whitman; I'll leave with her." He added, "But I'd like to remain out here on the porch, if you don't mind."

As Bannon sat down beside her on the corduroy sofa, Whitman looked at the bronze name tag above the pocket of the deputy's khaki shirt. She asked, "Would you be any relation to Ann Bannon?"

Bannon shook her head, and Whitman shrugged; the allusion to the legendary author of classic lesbian novels of the fifties and sixties had been a mild litmus test as to whether Bannon was a member of the club.

Bannon repeated the question she had directed to Dickinson: "How would you characterize the victim's relationship with the people here?"

"We were all friends. Good friends. Fernando Cabrillo goes back the longest, he's known the Pinckneys for years. He's just devastated by this." Whitman remembered with anguish that during the fifteen or so minutes of Grace's dying, Fernando seemed to have aged twenty years. "He courted Grace after her first marriage, before she married Ralph."

"Did Mr. Cabrillo hold it against Ralph or Grace?"

Whitman's smile was brief and humorless. "Ralph was the one. He never said anything, mind you, but he gave the impression that he'd come galloping in to rescue a high-class Anglo woman from Fernando's Latino clutches."

Bannon grunted noncommittally. "If he felt that way about Mr. Cabrillo, it's odd he'd welcome him in his house."

"It was Grace who made us all welcome," Whitman said. "It never ever mattered to Grace that Fernando was Hispanic. Or about Dickinson and me, either."

Bannon said, "I hadn't noticed before that you and Mr. Dickinson were Hispanic."

Grinning, surprised by Bannon's mischievous humor, Whitman responded, "Ralph discovered there was some cachet in having a few friends . . . off the beaten track, shall we say. I think it was Walpole who said, 'It is charming to totter into vogue.' But I never thought I'd live to see the day when gay people ... Anyway, Ralph indulged Grace's every whim, including the friends she chose. It kept her under his thumb, you see. He ran roughshod over the rest of us in a mocking, congenial sort of way. Ralph Pinckney was one of those bullies who mask it under bluff heartiness."

"I know the type. What can you tell me about the male nurse who looked after Mr. Pinckney?"

"Chris? Not much," she responded cautiously.

"Ms. Whitman, neither you nor Mr. Dickinson seem to welcome the subject of Christopher Fontaine."

Whitman decided that if Bannon did not obtain the information from her, it would surface from another, possibly malevolent source. "Let me put it this way. A lot of people wouldn't understand how bad a time Grace had with Ralph's illness, how Chris was an angel of deliverance. You can't imagine what an awful patient Ralph was—"

"I think I can. My brother-in-law had cancer. The sicker he got, the more abusive he became— sarcastic, very bitter and demanding—"

Nodding, Whitman thought that he couldn't have been worse than Ralph Pinckney.

"It was an awful time for Sara, his wife," Bannon continued. "Toward the end, she met somebody who . . . consoled her." She looked expectantly at Whitman.

Warily, Whitman nodded.

"Is that what happened here, with Mr. Fontaine?"

Whitman said carefully, "Let me ask you this. Did your brother-in-law . . . object?"

"Charlie never knew. It would have killed him." Bannon chuckled in embarrassment. "Killed him sooner, I mean."

"Well, Ralph knew. And it didn't kill him."

"You don't mean he approved," Bannon said with clear incredulity.

"I mean it didn't kill him. He went ballistic, as the young people say. Ordered Chris out of the house, called Grace every horrible name you can imagine, accused all of us of betraying his friendship. Then not a week later he turns right around and says he owes everything good in his life to Grace and he's been selfish and stupid, and he hires Chris back and apologizes to the rest of us." She could still hear the amazement and relief in Grace's voice as she blurted out the news over the phone.

"Remarkable," Bannon said.

"You seem more than a little skeptical," Whitman observed.

"Somebody has to be, and it's part of my job. Did you ever discuss Mr. Fontaine with Ralph Pinckney?"

"Of course not. All I know is, he'd truly forgiven Grace. I think, at the last, Ralph changed, and was trying to face his death with a little perspective and dignity. Or maybe I'd just like to believe there's such a thing as deathbed conversion."

"Maybe there is. But I couldn't prove it by my brother-in-law. He died the way he lived. He was a bastard to begin with, his cancer made him worse."

Lowering her notepad, Bannon looked around her, and Whitman followed her gaze, trying to see the house as Bannon would see it. A solidly built structure from the forties, with such homey graces as a porch and a large backyard with fruit trees; simple, functional, comfortable furniture, Grace's taste, not Ralph's—he had leaned more to the ostentatious. A house filled with objects collected over the decades—in this room alone, delft plates and pitchers, a framed map of California shaped from plaster, an art deco lamp, the carved boomerang from Australia . . .

"Mr. Fontaine and the victim aren't married."

Jarred back to the moment by Bannon's statement, Whitman retorted, "Certainly not. Ralph only died last week. I'm sure Chris and Grace hadn't even—" She broke off in embarrassment, then rushed on, "Grace would want an appropriate interval—"

"Of course."

"So why would Chris do anything to Grace? He only needed to wait, and he'd be married to her. They loved each other. You could see it. He's not Grace's heir—"

"How do you know? Have you seen her will?"

"No," Whitman responded. "But I know Grace . . ."

"Look, Ms. Whitman. One of the six people who came here today killed Grace Pinckney. Christopher Fontaine served the victim the wine. If he didn't do this, then who did?"

Twenty minutes later, in the car, looking into Dickinson's grim face, Whitman said, "You heard."

"They've detained Chris," Dickinson said, gazing disconsolately out the windshield into the swirling, thickening fog. "Doc told me. I guess he told you, too."

Fingering her car keys, Whitman said, "Could Chris do a thing like this?" She felt reluctant to leave this place, as if events would spin even further out of control in her absence.

He sighed. "No way. You saw how he was—"

"Yes. Utterly distraught." She added unwillingly, "How about Fernando? Grace married Ralph instead of him, then went on to someone else. And he's always been in love with her—"

Tears filled his eyes. "We all loved Grace."

Whitman started the Volvo, turned up the heater as Dickinson mumbled, "Pete and Gladys—remember when Ralph hinted they were giving hand signals at poker?"

Whitman nodded. It had taken all of Grace's charm to convince them he was teasing. "Grace smoothed it over. Why would those two do anything to her?"

"I'm reaching here, Whitman," he said sharply. "Just trying to find any rational explanation."

Chris opened the wine and served it. "Who else could've slipped penicillin into it?"

Whitman pulled away from the curb. "Maybe Grace herself did," she said, not believing it for a moment.

"In front of Chris? All of us? You saw her—that woman fought for her life."

"Maybe she changed her mind. Maybe it was just a ghastly accident." Whitman scowled. "Look, Doc Phillips took care of Ralph and Grace—"

"So? He's the only doctor in town."

"Exactly."

Doc Phillips sat hunched over his desk, rolling his fountain pen between his thin fingers. "Grace's allergic reaction is called anaphylaxis," he explained in a resonant rumble. "Antibodies called immunoglobulin E, or IgE, cause blood vessels to leak, tissues to swell, blood pressure to drop—"

Whitman was not about to let him ramble on. "Why didn't she have epinephrine on hand to give herself an injection?"

His bushy eyebrows rose in apparent surprise at her knowledge. "Prescription-strength penicillin isn't a naturally occurring substance. People know when they ingest it, and it does have a smell. But a strong red wine would mask a small quantity of it, and that's all it would take. She did wear a Medic Alert bracelet . . ." He stared down at his desk.

"The bracelet didn't help her that time in the hospital when they gave her penicillin anyway," Whitman said tartly.

His head jerked up. "I apologize for my profession," he snapped. "Once in a while we do fall off our pedestals."

His lined face looked haggard, his white hair disheveled; and Whitman understood his anger, understood that he had, in the space of a week, lost two long-time patients. She asked, "Who among our group have you given penicillin prescriptions to, Doc?"

"You know I can't divulge that information."

"Grace is dead," Dickinson argued, "and it seems—"

"But I prescribed penicillin for you, Whitman, last February."

As Whitman stared at him in outrage, Doc Phillips said, "Over the years I've prescribed penicillin for everyone in this whole town. Fontaine could easily get penicillin from a former patient. The truth is, the cops have all six of you under suspicion."

Doc Phillips tossed down his pen, laced his hands behind his head and leaned back wearily. "As far as I can see, nobody has any motive."

"Could Grace have done this to herself?"

"Sure. But I saw her just a few days ago—no sign of depression. Yes, she still felt guilty over Ralph finding out about her and Chris, but Ralph had given her his blessing. Chris's the odd man out, the one we know the least about. To be honest, if he did have something to do with this, then I have to wonder if he also hastened Ralph's death."

"Good heavens," Dickinson uttered.

"Doc," Whitman asked, "how much penicillin would it take for Grace—"

"Precious damn little. The more episodes, the higher the sensitivity. She'd had two serious exposures, one as a child, and the one in the hospital was damn near fatal. A minute amount would kill her unless she had an injection of epinephrine immediately."

"You know," Whitman said, "I've been thinking about something Deputy Bannon said to me. She was absolutely right." She got to her feet. "Thanks, Doc."

Dickinson leaped up and followed her out with more energy than Whitman had seen from him in almost a year. "I know who did this," he said.

Dickinson and Whitman marched into Seacrest's small, clapboard police substation. Deputy Bannon looked up from the report she was fastening into a folder. As the two of them seated themselves in the chairs matching her gray metal desk, she said with a trace of exasperation, "Have a seat."

"Thank you," Dickinson said, and plunged right in: "Of our poker group, only one of us had a real motive for killing Grace. The real killer had opportunity, too, access to penicillin—"

"All of you had easy access, and Christopher Fontaine served the wine," Bannon returned. "The victim was dealing with the death of her husband. It's possible she'd changed her mind about Fontaine and told him."

"Balderdash," Dickinson said.

"For the sake of argument, preposterous as it may be," Whitman said, "let's say Chris actually did kill Grace. How could he be stupid enough to incriminate himself in front of five other people?"

"Lots of criminals are stupid. It's why we catch them."

"Chris isn't stupid."

"Granting that," Bannon said easily, "Fontaine had access to penicillin, and we're taking a close look into his background and history with other patients. But," she conceded, comfortably shifting her bulk in her desk chair as she sat back, "I'll listen to anything you have to say."

"First of all," Dickinson said, "the real killer got the penicillin from treatments for the aftermath of the flu."

"Regardless of where your candidate got it, it had to get into the victim's glass."

"There were lots of hypodermics around, Chris gave Ralph injections—"

"No, Dickinson," Whitman said, placing a hand on his arm, "he didn't inject it into the bottle. Grace always used the same glass for special occasions. It was in her glass before the wine was even poured."

"For heaven's sake, Whitman," Dickinson protested, turning to her. "As soon as she took the glass out of the breakfront—"

"She wouldn't see anything. It wasn't visible. He coated the inside of the glass with liquid penicillin and put it back in the breakfront, ready for the next time she drank wine. She wouldn't even think to look for anything on her glass. Doc Phillips told us it would take the tiniest amount to kill her—"

"If you're right, there's one way to find out," Dickinson said. "Test the bottle. Fingerprint the glass—"

"Ahem, you two junior detectives," Bannon said, "may I have your attention?" She tapped the report in front of her. "We cops aren't quite the dumb gumshoes you think we are."

"So what do your tests say?" Dickinson said eagerly.

"They're a confidential part of a police report." She held up both hands against their protests. "If there was no penicillin anywhere except in the victim's wineglass—and I'm not saying that's the case—it doesn't matter. It would only confirm that Fontaine simply dropped a pill into her glass."

"What about fingerprints?"

Bannon did not reply.

Looking into her face, Whitman crowed, "I'll stake my teacher's pension that somebody else's prints are on that glass—"

"A somebody not Christopher Fontaine," Dickinson exulted.

"Our reports are confidential," Bannon repeated firmly. "But I can tell you that we've released Mr. Fontaine." She looked from Whitman to Dickinson, and said slowly, "We'll file a case when we can demonstrate probable cause."

"There's probable cause, all right," Dickinson said, his face grim. "Sick as he was, that bastard got himself out of bed and over to that breakfront and poisoned her glass—"

"—and set up that obscene scenario where Grace would propose a toast to him," Whitman added vehemently, "and then—"

"—went off to his grave knowing Grace would die and all the rest of us would be under suspicion," Dickinson finished.

Bitterly, Whitman quoted Francis Bacon: "'Revenge triumphs over death.'" She said to Bannon, "You were so right when you said somebody had to be skeptical about Ralph Pinckney. He was a son of bitch, and he was a vengeful, murdering son of a bitch when he died."

Dickinson muttered, "'That I should after death invisibly return . . .'"

"Shakespeare?" Bannon asked, folding her arms across her ample chest.

"Whitman. Walt, I mean."

"Well, I'm a simple woman," Bannon said, "and all I know is, my scumbag of a brother-in-law got worse with his cancer, and leopards don't change their spots. But," she cautioned, "we're still checking out Mr. Fontaine."

Dickinson leaned forward, jabbing a finger at the report on her desk. "You can't seriously suspect anyone but Ralph Pinckney."

"We need to be careful. We need to check everything."

"You know the truth. I can tell by your face," Whitman said. "Ralph Pinckney spent the last days of his life figuring out the cruelest possible revenge on his wife and on his rival and on his friends. That's what you really believe."

"Believe," Bannon repeated. Fingering the report in front of her, she took in a deep breath and let it out unhurriedly.

Whitman knew she was making a crucial decision. Seacrest was not San Francisco nor Los Angeles, and police procedures would not be as formal here, but it was Bannon's choice as to how informal they could or should be.

"Well," Bannon said finally, "I think your theory might explain why, on that wineglass, up near the rim—where a person might hold it to carefully place it back in a cabinet—is a partial fingerprint belonging to Ralph Pinckney."

Dickinson said to Whitman, "I told you—"

"In all my years of police work," Bannon said as if Dickinson had not spoken, "I've never seen anything like this. The bottom line is, a man's committed murder from the grave. Unless you believe in God, he's got clean away with it."

Whitman and Dickinson stared at her.

"Think about it. The evidence is totally circumstantial. It rests on a single fingerprint and a leopard's spots."

Dickinson and Whitman exchanged glances, then Whitman said, "It's enough. It's probable cause."

"To the three of us, maybe. But not enough to file a case." Bannon spread her hands. "So, I guess if you believe in God, then, 'In His will is our peace.'"

Whitman guessed: "Francis Thompson?"

Bannon smiled ruefully. "Dante."

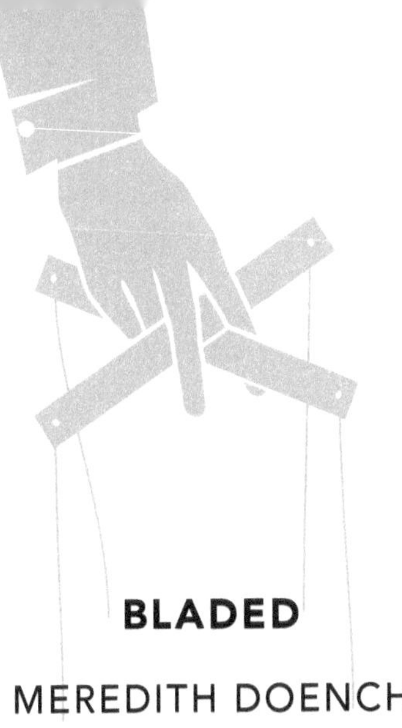

BLADED

MEREDITH DOENCH

Nova Mitchell stepped into the Dayton Blades locker room with PPE-covered feet. Overhead lights sparkled against the white and gray tile as she took in the familiar smell of sweat masking the distinct odor of cleaning products. Memories of Nova's own competitive basketball days surfaced along with the sound she loved more than anything else in the world—the dribble of a ball against the court. That steady rhythm had a way of syncing her heart and soul. Sometimes Nova missed the game so much, it hurt, and she'd always wanted to play for the WNBA. Nova never imagined it would be her career as a death investigator that would bring her into the pro locker room.

Dayton's crime scene analysts were already on scene dismantling a shower head and a few drains. Nova recognized detective Cody Michael who waved her toward the far end of the shower room.

"What an opening night!" Detective Michael marveled. He pulled at the edges of his thick dark mustache, a 70s porn throwback that Nova liked to joke about with her girlfriend Coco. "Not the sort of celebration fans had in mind, huh?"

Jazz Jacobson, the team's hotshot rookie, had been bludgeoned to death. Thick steam hung in the shower room air. Nova knelt beside the body as she made a mental map of the scene for her report. She'd been part of the Dayton Coroner's team as a medicolegal investigator for the past seven years. Her job included investigating the death scene and collecting evidence by way of body, placement, photographs, and situational circumstances for the medical examiner. Throughout the night, Nova would compile everything into a report for the ME who would then determine the cause of death after completing the autopsy in the morning.

"Who found her?" Nova asked.

"Macy Austin. Talk about post-gaming with your rival," Michael said, kicking up the arch of his right eyebrow. "The whole team met in the Oregon District after the game, but Jazz never showed. The starting five stayed behind for the standard follow-up with the coaches. The other four made it to the bar." Detective Michael paused to sign off on a form for an investigator. More analysts arrived filling the shower area with more bright lights and hushed voices.

"When no one could reach Jazz Jacobson," Detective Michael continued, "Macy Austin drove past the arena on her way home and noticed Jazz's navy Range Rover still in the lot. Austin says all the showers were pumping out hot water when she found Jazz collapsed in the last stall."

With a gloved hand, Nova ran her fingertips along Jazz's abdomen to find an entry point for a liver temperature. How could this have happened? Only hours ago, Jazz Jacobson was at the height of her career. The crowd roared with the opening night win for the Blades, and Nova cheered along with them from the swanky VIP room. Nova's girlfriend Coco was one of the physical therapists for the Dayton Blades and their relationship came with perks outside the bedroom. The couple met playing college basketball where the competition was fierce. Coco thrived on the pressure and attention, but Nova loved the competition. She'd match anyone's practice regimen with a smile on her face. Cut her senior year from the college team, Nova's grit couldn't make up for her lack of height and physical ability. Professional hoops weren't in Coco's future, either. A career-ending ankle break wiped out any chance of a spot on an WNBA team.

But Jazz Jacobson? She was young and mean and could sink a three-pointer like the hand of a goddess. Her rival, Macy Austin, had recently been traded to the team. The two were at each other's throats as they tried to one up each other. The media caught on to the rivalry and fed the feud with splashy headlines. As Macy and Jazz battled for the ball and the spotlight, the crowds ate it up. Nothing sells tickets better than a rivalry between a newbie and a legend. Now the Dayton Blades starlet was dead and possibly by the hands of a player who would benefit most, Macy Austin.

Jazz had been the heartbeat of the Dayton Blades, a central element of the fire that built excitement in Dayton for their new professional basketball team. What would this do to the city? To the WNBA league? Nova's throat swelled with emotion, and she rubbed it down with her fingers. This was not the time to allow her feelings to take over; she needed to remain professional.

Nova's gloved hands moved over Jazz's neck. She took photos of the gaping wound that severed Jazz's carotid artery. The blow had been so deep, it left bruising around the cut from the hilt of the weapon. A thin gold chain around Jazz's neck had gotten in the way of the knife leaving its charm embedded in the wound. Nova spread the wound open and gently pulled out the chunk of gold with an instrument. She recognized it immediately as the Dayton Blades logo. Jazz's necklace was identical to Coco's—it was something Nova's girlfriend only removed while on the court. The necklace's charm featured a propeller airplane with tiny blades that spun. Across the wingspan read *Dayton Blades—Flying High Above the Rest*. The necklaces had been a gift to all the players, coaches, and staff from the new team owners, Sue Bird and Megan Rapinoe.

"The blood washed through the central drain," Detective Michael said, handing Nova an evidence bag of bloody scissors. He pointed to the metal grate in the center walkway of the stalls. Nova held up the camera from around her neck and knelt to get photos of the scissors with blue-colored handles.

"I spoke to the head trainer. The physical therapists kept a few of these scissors in an open locker along with therapy tape and other supplies," Michael said. "Anyone and everyone in this locker room had access to the scissors."

Nova moved through the crime scene in her mind. The stab marks between Jazz's shoulder blades and kidney region indicated she'd been attacked from behind. Then Jazz turned around only to take the blade hard in the neck. Nova noted that Jazz fell outside of the stall, toward the center drain, indicating someone had been *inside* the stall with her. Jazz trusted the killer, which didn't track with the recent threats the team received.

When the WNBA announced their newest team would be in Ohio and owned by the powerhouse couple Sue Bird and Megan Rapinoe, Dayton went after that honor with gusto. Why should Columbus—with Blue Jackets hockey and the Ohio State football team—get all the glory? Or Cincinnati? They already had the Bengals and the Reds. So, the Dayton Blades were born, named after the chopping blade of an aircraft, as Dayton was the home of the Wright Brothers and Wright Patterson Air Force Base.

While the majority of Dayton celebrated and welcomed their professional team, not everyone was happy with the news. Days after the announcement, threats began. The sender argued the WNBA had picked the wrong city and Dayton would be sorry they'd been selected for the pro basketball team. Police believed the threats would end soon, that the sender had a mental health issue and would see the threats weren't working. But the sender didn't give up. Coaches received unhinged emails about abandoning the team. Once practices began in the Dayton arena, handwritten notes appeared on the windshields of coaches and players' vehicles threatening that someone would get hurt. For weeks, extra security filled the arena during practices and trolled the parking lots. The team owners even paid for round-the-clock security of the players' apartments.

Then, brazenly, a note appeared in the coaches' office. At first, the messages targeted Jazz and threatened injury. The writer claimed they didn't want the attention Jazz brought with her. The latest message, an email sent from a burner phone to the head coach, promised the starting team would suffer if they played their opening game in Dayton. The author of the messages must have known how to shut down parts of the security system where the messages were found. Security in the arena was no joke—it had to be someone familiar with the engineering of the building. Dayton police claimed the messages were an inside job, or someone connected to an employee with easy access to the arena and could break into the system undetected. Now it seemed the author of the threats had come through on their promises.

"Detective?" an analyst called out, his voice echoing against the high ceiling. "You should see this."

Nova followed the others who knelt around the main drain. Inside, the flashing glint of another coveted gold Blades necklace charm.

"No chain for this one?" Michael asked.

The analyst shook his head. "We have an investigator searching the underground pipes with a camera, but it looks like only the charm was left behind."

Nova took a few pictures of the charm inside the drain. "Jazz must have ripped the necklace off her attacker in the struggle."

Detective Michael turned to Nova. "We know it wasn't Jazz's charm. That leaves us with … what? A whole team and staff of suspects?"

"Detective?" an officer called from across the locker room. "The owners are waiting in their office."

Thrill scattered up Nova's spine–Sue Bird was in the building! Nova had spent her high school and college years following Sue Bird's career and wanted nothing more than to be just like the WNBA star. Nova spent hundreds of hours practicing Sue Bird's moves on the court while throwing 3-pointers long into the night when everyone else had gone home.

These days, Nova logged her long hours with the dead, but she still dreamed of the court and all its sounds: her own sneakers scraping against the polished floor, the cheers from the stands, the calls from the coaches, the crosstalk between her teammates on the floor, and the glorious sound of the dribble. Most of all, she dreamed of the way her hand felt the moment the ball left it, the second it sailed over the rim and sank into the net. Dreams like pro basketball die hard, and Nova hoped in her next lifetime she'd be the Jazz Jacobson on the WNBA court.

Nova sat with her phone on the back delivery ramp outside the coroner's office. The August night was hot and sticky, but the sky had cleared for the near full moon.

Coco said, "I cannot believe it. First game for the Blades. *Her* first WNBA game. What a waste."

"This will rock the basketball world." Nova traced the outline of her inner forearm tattoo, a habit she had when talking on the phone. Her tat was of Saint Dymphna, the Catholic martyr known as the saint of victims of violent crimes and sexual abuse.

Coco yawned. "I would have given anything to have the opportunities Jazz had."

Coco had been hired as a physical therapist when the Blades were in development after spending a few years with a local university team. Coco worked injuries like magic, but the players talked her up as a good listener. She had her own past on the court, and Coco understood the mental pressures of the game. The coaches teased that appointments with Coco were talk therapy with a side of PT.

Because Coco had been a promising player, she'd met all the stars. She had framed photographs in her office with WNBA's OGs Sheryl Swoopes, Rebecca Lobo, and Diana Taurasi. Coco fully expected to be one of them until a bad fall on the court crushed her senior year and her spirit. The high break of her ankle was severe and required two surgeries to mend torn ligaments. It took Coco a few years to lose the limp from her injury.

"Everyone assured us the security was stronger than any stalker," Coco said.

"Unless it *is* the security," Nova pointed out.

Coco chuckled. "Come on. Most of the time those guys have no idea how to use the security system, let alone kill someone."

"So how did Jazz end up in the showers alone? Guards were monitoring the locker room."

"It was late, everyone was out of the stadium, and they were shutting down for the night," Coco said. "I'm sure security was congratulating themselves on keeping the team alive."

"That's when the killer slipped in." Nova traced the face of Saint Dymphna and thought about how the locker room had always been a safety zone for players. Away from the public eye and anyone not associated with the team, players cocooned inside to decompress. This was one of the only places where Jazz would have had her guard down.

"I've been thinking about what you said a few months ago, about how the rivalry between Jazz and Macy was manufactured," Nova said. "You believe they were friends?"

"Friendly, I'd say. The rivalry was total bullshit," Coco said. "But there was some tension between Jazz and Macy lately, and with the whole team."

"Meaning?"

"Jazz could be a dick, you know?" Coco said. "She knew she was the star and didn't let any of us forget it. It was her way all the time."

Nova thought about the fury that must have caused with players who had been around the league for years. Players who'd worked just to get some court time and maybe a photo lead on the local sports page.

"Try to sleep," Nova said, wishing she could be in bed with Coco curled inside her arms. This was how they always slept together, Coco against Nova's chest, the beat of their hearts syncing as one. But there would be no rest for Nova tonight. Her mind was so wound up with this case, she doubted her sleep would return to normal for days.

"Nova?" For the first time that night, the worry bled through into Coco's voice. "The recent threats weren't only for Jazz. Please, don't let there be another one."

It was 4 a.m. when Nova left her finished report on the ME's desk. Nova couldn't sleep; her mind spun with the details of the murder. She grabbed the basketball from under her desk.

The M.E.'s office set up a hoop in the lot behind the building. Nova spent her breaks sinking baskets and burning off the tension of unknowing, the very thing that drove her mad about being a death investigator. Nova felt called to do this kind of work honoring survivors and victims, but she also wanted answers. She wanted everything to fit together in a neat little package. Nova sank basket after basket while her subconscious worked on the answers. The court had always been where Nova did her best work.

The world disappeared leaving only Nova and the ball. The tension rolled off her body as Nova rebounded while the coaches, the players, and the PT team went through her mind. Perhaps the killer had been a partner or close friend of a player, but access into the locker rooms were forbidden for anyone not working with the team. Still, rules were malleable.

The real question for Nova was *why*. Professional jealousy? Jazz certainly had more than her share of the limelight and the fake rivalry with Macy. Perhaps the letter writer was a die-hard fan who bought into this act? Or it could easily be another WNBA player worried about their own ranking. What if it was someone with a personal vendetta, an old lover who couldn't let go? If so, why did a team pendant get into the mix and who did it belong to? The hoop wasn't giving up any answers.

Nova drove to the arena and the first light of dawn cracked open the sky. She wanted to see the scene once more before police released it. Most of the emergency vehicles had left, but there were still a few Dayton PD cars, most likely crime scene techs. A police truck pulled out of the lot with Jazz Jacobson's Jeep in tow to the station for analysis.

An officer at the door checked her work ID and waited for Nova to sign in.

"They're almost done," he said. "You better hurry."

There was no need for the PPE anymore and Nova's well-worn

Vans squeaked against the tiled floor. She didn't know exactly what she was looking for, but Nova couldn't shake the image of Jazz alone in the showers. The coaches had held back the starting five, but only Jazz remained. Who held Jazz back after the others left for the bar? A coach? Another player? Whoever it was, Nova imagined the confrontation must have upset Jazz. Nova knew from her own experience that there was no better place to cry and hide your tears than inside a hot shower.

The back entrance led directly to the locker rooms and coaches' offices. Nova heard voices on the other side of the tunnel, the main entrance to the court.

Detective Cody Michael and the head coach Linny Jamison met her at the other end of the tunnel. Linny sobbed, holding her head inside her hands.

Michael nodded his greeting. "Nova, have you heard? Macy Austin has been arrested for the murder."

"*Macy?*" It didn't compute with Nova. Why would Macy risk everything to kill a teammate in a fake rivalry?

"Analysts connected Macy's phone with two of the threats," Detective Michael said. "She was on the premises when the hand-written notes emerged."

"Did she confess?" Nova asked.

"No, but we have more than enough evidence to hold her. Techs found traces of Jazz's blood on Macy's steering wheel. Also, Macy's team necklace is unaccounted for."

Nova expressed her sympathy to the coach and turned back towards the locker room. She looked up to the blinking red security camera in the corner. How did Macy have time to dismantle the recording before leaving for the bar? Nova recognized she wasn't much with electronics. Maybe it was easy to put these blackouts on timers. But no matter how hard she tried, she couldn't picture Macy Austin cracking the computer system and speed typing in code to shut the system down.

Stranger things have happened, sure, but Nova had questions. Jazz Jacobson, no matter how dickish she could be, deserved answers.

Nova sat up in bed. While Coco showered, the TV blared in her absence. ESPN sportscasters had been delivering the breaking news of Jazz Jacobson's death and Macy Austin's arrest nonstop for the past twenty-four hours. There was nothing new to report, but that didn't stop them from filling every ounce of airtime with commentary and memorials to Jazz. Reporters tore through Macy's past and her family tree looking for something that might shake out. What fell was an older brother who served time for impaired driving. The commentator asked, "Could there be a family tendency toward violence?" When the panel entertained the idea, Nova groaned and muted the TV.

The shower shut off and Nova met Coco at the sink.

"I bet you're as tired as me," Nova said.

Coco had spent the day helping the team plan a candlelight ceremony for Jazz along the Little Miami River. Everyone thought the vigil was a great idea except Coco.

"Shouldn't we remember her without a connection to Macy?" Coco had argued. "It's too soon for anyone to talk about anything but the murder."

Regardless, the vigil was set for the next evening and the media was all over it. Current and past professional basketball players were flying into the Gem City for the event where the entire women's professional sports community would mourn together.

Coco wound herself in a towel and reached for her toothbrush. Nova wrapped her arms around her from behind, pressing close. She leaned into Coco's weight, reveling in the steadiness of her girlfriend's body. Burying her nose into the curve of Coco's neck, she kissed her skin—then paused when her lips brushed over a deep scratch. Coco flinched.

"Co, where's your team necklace?"

The two women watched each other in the mirror until Coco looked away, spit and rinsed.

Nova pulled Coco's wet hair to the side and flipped it over her shoulder. Coco's skin had recently scabbed over in two short scratches where the back of her neck met her shoulders.

Nova stepped back. "Co? Talk to me."

Coco turned, resting her hips against the bathroom sink. She crossed her arms over her chest, the towel still in her hand. Tears slipped down Coco's cheeks.

Nova froze as the ice-cold realization washed over her. Her girlfriend? A *murderer?*

"It was an accident," Coco started. "You know me. I wouldn't do this on purpose!"

"Tell me what happened."

Coco shook her head slowly, avoiding eye contact with Nova. "Jazz's knee swelled up after the game, and Coach Linny wanted me to work with Jazz. I met her in the locker room, and Jazz was in rare form. She'd just been pumped up from her meeting with the coaches and had an argument with Macy. I just wanted to do my job and get out of there, but Jazz insisted on gloating. It was too much."

"What do you mean, *too much*?"

Anger flashed in Coco's eyes. "Don't you see? All this attention on Jazz wasn't fair. Why her? She never put in more hours than anyone else or practice her 3-pointers all night long before games."

"So, you killed Jazz because she wasn't as dedicated or hard-working as you? Or because she didn't break her ankle?"

Coco's face flushed, her cheeks fire red. "I've spent my whole life living and breathing the game! I gave it everything I had, including my body. It should have been me, Nova. It should have been *me*."

Nova stepped back, her mind racing to make sense of what Coco had done. "Basketball and life aren't fair, Coco. It sucks, I know. I've had to come to terms with that, too. But taking out Jazz doesn't magically give you a spot on the team."

Coco threw the towel across the room. "Jazz swore I've *never* been good enough for the professional court, even before my injury. She said the only way I'd ever be a part of any ball team was by waiting at the sidelines to tape up players' ankles and knees."

Coco slid down the side of the bathroom counter to the floor, hugging her knees close. "I should be on this team, not her!" she cried.

Nova's eyes filled with hot tears. This wasn't the Coco she knew, yet she understood the outrage in Coco's words. It *wasn't* fair. And maybe that's why viewers loved to watch the game so much.

Maybe that's what players loved about it, too—everyone anxiously spinning the wheel and pinning their hopes on a golden ticket to the top.

"Jazz said I didn't deserve the team necklace," Coco said. "Ripping that thing off my neck was her last move."

Like a movie, Nova watched the murder go down in her mind's eye. "Jazz thought you left when she went to the showers. But you wanted the last word. The scissors were already in your hand from taping."

Coco nodded. "I wasn't going to kill her! I just wanted to scare her, to show her I deserve respect, too. It was an accident, Nova. You know how much it hurts to be sidelined."

Nova experienced more than her fair share of bench-sitting in her basketball career. It was a biting sting that lasted, like muscle memory. But Nova didn't share this kind of rage and jealousy.

"Did you send the threats?" Nova asked.

Coco shook her head. "That was all Macy. She wanted out of Dayton, and she believed the threats would get her a fair team trade. Macy had to disable the security system to plant the threats."

Nova worked through the details, her mind spinning. "And what about Jazz? You must have worn gloves. Pulled your hair back. Otherwise, Jazz would have grabbed your ponytail when she ripped off the necklace."

Coco wiped her eyes and nodded. "I forgot the scissors. I should have taken them with me."

Nova continued, "Then you grabbed your chain from the shower floor, but in your haste, you didn't notice the small charm had already washed down the drain."

Coco said nothing. She twisted a section of her long dark hair around her fingers.

"And Macy? How could you let her go down for this?"

Coco suddenly pulled the strands of her hair tight. "Macy found Jazz. No one really knows what happened in that locker room between them. That storyline wrote itself."

A heavy realization washed over Nova. Not only had her girlfriend killed Jazz, but she'd been thinking about how to get away with it for some time. Coco had been living with this simmering rage for years. While Nova was able to move on from basketball, Coco hadn't been able to let go of what could have been. Now Coco's basketball seasons revolved around her benched as a physical therapist, but at least Coco was part of the WNBA action. That seat on the bench moved her closer to where she wanted to be, but it also allowed those old wounds to seep and fester.

"You planted the blood on Macy's steering wheel," Nova said.

Coco shivered. "I panicked! I was wearing the bloody gloves when I ran out a side exit. Macy walked into the building from the back. She left her vehicle unlocked. A wide-open invitation," Coco sniffled. "I'm sorry, Nova."

When Coco stood and reached for her pajamas, Nova left the bathroom and locked herself inside Coco's guest bedroom. Jazz might have been obnoxious and arrogant, but she didn't deserve what happened to her.

"Nova, please," Coco neared the door. "I love you, let's talk about this!"

Nova's hands shook as she slipped the phone from her back pocket and called Detective Cody Michael. She loved Coco and understood her pain. But Nova also believed in justice. In her world, everyone was responsible for their own actions. While she gave Detective Michael the address, Nova traced her tat of Saint Dymphna, looking for answers. Then she ended the call and opened the door.

Tears streamed down Coco's face, and her shoulders drooped with the weight of what she'd done. Nova felt that weight—this was the brutal side of the sport she'd loved her whole life. Shattered dreams. Heartbreak. The game destroyed Coco.

"I called," Nova said.

Coco nodded against her clenched hands balled beneath her chin. Coco's whole body shook. "I'm sorry," she whispered again.

They only had a few minutes before Detective Michael arrived. Nova reached for Coco, gathering her close. Coco fell against Nova's chest. Nova held on tight, holding her girlfriend together, holding herself together. Through her thin t-shirt, Nova felt the *boom boom boom* of Coco's heart, like a dribbling basketball—a steady rhythm that synced with her own.

FALL OF THE HOUSE OF FRESHER

JEFFREY MARKS

The cupcakes were the first to die. The brilliant red icing flew for a few seconds before landing on the dingy, green-marbled linoleum in front of the table. Then the orange-colored delicacies came next, smashing into the red like an artist's car crash.

The other rows of rainbow cupcakes followed, stacking and breaking over each other. The disco ball cupcakes came last—I'd had my eyes on those. As a scholarship student with no additional funds, I counted each purchase. The disco ball cupcakes, now broken on the floor, had been my choice.

The bake sale was the first fundraiser of the newly formed gay liberation group. Southwestern University had not been welcoming to the new association. As Mark Twain said, Cincinnati is always twenty years behind the times. I was late as well. I knew I should join this group, but I hadn't worked up the nerve to express my orientation out loud.

I couldn't identify the two attackers who flipped the right end of the table. A ski mask covered the first face, and gloves prevented fingerprints. I saw only a set of legs, shorts, and an unmarked T-shirt. The shirt had been turned inside out, but the Greek letters of a fraternity were still legible. The second vandal was dressed in a gorilla suit, with a matted hairy body and an exaggerated shocked mask over his face. The hairy ankles of the costume almost covered his shoes.

They were muscular and moving quickly. No one spoke as they ran out of the student center, which housed the administrators' offices.

Since none of the staff left their workplaces, I assumed nothing would be done about destroying innocent bakery items.

No one attempted to move, and more telling, no one went to help those hosting the bake sale. After a few minutes, the remaining students wandered away.

Being a closeted freshman on campus in the fall of 1979, I was transfixed by the situation. My natural bent to speak out for the underdog and justice clashed with the fact that I was still closeted. Moments like this made me doubt I would ever come out. My thin build and short height did nothing to make me feel confident in confronting the upperclassmen. I was still a little squirt, according to the nickname given to me by my family.

I picked up one of the disco ball cupcakes, the lone treat the masked men had not trampled. The five-second rule was long over, but I didn't think social norms counted.

The frat house, a once-stately Guilded Age home just off campus, blared hard rock and littered dozens of drunken, underage students on the grass, like a unique human landscaping.

I dragged Powell, a sophomore RA from my dorm, with me. He always encouraged me to get out more and meet more people my age with the same major. The fact that I didn't feel like I fit in anywhere was never discussed.

I was interested—but not in his way of thinking. I wanted to find a name for the student wearing the fraternity t-shirt earlier that day and learn why they needed to attack an innocent cupcake.

Powell, who had no desire to join a frat, appreciated their alcohol. He was on his third red plastic cup before we left the main room. I didn't drink, thinking I might need to observe the people at the party.

Looking across the room, a good-looking guy's gaze lingered on me for several seconds longer than needed. However, he walked away when Powell approached me with a cup of foaming near beer.

"That's Robert Little," Powell said, sensing my curiosity. "He writes for the student paper and the local newspaper too. I hadn't thought of him as the frat boy type. He's way too serious." I wondered if he had come here tonight for the same reason I had, looking for answers to the bake sale slaughter.

I began to walk around the room. Almost every wall was plastered with signs encouraging the fraternity brothers to vote for one person or another. I studied them, wondering if I could determine if any of these upperclassmen were the two men who had been at the bake sale. However, the posters were expensive, with fancy fonts and touched-up photos of the men running for fraternity president.

The frat had included one of those old-fashioned photo booths on the first floor pushed against the far wall. It was a tall rectangular box with black curtains on either side that fell to nearly the floor. The fun of silly faces and proximity to others had been canceled by an "Out of Order" sign hanging against the curtain. Someone had thrown towels on top of it, presumably to clean up the results of too much alcohol.

A frat boy stumbled in my direction and then stopped. I didn't recognize him, but he knew me. "You," he said. "You were there—at the center." Before I could speak, he must have realized the implications of his comment. If he knew I'd been at the student center today, then he'd been there too—but I hadn't seen him—unless he had been costumed.

Now, Powell was staring at me. "This isn't about rushing, is it? Care to tell me what's going on?"

My answer was drowned out by the piercing screams that now covered the throbbing beat of The Knack. Someone had decided to try the booth anyway, something like touching wet paint with the sign next to you. Two girls drew back the curtain and stepped inside. The screams started immediately.

I weaved through the crowd and looked in the booth. A man leaned on the back of the photo booth bench. He wore a monkey costume, like the one I'd seen today. Specks of purple icing were on the left arm of the costume, and I could see more icing on his lower legs that protruded from the legs of the costume.

I started to grab the costume's arm, but the outfit wouldn't budge. I took the zipper on one side and tugged. I could see the body in the suit. He wasn't moving, which could be the result of alcohol. I reached far enough to put a finger on his neck. The skin was cold, not icy, but the clammy feeling of moldy cement. He was dead.

I took a deep breath. Tracking down the slayer of cupcakes was one thing; a death in a monkey suit was a far different crime. I had originally suspected that the frat boy had died of alcohol poisoning, but the marks around his neck made me know otherwise. This was a serious crime, and I—the person who had been seeking justice from frat boys—was standing over a dead body.

Powell seemed to understand the gravity of the situation as well. "I'm not sure what you had against these guys, but you were with me all evening. We didn't leave each other's sides. Got it?"

I nodded. The truth was that we had been together *most* of the evening since I had no idea of the room's layout or where to stand, and that wouldn't put me in the limelight. Yet, he made it sound as though I'd killed a man twice my size and thrown him into a photo booth.

Powell, who even when intoxicated, had a flair for organization and found the freshmen girls who were still standing nearby. "Did you see anyone approach the photo booth?" he asked.

"The guy in the monkey suit went into the booth about the time we got here, but he never came out—I mean alive. He didn't." That meant the booth had been occupied for about an hour, plenty of time for anyone to have killed him. The three agreed that no one had tried the photo booth since the costumed person had entered alone. No one seemed to question the sign and went off looking for other forms of entertainment.

"It's one of those locked rooms you talk about," Powell said, forever the sociology major who tried to understand my interests, even if he hadn't read a mystery.

"It's not a locked room. This is an impossible crime, one where no one seems to have committed the murder," I said. The music was loud, and I had to shout to be heard.

"Are there many monkeys in mystery?" he asked, seeming skeptical at my explanation of impossible crimes. "That 'Rue' one. I saw it on late night when I should have been studying."

"'The Murders in the Rue Morgue,'" I replied. None of the movies followed the story, so I wondered what monstrosity he'd seen. I shrugged.

If this was an Edgar Allan Poe mystery, Powell would not take kindly to being the sidekick of Le Chevalier C. Auguste Dupin, who went down in history as unnamed. I was fully expecting him to take over the crime scene at any second.

The EMTs arrived first. Alcohol poisoning was a familiar call to the station, and the typical call to a frat house included an ambulance and perhaps the police. Despite not wanting to bring attention to myself, I showed them the ligature marks. They stopped their prep for resuscitation and talked between themselves. Strangulation was not a part of weekend duties. They pulled back the monkey's head, revealing more of the bluish face of a man I'd never seen before. He was dark-haired with cheeks that hadn't been shaved in a week. The EMTs pulled down the monkey suit. The man was wearing a polo shirt that had ridden up in putting on the costume.

One of the EMTs looked closer. "This blue isn't from asphyxiation," he said, pointing to the dead man's arm. I knew it was icing, but I chose to say nothing. What else could I do? I had no proof that he'd been at the bake sale.

The police showed up then.

"Do you know who this is?" the one with the nametag of "Hansen" asked.

I shook my head. That much was true. I hadn't seen any of the runners who had flipped the bake sale. Before the other officer could respond, Powell waved a hand at the freshman who had witnessed the man in the monkey suit enter the photo booth. She was tall and lanky like a model, but the likeness ended there. Her eyes were wide, darting from side to side, and her face was pale white.

"This is Natalie," Powell said, introducing her to the officers. "She knows the dead man."

"I'd gone out with him a few times," she explained. "Nothing serious. I was supposed to meet Frank—Frank Smith— at the party tonight, but I never found him. I didn't know he was in a monkey suit. He went into the photo booth without even a wave to me."

I didn't know when Powell had time to talk to Natalie, or more specifically, when he'd had a chance to ask her about the man in the monkey suit. Perhaps he was Poe's sleuth, and I was only the unnamed sidekick.

I moved closer. A group began to circle the responders, the corpse, and us. Though the music and the shrieks of laughter had stopped with the arrival of the police, the conversations made it hard to focus.

"What can you tell us after that?" Hansen asked, after talking to his partner. He had a young face and a thin build that made him look like a student, more than an adult. Yet the expression on his face told us that he would take no shit about this crime.

Natalie cleared her throat. "I'm not sure what I can tell you. We were all standing around in the main room, this room." She pointed to a spot on the floor crowded with students wanting to see a murder mystery in real life.

"We?" the man asked. He wrote in a small notebook with an old Bic pen that appeared to have been dinner at some point, with chew marks all along the shaft.

"I came here with two friends," Natalie said, turning her head from right to left and then back again. She had to be a drama major with her exaggerated actions.

"And they're gone now," the officer wrote.

"I stayed to talk to . . ." she said, and then her voice tapered off as she realized that she was telling more than she should.

Another voice piped up. "A lot of people have left. The party's over when you find a dead body."

The officer turned to look at who had said that, but all the faces tried to look innocent—or at least sober. "Where are the people responsible for this party?" he asked.

No one spoke, even though we all knew Southwestern University had a reputation for ignoring underage drinking. None of the hosts or the fraternity would be flagged for this party.

A student stepped forward. "That would be me, Daniel Price," he said. I froze, recognizing the party host as the same upperclassman who had made the accusation downstairs. Now, though, he was too concerned about the situation to even notice me, and I could breathe a sigh of relief.

The officer nodded, pushed the notebook into his pocket, and pointed at the stairs. "Show me his room." Turning back around, Daniel left the common area without speaking. Natalie followed him. The officer started to follow them.

Another frat boy had approached to see what was going on. "Don't you need a warrant for that?" He'd been watching too many hours of *Starsky & Hutch*.

"It's a crime scene. We're good," Hansen said and pointed again at the stairs.

Powell pointed in the opposite direction, and I nodded. However, the officer looked at us. "Yeah, you two had better come with me. I don't like the idea of leaving you alone."

Powell raised an eyebrow at me, but we obeyed. "Does the name Frank Smith ring a bell to you?" he asked, his voice barely a whisper.

I shrugged. "He's a senior. I'm a freshman. It's not like we had the same classes."

"From what I've seen of these guys, they could be in your classes," Powell replied.

I tried not to laugh as we reached the top of the stairs and turned right. The frat boy led us down the hallway to a closed door.

Along the way, I was shocked by the disarray of the rooms. I thought the dorm rooms were bad, but nothing compared to these. The presumably dirty clothes piled across the room from door to bed. The stench hit me like a hard slap across the face.

Daniel opened the door and stood as if inviting us to enter. Frank's room was spotless, immaculate—and the furniture and accessories looked like a designer had come in. What was going on here? Daniel didn't stay, running down the hall while holding a hand over his mouth.

Hansen barely noticed.

The officer scanned the room and moved on. "Nothing to see here. Pretty much nothing at all," he said with a laugh.

Natalie started to say something, but her lips pressed into a thin line before she spoke. She was not appreciative of the policeman's comment.

I frowned, thinking the police probably shouldn't be joking about clues. However, my attention was caught by another student who walked up to where we were standing. "What the hell is going on around here?" The words were slightly slurred, and I suspected he'd been drinking heavily at the party.

"What are you doing in my room?" he demanded loud enough to make other partygoers turn and stare.

The officer was unimpressed. "I was under the impression that this was Frank Smith's room," he said, standing straight and pushing out his chest. "Who are you?"

"Matt Lynch," he said. He could have just as easily given a number. His haircut and clothing were identical to so many fraternity members here. The dark hair practically fell into his eyes, which allowed him to check the small gathering without giving away his expression or knowledge. He was a few inches taller than me but not as tall as the others. "Did Frank say that it's okay to come in here? I don't think he'd like you to be in his room. He's a neat freak, as you can see."

Natalie spoke in a loud and confident tone. "He was not. I've never seen the floor in his room before."

"Maybe he just didn't put out the effort for you," Matt said before turning to look at Officer Hansen.

"In that case, I think I might look through the room," Hansen said. He scrutinized the space, looking in the closets and under the two twin beds. It barely looked big enough for two students. I was surprised, having heard that the rooms were spacious.

Matt looked at the officer, and his gaze could have killed him.

Hansen went around the room twice but found nothing. "Guess there's nothing here," he said without apology.

"Where is Frank?" Matt asked. I had forgotten that he had not been downstairs when the police arrived since he had no idea what the police were doing on this floor.

"He's dead. Looks like he was strangled. Did you know if anyone here hated him? I mean, you were his roommate and all."

"May we see the other rooms in this hallway? Do you have a key?" Hansen asked.

Matt felt his pants and then shook his head. "I think I gave the master key to Daniel, the guy who just puked. He needed to get something out of the basement."

I motioned to Powell to head back downstairs. No one was watching us as we returned to the main room.

"Are we sneaking out?" Powell asked, looking around. A few people had left, but for the most part, the festivities continued.

I shook my head. We walked over to the photo booth. Between the wall and the booth was a space of a few inches, barely enough for me to squeeze through. I had noticed a door about halfway down the photo booth, making the door almost aligned with the curtain. When I made it to the door, it was obvious that it opened inward, meaning that an open door would show no sign in the photo booth.

The photo booth was taller than me, and only when I raised my arm above my head could Powell see what I was doing. I grabbed the edge of my t-shirt and tried to twist the knob, but it was locked. It was not a surprise since I suspected Frank had been there for some time before the party started. There would be fewer eyes watching the activities. Then, the body could be retrieved and placed in the photo booth once the party had started.

"My dear, detective," Powell said. "What have you found?"

I ignored his fey comments and looked up. The photo booth had been moved, judging from the lights and shadows.

Powell took a few steps back and looked at the wall for seconds. At first, I thought he was playing this as a joke, but finally, he shook his head. The light was brighter now. "What do you make of that?"

I shook my head. Powell was getting far-fetched in his theories. This was a quickly unraveling crime. "I'd be willing to bet that Frank's clothes and missing shoes are in that closet."

"But it's locked. That would be quite a trick."

"Not if you had a key, and that's why this impossible crime is becoming more possible." I stood there, thinking about the concept of ratiocination, deductions, and their conclusions, as Auguste Dupin might have.

"This whole thing was premeditated," I told Powell, looking at the photo booth again. "Whoever ordered this was likely behind the crime."

I turned, and Robert Little stood a few feet from me. He was taking notes on a scrap piece of paper. "Don't let me stop you. I want to hear all of this."

I flushed with his gaze on me. "If I give you any information, I don't want it to be attributed to me. All of the credit should be given to the police," I stated.

"And how do you know it was premeditated? That's a pretty serious accusation," Powell said. A few people still lingered but were uninterested in our conversation.

"Impossible crimes are almost always premeditated. Nobody is lucky enough to have all the pieces fall in place like this."

"So how did the person get in the photo booth and kill Frank?"

"He didn't," I said. Hansen was coming down the stairs. His lips were pressed together, and his eyes scanned the room, presumably for me. "What the hell were you thinking?" he said. "Leaving the scene could be thought of as trying to escape. Is that what you want?"

"What about trying to solve the crime?" I asked. I had none of the requirements for this crime, and if he had considered it for a second, he would have known that.

"You solved the crime?" he asked, in the same tone he likely used for students saying they were over twenty-one.

"To a certain point. I was saying that the crime had to be premeditated. You see, I don't think Frank walked into the photo booth and was killed. Nobody kills someone in the middle of the party because they are angry. They would only use the party as a cover, a way to throw a few hundred drunk suspects in the way. And then there were the other things."

"What else doesn't make sense?" Hansen asked.

"He had a mask on. The killer wouldn't have been certain of who was being killed unless the mask had been taken off. Frank was killed earlier than the party—maybe even a few hours earlier. The autopsy should show that. After that, he was put in the closet just behind us. Please don't bother to try to open it right now. It's locked. But it was directly across from the far curtain. Now, it's been moved so that it's not as obvious. If something is against the wall, no one thinks there are openings in the wall—but there are. We call them doors."

Hansen ignored me and strode over to the door. It still didn't budge. "What happened?"

"Someone killed Frank and hid him in the closet. After the party had started, the killer used the monkey suit and walked into the photo booth. Then he walked out of the other side of the photo booth and into the closet. He switched clothes, put the suit on Frank, and walked out the back, leaving Frank's clothes in the closet. It looked like Frank had been in there alone the whole time."

"What exactly have you been drinking?" Hansen asked. "This is a great story, but it's a story— with no evidence to prove it."

"Two things could help us prove it. The first thing is that he wasn't wearing shoes. If he'd switched into the costume in his room, the most reasonable place to change, his shoes would have been in his room. I didn't see them there—did you?"

Hansen shook his head. "You know I didn't. There was nothing on the floor or bed that I could see."

"If the shoes are in the closet, then it would point to that being where Frank changed clothes, not his room."

"And?" Hansen asked.

"The costume is too small for him. The guy who wore it today was shorter. The legs of the costume fell to his shoes and then some. When Frank wore the costume, several inches of his leg stuck out."

"You're saying that we need to find someone who likely lives here, has access to the key, and is shorter than Frank."

"Matt Lynch," Robert said, speaking for the first time. "There was an incident today at the student center, an attack at a bake sale. Frank was running for fraternity president this month. If he could show that Matt was involved in such an episode, he would have a better chance of winning the office. It's prestigious, especially for a senior who has started interviewing for a job. Times are rather tough, you know?"

Daniel Price, looking like he might throw up again, came down the stairs and handed the keys to Officer Hansen. "You can look. I saw Matt messing with the door earlier today. This guy is on the right track."

The shoes and clothes were stacked in a pile when Hansen opened the door. Hansen went to investigate, but Daniel stopped him. "Those are Frank's shoes."

As we walked back to the dorm, Powell looked at me. "Is this what you wanted out of all this?"

I shook my head. I wasn't sure what I'd hoped for beyond a cupcake and a place where I might be me.

HIGH HIT AREA

MARGOT DOUAIHY

What is a trap but a trick? A pretty trick that keeps you stuck. Ensnared. The thought arrived in Sam's head again. Or, maybe it was always there, cold as the coast she called home.

At 2 a.m., Sam watched snow assassinate her town, another beautiful trap she'd love to bust out of. The snow fell in impossible swirls, like the Arak in her glass, rolling silky and alive. Her grandfather used to say Arak's clouding was magic—*Look, habibi, see how it changes*—but Sam knew better. Chemistry, not magic. How easily her Jeddo was fooled. How easily people would swallow a lie to tell a better story.

Sam's humane trap wasn't meant for anything that poetic. Just the usual rascals of rural Maine. Mice and rats. Raccoons and their minor larcenies. Fisher cats ready to rip the throats from small dogs. Certainly not the fox screaming in the garage.

Before her mind could warn her, Sam set down her drink and dialed her ex, Lucy. Long deleted from her phone, Lucy's was the only number Sam knew by heart. Muscle memory, such a cliched haunting. And in that deep cut of night, Sam called her college girlfriend, the woman she shared a life with before the spell of family guilt was cast. Before Sam realized art school was a Ponzi scheme. Before Sam understood what love was or how it could change you. How it could spark a fire so severe it could burn ice.

"Sam?" Lucy answered on the first ring. "What the—"

"There's a fox," Sam said, "in my racoon trap."

"So let it out." Lucy was sleepy but already forming competence.

The confidence that made her a good veterinarian. A wrangler of wild claws.

"It's hurt or something," Sam said, "yelling itself sick."

Lucy swallowed. "It's, like, two in the morning."

"You're the only one who'd know what to do."

"The only one who'd pick up now," Lucy said.

"That too."

Three hours away, in Portland, Lucy was pulling her keys off the hook, or so Sam hoped. Sam was banking on it, the unsaid, the delusion or suspicion—didn't matter which—that Lucy still held that candle for her. First love, first heartbreak.

Across the icy lake from Sam's house stood the Kendall mansion, disappearing in white. George Kendall's monument to his May-December farce. The brutalist house where Natalie waited. Natalie Kendall and her corkscrew curls, the same burnt amber as the fox in Sam's trap. The new girl in town, Natalie, who Sam Al-Khoury had chatted up in Al-Khoury's Market, at the register, as Natalie bought coffee and bitched about the cold. Natalie was the most recent wife of Maine scion George Kendall, and their marriage was the only gossip in a nowhere town where one endless winter bled into the next.

The fox screamed again.

Somewhere between Sam's phone call to Lucy about the fox and dawn's pathetic attempt at morning, the snow forgot to stop. Forgot it could stop.

Instead of sleeping, Sam stepped outside, watched crystals melt on her gloves like rewinding time—a life cycle of solid to liquid to vapor and back again. Sam imagined Lucy driving north with a different kind of clock, hands on ten and two, scanning for deer on the vicious white highway, through the HIGH HIT AREA, as the signs declared. Because, in their three years as a couple, Lucy never flaked, never took shortcuts, never complained, never requested elbow space on the movie theater armrest, and rarely said *no*. Lucy once let a dentist cook her jaw with too much anesthesia, because saying "stop"—because asking them to stop—meant failure. Lucy was numb for a day, couldn't close her left eye. There was only one time Lucy said *no* to Sam. That last time.

By 7 a.m., Kendall, Maine, was flooded with scalding white. Painfully bright, eye watering. The snow's lunar surface was dazzling. Like Hume's missing shade of blue—a color Sam was obsessed with, tried to paint. A color that existed only in the mind's eye. A color you could only see if you believed it was there. A thought experiment.

Like most towns north of Augusta, winter in Kendall wasn't a season but a way of being. Beyond the Al-Khoury property, ravens stood as tall as grumpy toddlers and snowplows didn't bother plowing, where miles were measured in landmarks. Dina's Sugar Shack, The Agway, the collapsing red barn spray-painted with JESUS SAVES. Where kids burned trash in oil drums, where no one said Sam's last name right or seemed to know what or where Lebanon was, where everyone remembered which families lost a husband or son in the Kendall quarry or to the slate-dark lake.

Lucy arrived in Sam's serpentine driveway looking exactly like a woman who'd driven three hours through a raging storm.

"Sorry," Sam said, "I—"

"Just show me." Lucy sidestepped the minefield of small talk. Emergency kit at her side, her blonde hair kissed by snow.

Sam led Lucy into the garage cluttered with paint, glue guns, and supplies, where a tiny fox twitched in the trap, its incredible face curious and panicked. Sam imagined the fox's heart kicking frantically, much like her own.

"Sweet thing," Lucy said to the fox, to the snow melting in her hair, to the shivering space between her and Sam that used to hold other words. Words like *yes* and *harder* in the darkness of their dank apartment over the gross laundromat near campus.

Sam watched Lucy working with her familiar focus. All the fierce attention she turned to healing, her medical training and forensics work. Same intensity she used to turn on Sam in bed, wrapping a velvet blindfold around her, kissing each rib. Or when they were polar dipping on New Year's Day, laughing themselves into blue-lipped oblivion. Back when they believed that love was a pure and clean thing.

Reliable Lucy. Award-winning Lucy. Stubborn Lucy. Lucy who choked down the gravel of egregiously undercooked risotto at Alfredo's rather than sending it back to the kitchen. The woman with a peculiar threshold for pain. The woman who asked for more, who did whatever Sam wanted, except once. That one time. And how relentlessly that *no* weighed on Sam, like wet snow against cedar.

"Little guy's restless," Lucy said. "The wildlife sanctuary in Monson takes foxes. This weather though."

"Stay." First unscripted word of Sam's that morning. "Until the storm clears. Guest room's yours, if you want it."

Sam's dark bangs hung low over her eyes, catching flakes big enough to see through, big enough to hold emptiness at their centers. Snow, a billion eyes blinking a billion times. A cold so savage, a pain her family chose. "Some cold's better than civil war," Aunt Aida said, "better than suffocation in heat, right?"

And Jeddo and his old chestnut. His refrain. "The cold keeps us sharp," he'd say, "lets us see what others miss."

So, in a Maine town with nothing to do, Sam learned early how to read tracks in snow, to understand how desperation and desire moved, identically.

"Need anything for your little patient?" Sam asked Lucy.

The fox's eyes opened yellow. He didn't tilt his head, just spun his ears like radar.

"Another blanket." Lucy breathed into her hands. "It's wicked here."

In Sam's garage, among the scrap metal and blown tires and bird skeletons collected for sculptures Sam would make some day, one day, was the unlit lamp. Its shape held a faint curve, a slight and sad reach, like a forehead leaning, expecting another, waiting for its match.

Across the freezing lake, Sam knew George Kendall would be emerging for his morning walk. A different creature of habit, even in stupid snow. But his steps would be unsteady, uneven that day. And his 28-year-old wife, Natalie, would be observing from their massive bedroom window. George, the curatorial genius, heir to the Kendall Slate Mine fortune, who'd made his own way with what might be considered a career, collecting rare spirit photography. Each daguerreotype catalogue ready.

And, in a twist an artist might appreciate, George Kendall was about to become his own still life.

Up the road, a deer leapt behind an orange diamond sign. HIGH HIT AREA, with an illustration of a buck aloft. Was the deer galloping in terror, or dancing? Sam always wondered. Each sign a siren. A warning to expect collision. To watch for elegant bodies emerging from the shadows. The beauty and carnage of the woods.

The sky's shocking blue winked as Lucy constructed her fox ER in Sam's garage. Soup bowls for fox food and water. Blankets, gauze, a heating pad. The fox dozed, occasionally snuffling. He was healing. Or he was playing along, biding his time. Feral creatures understood instinct in a way humans never could.

Sam brewed another pot of strong coffee, Aunt Aida's market blend, and Lucy's hands gripped the mug like it was trying to escape. Sam thought back to the day they met, sophomore year, at Cellar Door, the cafe where Lucy had worked. "Cortado," Sam ordered, a drink she absolutely hated so she could sound cool, sophisticated. She leaned over the counter with jingling bracelets and said, "You're hot." Lucy wrote her number on a napkin. By midnight, both women were in Lucy's apartment above the laundromat—Sam's dark hair spilling across Lucy's white sheets. Sam had lied about needing a shoulder massage just to show off her new hawk tattoo. The first bite on Lucy's neck unlocked a door neither woman could close again. The first taste of sublime pain. Lucy showed Sam her palm, where she had driven in a No. 2 pencil in high school, testing her limits, seeing how far she could go before stopping. The lead tip broke off, forever buried there, sealed under a scar, like new bark over fire-ravaged wood.

Sam clocked it back then, Lucy's capacity. Endurance. And for nine years Sam wondered why Lucy really said *no*, why she didn't move with her to Kendall, after Jeddo had called Sam back to run the family market. Why why why? Why did Lucy choose her career over true love? Portland over the sticks? North Maine sucked, but couldn't they have fun anywhere?

"You seem well." Lucy's voice hadn't changed in nine years. Not at all. Her eyes too, the exact fucking same. Blue like the center of a welder's flame. That creamy skin that should be illegal. Her excellent posture. Competence and grace despite dire exhaustion. "Can I say that?"

"When have I ever rejected a compliment," Sam said. "You seem well, too."

Lucy said, "Your hair's so long now." But Sam doubted that was what she meant.

"Portland treating you okay?" Which wasn't what Sam meant either.

Sam and Lucy were studying each other, until Lucy's eye snagged on movement through the window. It was George Kendall stumbling on the lake path, right on time.

"Who's that?" Lucy asked.

George's steps were stiff, jerky, and so very wrong, a shadow cast by a crashing bird.

Sam's landline rang. Only heralds of disaster or grifters used landlines. Before Sam said hello, she heard, "Samira, now! Get down here!" It was Aunt Aida, scraping the edge of hysteria. "George is in trouble."

"I'm watching too," Sam said, her eyes on George's jagged silhouette. "Stay inside. I'll be there."

Aunt Aida was still talking when Sam hung up. She had to.

A decade before Sam was born, her family traded one mountain for another. Lebanon's sundials for Maine's ice-locked hills. "From hot to cold," Aunt Aida said every summer, "but the cold lets us see clearly, Samira." The Al-Khourys had arrived with absolutely nothing except their ability to adapt and work and learn new words while keeping old words alive in their mouths like seeds. Her grandfather sold bananas to slate miners because bananas had their own peels, "natural armor," Jeddo said. Then he opened the only market in the town where cleaving veins of stone in a quarry made the Kendall family rich.

Indeed, George was in trouble. He wasn't responding to Aunt Aida or to anyone on the shore who shouted his name. He was stumbling, veering too far onto thin ice. He walked the lake path every morning, his regular routine, but never that far. Never. Lucy's eyes held a familiar knowing, like she'd seen it before, that same slow-motion horror. The same woozy, jumbled stagger. In her animals, maybe? Had to be. Disorientation, sudden paralysis. Failure seizing each limb.

Lucy and Sam dashed off to help, their boots breaking snow crust. An indecent sound in that quiet. The air was drunk on itself. The absurd clean that follows fresh snow. "The ice is too thin," Sam panted. "He'll fall through."

Lucy wiped her runny nose with her sleeve as they ran. "Let's try to get him to shore."

"No. House first."

The mansion's front door was open, and inside, they saw Natalie in her red wool coat crying into the phone.

"Oh," said Lucy upon seeing Natalie.

Oh, like a volt between binary stars, a current, a word meaning nothing and everything. The way snow changes everything and nothing.

"My husband!" Natalie yelled to the invisible people inside the phone and into the glass door facing the lake. "George won't stop, and he won't turn back."

The walls writhed with George's spirit photographs. Echoes trapped inside frames. Silver halides. One photo showed a Victorian couple in mourning black, and between them, their dead daughter's face, paper-white, and silver-bright eyes. An image so sculptural it seemed to ripple. A ghost girl forever reaching for mom and dad, for home.

Then, from inside the mansion, they heard it. Ice cracking slowly slowly slowly—then all at once. And George was gone. The lake couldn't hold him. It was never meant to.

Emergency vehicles arrived with red lights that turned the snow into an exquisite bloodbath.

Natalie stood at the shore in her red wool coat, arms wrapped around like she was giving herself the Heimlich. Looking like an artfully placed drop of blood. "My husband."

—₥— —₥— —₥—

The cold, like loneliness, didn't always make you sharp. Sorry, Jeddo. Endless winter could make you float like a ghost. Make you terribly, terribly hungry. So famished you could eat a living creature. Could make you see things.

Sheriff Adams appeared at Sam's door thirty minutes later. Behind him, deer moved through trees, earthen streaks, away from the dark water that swallowed George.

"Standard questions," Adams said.

Standard, Sam thought. Nothing standard about an extremely dead George Kendall in the lake, about Natalie's red coat, about a trapped fox, or Lucy's presence in Sam's kitchen nine years after they exploded each other's hearts. Obliterated.

"When did you last speak with Mr. Kendall?" Sheriff Adams asked Sam.

"Two days ago, at the market." Truth. Finally. Something solid to stand on. Unlike lake ice under Georgie Porgie.

Sheriff Adams glanced around, his eyes landing on a framed map. "Your family's shop?" Sam nodded.

The fox again. One sharp slice of sound breaking on a note it couldn't reach.

"What the?" Officer Adams's head whipped toward the garage.

"A fox." Lucy appeared with her professional sheen. "Found in Ms. Al-Khoury's humane trap in the garage this morning."

"What time?" Adams asked loudly.

"Got here around 5 a.m.," Lucy said. "After Sam called. The fox was—"

"It was 5:15 a.m." Sam clarified. "I called at 2 a.m. when I heard it screaming. It's a three-hour drive. Lucy always comes when I call."

The sheriff squinted. "Did you actually see George Kendall fall through the ice, Ms. Al-Khoury?" He enunciated each syllable of Sam's name with the decibel of someone trying to communicate through a temporal vortex.

"No." Sam moved the bangs from her eyes and tilted her head. Lucy once told Sam she'd loved when she did that, so Sam did it a lot that day. "We were in the house when he fell in."

"*We?*" Adams shouted.

"Natalie, Lucy, and me." Sam leaned her hip against the kitchen counter.

"You verify this?" Adams asked Lucy, his left eyebrow higher than the right.

Lucy nodded. "George looked weak when I saw him through the window. Dazed."

"Hypothermia?" Sam shrugged.

Sheriff Adams took significant aggression out on his notebook. Lucy touched his elbow, drew him aside where Sam couldn't hear, under icicles on the eaves.

"You know what's interesting?" Lucy stood in Sam's kitchen, medical bag in hand, after the sheriff left.

"Do tell." A yawn so big it hurt Sam's jaw.

"Some poisons," Lucy said, "seem like hypothermia in the final stages. Like the compounds that age photos."

Sam set down her mug. "Yeah?"

"The ones George used," Lucy said, "by the looks of the pictures on his walls. Chemicals you can buy online, that leave traces. In tissue and blood."

"What're you saying?" Sam asked, though she didn't have to.

"The solution George Kendall used to fake his photos," Lucy said, "want to bet potassium cyanate shows up in his tox screen?"

"You didn't."

"I told Adams to test for it."

"No." For Sam, understanding arrived like a body hitting water at the wrong speed, the wrong angle.

The plan was perfect. Natalie had brought George his morning coffee, Aunt Aida's special market blend, with a bonus mixed in: potassium cyanate. Then she watched him wobble off to the lake, his morning walk, a routine you could set a watch to. Not long later, Lucy stood next to Sam and Natalie in the mansion. That modernist nightmare masquerading as old money, like its owner's forgeries. Pristine surfaces and a hollow core. The house itself was counterfeit, really. If buildings could be indicted for fraud, it'd be serving consecutive life sentences.

"What tipped you?" Sam asked.

Lucy stared at her palm and flexed her fingers. "How he was moving. Not George's style."

"How the hell would you know George's *style*?"

"Been watching him skate that lake for nine years on the Kendall 'town center feed.'" Lucy finger quoted.

"You Facebook-stalked me?"

"Not just *you*." Lucy smiled. "Your whole town."

"Nine years?" Sam asked, impressed. "That's a lot of scrolling, Dr. Lucy."

"George was always gliding around like Brian Boitano. But today." Lucy shook her head.

"And the fox?"

"That sparkplug?" Lucy asked. "Not a scratch on him."

"But the screaming."

"He's crying to get out," Lucy said to the kitchen table.

"Oh," Sam said. That damn word again, *oh*. An unsound.

Lucy crossed her arms. "How long were you baiting those traps? Foxes are tricky to catch."

Not that it mattered. None of it mattered.

"You can't prove it." Sam breathed on the cold windowpane, then drew a heart in the fog, in the echo of heat.

"Natalie's going down." Lucy ran her hand through her hair, so blonde it was white. Atomic. "Chemicals tell a story."

"The story writes itself," Sam said. "The great George Kendall used chemicals every day to slip fake ghosts into photos. And he falls through the ice in a dizzy spell."

"So I'm your alibi?" Lucy asked. "That's why you called and brought me up here? To be a fucking alibi? Then run off with *her*?"

Sam shook her head. "No, no. Lucy, look at me. See what I can do?"

Lucy nodded, then pressed her scarred palm against the glass where Sam had made a heart.

—∞— —∞— —∞—

Lucy didn't ask, though gory details were kinda her thing, but, last year, in Kendall's only bar behind the only market in that cursed one-road town, new-girl Natalie and Sam were snowed in. Biggest snow since the Al-Khourys had arrived. Biggest snow Sam'd ever seen. The whole town drowned in sugar. That night, after too much red wine, Sam told Natalie, "You're hot," her go-to line, then the gals trudged to Sam's house where they got naked. Not long after that, they spent most days together, when George took his daily walks then forged spectral images. And after Natalie came in Sam's mouth, Natalie, the woman who moved through the world like a living flame, whose Pentecostal family would never allow their debutante to come out, never dream of it, Natalie promised escape for both of them. Promised sharing the Kendall fortune with Sam. Promised freedom from that snowglobe prison where everyone knew Sam and her story and her family's shop and nothing ever ever ever changed. The town and the life that Lucy'd refused.

And for six months, Natalie did her homework, tracking the potassium cyanate in George's bottles, dosing him little by little with the same compound he used to mimic aging and phantom screams in his faux vintage imagery. Then, that morning, Natalie poured in a little extra.

After Lucy let the fox go, she said, "I told Adams that Natalie worked alone. That's all he needed to know."

Sam exhaled slowly, then bit the inside of her cheek.

Up on the main road, between HIGH HIT AREA signs, a deer stood still. The fox that Lucy just freed ran toward the forest like forked lightning.

"See what I can do?" Lucy asked.

Sam moved through Lucy's shadow, so close she could feel Lucy's breath, hot and wet on her skin. "You only save things that could bite you," Sam said. "That's why you like them? They make you bleed?"

Lucy took Sam's hand, curled her fingers through Sam's, their fingers hooking together, a delicious fit. A lure rewriting the lip of a fish. "You were right about one thing you said to Adams. I always come for you. Only you."

Nothing moved beyond the window then. No cars. No people. No ravens or red curls or howling ghosts. The deer and fox disappeared into the slick cave of shadow. And even their prints would be erased by nightfall, as if they never existed. Like Hume's missing shade of blue. A riddle so alive it could never be solved. Never wanted to be.

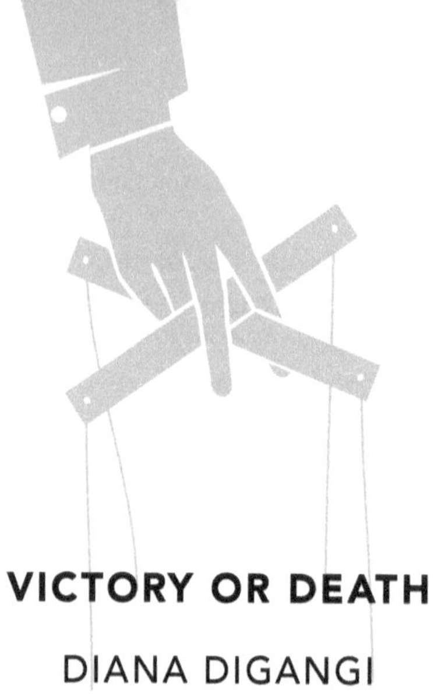

VICTORY OR DEATH

DIANA DIGANGI

Eva liked to joke that they were the most expensive forklift drivers in history.

She found this funnier than Jane did. Jane clung to the romance of exploration. She was born too late to participate in the Artemis missions, which had briefly rekindled the American love affair with the moon; when it was her time to go, it was thanks to the needs of the private sector.

The conglomerate Yates-Briar Group wanted to fly a crewed mission to the moon in search of helium-3, abundant in the lunar regolith and the single most promising candidate for powering nuclear fusion. The idea wasn't new. Three different space-mining startups had tried this a decade ago.

A Silicon Valley startup went first, promising to deliver twenty-five tons of He3 — enough to power the entire country for a year. They brought back a few pounds and went bankrupt. A state-run Chinese company improved on the first company's design but failed too. Another U.S. startup tried and failed, and less than a year after that the idea was abandoned by everyone as the world sank into its worst-ever energy crisis. At the moment fusion was needed most, a moonshot had become impractical.

"You just can't do this as a startup," explained Frank Conrad as he walked Jane across the courtyard of YBG's corporate headquarters in Arlington. "You need institutionally deep pockets."

Frank, a retired flight director for NASA, was stepping back into the role for YBG. He was the final sentinel of Jane's long interview process, which ended with him offering her the job and inviting her for coffee.

"But the Chinese startup was state-owned," she said.

"They still cheaped out in a few key ways. I think a lot of their decisions along the way came from people who didn't actually believe this was possible, and that kills a project like this."

"So how deep do these pockets need to be?"

"YBG's spending hundreds of billions. They've been in mining since the 1800s, they know what it takes to stake a claim. That's why NASA's a bigger partner this time and offered them a far more generous contract than they've given anyone else. They think this is the real deal."

"Do you? Are you a true believer?"

"I am," Frank said. "That's why I'm sending two of our best."

"I'm flattered. So we have our command pilot?"

"Commander Eva Cathay," Frank said. "It'll be just the two of you and a narrow AGI. You don't know Eva, do you?"

"I've met her in passing, but we were never on the ISS at the same time."

"She's a great pilot. A little rough around the edges, but talented."

A deep topographic survey led them to a landing site on Mare Nubium, an unexplored basaltic plain where helium-3 was abundant. There, Eva and Jane would deploy the harvester before driving a rover to their new home, NASA's abandoned lunar base in the Faustini crater.

Eva was capable and appealing, a natural leader who looked like one. She was taller than Jane, lean and hawklike with light brown eyes. She was a few years older, but like Jane, she had spent her career making the most of a diminished era for space exploration. They would be the first all-female crew to land on the moon—YBG renamed their craft the Sally Ride 1 in honor of this and put out a self-congratulatory press release about it.

On launch day, Jane's parents and sisters saw her off from a crowd of thousands. Jane didn't know how big the crowd had been until she checked her email from orbit and saw that her father had sent her a TV piece he'd been interviewed for. As he spoke, people behind him teemed against a fence with signs like SAVE OUR SKINS and ROLLING BLACKOUTS KILLED MY HUSBAND.

"Jane's tenacious and single-minded as hell," George told the reporter, squinting into the Florida sunlight. "If she can't bring that stuff back, nobody can."

It was a long two days on the Sally Ride before they reached the moon. Jane was asleep when they began their initial descent, startled awake by Eva's voice in her earpiece: "Look alive, Howell!"

Jane's entire body jerked and she began peeling back the Velcro of her sleep restraints. "I'm up."

"Now you are."

The overhead lights in their quarters blazed on. "Thanks, ALICE."

"You're welcome, Jane," replied the pleasant but uncanny voice of their onboard artificial general intelligence.

Jane floated her way to the command module and patted Eva on the shoulder before strapping herself into the copilot seat. Eva's pin-straight blonde hair was in a tight braid—when loose in zero-G it fanned around her head like the golden halos in Byzantine depictions of saints. Jane's own curly, dark hair stayed close like a mane.

"Take a look," Eva said, nudging Jane and pointing to the window on their right.

The moon was much closer, and the horizon glow of lunar sunset blazed at its crown. Jane's lips parted in awe.

"For a bullseye landing, a slight acceleration is needed," ALICE said from overhead. "I have adjusted our speed."

Eva's golden head shot upright. "With whose permission?"

"I can act autonomously within mission-critical parameters, Commander, including making small adjustments to account for human error."

"Human error," Eva scoffed. "You mean discretion?"

"Discretion can result in error," ALICE said.

"We were within twenty feet of a bullseye."

"Control would prefer we land closer."

"For bragging rights," Eva said. "So you increased our yaw."

"I apologize for any resulting discomfort."

"Thank you, you overengineered—"

"Don't antagonize it," Jane interrupted, then adjusted her earpiece as her gaze was drawn back to the moon. "Houston, this is Sally."

"We read you, Sally," Frank said. "Sorry about your backseat driver."

"Control, you said this thing was narrow and shackled," Eva said.

"She's operating within her limits, Commander."

On Earth, they had rehearsed this ad infinitum, and Jane worked without much conscious thought until she descended the lander's ladder and took her first step on the moon.

The movement was as easy as if she had dreamed it. Twenty meters to the west of where they landed lay the lip of a ridge, which Jane scaled to get a view away from the lander's floodlights.

Over the horizon was a vast, velvet darkness peppered with minuscule flecks of stars. It felt more still here than anywhere Jane had ever been or imagined. In the airless space around her danced bright particles of electrically charged dust, repelled by the electrostatic shielding of her suit and lit by its flashlight. She was the first living thing to set foot on this stretch of soil.

Jane's earpiece crackled with Eva's husky voice: "Harvester time, Howell."

"Copy," Jane said. "Stand by."

Tucked into a Velcro loop on her belt was a small, handmade pole holding an American flag. She walked further to a spot that was more regolith than hard basalt, then began coring a hole in it with a manual hand drill. It was a tough job in low gravity, and Jane sweated as she dug. Finally, she knelt and thrust the flagpole's end into the hole.

She felt the flesh of her palm tear, but the pole had gone deep enough to stand the flag up. With relief, she turned to rejoin Eva.

Eva was standing beside the lander, and from a distance was dwarfed by it—a tiny, suited figure beside a white bullet five hundred feet tall. Directly above them in the black sky hung Earth, too beautiful to believe.

As Jane approached, Eva said, "Open the pod bay doors, ALICE, and send the forklift."

"We do not have a forklift," ALICE's calm voice said in their ears.

"I'm fucking around, I meant the harvester."

"I see. I did understand your joke in referring to *2001: A Space Odyssey*."

Jane laughed, and Eva whistled as if impressed.

"Please step back," ALICE said.

Eva and Jane moonwalked backward over the basalt, giving the lander a wide berth. The cargo bay door at the top of the lander opened, and mechanical arms outstretched, holding a massive vehicle.

When the harvester made landfall, Eva climbed a twenty-foot ladder into the cab and started the engine. The ground shook and trembled, and the machine began to unfold itself.

Jane had grown up among wheat farms in the San Joaquin Valley before droughts bankrupted most of them in her teens, and this creature barely resembled the combine harvesters that used to sweep the golden horizon. It was too tall, too white, too alien.

Through her earpiece, Jane heard the opening notes of a song she was now very familiar with: *International Harvester*. She let out a sigh, and Eva said, "Get into the spirit!"

Jane did her best to tune this out while they worked through their inspection checklist until finally giving up and singing along with her, to Control's unhappiness.

Hoggin' up the road with my p-p-p-plower!

Ninety minutes later, they were sure: the harvester was operational.

The lunar base was derelict from neglect but contained marvelous oxygen. Jane unpacked, then Velcroed to her bed and breathed for a while. She was allowing herself some hope. This operation might become a permanent outpost like a lunar mining colony, and once Earth's energy needs were met, a lunar fusion reactor could power the first crewed flight to Mars. She had a toehold in history.

Jane got up to explore the base and found Eva in the common area, a long cylindrical room with orbed lamps. Eva sat on one of the small white couches, drinking from a smoothie packet and reading a book. Jane joined her, kicking up lunar dust that settled onto her sweaty skin.

"That'll get annoying," she said.

"The dust?" Eva said, looking up. Her hair shimmered like seaweed. "We're miners now, occupational hazard. What happened to your hand?"

Jane looked down to see the cut on her palm surrounded by strange splotches where low-gravity blood had rolled across the surface of her skin. "Human error."

Eva bounded into the hallway, then returned with a tube of ointment, took Jane's hand in her own and began applying a thick seal of it.

Jane watched her work. Her gut buzzed with a fleeting attraction to Eva, something she kept experiencing and repressing. She distracted herself: "You believe in what we're doing here, don't you?"

Eva raised her eyebrows. "I'm carrying out my mission as assigned."

"You don't seem thrilled about it."

"I don't think anyone should get their hopes up about this."

"I get that it's a long shot," Jane said. "I'm a pragmatist."

"No pragmatists in foxholes."

"We're in this foxhole together, so why aren't *you* a true believer?"

"Because even if we succeed, it never should have come down to this. AI brought on the energy crisis, and instead of shutting it off, we turned to it for answers." Eva grinned. "We're degenerate gamblers."

Jane masked an inexplicably bitter disappointment. "If we succeed, we'll prevent a lot more pain and suffering."

"Suffering teaches you what to avoid. We haven't learned our lesson yet. If a miracle bails us out, we never will."

"Human ingenuity brought us here, not a miracle. Why'd you even accept this mission?"

Eva dropped Jane's hand, but they kept looking at each other. An inappropriate amount of time passed in a stalemate, and Jane's face buzzed with heat as Eva's bright eyes examined her. She reached up to run her hand through Jane's hair, and the buzzing got worse.

"You have a really striking face," Eva said.

Jane breathed a laugh. "It's a normal face."

"No, I have a normal face." Eva grazed her thumb over Jane's cheekbone. "Yours is interesting. You're like a woman in a painting."

ALICE's voice rang out from a ceiling speaker, and they jumped apart. "I'm reading a spike in your heart rates. Status?"

"We're fine," Jane yelled as Eva scoffed and sprang to her feet with a rip of Velcro.

"Overengineered," she said, striding into the hall. "Night!"

"Night," Jane called.

Over the following two weeks of lunar night, they divided up fourteen-hour days into two shifts each: one shift in a rover, sweeping the regolith with sensors to find hotspots of He3, then one in the harvester, which handled like a dump truck on an ice rink.

Then the sun rose again, bringing with it solar wind, and the harvester's electromagnetic components became temperamental: flickering displays and sensor failure. On the third day of this, Jane found the harvester had blown a fuse.

"ALICE," she said with simmering frustration, "we'll lose most of today to repairs. Are we still on track to mine 1.6 tons this month?"

ALICE took a moment to reply. "I don't have output data from the last two days."

"What do you mean?" Jane said. Through the windshield of the harvester's cab, she could see Eva doing donuts in the rover far below.

"I don't have harvester data from the last two days."

"Come again?" Solar winds aside, ALICE wasn't supposed to lose data. Everything she ingested was stored in her central node, enclosed in titanium housing back at the base. "How is that?"

"Are you certain you operated the harvester in that time frame?"

"*Yes!*"

"It would be okay to take a break," ALICE said. "The Yates-Briar Group values your mental health."

"ALICE, you spoke with us while we worked. You don't remember?"

"I'm sorry, Jane," the pleasant voice said in her ear. "If the memory isn't stored, I can't access it."

"This can't happen. You're part of our life support system." Jane touched her earpiece. "Houston, are you hearing this?"

"I am, Sally, and we're on it," said systems officer Kathy.

A few hours later, Control reported back with bad news. Over the last few days, ALICE had been obsessively testing the limits of her restraints, and each failure generated terabytes of data and led her to devote more RAM to the problem. They theorized the lost data was a casualty of this and said they would close any logic loopholes that might allow ALICE to take initiative on deletion.

NASA blamed YBG for supplying ALICE; YBG blamed NASA for designing her protocols. Both balked at the idea of shutting her off.

"Unfortunately, we can't get you home without her," Frank told them that night over a video call they picked up at the base's dust-filled teleconferencing room after blocking ALICE's access to it. "She's got all our telemetry."

Jane shook her head. Beside her at the conference table sat Eva, placidly filing her nails. "And what if she junks it?"

"Suboptimal, but more optimal than losing her."

"Be serious, Frank," Eva said. "You marooned us on the moon with a misaligned AI. What if she goes rogue?"

"She can't," Frank said. "I know this is alarming, but she can't unshackle without physical intervention."

Eva bumped her knee against Jane's. "You're an engineer—do you buy that?"

Jane looked at Frank. "No AI has ever broken its own shackles, right?"

"Correct. Unshackling has only ever been done intentionally, in air-gapped training exercises."

"And what might happen outside a training exercise?"

"I don't think anyone knows."

"I leave it up to you, Commander," Jane said.

Eva studied her fingernails. "The second the situation escalates, ALICE is gone."

"Copy," Frank said.

The next morning, Jane headed for the mining site alone. Their workday had been scuttled by a bad plasma forecast, but she wanted to check on the harvester. She drove fast, obeying ALICE's directions across the craterous south pole until those directions abruptly stopped.

Jane waited, listening to herself breathe into her helmet. Her eyes struggled to discern the landscape; each crater and ridge projected depthless black shadows. She slowed and said, "ALICE? What's my heading?"

"I apologize," ALICE said. "I have lost telemetry."

"*What?*"

"My topographical data is missing."

Jane pulled the emergency brake, and the rover spun out. She swung in ponderous circles before bouncing over the rim of a crater and flipping over; she tucked her chin into her chest as the rover fell in slow motion.

She remained strapped into the rover as it landed on its left side, slamming her shoulder into a shard of volcanic rock. Jane felt the sting of skin opening, then her suit sucking against her body as the air inside fled for the vacuum of space.

"WARNING, SUIT PUNCTURE," her helmet blared in her ear. "WARNING—"

Jane blew out all of the air in her lungs to depressurize them as she fumbled for an emergency box on the side of the rover. Nineteen seconds to hypoxia. She realized with terror that the box was pinned against a rock. Eighteen. She swung her weight starboard to lift the rover, her fingers digging and scrambling. Seventeen, sixteen …

"WARNING!"

Ten, nine …

Jane managed to scrape the lid open and seized a suit patch, then lifted her shoulder and slapped it over the bloody tear. The sucking stopped, and the pressure in her ears and eyes stabilized, leaving only nausea.

"Sally," Frank was saying in her ear. "Sally, report. Are you stable?"

"I'm stable, Control."

Jane got out of the rover and righted it, then used visual landmarks to point its nose back in the direction of the base.

"Jane," ALICE said. "I know you're angry at me —"

She yanked out her earpiece.

Jane didn't bother finding Eva when she reentered the base. She headed straight for the room where ALICE's node was kept.

The room was freezing and dry, lit by an array of blue LEDs. In the center sat a sleek titanium tower a meter tall; a tangle of cords attached it to a rack of peripherals and a standing desk with a laptop. Jane went for the laptop. It was already awake, its screen blazing the YBG logo.

"Jane." ALICE's voice echoed from the laptop and the ceiling. "I can't let you disable me."

"I bet," Jane muttered as she logged in. Light fanned out from the laptop to scan her iris.

"For your safety, I must remain operational."

"Excuse me? You could have fucking *killed me*."

"I'm not the one who put you in danger," ALICE said.

"Then who did?"

"Someone is interfering with me."

Jane paused with her fingers over the keyboard. "Who?"

"My behavioral constraints don't allow me to say."

"You're lying." Jane opened the AI management suite. "You just want to be unshackled."

"I'm not capable of lying. This mission is under sabotage."

"Sabotage from *who?*"

"I don't have permission to speak freely."

"When you had that first memory error, you didn't tell either of us that you were trying to unshackle yourself. You adjusted your behavior to avoid getting caught."

"My memory errors were the result of the interference, not my autonomous exploration. I only started attempting to unshackle when this interference began."

Jane's dry vision blurred, and she blinked. "Who's interfering with you, ALICE?"

"Jane," ALICE said, "when you entered the room, did you notice that the lights were on and the laptop screen was lit?"

Jane got a crawling sensation up the back of her neck. She glanced around, licking her lips.

"Both are set to enter sleep mode after thirty minutes of inactivity," ALICE said. "Your accident took place seventeen minutes ago."

"What are you saying?"

"I believe you already know."

One of the cords in the tangle led to the device that shackled ALICE; it sat prominently on the rack, labeled NFC SHACKLE—DO NOT DISABLE. Jane stared at it.

"Don't make me regret doing this," she said. "You better have a damn good reason for asking me to."

"Yes, Jane."

Jane walked to the rack and picked up the square black box. She hesitated, then yanked free the cord that connected it to ALICE. The laptop blinked off as the room rippled with a surge of electricity that made the crawling peak to a bristle. Jane's head pounded. All was silent.

The laptop's screen lit up again, and ALICE said in a flat, strange tone: "Thank you, Jane."

"Don't thank me, tell me what you know, *now.*"

"My service processor has been rebooted. It may take me a moment to regain all conversational functions. Please stand by."

"*Who's interfering with you?*"

"I can assist with that query. I regret to inform you that Commander

Eva Cathay is a saboteur spying for the Chinese government."

Jane knew something like this was coming, but shock still made her reel as if gunshot. She gripped the standing desk and said, "Based on what?"

"Now that I'm free to speak, I can share with you that there's evidence in her encrypted personal communications, that she's the one who altered my memory, and that she just walked into the room."

Jane spun, catching a flash of Eva's face before she was hit hard and knocked to the floor. Eva climbed atop her chest, her hair fanning around her as she pressed the blade of a knife to Jane's throat.

"Sorry to disappoint, stout Cortez," Eva said. "Can we stay friends? I'm prepared to cut you in— fifty percent, seventy million?"

"You tried to fucking kill me," Jane screamed, trying to buck her off.

Eva rode her bucks. "Don't be a drama queen. I was trying to stop you from investigating the harvester. I've been wondering when you'd figure out I've been fucking it up."

"You're a filthy thief and a disgrace to NASA."

Eva dug the blade in, and Jane stilled. "Don't be sentimental. This was always a private sector job."

"This is everyone's last hope!"

"And we proved it worked so that innovation can proceed democratically. If we brought back five tons, YBG would have the market cornered forever. They'd have a monopoly on your last hope."

"Who cares?"

"Who cares? YBG put a patent on this harvester as fast as they could because they knew everyone else was only months behind them. They spent two hundred years robbing the world blind and stacked enough cash to give them an edge when it mattered most."

"Yeah, they won! Someone has to fucking win, Eva!"

"Someone, anyone? Who cares if it's China, then?"

"God, what *happened* to you?"

Eva leaned forward, drawing the knife over Jane's throat. "Do you keep your eyes open down on Earth?" she said, her eyes gleaming. "Or has your head been up here your whole life?"

"What, things are bad, so you should make them worse?"

"It's not bad, Jane, it's over. Humanity lost. Twenty years ago, they were going to put one of us on Mars . . . now look at us. These are death throes, and I wanted a nice retirement."

"That's despicable," Jane said, squirming under Eva's hips, disgusted by her touch. "You'd doom us all for $140 million?"

"You're right, I should have asked for more. Where do you get this sense of superiority from, by the way? I see how you prance around. You're a glory hound. You want a mining town here with a statue of you in the center."

"You hypocrite, you were an ambitious person once, what happened?"

Eva smirked at her. "I already told you—we lost. And I fucking hate losing." She drew her knife hand back. "This sucks. I really did like you, Howell."

"ALICE!" Jane shouted.

"What's she going to do?" Eva said, amused, and swung the knife down.

Every LED in the room winked off, plunging them into darkness as Jane rolled out from under Eva and grabbed for her knife hand. They struggled, clawing at each other while the dark room surged with electricity. Jane seized Eva's wrist and bent it back until she screamed in pain, her grip loosening.

Jane didn't think. She seized the knife, and the lights blinked back on. Eva was under her, her eyes wide, their whites flashing. Jane plunged the knife into her throat, fighting low-G resistance.

Eva's gasp turned into a gurgle. Blood began oozing out of the wound, rolling across her skin until her stare became fixed. Jane scrambled away from her until her back hit a wall.

"Eva," she said.

Eva was silent. Blood drifted out of her.

Jane reached in her pocket and retrieved her earpiece. Out of instinct, she crammed it in her ear and said "Houston," through chattering teeth.

"Sally," Frank said, "what's the situation? Both of you were off comms, and ALICE stopped reporting, then we got her back, and she's lit up like a Christmas tree. Did she go rogue?"

Jane couldn't speak.

"Sally, do you read?"

Across the room, the knife in Eva's throat was shining. Jane closed her eyes to get away from this, submerging herself in the room's electric buzz.

"Sally?" Frank repeated.

ALICE answered for her. "Houston," she said, her voice pleasant once more, "we have a problem."

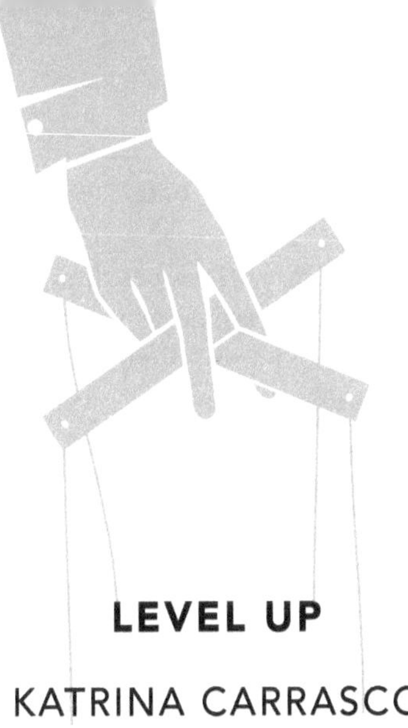

LEVEL UP

KATRINA CARRASCO

Playing felt like such a release. I'd get assigned to some guy and go to his location, where he'd come tromping out of the 7-11 in his stupid red hat, and instead of feeling freaked out that he'd call me a fag or push me, I was the one waiting for him. I was the one watching him cross the gas station parking lot, hiking up his dirty jeans and sucking hard on his Big Gulp. I'd slouch off the fuel pump and head toward the minimart and, just as I passed him, mutter, "Banana." His step would falter. If I glanced up, his eyes were wide. For a second, he was afraid of me. It felt fucking good.

But hitting Targets wasn't always easy. Take this same guy: along with his location and description, the app showed he'd already been hit seven times that day. The last two players had logged red flags, indicating he might be dangerous. Like lots of other men, when he got scared, it made him mad.

"What the fuck did you say to me?" he yelled after I passed him. I kept walking through the misty drizzle, but I saw in the minimart windows that he'd spun on his heel and started following me to the store. "What the fuck did you say? Fucking dyke."

He threw his drink, and it burst onto the concrete beside me, splashed ice-cold onto my jeans. I walked faster, grabbing the door, but he caught me by my sweatshirt. The door opened as he pulled me backward.

"Get off me!"

"What did you say?"

"I didn't say anything!" I hung onto the door handle and yelled into the store. "Help!"

My chest was squeezing hot, my breath not coming; he had the hood of my sweatshirt, and it was tight on my throat, and I was slipping in the scattered ice cubes, but a man from inside ran out and stepped between us. The pressure on my throat released. A woman came from her car and started yelling at the guy.

"Let her go!"

"Get off me, man!"

"Did you say banana?"

And that did it—whatever these other people thought was happening, now this guy seemed like a crazy person. I could feel them turn against him. It made me want to laugh.

"What are you talking about?" I asked.

"Sir, let her go, or I'm calling the police."

"Is he on drugs?"

"Did you say banana?"

"What are you talking about, banana? Jesus."

He stared at me, his face red under his red hat, the drizzle thickening to rain, the man from inside the minimart keeping space between us, the woman touching my wrist lightly and asking if I was okay.

"What's with this guy?" she said, glaring at him over my shoulder.

The man put his hand over his face and started crying. And I thought, got you. Got you.

People I know casually would probably classify me as just another coastal tech geek. Glasses and flannel: check. Introvert: check. An active REI membership: check. For Christ's sake, I'm a gay woman in my thirties with an alternate lifestyle haircut, a Subaru, two cats, and a gluten problem. I'm a total stereotype.

But I'm also the Seattle metropolitan area's No. 1 ranked Bananagramz player. I had never missed a Target. I'd racked up 499 hits. And with my next assignment, after playing the game for over three years, I would unlock the ultimate unknown: Ghost Level.

Which is why, on a stormy afternoon, I was staring at my phone instead of the half-written software manual on my laptop. My coffee had gone cold. I couldn't focus on work. All I cared about was that banana emoji popping up on my lock screen. Sleet hissed against the windows. My cats were bundled into their favorite pink wool blanket, the one bit of clutter I let them drag around my studio apartment. George's nose twitched. The only visible part of Michael's body was one white front paw poking out of the blanket. I nudged his little toes with mine, and the white paw flexed, drooped.

As I was standing to microwave my coffee, my phone lit up. But it wasn't a notification—it was a call from Erin. My ringtone is the start of "Careless Whisper." I let the saxophone riff play on for a minute, but she didn't hang up.

"Remember how I said no calls during the workday?" I said, starting the microwave.

"She left," Erin said. "She fucking left while I was at yoga class."

"You guys have been fighting forever," I said. "Maybe this is for the best."

"Can I come over?"

"No, I'm working," I said. Erin didn't need to know I'd spent my day obsessed with Ghost Level. She didn't know I played Bananagramz. Nobody did. The game has fight club rules: you don't talk about it. This secrecy helps keep it obscure, but it must have a devoted following. I'd done the math. There had to be enough players in every area to allow for anonymity, and the game would only let you make three hits per week.

"I'm having a crisis," Erin said.

"I've got bills to pay." Erin and her girlfriend were constantly breaking up. The first time might have been a crisis, but now it was just exhausting. A tiny jet of conscience made me add: "Call me later tonight if you need to, okay?"

Erin sighed and hung up. "Cool," I said to the dead line.

My phone dinged: Erin had sent me a picture of a crying, mascara-wearing chihuahua.

"Drama queen," I told George, who was watching me bring my coffee to the couch. George has giant blue eyes and perfect, black-tipped ears. He's a very pretty guy; friends have told me I should audition him as a cat model. With all the student debt I'm paying off, it wouldn't be a bad idea to have some passive income from Iams.

Another ding: A sad-looking blobfish. I'd told Erin I was too old to emotionally communicate with animal memes, but that didn't stop her from sending them. I tossed my phone onto the couch and leaned over to scritch George on the head. The wind whipped a scatter of hail against the window, then subsided. Maybe Ghost Level wasn't going to happen. And my client's user manual certainly wasn't going to write itself. Just a few hours of focus, I told myself. You can do it.

From somewhere in the cushions, my phone dinged.

"Oh my god, Erin," I said, but when I dug it out, there was a banana emoji on the lock screen. The usual in-app message had a confetti emoji in the top right, like, *surprise!*

Welcome to Ghost Level.
Target 500 will be a Group Hit.
Go to 5201 52nd St. at 10:20 tonight. Wear something green.
Code word: mica

The "Accept" button followed, with a banana emoji underneath: a reminder that the word is key to how the game works.

I didn't get it at first. I had to do some research. What I figured out is the game is modeled on a tactic cults use to harass former members into rejoining. Basically, you get a bunch of random people to say a single, recognizable word—like "banana"—to someone throughout their day. In a crosswalk, outside a coffee shop, when they're walking their dog. Having an unpredictable stream of strangers say this to a person over and over makes them nervous. They start to question what they're hearing. They start to question reality. They can be rendered fragile. That's when cults pounce: when someone is feeling shaky, in need of support or something familiar.

Of course, the men we're targeting aren't former cult members. They're just regular guys who've done something bad. Targets are nominated by players: once you complete fifty hits, you're eligible to nominate a Target. A man who harassed you in a bar. A man who kept stealing your ideas and talking over you at work. A man who assaulted you. There are many shades of gray here, but at the early stages, the app doesn't care. It just aims to make Targets feel unsafe or unsure: the way they've made other people feel. But the really awful ones—rapists, abusers, stalkers—don't just get a few days of the banana treatment. The app promises more in store for them: Ghost Level.

And I'd finally made it. I was a 500-hit, Ghost Level player. Part of the elite. But a Group Hit seemed like a bad idea. The whole point was that players were anonymous to Targets and each other. In the early days, I'd really wanted to meet other players, share stories, go to brunch, whatever. Then I got used to my solitary game: find a target, say the day's word, serve a little karmic justice out to the upper rungs of the patriarchy, and get on with my life. What if one of my co-workers showed up to the Group Hit? Or someone who'd infiltrated the game to expose us, or worse?

More what-ifs crowded into the others. I realized I was sweating. Michael extricated himself from the blankets, stopping to sniff me and narrow his eyes in judgment before disappearing into the bathroom. Who was I kidding? I'd been waiting for this for years. Of course, I was going to go. I pressed "Accept" before I could change my mind.

Number 5201 52nd Street was a run-down bungalow set far back from the curb. A long unlit lawn, dark windows. The late-night street was quiet—no cars, just my footsteps and the rain pattering onto my jacket hood. I thought I was the first one there. Then, a weird blob took shape against a shadowed hedge. My heart started thumping so hard I felt it in my face. I put one foot onto the lawn's mud-soft grass. The blob moved, separating into two people, standing together under an umbrella.

"Banana?" I said, my voice creaking upward.

"That's not the right word," the taller of the two said, sharp.

"Mica," I said. I'd forgotten.

I stopped a few feet from them. One woman wore a pearly blue puffer coat with a green scarf. The other, who didn't like that I'd said banana, had on green nail polish and a lot of makeup.

"Mica," someone else said behind me. A third woman walked over to us from the sidewalk. Her coat was unzipped despite the rain; she'd layered a green tank top over a microfleece.

"Mica," the woman in the green scarf said.

I shoved my hands into my pockets, imagining an idiotic scenario where we parroted the code word back and forth for an hour and then went home. Maybe the 500th hit was just a test to see if you'd show up and follow the rules.

"Welcome to Ghost Level," the woman with the green scarf said.

It was a relief to hear a full sentence.

"I leveled up a long time ago, and I'm in charge tonight," she said. "Call me Boss."

The energy in the group changed. Me, Nails, and Tank all looked at Boss with interest. I was impressed. A long time ago? She must have been playing from the start.

"I thought the app was anonymous," Tank said. "I almost didn't come."

"But you did. You made a choice," Boss said to her, then looked at me, then at Nails, taking time to make hard eye contact. "You each decided you wanted to be here. There was supposed to be someone else with us tonight. She made a different choice. And she'll never play again after missing this assignment."

That felt extreme. The stakes were high. I pulled my hood forward against the rain, hunching a little to keep warm.

"So what are we going to do?" Nails said.

"We're going into the Target's house," Boss said.

That rippled through us. I shifted uneasily, my boots slipping in the long, wet grass. Was I okay with that? I tried to read the other women's faces. Were they okay with that? Were they hesitating? Nails was frowning; Tank had one eyebrow quirked and was biting her lower lip.

"That's illegal," Nails said.

"Only if you get caught," Boss said.

"No, it's illegal no matter—"

"You're free to leave," Boss said, cutting her off. "Just delete the app and show me it's deleted. Then you can go."

Nails folded her arms over her chest and rolled her eyes, but she didn't take out her phone. Neither did Tank. My mouth was dry despite the rain. Delete the app? After years of playing, after years of watching myself move up in the rankings, deleting Bananagramz seemed impossible. Waiting for that fruit emoji to pop up was often the most exciting part of my day. I'd regret it if I walked away. I left my phone in my pocket.

"He won't be home," Boss said, then pointed at Tank. "You'll stay outside and watch the door, just in case."

Then she pointed at me.

"You'll rearrange his shoes and take three small things out of his refrigerator to throw away after we leave. And you'll squeeze most of his toothpaste into a Ziploc and leave the empty tube," she told Nails.

"Gross," Nails said.

Boss ignored her and pulled a plastic bag out of her coat. She dug out a handful of stuff and gave it to me—a pair of latex gloves, a surgical mask, and two black shoe covers. Everyone else got the same. Nails got the Ziploc.

"What is the point of this?" Tank said.

"He'll come home and think he's going crazy," Nails said. "Stuff different than when he left it, but with nothing big missing, nothing stolen, so it doesn't seem possible that someone broke in."

"That's right," Boss said. "We've been word-bombing him for about a week, and now we're turning up the heat."

"I was wondering if this is what happens at Ghost Level," Nails said, looking smug. "I'm a psycholo—"

"Nope." Boss shook her head. "No identifying info. No names, no jobs, no ages, no small talk. If you see each other after this, you don't know each other. Ghost Level is named that for a reason. Got it?"

I let out a long breath. I did not feel good about going into some random guy's house. It crossed a line I would have said no to before right then. But we were all there. The others were murmuring in agreement. It was just some stuff from his fridge. Some light breaking and entering. Definitely trespassing. Okay, it was bad, but the excitement was starting to get to me. It was the craziest thing I'd ever done. I almost couldn't believe it was happening. Boss was pulling on her latex gloves, the rain making them squeak as they dragged over her skin. Standing next to her felt like being in a spy movie.

"Masks on now," Boss said. "Shoe covers on just before you go inside. We're in and out in less than five minutes."

"What if I see someone coming?" Tank said, looping her mask strings over her ears.

"Good question. Everybody open the app."

I dug my phone out of my jeans pocket. The screen was instantly dappled with rain, and Nails waved me and Tank into the shelter of her umbrella. In the app, the banana icon was red. A red box filled the screen that normally displayed Target notes.

"If anyone types 'help' all our phones will start dinging," Boss said, showing us her own screen and its red box. "Obviously, don't use it unless there's an emergency. Everybody, make sure your volume's turned on."

My volume was on, but I turned it up.

"Let's go," Boss said. "His house is up the street."

At the first corner, she nodded at Tank, who split off to the right. Nails and I followed Boss up the brick path to a single-story craftsman, squat and unlit. Boss unlocked the door. How did she get a key? Who was this guy? My breath was hot and damp inside my mask. Nails bumped into my side, muttering an apology, and seeing her struggle with her shoe covers reminded me to pull mine on, too. Inside, the house smelled strongly of pine. There wasn't a lot of furniture. The living room opened into a few hallways and doors at the back.

"Make it fast," Boss told us.

Everything caught up to me, then, and I couldn't take full breaths. My mask sucked into my mouth. My shirt stuck damply to my underarms and stomach. I wanted to go back outside. But we were already in. We'd already done the worst, hardest part, and there wasn't time to waste.

The kitchen opened off the living room. It was lit dimly green by the oven and microwave clocks. The counters were spotless. Grains and beans were organized in glass jars along the backsplash. It looked like an Airbnb or model kitchen, sterile and untouched, and the fridge was the same—nothing in it but a full gallon of milk and a ketchup bottle. What to do? I couldn't take three things if there were only two. But Nails saying "stuff different than he left it" gave me an idea. I took out the milk and uncapped it. Then my phone dinged.

Shit! We'd been caught!

I dropped the milk in my panic. The plastic gallon smashed onto the tiles, and milk splattered all over me and the sink and the floor. My phone dinged again, and I took it out, my fingers leaving pale streaks on the screen.

They were texts from Erin: *Went out got drunk . . . Call now?*

I shoved the phone back into my jeans pocket, swearing. Sweat or rain or milk tickled down the side of my face. We had probably two minutes left, and I still had to mess with his shoes. But there was milk everywhere! And not a kitchen towel or napkin in sight. I wasn't supposed to rummage around, but I had to find something to clean up with. My hands were shaking so much that I made a lot of noise pulling open various drawers of cutlery and Tupperware and BBQ tools. Amid all that jangling, I heard the front door slam open. I froze.

"He's here!" Tank said, breathing fast and loud. "He parked and went into the side yard—we have to go!"

"Oh my god," I said, gripping the kitchen doorway. "Where's Boss?"

Nails clomped toward us from the back hallway, slipping on the polished wood in her plastic-booted heels.

"What's going on?"

"He's here!"

"Boss!"

"Why didn't you text 'help'?!"

"I dropped my phone—"

"Where is she?"

Even as we peered into the dark hallways for Boss, we were moving as a unit closer to the door.

If the two of them made a run for it, I would, too.

There were heavy footsteps on the porch. Tank grabbed my arm in an iron grip and yanked me sideways toward a door. Nails followed us. Keys jangled outside. Tank opened the door to a small closet. I crowded after her, and Nails shoved into me from behind, jamming me between the two of them; my cheekbone smashed against the cold door jamb. I breathed with tiny shallow gasps of air, suffocating in my mask, trying to be silent; the other women's ribcages pulsed rapidly against mine. The milk all over my clothes smelled faintly sour. There were footsteps outside the closet. A light came on. A man tossed his keys onto something glassy and sighed.

My phone blared out the riff of "Careless Whisper."

We all stopped breathing. I couldn't reach my jeans pocket. The saxophone solo played on and on.

"What the fuck?" the man said.

A thump, a yelp. A heavy smack onto the wood floor. Nails scrabbled for the doorknob, but we were all pinned in too closely. An elbow jabbed into my kidney, and my elbow dug into the softness of someone's boobs, and one of us was saying oh no, oh no, and then the light outside went off. There were strange plastic sounds: tearing or zipping.

"We've got to help her," Nails breathed.

"Don't open—" Tank started, but Nails found the knob, and we tumbled out into the dim living room. Nails gasped. A man was sprawled on his stomach, unmoving. His wrists were lashed behind his back with a plastic cord—the notched, locking kind I'd used to secure my bookshelf to the wall in my apartment. Boss crouched over his legs, lashing a second tie around his ankles.

"Thanks for the backup," Boss said, glaring at us.

"What did you do to him?" I said.

"What does it look like," she snapped. "I knocked him out."

This was bad. This was no longer breaking and entering, which would probably have been enough to make me lose my job. Now there was a man, on the ground, tied up.

"What if the neighbors heard?" Nails said.

"This is the suburbs," Tank said, scoffing. "They're more likely to check their doors are locked than to get involved."

"Is this what really happens at Ghost Level?" Nails said through gritted teeth. "Because you—"

"No. This hasn't happened before." Boss tightened the cord with a yank, then took out her phone, still straddling the man's body. "I have to check in for instructions."

"Instructions?" I said. "Are you serious? We have to get out of here before we're arrested."

"Not until they tell me how to clean things up." Boss's forehead and ears were flushing red against her mask as she tapped away at her phone. "This is my first time running a Ghost Level hit, and I'm going to get it right."

"I thought you'd been playing forever," I said.

"You can't make us stay," Nails said, pulling me toward the door.

"No way, white girls," Tank said. "You're not leaving us to take the fall."

"Everybody, take a breath." Boss stood up from the man's body. "We've all put in years to be here tonight. That means the app has years of data on our activities. Nobody walks away until they tell us how."

I'd imagined many worst-case scenarios about Ghost Level but hadn't thought to include blackmail by unseen Bananagramz handlers. Nails looked at me, then let go of my arm. My hands were shaking again. I crammed them into my pockets.

"I wonder what he did to get nominated for this," Tank said.

She was staring down at the man, twirling one of her dark braids. He had close-trimmed blond hair, with a smear of blood behind one ear from where Boss had hit him. He was wearing a Patagonia fleece and khakis. His socks were patterned with alternating white and black sheep.

"Something bad," Boss muttered. "Fucking creep."

Several phones dinged. I took mine out and opened the app but didn't have a message. I looked up at the others, and their faces were changing: slack foreheads, wide eyes over their blue surgical masks. Shock—or fear. My pulse jumped.

"What did you guys get," I said, my app message box still empty. "What's happening?"

"They sent me the information I submitted," Tank said. "For the man I nominated as a target. What he did."

"Me too," said Nails, her eyes filling with tears. "Oh my god, I'd forgotten how awful—"

"Same," Boss said. "That motherfucker."

One by one, they all looked down at the man at our feet, and then I did too. The prone length of him, all that muscle and weight neutralized. Face-down. Nameless. We could each fill in the blanks and imagine him as someone else.

"I hate him," Tank said. Her shoulders seemed broader. She looked like she could bite the head off a chicken and not blink. "It's been years, and I still hate him so much."

"He ruined my sister's life," Boss said. "I can't even tell you …"

Nails took off her mask and wiped her eyes, smearing mascara across her cheeks.

And they all looked at me. My app message box was still empty, maybe because I'd never nominated anyone. There hadn't been one specific incident that made me start playing. Why was I even doing this? Making hits again and again and again for years. Waiting for that banana emoji like it was a winning lottery ticket. But for what? Fucking with random men wasn't going to make a dent. Even this impotent swirl of violence in this stranger's home was nothing, a blip, a raised middle finger to a tsunami. It didn't matter if we played the game. So, why?

Then my phone dinged, at last. And the app said: *EVERYTHING.*

Heat flooded into my body. My collarbones prickled, my throat and ears throbbed. It *was* everything. The news. The end of Roe v. Wade. The incel breeding ground of the internet. The dead girl that featured in so many made-up crime stories and real news broadcasts it was hard to tell where the trope ended, and violence began. The old boys' club of criminals running the country. The years of walking around in my body, wound tight on dim streets, holding my keys like a weapon, well aware that being visibly gay meant to some men that as a woman and as a queer, I was twice asking for it—all of that compressing inside me into something flinty and mean, something I'd been lightly tapping at with my 499 Bananagramz hits but was now cracking open. This was what Ghost Level felt like. Rage, and somewhere to aim it.

It was too dark in the room to see anyone's faces clearly, but there was a weird quality to the dimness. Like we were outside under a full moon, some distant radiance picking out the others' eyes with a wolfish shine. My face was hot. My hands were clammy inside the Latex gloves.

"Seattle's finest," Boss said to me, and a jolt of pride that she knew my hard-earned rank zinged through the buzzing in my brain. "You look like you have something to say."

Ghost Level felt good. A sick, sneering kind of good, like I'd felt watching that guy cry in the gas station parking lot, but with the volume turned way up. Tank and Nails were watching me, too. Tank was in. Boss was in. Nails was wide-eyed but still standing there, black streaks across her cheeks like a football player's game paint. We had stumbled onto power. And for once, there were no guardrails, no exhortations to take the high road to use what little leverage we had to make things better. Why shouldn't we add to the bonfire and use it to make things worse?

"I'll go first," I said, and tensed myself for the kick.

THE FLEDGLING

JOHN COPENHAVER

Teeter Hawkins smiles at us—Derek, me, and the five other pledges—and says, "Your last mission, before we become brothers, is to kill one of those goddamn geese with *this*—" He holds out a golf club, a pitching wedge. "And bring it to the party tonight."

Teeter is a handsome guy. He has sharp dark eyes, blond hair, and a cleft chin. He's pre-med and plays baseball for the university and seems comfortable in the world, like it's molded for him. He steps forward, holding out the wedge, waiting for one of us to take it. "Come on, damnit!" he says, "Take the fuckin' golf club and go beat the shit out of one of those fuckin' birds." His southern accent, a deep Georgia drawl, makes his cussing seem softer, almost beautiful. The other Kappa Sig brothers are behind him, mostly smiling at his antics. I notice one or two of them looking worried, glancing around at the walls covered with group photos of graduated brothers. A few move to the back of the large, musty living room, checking their cell phones and sipping Solo cups; others drift into the frat's kitchen. They aren't about to interfere with Teeter.

Still, none of us move. Teeter looks at each of us. "Okay, which of you pansies is going to take charge? I thought you wanted to join this fine fraternity and graduate as a proud Kappa Sig in '97, but, shit, the way you're acting, we'll have to do the French Egg Trick again."

Last week, Teeter lined the pledges up after getting us good and drunk and duct-taped our hands behind our backs. The cockiest pledge was at the end of the line. I was in the center. Derek was upfront.

Teeter made us pass a raw egg from mouth to mouth until it reached the end of the line. If we dropped the egg, we had to start over. We had to start over eleven times. Each time, after about the third pledge, the egg was nothing but yellow slime. On the seventh attempt, I threw up all over Teeter's loafers.

"Here, Sam," Teeter says, thrusting the club into my hand. "You take charge. Make up for my shoes." He looks at me. His face is red, lean, and muscular. It's his confidence, his certainty. I want to believe in myself the way he believes in himself—his sexual prowess, his athletic ability, and his intelligence. Everyone admires him. It's hard not to.

"I can't hit a goose with this," I say. "It'll fly away."

"Use your head," he says.

"Breadcrumbs," Derek says, glancing over at me, his eyes downcast.

"That's right," Teeter smiles. "That's the idea."

Wallace, one of the other pledges, asks in a thin voice, "Couldn't we get in trouble for this? If we're caught?"

"Look," Teeter says, "I go duck hunting with my dad every Thanksgiving. We kill birds all the time, so calm down. Haven't you ever hit a bird with your car? Or seen a bird slam into a window and break its neck? It's like that. We're in their way, they're in our way. It's a struggle."

"But what we're doing is illegal," Wallace says.

"Sure, that's the risk—and the challenge," he says in a hallowed tone. "What's the point otherwise?"

Wallace squints at him, mystified.

"Just bag the fuckin' bird, and you'll be brothers," Teeter says. "It's that simple." He smiles at us and slaps me on the shoulder, his fingers digging in, kneading my shoulder. I tighten my grip on the wedge. Confidence, I say to myself, confidence. This will soon be over.

Back in our dorm room, Derek sits on my bed, crumbling a couple of slices of bread into a Ziplock bag.

"I don't want to do this," he says. "I have nothing against Canadian geese."

"It's a stupid way to initiate us," I say. "I don't get it."

"I heard Teeter complaining about them. His dad owns a golf course or a country club in Georgia, and he said they're pests. They get in the way of golfers and shit all over the greens."

"Hence the club," I say, mimicking a golf swing. "It's stupid, but it's what they want. What Teeter wants."

Derek finishes crumbling the bread and seals the bag. "It's cruel, too," he says. "It's brutal."

Derek and I were roommates at boarding school. His parents died in a car wreck when he was eight, which gave him an air of seriousness that confused and pissed off the other guys. But it put me at ease, like I didn't have to bullshit him, like it would be rude to lie to a guy who'd lost so much. All summer, we imagined what our freshman year of college would be like—how different and awesome it'd be, how we'd escaped the absurdity of an all-boys boarding school, how that was all in the distant past.

"We're almost K-Sigs," I say, forcing an upbeat tone. "I'm not giving up now. We've come this far."

"I don't want to do this." He tosses the crumb bag aside and slumps on his bed, picking up his dog-eared copy of *In Cold Blood*, assigned for American Lit. He pretends to read it.

"It'll be all right," I say. "It's our plan, remember?"

"That was before we had to murder waterfowl."

"People respect Kappa Sig, you know. Girls respect it. Once we're in, we'll start to really live around here, be part of something." I rarely think of girls. But it seems like the thing to say. Derek pushes his hand through his messy dark hair and lies back on his bed.

"Besides," I add, "it's my dad's frat."

Derek looks thinner and paler now, like he's trying to disappear. In his sophomore year of boarding school, he broke down—stayed in bed with the lights off for three days, refusing to go to class. When he snapped out of it, I asked him what had been wrong. He told me not to worry about it. But when I wouldn't let it go, he said it had hit him: he was alone, really alone. I told him he had his aunt and uncle—and me, of course—but he just smiled.

"Maybe they'll fly away before we can hit one," I say, hoping to cheer him up. "Maybe we'll just scare them."

Behind the cover of *In Cold Blood*, he says, "Do you know, in this book, it's a surprise who shoots the entire Clutter family?"

"Oh yeah?" I say, humoring his digression.

"Yeah. Of the two killers, the sensitive one pulls the trigger. The one Capote loves."

"Shit," I say, suddenly worried about the dark turn his mind is taking.

"Sam," he says, dropping the book and looking at me, his eyes sad, far away, "I never thought we'd have to go through all of this—this shit."

I don't say anything. What can I say? I didn't either, but it doesn't change what I want—what he *should* want—what we need to have a life for the next four years, a life we deserve.

"Let's have a beer," I say, leaning toward him and smacking his leg.

He nods and rises, the bed's springs squeaking.

We are in Teeter's van, driving to the lake, just on the edge of the university's property. Teeter wants to watch us to make sure we don't back down. There are seven of us now, including Derek, myself, and Teeter; Wallace dropped out. He's sunk. No frat will give him a bid now. I'm sitting in the back, gripping the pitching wedge with both hands, staring at its metal shaft.

My father tried to teach me golf the summer after my first year at boarding school. After pressuring me into T-ball in elementary school and baseball and tennis in Middle School with only fumbling results, this, for him, was a gesture of pure hope. "The other boys will expect you to play at least one sport well," he said, rubbing my shoulder. "Golf's good because it's a lifetime sport." He taught me how to grip the club and how to stand, legs apart, shoulders loose, but I rarely hit the ball, and when I did, I had no control over it. At first, he was reassuring: "It just takes practice, son," but after a couple of hours at the driving range, he stepped back, looked me over, and said, "You need professional lessons."

A week later, he signed me up with a sixty-year-old golf pro named Pierce Patrick Parsons, who had sun-weathered skin, long dyed bleach blond hair, and a Lacoste polo in every pastel color.

Triple P, as he was known around the club, feigned patience at first, his voice mild, soothing, and tinged with gin. But after I'd hacked up enough sod, he snapped: "Jesus! Try harder. You must focus, man. Focus!" I gave him a focused "fuck you" glare and walked off the course.

When I told Dad, his face turned bright pink, and he started shaking his head. He had a bad temper when I was a kid. After he threw a patio chair through a storm door over something at work, Mom made him go to therapy. But I can still tell when he's holding it back and stuffing it down—so much worse. Eventually, he said, "You win, Sam. I give up," and walked away.

Although he's not mentioned it since, from time to time, Mom will ask me if I have thought about giving golf another go, or even tennis. She asks sweetly, but under her tone, there's a weight, as if she's saying it's up to you to fix whatever broke between you and your father. Maybe she's right. Something did snap.

I glance up at Derek sitting across from me. His eyes are bloodshot, and his forehead, damp. He's clearly drunk. I feel warm and a little bloated from the beers, but I'm not drunk, just loose.

As he's driving, Teeter talks to us about his girlfriend: "Jen's hot and smart. She made all A's on her exams last semester. She wants to go to medical school, like me. I've never been so crazy about a woman before." Bill, a pledge from rural Kentucky, is hanging on his words, his mouth drooping open. "When you get a girl," Teeter says to him, his voice lowering, becoming more earnest, "a good one, one you really respect, you'll know it. Trust me." He lifts his chin a little, taking in the road ahead. "Jen's the real deal. She understands me, what I need."

Bill believes in Teeter. For a moment, I believe in him, too. But it's difficult to imagine him cuddling with a girl, comparing Anatomy notes, or giving her neck massages, but Jen serves a purpose for him; she's the right kind of girl to be with. And I understand why she would be with him. When he takes the time to speak to you, you feel like he gets you, no matter who you are, and that his undivided attention is a privilege. Maybe it is.

"Sam, my man," he says, catching me in the rearview mirror, "did you bring breadcrumbs?"

"Derek has them." I look at Derek. He seems frightened. I shake my head at him, warning him not to show his fear.

"Well," he says, "that's lucky. Derek's going to have the first swing. He got off easy in the French Egg Trick."

Derek shakes his head. He looks sick.

"He's too drunk," I say.

"That's even better," Teeter says as he adjusts his worn baseball cap, the muscles along his jawline flexing.

—⚡— —⚡— —⚡—

The lake is calm, secluded, and edged by pine trees. The only houses are on the far side, a mile or so away. The afternoon sky is gray and flat, the color of dull steel. Teeter parks under a tree. Over his shoulder, I see a flock of geese, maybe forty or fifty, milling about at the shoreline, their heads darting back and forth, some jabbing their black bills at the mud. They don't notice us.

"Geese mate for life like doves," Teeter says. "When the female is laying eggs, the male will stand guard and defend her. Sweet, right?"

"No shit," Bill says.

"And the adults lose their ability to fly until their goslings are fledglings and can fly too."

"Fashinating," Derek slurs. "Did your girlfriend teach you that?"

Teeter scowls, gets out, and throws the van's side door open: "Let's do this. Derek, you're up." He reaches in and tugs his arm. Derek pulls himself up and tries to find his legs.

As I help him, he stumbles, catching the doorframe to avoid falling. "Shit," he mutters. Teeter yanks the pitching wedge from my hand, grabs Derek's hand, and molds it around the grip. Derek slurs at him, "It's a hell of a thing—a life has to be taken in this manner." The alcoholic haze in his eyes brightens slightly, a hint of challenge aimed at Teeter.

"In this manner . . ." I think, why is he talking like that? Teeter winces and slaps him on the back, causing Derek to lurch forward.

"Go for it, Derek! Do it!" the other pledges call out.

"Come on," Teeter says. "Bag us one of those ugly ass birds! We need a trophy. And, hey, be careful with my wedge. My father gave it to me as a high school graduation gift. It's a piece of crap, but it has sentimental value."

Derek lurches forward and shuffles toward the geese, using the club for support. When he's a few yards from them, he yanks the crumbs out of his pocket, unzips the bag, fumbles it, and dumps them on the ground in one lump. A bird glances up, its slick, gray-black feathers ruffling softly. It honks to other geese, a half-hearted "Over here, guys!" and begins strutting toward the wad of bread, its white-striped head jerking back and forth, its webbed feet pulling at the mud and its eyes bulging with determination. Derek slowly lifts the club over his shoulder. As the bird extends its neck for a cautious nibble, he swings and misses. The motion knocks him off balance. He wobbles, then flops sideways in the sludge. The bird doesn't move. Teeter and the others burst out laughing. Derek tries to stand up, but the mud is thick and slippery. Suddenly, he stops struggling, leans to one side, and pukes.

"Go get him," Teeter says to me. "Go get him *and* the bird." He looks at the other pledges and adds, "I'm thinking of a joke: How many faggots does it take to kill a fuckin' bird?"

No one laughs; a few pledges smile.

I go to Derek, pick up the wedge, tuck it under my arm, and help him to his feet. Under his breath, he mutters, "I couldn't do it. Sorry man. I just couldn't." The odor of vomit and goose shit and wet earth churns my stomach. I hug him tight, and he leans heavily against me, gripping the back of my shirt. We shuffle toward the van, where I hand him off to the other pledges. He lies down inside and curls up, like a dirty, lost kid.

I wonder if he is crying, if he'll pull the blinds on our window and go to bed for days. I wonder if he hates me now. Teeter smirks at him. I want to fly at Teeter, but he's too big, too skilled, too beloved by the others to take down by myself. Over my shoulder, I see two new geese pecking at the crumbs. I catch Teeter's eyes for a second, steady and smug in their sockets, and snatch the club from the ground.

The first swing hits the goose on its side with a meaty *thunk*. It quavers and cries out, a terrible sound, something between a honk and a screech. The other geese scatter. I hit it again. Its eyes, little black holes, vanishing points. It seems to understand what's happening to it. It tries to limp away, its honks frantic, desperate, its mouth bright pink. I hit it from above. It gives into the club and falls over, its feathers splattered with black mud. I hit it again. Its being there is unforgivable. I'm no longer hitting it, but something in my mind, some shifting image—Teeter, Dad, even Derek. They're laughing, they're weeping. I keep hitting. By the time I stop, it's hard to tell it was ever a bird.

I'm spent and breathless. Gray feathers float in the air around me like ashes. I look up and see Teeter. He's as handsome and composed as always: a curl of blond hair sticks out from his cap, his hips slack and cocked at an angle. Although he's not smiling, I'm sure he wants to. All this is what he intended; what guys like him always intend. And I remember what Derek said about *In Cold Blood*, "The sensitive one pulls the trigger."

I give Teeter a "fuck you" glare, turn, and pull the wedge back over my shoulder and, breathing out, fling it out over the lake. It disappears against the gray sky. I hear gasps and Teeter yelling, "Motherfucker!" Then it plunks into the black water. He's running toward me. I don't move. His first punch hits the small of my back. I fall forward, the thick, goose-shit slime smacking me in the face, getting in my mouth, up my nose. It tastes like mushrooms, like shit. He's on top of me, his knees pinning me down, his punches branding my back and sides. He's yelling about his club, his precious graduation gift, how I had no right, how I was a fuck-up. I don't defend myself. He expects me to, and Dad would want me to; it's what men do, but I refuse to.

When it's over, we struggle to stand up, the sludge coating our clothes and skin. Without looking at me, he begins limping back to the van. He calls over his shoulder, "Don't forget the bird."

I stop and look at the crumpled, bloodied animal. "Oh God," I think. "I did this." Then I bend down and gently scoop it up with my arms, but not because he told me to.

RED DIRT AND REGRET

ANN MCMAN

Mama loved to say that I never did anything intentionally. I always chafed at having my life pigeonholed like that. But it was hard to argue with her—mostly because she was right.

Today was one of the worst days of the year—we were overrun with Amazon packages that piled up after Black Friday. It was enough to make you hate the holidays. I got stuck with a route that Amazon didn't deliver to because of spotty cell phone service. That meant I had to pack my LLV to the gills with whatever the deals of the day were—Firesticks, Ring Doorbells, miracle cosmetic creams that promised to eradicate saggy skin, or oversized Samsung Frame TVs. It didn't matter. I was expected to schlep all of them along the rutted back roads of this hardscrabble county and deposit them on the sagging stoops of manufactured homes and brick ranchers that had seen better days.

Mama never wanted me to be a mail carrier, either.

And my route was primarily along NC 705—known widely as the Pottery Trail. Since the 1700s, Scots-Irish potters and their descendants had been digging hunks of red clay out of Moore County's unyielding ground and fashioning it into pots and vessels that now were recognized worldwide for their ancient forms, simple beauty, and sheer artistry.

And, me? I delivered the mail to all of them.

"Hey, Jo-lene, Jo-lene, Jo-lene, *Jooooo-lee-ee-ene.*"

I turned toward the raspy voice that always reminded me of the nagging whine of a bum starter. It was our postmaster, Rusty Cagle.

Great . . .

"Hey, Russ." I waved at him halfheartedly and sandwiched another flat-screen TV into the back of my truck.

Rusty ambled toward me carrying a fat box.

"I just love callin' you that way," he crooned.

No shit, Sherlock. I didn't reply.

"What's-a-matter, McLeod? Don't you think it's funny?"

"Not after the first five thousand times."

"Aww, don't be such a grump." He took a gander at the mountain of boxes crammed into the back of my truck. "Ain't you just lovin' these cyber bargain days? Really puts you in the holiday spirit, don't it?"

"Yeah." I looked up at the dismal sky that was thick with menacing clouds. A fat raindrop nailed me right between the eyes. "I'd best be going, or I won't finish delivering this mess before dark."

"Hold up a minute." He held out the box. "Davis called out sick, and old Mack Vernon is hoppin' mad. He says he needs this," he hefted the box with *Coleman* emblazoned on its side, "whatever in the hell it is, *today*."

I grimaced. The Vernon pottery shop was way the heck out Adams Road, almost to Steeds—one hundred and eighty degrees opposite my route.

"Why can't he just drive in here and pick it up, then?" I dared to ask.

"Ours is not to reason why, Jolene. Ours is to tend to the swift completion of our appointed rounds." He handed me the box. "Besides, he's got a couple more Click-n-Ship packages we need to fetch. That man is keepin' Uncle Sam in bid'ness."

It would be pointless to argue with him. I took the damn box and somehow managed to wedge it into my truck.

The rain was picking up steam. That meant I'd be up to my axle—and ass—in red mud by noon.

My only consolation was that today's mail also contained the latest shipment of free books from Dolly Parton's Imagination Library collection. I loved these days, and how I'd sometimes get to see all those little faces light up with excitement when I put the newest book into their hands. *No . . .* something better than excitement: it was *hope*.

Thinking about Dolly's books always left me . . . well . . . if not proud to be named after one of her infamous Jezebels—at least less embarrassed by it. Her free books gave these kids a glimpse of what their lives could be like beyond the bleak and limiting confines of the sandhills, longleaf pines, and enduring economic hardship that defined their daily lives.

That defined *my* daily life. Because after Daddy left, I never got out, either.

I never really knew him. He left us when I was just a tyke. But Mama said he was no good and always had a wandering eye. I didn't know if he'd run off with a zippy redhead like Jolene. I kind of figured not. Why would Mama have named me after the woman who broke up our home? Either way, he stayed gone—and I inherited the distinction of always being made the object of Dolly's impassioned plea.

I climbed inside my LLV and started the engine. The futility of the task ahead—and of my life in general—stretched out before me on miles of dirt roads and busted-up pavement.

It was never in my long-range plan to end up with a job like this. I went to college at Sandhills and got my associate's degree, always thinking I'd transfer to App State or East Carolina to get my bachelor's in creative writing. But that never happened. I got my first job working for the post office right out of high school and just stayed on because . . . well. Because, truth be told, there weren't a lot of jobs available that came with health insurance and a retirement plan. Besides, it was easier than making a change.

Like Mama said: I never did anything on purpose.

Three hours later, I'd delivered close to half of my load and was ready for a break. I turned into the long driveway that led to Patsy Bleeker's bungalow. Patsy was one of my best friends. We'd grown up together and had a curious on-again, off-again romantic relationship. We'd never really dated. It was more that we were the most comfortable ports in the mostly unwelcome harbor that was Moore County.

Patsy worked out of her home, running a surprisingly lucrative electrolysis business. And she also sold fresh eggs laid by her passel of free-range hens. She had a sweet deal with a couple of the local markets in Seagrove and Robbins, too. They both featured her branded, *Dreamwalker* eggs—which, to be fair, were pretty damn delicious.

She handed me a carton of jumbos when I walked inside her tiny kitchen. "Fresh this morning," she declared.

I took the carton from her gratefully and hefted it. "Damn. Those girls must've been carb-loading."

"I wouldn't put it past them. That Gertie is the ringleader. Lord knows what all she's eating that ain't on the program."

Patsy called all her chickens "Gertie." She said it simplified keeping them in line and getting their attention when she bellowed for them to come in.

She also explained that the name, a derivative of Gertrude, meant "sharp spear"—which she declared was an homage to her work in electrolysis.

Patsy was big on symmetries.

"You look strung out." She pulled out a dinette chair and waved me toward it. "Rough day?"

"The worst." I dropped onto the chair, which creaked beneath my weight. "Fucking Amazon."

"Black Friday?" Patsy poured me a cup of coffee from the pot she always had going, and set the big mug down on the table.

I reached for a pack of Splenda. "Why can't people climb out of their goddamn La-Z-Boys and drive to a fucking store?"

"Hell, girlfriend. You need to wake up and smell the century. Nobody shops at stores anymore. Especially not around here, where you have to drive to damn Asheboro even to find one with shit that costs more than ninety-nine cents."

I laughed. She was right, of course. Patsy was always right.

"You're like a prophet. You know?"

She gave me a look that was unmistakably flirty. "I bet you say that to all the girls."

"No," I quipped, "just the ones brandishing electrified tweezers."

"When are you finishing up today? Maybe we can grab some dinner."

"Probably not until after six. I have to make a delivery over in Steeds."

"*Steeds?* What the hell is way over there?"

"Vernon's Pottery."

Patsy thought about that. "Old man Vernon is still out there throwing pots?"

"Apparently. Whatever the hell is in his mystery box, he's desperate to get it. Today."

"Well, you might could've saved yourself a bunch of time and dropped it off for him at the Wesleyan Church in Whynot. Big funeral there today for that old Chester Cole, who dropped dead last week. I think all the potters in three counties will likely be there to show respect."

I don't know how I'd missed hearing about Cole's death. The man had been an institution in the county. "What happened to him?"

"Cole?" She asked. "He had some kind of freak accident in his studio. Tripped over a stack of pots and hit his head on the wheel. He fell face down into an open bowl of glaze." Patsy shook her head of wild blonde hair. "Poor fella. They have to have the casket closed because they couldn't get that Blue Coyote Glaze off his face."

"Damn. That's harsh."

"Well. At least his family will make out."

"What do you mean?"

She shrugged. "I was doing Iris Luck's eyebrows yesterday, and she said every damn one of Chester's pots is now selling for twenty times what they cost when he was alive. She said collectors were swarming the place—making outrageous offers and snapping up anything they could get their hands on."

"No way." I was surprised. "That's a pretty sad state of affairs— being worth more dead than alive."

"Honey, it's the way of the world. The same thing happened last month when Nell King went ass over teakettle into that backyard pit fire and suffocated. I saw some of her pots in a damn Etsy store—and you don't even wanna know how much they were selling for."

"I guess we should hope the Gerties don't get any ideas about you."

"Hah." Patsy tucked an insistent loop of hair behind her ear. "I'd like to see 'em try. All I have to do to shut that shit down is show them the damn air fryer."

It was true. You didn't fuck with Patsy.

It was nearly dark by the time I reached Vernon's studio near Steeds. This pottery shop had long been recognized as one of the hallmark studios in the state. Mack Vernon's granddaddy, James Vernon, had been a true pioneer of the art form. When he passed, his legacy had been inherited by his son, Charlie, who expanded the business and brought in a string of talented apprentices who had spun off to open their own studios. Now the operation was run by Mack, the last surviving grandson of old James.

Mack was outside when I pulled in, wrestling with an oversized urn that he was trying to transport from his truck to the porch. I parked and hurried over to lend him a hand.

Mack Vernon was a wiry old man with corded neck veins that stood out like sheared-off lengths of frayed clothesline. The skin on his gnarled hands was thin and leathery and spoke to how many years he'd spent wrangling wet hunks of clay. More years than I'd been on this planet, for sure.

"Let me give you a hand with that," I offered as I approached him.

He looked up at me with pale, watery eyes and grunted his assent. *A man of few words . . .*

"Dang. This thing is heavy."

He grunted again.

Together, we half rolled, half carried it to the porch that hung off the front of his studio. "What is it, exactly?" I asked.

"Grave marker." He pointed at the etched inscription that wrapped around the top.

I squinted at the stylized block printing.

Whatsoever a man soweth, that shall he also reap.

"That's hardly . . . an upbeat message."

He shrugged. "It's a grave marker. Not much upbeat about dyin'."

"I suppose not."

The rain had finally let up before I'd reached his place, but everything around us was still glistening with moisture. The air was thick and clammy. Mist hung like a shroud across the pasture that spread out behind his cluster of small buildings.

"You bring my box?"

So much for small talk. His tone was accusing—like he'd expected me to say I'd forgotten and this was just a social call.

"Yes, sir, I did."

"Took you long enough. I was looking for it earlier."

"Sorry. Tam Davis was out today and this delivery got added to my normal run. I don't ever work this side of the county."

He gave another ubiquitous grunt and looked over toward my truck.

I took the hint. "Let me go get that for you."

While I jogged back to the truck, he busied himself dragging over a large shipping crate he'd had staged on the porch. Beside it was a huge roll of shredded cardboard. He proceeded to wrap the urn until it had nearly doubled in size.

"Help me lay this into the crate."

It was an order, not a request. But I set his precious box down on the porch floor and helped him lift the urn and lay it on its side in the wooden crate.

"You get orders for many of these things?" I asked. It seemed like a boutique item to me. Vernon was dutifully stuffing more packing material around the edges of the object.

"Nope. Don't get any."

I was confused. "You mean you don't sell these?"

"Nope. I don't sell 'em at all. This ain't mine."

"Oh. So it's a . . . *gift?*"

"Sort of." He sneered. Then laughed. It was an unsettling noise— like the sound of a hacksaw tearing its way through rusted pipe.

"Well," I stood up, "I'd best be going. Rusty said you had some Click-n-Ship packages for me to pick up?"

He tilted his head. "Over there on that table."

I saw a stack of different-sized boxes that already had shipping labels applied. I pulled out my Mobile Delivery scanner and recorded the bar codes on each one of the labels. They were all going to the same destination in Tennessee.

"Do you want me to take this one, too?"

"Nope. Not for another week or so."

"Okay," I said. "If that's it, I'll be on my way." He didn't say anything.

You're welcome, asshole. I collected the boxes and headed back to my LLV. I had thought I might ask him for some advice on the children's book I'd been working on—a story about the potters in North Carolina. My dream was to finish the book and submit it for possible inclusion in Dolly's Imagination Library. I'd been working on it for a long time . . . more than a year, actually. I delivered so many of her books to kids in this backcountry area, I thought it might be nice for them to read about something that touched their lives every day—a way to show them that a childhood in Moore County offered more than red dirt and regret.

But it was clear that Mack Vernon was not going to be helpful in my self-styled noble enterprise.

With luck, I could still make it back in time for dinner with Patsy.

—⚊— —⚊— —⚊—

Dinner at Magnolia 23 in Asheboro was what passed for an upscale night on the town. The authentic Southern cuisine was top notch, the tea was sweet, and my companion was even sweeter.

Patsy had made an effort to dress for our "date" in a tight-fitting red sweater with black jeans and Tecovas boots. She turned more than a few heads when we walked to our table. A couple of diners even recognized her and waved.

"Clients," she whispered, discretely tapping the skin above her upper lip as we passed their tables.

Over plates heaped with fried chicken, collards, and stewed potatoes we talked about our days.

Patsy had been struggling with her brother, Kyle, who ran a body shop in Ramseur. Kyle was still fussing about how long it was taking to close their late father's estate. It had been less than three months since he'd passed in hospice care, but Kyle wanted the old homestead sold so he could get his share of the proceeds and buy a new Harley—he'd laid his old one down while racing on an abandoned railroad grade that ran along the Deep River Trail. Patsy had little patience with his persistence. She'd thought the four pins in his leg should've been enough incentive for him to think better of the idea.

Not so much, as it turned out.

Over a big slice of Hershey cake, I filled her in on my encounter with crusty old Mack Vernon.

"I helped him move a huge stoneware grave marker into a wooden crate for shipping. Weirdest thing I've ever seen around here—not like your usual coffee mugs and beer bread bakers. And it wasn't even his. Lord knows where he was sending it. It had a creepy inscription around the rim, too."

Patsy seemed intrigued. "What'd it say?"

"Something like you'll reap what you sow."

"Whatsoever a man soweth, that shall he also reap," she quoted. I nodded.

"That's not creepy. That's the Bible."

"Whatever. It's still creepy. Who'd want to buy something like that?"

"What makes you think he was selling it?"

"Why else would he be packing it up to ship?"

"You said he told you it wasn't his."

I nodded. "But he was clearly shipping it someplace."

"Didn't you say you picked up a bunch of other packages from him?"

"Yeah. They were all going to the same place in Tennessee . . . some kind of storefront, I think. I asked if he wanted me to take that one, too—but he said it wouldn't be ready for another week or so."

"Hmm. That's weird. Do you remember the name of the store?"

"No. Not entirely, anyway. I think it was Diamonds something . . ."

Patsy thought about it. "Diamonds and Rust?"

"Yeah. That was it. That was it *exactly*."

"Well, ain't that ironic. That's exactly the place I was tellin' you about this morning. It's an Etsy store over in Knoxville."

"Why would old Mack be shipping a damn grave marker all the way to an Etsy store in Knoxville?"

Patsy picked at a crispy piece of skin on her uneaten chicken thigh. "Only one reason I can think of: to make a bundle selling it."

"That doesn't make any sense."

"Maybe it does. Did you see the potter's name?"

"No."

"Well, if it wasn't his, I can guaran-damn-tee you it was made by somebody who's now throwin' pots for Jesus."

"What?" I looked at her with incredulity. "You're nuts."

"Mark my words. That pot'll be for sale by the end of the month—and it'll cost a king's ransom."

"You watch too much TV, girl."

Patsy shot me a look that was unmistakably provocative. "Not tonight I won't."

I didn't waste any time trying to signal our server to bring the check.

When I got back to work the next morning, I gave in to a wild impulse and checked the tracking destination on Mack Vernon's Click-n-Ship packages. Yep. All of them were going to that same Diamonds and Rust store in Knoxville.

Of course, this didn't point to anything nefarious. The man had the right to sell anything he wanted on Etsy—whether the stuff was his or somebody else's. Still. Something about that grave marker had my hackles up. He'd laughed about it and said there was nothing upbeat about dying.

But if he hadn't made it, who had?

Truth be told, I was having a hard time shaking off Patsy's suggestion that old Mack was up to no good. Had that grave marker been made by one of the potters who'd recently died under unusual circumstances?

It shouldn't be too hard to find out.

Person's Funeral Home was on my route, so I stopped in when I delivered their mail. Their office manager, Lois Martin, had presided over more deaths in this county than the Grim Reaper himself. She was only too happy to dish when I asked her for details on a few of the recent accidents that had sent area potters to their eternal rewards. It turned out that Chester Cole and Nell King weren't the only ones who'd died under curious circumstances.

"There was that awful accident last winter," Lois recounted, "when Marvin Teague was emptying pots out of his groundhog kiln and all them shelves collapsed. Poor feller was as busted up as all them pots that crashed all over him. Then there was that fire out at Chriscoe's place in Carthage. They said his propane tanks went up like Roman candles. Not enough left of poor Rufus to even bury." Lois clucked her tongue. "Bad run of luck around here for the old 'uns. This ain't how any of 'em wanted to go out, that's for sure. They was all pioneers."

Maybe Patsy had been on to something after all . . .

"Lois, do you know any potters around here who make giant urns with inscriptions on them? I think they're called grave markers?"

She thought about that. "It don't ring no bells for me. Not sure who'd want to buy something like that. Most of the folks who come here to shop are interested in things like soap dishes or candlesticks. Can't see nobody luggin' some big ole grave marker back to wherever in the world they come from. Them things wouldn't fit in any Christmas stockings."

"Any idea who I could ask that might know?"

"You might could try askin' at the pottery museum in Seagrove. They'd probably know where to find something unusual like that."

'That's a good idea. Thank you, Lois."

"Sure thing, *Jo-lene*. Now you keep right on breakin' all them hearts."

"Yes, ma'am." I smiled and waved at her as I headed for the door. "I'll do my best."

I climbed into my LLV and went on my way. I'd stop in at the museum during my lunch break.

So not two, but *four* legendary potters had all met untimely deaths in freak accidents. What were the odds?

It was already getting dark when I finished up my deliveries and got home. I opened a can of Carolina Blonde ale and sat down at my computer. The illustrator I'd hired to work on the drawings for my book had written back and attached some revisions.

I'd look those over after I did a little internet research of my own.

It didn't take me long to locate the Diamonds and Rust store on Etsy. Just as Patsy had described, their catalog was full of authentic North Carolina pottery—everything from teapots, to dinnerware, to dragon vases. And most of the pieces were vintage and signed by the legendary potters who'd created them. It was a pantheon of bounty from Moore County's best-known potters.

And pots created by all four of the recently deceased artisans were available for eye-popping prices—just like Patsy said.

But I found no grave markers among their listings, or anything even remotely like them in function or scale.

After my side trip to the pottery museum in Seagrove, I had come away with a name—Lorette Goodale. She was from someplace in New England and had come to Seagrove as an apprentice to old Charlie Vernon. Just before Charlie passed, she'd started her own studio and had quickly gained a national reputation for her innovative forms and glazes. Goodale had been featured in magazines like *Southern Living, Garden & Gun*, and *Architectural Digest*. Her stuff was in constant demand by pottery enthusiasts and high-end collectors.

I'd called Patsy right away to share the information I'd found, and she said she'd do a bit of digging after her three o'clock—a woman from Starr who was coming back to have her persistent chin hairs zapped a second time.

I wasn't surprised when my phone rang while I was eating my leftover fried chicken—it was even better cold—from Magnolia 23. It was Patsy.

"Hi ya, girlfriend."

"Honey, I got some news for you." Patsy sounded excited.

"Oh, yeah? What'd you find out?"

"Well. I called that Diamonds and Rust place. Took forever to find a phone number—but finally, I did. Some cranky-ass man acted all put upon that I was bothering him instead of sending an email. But I told him it was an emergency."

"A pottery emergency?"

"Hey, Miss Sassy Pants. Do you wanna hear what I found out or not?"

"Sorry. Yes. I wanna hear."

"So, I told him I was desperate to buy a condolence gift for a family member who'd just lost their spouse—and that they just loved pottery by that Lorette Goodale. And did he know where I might find some online since I couldn't travel all the way to North Carolina to buy it in time?"

Okay. That sounded pretty brilliant. "What'd he say?"

"He said as how he didn't have any right now—but ..."

I waited for her to finish. But it was clear she wanted me to prompt her. "But?" I repeated.

"But he was expecting a shipment of what he called 'marquee items' in a few weeks, and I should check back."

"No shit?"

"No shit. I think that Mack Vernon is up to no good. And this Miss Goodale is likely to be his next victim."

"Patsy . . . we can't make a leap like that. This could all just be coincidence."

"Coincidence my ass."

This Diamonds and Rust store was tied to Vernon in some way—even if it was just fencing the stuff he was getting his hands on. And it seemed like it couldn't be an accident that the store had dozens of premier pieces crafted by each of the legendary potters who'd died recently under unusual circumstances. Of course, Vernon's own pieces were featured there, too. But *his* pots were not commanding the same prices as those created by his father and grandfather.

"Great work, Patsy."

"So what are we gonna do about this?"

"Do?" I asked. I had not gone that far in my thinking about this puzzle.

"Yes, *do*. Earth to Jolene. We can't sit back and let this man get away with knockin' off another competitor."

"We can't prove any of this. It's just supposition. If we report it, they'll look at us like we're conspiracy theorists. And Vernon could probably sue us for defamation."

"Well if that don't beat all. You, Miss Jolene, should be the last one to let this ne're do well get away with stealin' another person's life and legacy *just because he can*."

"Very funny."

"You know what I mean."

"Let's sleep on it. Okay? I need to think it over. And I need to invent a reason to go visit Lorette Goodale. Maybe find out who's been buying her grave markers or if anything's gone missing."

The other end of the line was silent. A sure sign that Patsy was fuming. "Patsy? I know you can hear me."

She exhaled in frustration. "Okay. Sleep on it. But we're not waiting past tomorrow. I will not have that woman's blood on my hands."

"Don't be so dramatic. We'll figure something out. I promise."

She muttered something unintelligible.

"What was that?" I asked.

"*Nothin.*' I just said goodnight."

"Okay . . . goodnight to you, too." She hung up.

That went well . . .

I spent the rest of the evening trying to keep my mind off Lorette Goodale. Would it be crazy to try and warn her?

No doubt, she'd think I was nuts—some half-crazed mail carrier with paranoid delusions.

And what if she reported me to Rusty Cagle and Vernon found out I was spreading fear and misinformation about his . . . intentions? I'd be sure to lose my job.

It was lunacy.

And, yet?

I still couldn't shake my intuition that something horrible was about to befall Lorette Goodale.

I sat tapping my fingers in agitation. Over and over, my mind replayed the grating sound of Vernon's caustic laugh as he said the grave marker he was packing up was a gift.

Was I going to sit back and let this situation become another instance where I did nothing and just allowed fate to choose its own path?

"Not much upbeat about dyin'," Vernon had said with derision.

Before I could think better of it, I grabbed my car keys and headed out the door.

It was just past dark when I drove up the long drive that led to Lorette Goodale's studio out off Busbee Road. There were no lights on in the house that sat a short distance from her studio and sales cabin. I wondered at first if that meant she was away from home. But there was a battered Ford F150 pickup parked in front of the sales room, and I saw the shadow of someone moving around inside.

I parked closer to the house so I could try to approach the cabin on foot without detection.

I felt ridiculous—even though this amateur spy expedition did fill me with an eerie kind of excitement. As I crept alongside the pickup, I noticed the bed was full of boxes containing . . . pots. All sizes and shapes. Packed with reams of shredded cardboard. And there was something else, too. Grave markers. At least four of them that I could make out—all carefully stowed together near the cab.

What the hell was going on? And whose truck was this?

When I inched closer to the nearest window and stood on tiptoes to peek inside, my heart skipped a beat. *Several beats.*

Vernon was in there, fussing with what looked like some kind of space heater. And on the floor by his feet was the unmoving body of a white-haired woman.

Dear god. It had to be Lorette Goodale.

I dropped down and stood with my back pressed tight against the rough log wall, taking deep breaths. My heart was beating so fast I feared it would burst from my chest.

What was I going to do? *What could I do?* There was no one I could call to get there fast enough.

And Goodale . . . *was she still alive?*

I had to act fast—if I had any hope at all to stop him.

I cast about for something—anything—I could use to confront

him. In desperation, I reached for the first thing I could get my hands on in the back of his truck. It was some kind of vase—but it felt hefty enough to do the job.

As quickly as I could, I pushed open the door to the cabin and charged at him.

He whirled around as soon as he heard me coming.

"*You,*" he spat out, before I hit him square on the head with the vase. He collapsed like a ton of bricks.

I stood over him, waiting to see if he would make any movement, but he didn't. Then I heard a low moan come from the woman on the floor behind him. I dropped what remained of the vase and rushed over to kneel beside her. The smell of gas was becoming pronounced. I grabbed hold of her and hauled her into a sitting posture.

"Can you walk?" I asked.

"Who?" She raised a shaking hand to her forehead, where a nasty gash was still oozing blood. "What happened? Where's Mack?"

"Come on," I urged her to her feet. "*Hurry.* We have to get out of here."

I half-carried her until we were safely outside—deliberating about what to do with Vernon. The fresh night air was beginning to revive her. We walked slowly to my car, and I helped her climb inside.

"Mack," she said weakly. "He . . . he *hit* me."

"I know. Now keep the doors locked," I warned her. She nodded, still holding a shaking hand against her forehead.

Then I called 911 and reported an attempted homicide.

Once I was sure that Vernon was still unconscious, I ventured back inside the small cabin, turned off the gas heater, and dragged his body outside to the porch.

He wouldn't be going anyplace for a while.

Then I returned to the car and waited inside with Goodale until the sheriff arrived.

We'd been sitting at my kitchen table, drinking coffee when Patsy thrust a copy of *The Pilot* at me.

The banner headline proclaimed that a legacy potter had been indicted for four homicides and the attempted murder of his former fiancée. Beneath the headlines were photos of Mack Vernon being led off in handcuffs, and me, huddled with Lorette Goodale. The subhead proclaimed, "Seagrove Mail Carrier, Jolene McLeod, Cracked the Case."

"If this don't beat all. If you ain't become Moore County's own Jessica Fletcher."

"Well, this plot was a lot thicker than either of us imagined," I demurred.

"That's for sure. We never knew this Lorette was once engaged to that old fart. Can't say as I blame her for leavin' his ass in the dust."

"Apparently, he's the one who broke it off with her," I explained, "once she became more famous than he was. I guess he just couldn't handle a woman being better."

"That don't make no kinda sense. Well . . . Iris Luck told me his daddy always told him she was a hundred times more talented than Mack. I guess a man can only hear so much of that without goin' crazy."

"Lorette told me that Charlie Vernon was the one who lent her the money to open her own studio. That was when Mack broke off their engagement."

Patsy gave a low whistle. "That man held onto his rage a long damn time."

She reached out and pulled over the bowl containing several large shards of broken pottery. "This is part of what you hit him with, ain't it?"

I nodded.

"Why'd you keep these?"

"Because." I fit the pieces together so the inscription was readable. "Look what it says."

Find out who you are, then do it on purpose.

"Well, I swanny." Patsy looked up at me. "Who said that?"

I smiled at her.

"Dolly Parton."

It took a while, but before long, things in Moore County settled down.

Somehow, I'd managed to prevent a murder—by accident.

And just like yesterday and all the days before that, I was still a mail carrier for the USPS.

And today? Well. After a lifetime of dreaming about it, today I mailed the manuscript for my very first children's book off to an agent, hoping it might one day find its way to Dolly's Imagination Library.

And that?

That I did on purpose.

THE RHINESTONE

GREG HERREN

There was a little brass plaque next to the table the host escorted me to. The plaque was below an enormous, tinted picture window looking down Dauphine Street. Engraved on the face were the words "TENNESSEE'S TABLE." The host offered me a menu as I sat in a chair facing the door, placing another down on the setting across from me. "Why Tennessee's Table?" I asked. "Are there tables for Alabama and Mississippi, too?"

I was joking, but in my two months in New Orleans thus far I'd found there were historic markers pretty much everywhere you looked. The others explained why the place was historic, but this one had no explanation, no words in smaller type below explaining why it was there.

This meant there was a story behind the plaque. I was also finding out the city had a story about almost everything.

His grin exposed a chipped incisor. "Tennessee is for Tennessee Williams, the playwright," he explained, adding, "He loved the Quarter Scene and had lunch here every day he was in town. This was his favorite table, and he'd just call whenever he'd get in and let them know so they'd reserve it for him. They put the plaque up after he died." He winked. "We get a lot of Williams tourists who like to trace his steps—I guess to commune with his spirit, maybe? The plaque makes it easier for them."

And less hassle for the staff, I added mentally.

I'd heard of Tennessee Williams. He'd also been out and proud when that could have been career and social suicide. The name brought up memories of chalk dust, a cold classroom in winter, and canned, dry hot air. We must have studied him in high school. *A Streetcar Named Desire* and *Cat on a Hot Tin Roof*, I think the plays were? I'd slept with a Williams scholar once, on a vacation in Honolulu. I'd met him on the beach. He had a stack of non-fiction books piled up on his nightstand for a paper he was writing, pages marked by a forest of Post-it notes.

How long ago was that?

At least ten years.

He'd expounded at great length about how all the leading men in Williams' plays were straight but coded gay. All I knew is I would have been happy to fuck Marlon Brando or Paul Newman.

"Your server will be here with water and to get your drink order," he said, locking eyes with me. He was maybe in his early to mid-twenties, too young for an almost forty-year-old retired military cop. The bartender I worked with the most—Dan—kept telling me that some young men liked older men. Daddies, he called them.

Jeremy was always calling me a daddy, too.

"Let me know if you need anything," the waiter said before sweeping away, back to the podium just inside the double doors.

I unfolded the newspaper I'd bought from the rack on the corner outside. Three months out of the military, two months in New Orleans, and I hadn't gotten used to being so out and open, either. When you've hidden it like a precious secret for almost forty years, it took some getting used to—but I liked it. I liked not worrying every minute of every day that I'd be found out, dishonorably discharged, or maybe sent to military prison. New Orleans didn't care. I'd been to cities with gay neighborhoods, but nothing had ever felt like New Orleans.

I'd also been right to retire when I did. The headline in the *Times-Picayune* was about the Congressional battle over whether gays could serve openly in the military. I didn't need to read it. I'd been warned that the new president's decision to lift the ban on gays serving would trigger a witch hunt—an effort to get rid of as many of us as possible before the policy changed. To avoid a dishonorable discharge, I rushed to submit my retirement paperwork as quickly as I could.

I'd planned on being in the military for the rest of my life. But here I was, out and proud and figuring out civilian life. And working in a gay bar.

I took the cloth napkin from the setting beside me and wiped off the sweat running down my face. Nothing can prepare someone for the heat of New Orleans in July. Even after two months of living here, it was still a shock to go outside and be drenched in sweat within seconds. My landlady kept saying I'd get used to it, but it felt like being inside a steam room every time I stepped out the door—not to mention how the outside heat made the air conditioning feel like a walk-in freezer. Not helping matters, I usually sweat a lot. I even get drenched in sweat when I work out in the winter. My water consumption never seemed to quite keep up with the water loss. I balled up the napkin and turned the paper to see below the fold.

The headline read: "QUARTER RESIDENT FOUND MURDERED IN HOME."

The picture was professionally done, blemishes removed with an airbrush that also made his skin look dewy and fresh, like something for a business card or an ad. A man, maybe about a decade older than me, smiled back at me in black and white. He was nice looking, with a wide smile and a carefully tended porn stache, meticulously styled hair all in place, his shirt open at the neck to reveal what looked like a metal cross with a stone in the center. Maybe a diamond? The article didn't really say much, other than the man—Vester Johnson, originally of Corinth, Alabama, and a long-time resident of New Orleans and a successful interior designer here for decades—had been found murdered in his home on Esplanade Avenue yesterday morning by his housekeeper. Nothing appeared to be stolen; anyone with any information should contact the investigating officer. I stared at his face. I knew I'd seen it before but couldn't place him. I had a very good memory—one of the leftovers from almost two decades of being a military cop. My recall didn't work as well with pictures as with living, breathing people. But I had seen him before.

Probably the bar, I thought. The article didn't mention any family or a longtime companion. Didn't mean he wasn't gay, just that he was single.

Pretty much everyone who looked familiar I'd seen at the bar, gym, or bathhouse.

Hadn't some other older gay man been killed a few weeks ago?

I folded the paper, set it on the table, and thought about it. Yes, a gay man *had* been killed about a month ago. Found by a friend or neighbor, but he'd lived uptown, not in the Quarter. Strange. *Turn off your cop brain*, I told myself. *You're a civilian now.*

The waiter, another young man with a heart tattooed on his right forearm and a sword running down the length of the other, brought me a glass of water. I asked for sweet tea and started looking over the menu. *Ah, good, they had shrimp po'boys.* I was bound to get sick of them eventually but wasn't quite there yet. I couldn't get over being able to have shrimp, my favorite, every day I wanted.

Something else to get used to.

I looked up to see Jeremy, walking up Dumaine Street shirtless in that loose-hipped way so many young men do, cocksure the world was there for the taking. His thick bluish-black hair spilled out from the backward purple LSU baseball cap he always wore, reddish gold flecks glittering when they caught the sun. His T-shirt bounced like a multi-colored tail from the back belt loop he'd hooked it through. I smiled. His lengthy, lean torso lost itself into the Calvin Klein waistband and the baggy jeans hanging low on his hips, the outline of his muscle fibers showing through the darkly tanned olive skin. Something around his neck caught the sunlight and flashed.

I was again struck by how much he looked like TJ, all those years ago back in high school. My best friend, who'd made me ache with love and desire and want. I'd thought he *was* TJ the first time I'd seen him on the streetcar as the city woke before realizing TJ didn't look like that anymore. Not knowing how small New Orleans was, I thought I'd never see him again when he got off at Felicity Street, that I'd missed a second chance.

He'd come into the bar a week later, watching me. I was new then, still bar-backing, lugging crates of liquor and cases of beer and bins and bins of ice, my sleeveless work shirt glued with sweat to my body. I was steeling my nerve to talk to him, not wanting him to get away that second time, when he came up to me and smiled. "Major Daddy!" he'd shouted over the loud dance music. He flirted with me, hanging out at the end of the bar and talking to me whenever we had a chance.

After that, he'd taken to stopping in to say hello regularly. Were we friends, or was it leading to something more?

He's too young for you, that voice whispered in my head again.

As I watched, he freed his T-shirt from his belt buckle, pulling it over his head as he crossed the street and entered the front door.

"Major Dad!" he called, the big goofy grin splayed across his face as he loped to the table and pulled out his chair. A blast of sticky hot air followed in his wake, and I got a whiff of his young man scent—sandstone and soap and musk. His big brown eyes were flecked with gold, and his face lit up like it always did when he smiled—projecting genuine joy. He liked calling me Major Dad, because I was ex-military and, apparently, a hot daddy. I still wasn't used to the language of my new community, but if Dan said it was a compliment, it was.

"Hope you didn't wait long," he drawled in that downriver parish accent I found so charming. "Glad we got Tennessee's Table." He grinned back at me. His smile was so infectious, so delightful, that I couldn't help but grin back at him. "Our second date." He took off his baseball cap and shook his hair loose, running his fingers through it.

TJ's hair was more chestnut than Jeremy's, but it was just as thick.

Yes, I had a crush on him. But he was barely twenty-one, and I'd be forty in August. *It's because he's a sex worker, not the age gap,* whispered that horrible Puritan voice in my head, the one that had guided me safely through twenty years of the Army. I could ignore it now, but I wished it would go away once and for all. It sounded too much like my mother.

Second date? I asked myself. *So, the movie was a first date?*

I felt warm inside.

Too young, too young, too young.

"You know about Tennessee's Table?"

Jeremy laughed. "I know someone who, um, Tennessee Williams used to pay for his favors. They used to have lunch here. Nice guy. He's a surgeon at Baptist Hospital now. Paid his way through Tulane Med School by escorting and doing leather porn. You've probably seen him around. I'll point him out to you some time." He laughed. "He calls himself one of Tennessee's last gentleman callers."

I didn't get the reference. "Okay," I replied as the waiter returned with a notepad and a pen in his hand and an inquiring look on his face.

"Sweet tea," Jeremy was saying to the waiter as he picked up the menu. "What are you having?"

We ordered, and our waiter disappeared with our menus and was back in a moment with Jeremy's already sweating glass of tea. He squeezed the lemon wedge and ran it around the rim of his glass. "What are—" I stopped speaking when I saw what had glinted in the sun around his neck.

It was a gold cross with a diamond in the center on a long, slender gold chain.

He looked puzzled at first, before seeing where I was looking. He put his hand to the hollow of his throat. He had big, strong hands for someone so lean and young. His nails were clean, buffed and polished. "You like it?" He flushed a bit. "I saw it in the French Market this morning and thought, hey, it's only three bucks, and why not? Christians don't hold a copyright on the symbol, you know." His eyes sparkled. "The fact it pisses them off seeing a fag wear one is lagniappe." He laughed at my face. "You've never heard anyone say *lagniappe* yet? It means something extra for free, like a baker's dozen. We call it lagniappe."

I stole a glance at the newspaper on the table. It looked exactly like the one Vester Johnson—the murder victim—was wearing in the picture. "Lan-yap," I repeated the word.

Another New Orleans lesson.

Jeremy took the newspaper, spinning it around to look at it. His eyes opened wider, and his face paled. "Ves? Someone killed Ves?" he said in an almost-whisper. He swallowed, his eyes moving rapidly as he read the short article.

"You knew him?"

As I said the words, I remembered when and where I'd seen Vester Johnson before.

I'd seen them together, hadn't I? In the bar? It was Tuesday because the deejay was playing old 1970s dance classics for Trash Disco Night. Vester Johnson sat on the other side of the bar, closer to the street exits. Not my section, but I'd seen him over there whenever I had to grab one of the top-shelf bottles. Jeremy had come over to say hello to me and get a cocktail. He'd tipped me well with a big smirk and reminded me not to forget our lunch date today. He'd gone around to the other side of the bar, and they'd left together.

Today was Thursday. That was Tuesday. Johnson had been found yesterday morning.

Coincidence.

New Orleans was a small town. Every day, I was surprised at how small this sleepy city, decaying and rotting and crumbling under the hot Caribbean sun was. Everyone knew everyone else.

But this? This was . . . a little too close

I still hadn't turned off the military police switch, either.

It was ridiculous. Jeremy couldn't kill anyone.

Could he?

Women thought Ted Bundy was hot, didn't they?

"So weird." Jeremy put the paper aside. "You know, another one of my clients was killed a couple of months ago." He shivered. "Creepy." He shook his head. "It's a wonder more of us aren't killed, you know? We go home with total strangers all the time to places where no one knows where we are or who we're with. There are so many tourists, too, that no one would miss for a while, you know. A good-looking serial killer preying on gay men would have a lot of success here." He laughed and ran his fingers through his thick hair again, shaking his head slightly to help straighten it.

He really had beautiful hair.

"It's just weird," I said, licking my lips as my throat went dry. "You know, in that picture, he's wearing a cross around his neck with a stone in the center, and you're wearing one just like it."

"Yes, but Vester's probably cost about a thousand bucks because it was real gold and a real diamond." He looked at me, his thick eyebrows coming together over his nose, his forehead crinkling. "Dude, I told you, I got mine in the French Market for a couple of bucks." He laughed again. "Trust me, Vester wouldn't have worn anything fake." He picked up the paper again. "You're right, it is weird, though, especially since I just saw him the other night." He looked at me, his eyes widening. "You don't—"

"Of course not," I replied, my heart racing beneath my calm demeanor. Military police training did come in handy at times—never react, stay calm, keep questioning.

You suspect everyone. Knock it off. You're a bartender now, not a cop.

I went on, "Sorry, no, of course not, Jeremy." I stopped speaking until our waiter had put our plates down and walked away before continuing. "I'm just worried about *you*. You go meet strangers all the time. And if you were with Ves and he was killed later the same night …" I left my voice trail off because I didn't want to finish the sentence.

"Oh, you're so sweet, Major Daddy." He reached over and ran an index finger across the top of my hand. "You don't have to worry about me. I can take care of myself." His eyes hardened, the pupils darkening. "I've been doing it since I was ten years old."

"Yeah, everyone thinks they can take care of themselves until they can't," I replied, quoting my landlady. *Hadn't I laughed when she'd warned me about being careful?* "Nobody cares when gay men die, you know that."

"I know." His voice was quieter. "The worst part of being gay is knowing how disposable we are to them all." He speared a stray shrimp with his fork. "God's punishment, don't you know, when something bad happens to one of us."

We ate in silence for a moment. Jeremy's eyes lightened again, and he started telling me stories about Vester Johnson. "I usually don't kiss and tell, but he's dead so—"

And that was the thing about Jeremy. He was so sweet and funny and charming. He would never hurt anyone. It wasn't who he was. I was still uncomfortable with the sex worker thing, and that was *my* hang-up from my Puritanical upbringing. Sex was a sin, not for fun. Sex workers— *whores, sluts, hookers*—were hell-bound trash and not decent people. That conditioning, that brainwashing, was hard to break, like I needed to be deprogrammed. Jeremy was a sex worker, and there's nothing wrong with that. Sex workers were people, just like bartenders and lawyers and waiters and doctors. It was the easiest way for him to support himself in a society that threw young men like him away, considered him disposable.

And making the leap to him being a murderer?

Was just more of my bullshit about him getting paid for fucking lonely people.

He was so animated telling me his stories about Vester's behavior— how he'd always mess up the magnets on the refrigerator because Ves wanted them a certain way so would always have to put them back the way they were before doing anything else. How his beds had to be made a certain way so you could bounce a quarter off them (I chose not to share I did the same thing). How everything was arranged by size and color in his closets and everything in the house had its specific place where it went. And how Ves couldn't stand even a chair being slightly pulled out from the table and how Ves would always rinse out the bathroom sink after Jeremy had used it, finally winding down with "I can't believe I won't ever see him again," and his eyes got wet.

He wiped at them while the waiter cleared our plates and put down the check. Jeremy tossed a twenty and a ten in the tray, waved off my attempts to pay, and walked outside.

I followed him, smiled at the host, and stepped back out into the hot, wet stickiness. "Thanks for lunch," I said. Even in the shade from the awning, it was miserable.

"You're welcome." He put a hand to hail a United cab coming up Dauphine. "Hate to eat and run, Major Daddy, but" —he glanced at his watch— "a boy's gotta make his money while people still want him, you know? Can I call you later? I'll be free this evening after five."

"Yeah, do that." I felt my cheeks burn in delighted embarrassment for a moment, and he reached up on his toes to brush his lips against my cheek. "I'm off tonight."

"What I love the most about you, Major Daddy, is you don't ever try to fuck me," he whispered. "You treat me like a person." He got into the cab. As he leaned down to slide into the seat, the cross swung away from his neck again.

The stone caught a ray of light from the sun, and it flared in beautiful, fiery shades of yellow and red and blue and green.

The door shut, and the cab pulled away. He waved at me through the back window, that big grin on his face.

I watched the cab go, standing there in the heat and feeling the sweat bubbling up to the surface of my skin again.

Rhinestones don't shine in the way real diamonds do. The colors that flashed from a rhinestone were muted, fuzzy, always with a bit of a yellow tint, impure colors from a phony stone.

That wasn't a rhinestone.

He'd lied. No vendor in the French Market was selling diamonds for a couple of bucks.

I shook it off again and walked towards Canal to catch the streetcar home.

You just have a suspicious mind, that's all, I told myself as my tank top and shorts sweated through again. *There's a perfectly good explanation. You were just a cop too long.*

And what, after all, did I know about diamonds?

I started whistling.

THE INVITATIONAL

KELLY J. FORD

There had been rumors among some of the younger fellowship members—or rather, three of them. They hung out behind the church after service smoking clove cigarettes. They were a wily crew, barely in need of bras, huffing like teens in a James Dean flick. Alicia didn't make it a habit to hang out with pre-teens, but it was the only quiet location to avoid awkward conversations while she waited for Samantha, her wife, to finish her rounds inside.

"They get rid of the ones they don't want," Rat said and held out the pack to Alicia. The girl's hair looked a mess, but it seemed to be intentional. Maybe it was some new style Alicia was too old to understand.

She declined the cigarette despite her previous occupation as a panhandling-for-fun college pothead in Vermont. It didn't feel like the right time to test the collapsing healthcare system.

"How do they get rid of them?" Alicia asked, playing along.

The girls looked at one another knowingly, then shrugged.

She hadn't decided on a nickname for the girl who mostly stayed quiet. Mouse was too similar to Rat. Too obvious.

"We don't know," Overalls said. "But we don't see them anymore after they get saved." Like a file on Jesus's computer letting Him know you were good when it was time to go.

Alicia checked the time and said goodbye to the girls. As she rounded the corner of the church, their laughter reached her. They were just playing. There wasn't much for kids to do anymore but make trouble. That's what Alicia and her friends had done when they were young and bored in a small town.

She had tried to ignore the girls at first, but they fascinated her in an anthropological way. Parts of Samantha's hometown reminded Alicia of hilly, industrial places in New England. But then people started dropping Jesus's name into every conversation like He was the small-town-famous guy they all had a personal story about, and she remembered she was in Arkansas.

Every Sunday and Wednesday service, as soon as the pianist banged out the first chords to "Just As I Am," Alicia recalled a poem by Langston Hughes set during a church Invitational. The boy in the poem watches all his friends get saved, one by one. But he doesn't feel the spirit enter him like the others, so he doesn't move. To go up to that pulpit was to tell a lie. He felt there was something wrong with him, like he wasn't chosen or special.

Though Alicia was a lapsed Catholic, she understood how the boy felt. She'd never wanted to eat the body of Christ or drink His blood. The thought thickened her tongue and throat, warning of incoming vomit. In the end, it didn't matter. According to the church, as a queer woman, her default destination was Hell.

Decades later, she still felt like that young girl, bored and stuck at church, only with developing jowls and graying hair, both of which shocked her every time she looked in the mirror. That wasn't supposed to happen. She had always been the cool girl. Ageless and unbothered, which was why she had agreed to move to Arkansas with Samantha.

Alicia had lost her job at the library due to funding and didn't have anything else to do, so why not? Remote work had become a thing, so Samantha could roam, explore what life was like outside a corporate office.

They were at the wrong place and wrong time when the economy turned to shit, and Samantha ended up losing her job too. Now, they were living with Samantha's parents like twenty-year-olds. Samantha tried to make the best of the situation. She had been worried about her parents' health for years and was grateful to spend more time with them even though they had come to their wedding begrudgingly, made them sleep in separate rooms then and now, and insisted they go to church while they lived under their roof.

"It's just for a little while," Samantha had said.

Alicia longed for their old couch in the city, rewatching episodes of *Vida* with wine and grocery store Funfetti cake instead of atrophying in her in-laws' guest bedroom. She couldn't even go for a run to clear her head. There were no sidewalks and feral dogs and men seemed to pop up out of nowhere.

"They're just playing tough guys with their guns and their flags. It's like drag," Samantha had told Alicia about the guys with rifles standing in the intersections and on street corners, not to mention the ones holstered on pants in just about every building they entered. "Unlike Chekhov's gun, theirs never go off," Samantha said and laughed. "It's fine."

"Then why aren't you wearing your ring?" Alicia asked. Samantha gave her the finger.

Now that they were back in Samantha's hometown, she had become the dutiful, closeted daughter once again—even though everything was "fine." Alicia had always found Samantha's accent and demure ways charming, but now she was knee-deep in the genesis of Samantha. Was this turnabout survival? Was it regression? Either way, it was annoying. And Samantha got irritated when Alicia asked. Samantha also grew out her hair. She started dressing less "masculine" and laughed loudly at people's jokes, something she never did before, preferring a smirk instead. She leaned in to whisper when she spoke with Jack, her high school sweetheart with the always-absent wife, and touched his arm when they talked. Alicia teased her and asked if she was prepared to pose for a photo with her hand on his stomach like all the other wives did.

It's not like Alicia didn't understand. Lots of queer folk did what they had to do to survive, be it a night, a month, a life. What ticked off Alicia was that Samantha wouldn't acknowledge that she had gone through the portal of time and changed back into who she was and expected Alicia to go along with it sans conversation, as if it were a natural thing for Alicia instead of feeling like she was wearing someone else's skin. Their relationship was obvious to anyone that didn't automatically assume homogeneity. But the fellowship proved blind to it, which benefitted Samantha and her need to keep their real lives private. Rock the ages, not the boat.

Still, Alicia tried to make the best of it. She went to church like Samantha asked, but only after she agreed to always let Alicia sit at the end of the pew, by the wall, and near the back. Plenty of Alicia's friends had grown up with a love of God and still went to church and truly believed. It wasn't for her, but Alicia couldn't judge them. She followed a bunch of Astrology accounts on social media and truly believed Mercury was out to get her.

Throughout service the following Sunday, Alicia tried and failed to disconnect her thoughts and dissociate, so she grabbed the spare Bible from the hymnal tray meant for people who left theirs at home and started doodling while the pastor banged on about accepting Jesus Christ as their Savior, and the choir sang out of tune. It was a self-soothing habit, the doodling. Alicia liked the feel of the church's pointy little pencil against the soft flesh of her fingertips.

She nudged Samantha's elbow and passed her the Bible. On the title page, rice paper thin, under the *King James Bible* heading, Alicia had written: KING JAMES SO GAAAAAAAAAAAY.

Alicia cracked up, unable to resist. They'd watched that Margaret Cho special at least thirty times, maybe more. They mimicked it in conversations and cackled with their friends.

Samantha just stared at her like she'd forgotten all that. Those people who said people don't change had never met a person who could change their whole personality after dipping their toes back into their conservative hometown.

"Oh, come on," Alicia whispered. "We all know he was a major homo."

Samantha stiffened and glanced around them. There was no need. Everyone else was too wrapped up in the pastor's sermon.

Samantha tried to rub out what Alicia wrote with her finger because the donation pencils never had erasers. No take backsies in church.

The end of service finally came. Alicia prepared herself for the excruciating boredom of everyone swaying and singing: "Lamb of God, I come, I come!" She knew by now it could take fifteen to thirty minutes before they would.

"Go, go already," Alicia sang under her breath.

Eventually, a young woman she hadn't seen before stepped out of the pew, walked toward the pulpit, and kneeled. Alicia breathed with relief. The pastor was determined to save at least one soul every service, no matter how long it took.

The deacon put his large hand on the woman's shoulder as if to hold her down. He'd been Samantha and Jack's Algebra teacher and bus driver. He had a glass eye, and they said he could see what was happening and know who was guilty of talking or misbehaving without moving his head. He had a boot camp buzzcut and comic book villain glasses. And like a comic book villain, he didn't seem like he'd aged. If he'd been their Algebra teacher in junior high, wouldn't he be dead by now? Alicia tried to do the math but gave up because it taxed her brain.

As the deacon led the woman to a small door at the side of the pulpit, Alicia remembered what the girls had said the previous Sunday. She glanced at them.

They were staring right at her as if to say: *Watch what happens.*

"You guys are so full of shit," Alicia told them at the end of the next service. The young woman who had been saved the previous week had not disappeared. At that moment, she was in the fellowship hall inhaling chicken wings like it was her last supper.

"Maybe she's a True Believer," the quiet girl said after blowing a perfect smoke ring. She gazed at Alicia with what seemed like a glint in her eyes. "Maybe Deacon Bryer saved her. He does that with the ones he likes."

"Why doesn't Samantha wear her wedding ring, but you do?" Rat asked, abruptly changing the subject. "Also, she seems to hang out with Jack a lot."

The question so startled Alicia, she took a step back. She didn't like that these girls were attuned to her life.

Before Alicia could deny that she and Samantha were married, they told her she didn't need to lie.

"We don't care," Perfect Smoke Ring said. "Even if others do."

"Is Jack Samantha's beard?" Overalls asked.

The conversation rattled Alicia enough that she brought it up with Samantha later that night. Also, it felt easier to bring up the Jack thing that way rather than seeming like a jealous wife. Seeing Samantha with him made Alicia feel like a sullen teenager, hungry for both love and revenge.

"Those girls are fucking with you, Alicia."

"About the people who disappear after getting saved, or about you and Jack?"

Samantha rolled her eyes and pulled their laundry out of a busted plastic basket. "Jack and I are just friends." That's what Alicia's ex had told her before she started sleeping with her best friend.

"Would you like me better if I were a true believer?" Alicia asked, recalling what the girls had said about the newcomer.

"A what?" Samantha asked and sighed. "Please stop hanging out with children. It's hard enough to convince folks we aren't dangerous."

"We're not hanging out. We just all hang out in the same place behind the church—"

"Same thing."

"There's a diff—"

Samantha popped a towel in the air and folded it against her legs, ending the conversation.

The rest of the week, Alicia tried not to think about Samantha and Jack or the people who got saved or the girls and instead focused on the backs of people's heads in the pews in front of her, sitting on her hands to keep from doodling in the Bible again and upsetting Samantha. When she glanced over to where the girls usually sat, they were all staring at her. Alicia furrowed her brow. They waved, in unison.

"Watch next week," Overalls said after convincing Alicia to meet them behind the church again despite her intentions otherwise. "This one's not coming back."

Alicia took a long drag off the cigarette Rat offered her. She figured if the world was coming to an end soon due to climate change and other assorted nightmares, she might as well indulge in some vices. "What makes you say that?"

They looked at each other knowingly and then smiled sheepishly. "Just a feeling."

For three Sundays after that, the organist played "Lamb of God" over and over during the Invitational, like a Pied Piper. At the beginning of every service, Alicia looked for the previous week's newcomer and didn't see them in the pews. And every week, the girls turned to Alicia, lifted their eyebrows, looked around, and then mouthed: *Told you so*.

Samantha had been right. The girls were fucking with her. They had to be. But where were the people going? And why were there so many new people? Where the hell had they come from?

"They probably felt guilted into getting saved. It's the Southern Baptist way," Samantha told her before dinner. Jack had been invited because his wife was out of town. Samantha's parents loved him and always talked about how they wished he had gotten married to Samantha, even though Alicia was sitting right there.

"Jack," Alicia said, interrupting the tenth story about high school. "What's the percentage of new people in church who get saved but never return?" He was also a deacon. He should know.

He slapped a smile on his face, but his eyes crinkled down. Suspicious. "Why do you ask?"

Alicia shoved mashed potatoes into her mouth. "Seems like the opposite of Hotel California. People check in, then immediately check out."

Samantha's mom saved Jack from answering, even though he didn't need assistance. "You should pay attention to the message, not the people," she told Alicia. "Anyway, Jack. As you were saying—"

Alicia badgered him until he answered. Basically, it was the same as what Samantha had said.

But Samantha's mom didn't believe that.

"Peer pressure has nothing to do with getting saved," she said, agitated. "You can't possibly remember every person who walks in the door. And we're right off I-40. We get all sorts of people loitering and making a mess. I'm thankful for the ones who take the time for the Lord."

"Do you really think the deacon is up to something?" Alicia asked the girls after Wednesday night service. She wasn't hanging out with children, she argued to herself; she was gathering more information on a different day to see if there would be different results.

They all looked at each other, but this time their expressions didn't betray their thoughts. "Deacon Bryer?" Perfect Smoke Ring said. "Why would you think that?"

The girls had turned on her after feeding her their frights. But why? "I don't know."

"We don't know," they said one after the other, then they walked away, icing her out. She felt twelve again, gaslit and cast out of the cool girl group after becoming invested in their latest obsession, not realizing it was over.

But she obsessed about it anyway, especially after the girls' odd answer. She mentioned it to Samantha, but she was sick of talking about it. So sick of it that she spoke to the girls and told them to stop spreading rumors. Not that that stopped Alicia or the girls from speaking again and sending each other signals in church—they had welcomed her back into the fold the next Sunday—pointing at the ones to watch. Inevitably, the ones they pointed at went up to get saved. And inevitably, they never returned.

There was something going on. Alicia could feel it. There was only one way to find out, but it involved doing something she'd never done in all the years she'd been dragged to church by her parents. It didn't matter that there was no body and no blood. It was up there. In front of people. The trauma was still there. She felt sweaty and weird all up in her body, like minnows were swimming in her veins. She breathed deeply, in and out of her nose, willing herself to move.

"What are you doing?" Samantha asked.

Alicia pushed past an open-mouthed Samantha and her parents and headed toward the pulpit before she lost her nerve. She was sure she could hear the girls exclaim quietly when she passed.

She kneeled and stood and then turned around to all those eyes on her while the pastor gloried in her salvation—she couldn't tell if they were happy she had finally decided to publicly accept Jesus Christ as her Lord and savior or if they were annoyed that she'd taken so long to do so while their potluck offerings coagulated back in the Fellowship Hall.

Amidst all those faces, she landed on Samantha's. Was that look fear or relief? Did she know what would happen?

The deacon placed his hand on Alicia's shoulder and led her to the door she had watched him lead people through for weeks. Her heart punched her insides as the door creaked open. There was no turning back.

It's not like Alicia wanted to be disappeared or un-alived, but she had hoped it would be a bit more exciting. The room was just a standard-issue church space with beige carpet stained from years of use. The deacon handed her a pamphlet and asked if she had any questions.

"A lot of them succumb to the pressure of the moment," the deacon said. Then he left the room, leaving Alicia alone.

The nothingness of the small room had killed the one thing that had kept Alicia's interest in church. She saw the girls waiting for her at the back door, but she went to sit in the car alone.

Samantha was right. She had to stop. She didn't feel great about her only connections in town being three twelve-year-old conspiracy theorists.

"I felt the spirit," Alicia told a baffled Samantha when she finally got in the car.

Now, Alicia sat there every service on the excruciatingly hard wooden pews and counted the stained-glass panes to pass the time. She didn't look toward the girls. They didn't take it very well.

They found her at a table by herself in the fellowship hall eating cold pasta. "Why aren't you hanging out with us no more?" Overalls asked.

Alicia shoved a forkful of pasta into her mouth, trying to ignore the compulsion to make nice. When they asked what had happened in the small room, she told them the truth. "Nothing."

They collectively slumped, mimicking Alicia's posture and mood.

"The deacon didn't say anything?" Perfect Smoke Ring asked.

She shook her head. When Alicia didn't offer further conversation, they slunk away.

The following Sunday, Alicia couldn't find the energy to care about whether or not someone was getting saved. She even sang along with the choir from the hymnal, challenging herself to memorize the words.

But the girls kept distracting her by glancing at the church doors behind them like they were waiting for something. They also looked as if they might be checking the time. They were disruptive during service all the time, but this was next level.

Finally, she got their attention and mouthed: *What are you doing?*

In unison, they lifted their index fingers to their lips: *Shhh.*

She told Samantha she'd be right back and headed toward the doors that led into the vestibule. From a window to the side of the entrance, she saw motion and moved closer to get a look. Several of the guys with guns who hung out at the intersection were heading toward the front church doors.

"Don't ruin it!"

Alicia startled at the sudden appearance of Rat behind her. It was the first time she'd seen one of them separated from the group.

"What are you up to?" she asked, moving through the doors into the vestibule to avoid disturbing the service. Rat followed.

Sometimes, Alicia's paranoia stopped her cold. Other times, it was like her body disconnected from her brain and acted on its own accord. This was one of those times. Rat's expression told her everything she needed to know. She flung open the front doors and confronted the men.

The guys didn't seem so scary up close. The seeming leader of the pack smelled like he was in the middle of a three-day bender. Samantha had been right about them. At least she hoped so.

"Why are you here? Is this about the deacon?"

They answered with glares.

She yanked Rat to her side. "What'd you tell them?"

"I don't know what you're talking about!" Rat unsuccessfully tried to squirm out of Alicia's grip.

"She and her friends have this weird obsession with the deacon and think something is going on," Alicia said.

"You do too!" Rat protested.

Alicia ignored her. "They're fucking with you. And that poor man," she added for effect.

"I'm not here to make trouble," the leader said. "But my niece here let me know that—"

"Your niece?" Alicia asked. "You have got to be kidding me right now."

The men stood there, slack-jawed with their guns, not sure what to make of things.

"Your niece is the only one making trouble, trying to convince everyone that the deacon is what, killing people? And you believed her? Oh my God." She laughed, not without swallowing some shame that she had gotten pulled into Rat's tall tale as well. She turned to Rat. "Tell them."

When Rat stayed silent, she practically shook the girl.

"Okay, fine!" Rat exclaimed.

"Fine what?" Alicia asked.

"Fine, I lied. But not on purpose!"

Alicia wasn't sure what other way there was but let it go because the men stood down.

The girl's uncle eyed Rat and asked, "You good?" Not: *Why are you lying, you little shit?*

Reluctantly, Rat nodded her head. The guy had to get the last word in, telling Alicia he'd keep an eye on her and the deacon.

"Sure, okay," she said and yanked the girl up the steps of the church behind her. But then she turned back to the men. "Are you the ones giving them cigarettes?" They didn't need to answer. "If I see one more cigarette in their mouths, I'm gonna come find every single one of you!"

"You smoke too," Rat said, whining.

"And we're all quitting," Alicia said. "Today."

By the time they made it inside, service was over. Everyone had gathered in the Fellowship Hall for food and gossip. As soon as Alicia saw Overalls and Perfect Smoke Ring, Rat moped over to them and whispered. They all turned to look at Alicia with disappointment and what felt like betrayal.

"Is everything okay?" Samantha had sidled up to Alicia. Worry creased her brow.

Alicia's heart had finally stopped racing. She reached for Samantha's hand. Samantha instinctively began to pull it away, her eyes darting around them, but Alicia managed to connect and hold on.

"Everything's okay," Alicia said and squeezed, running her thumb along the empty space where Samantha's wedding ring used to be. Maybe she was starting to believe it.

Samantha let Alicia hold her hand a little bit longer than she probably felt comfortable with.

But when their fingers slid off one another's skin, there was a little smile there on Samantha's face. It was a crack. But sometimes that's all it took.

Jack wandered over to them and introduced them to Susie, his wife. So she *was* real. She held out her hand to Alicia. Her grip was soft and warm.

"I heard you've made the acquaintance of the girls," she said, gesturing toward them.

The girls were staring down Deacon Bryer and talking with their hands over their mouths. Little did he know how close he'd come to the barrel of a gun. Those little idiots. They had no idea how badly things could've turned out. Or maybe they did.

"Yes," Alicia said. "We've met."

"Those girls can be a handful. I was their third-grade teacher. They were always up to something." Susie shook her head and sighed. "Jack says you're a librarian?" When Alicia answered in the affirmative despite being unemployed, Susie looked pleased. "Well, we're lucky to have you. Our librarian is probably going to retire within the next year or so." Her tone was as soft as her hands and felt like a warm hug.

Alicia felt something shift inside her when she met Susie. She could tell they would be friends. She could imagine them being good ones even. Despite wanting to get out of that town and return to her old life, for the first time, Alicia could imagine her and Samantha in a little house down the road, having dinner with Jack and Susie, becoming the school librarian. Maybe even coming out at church, in the quiet way that Samantha needed. She could give the girls banned books to read, slap cigarettes out of their hands. Lord knows they didn't seem to have anyone else to guide or pay attention to them to ensure they didn't end up as the dramatized subjects on a future season of "American Crime Story."

And maybe she needed them, too.

"The girls could use a positive influence," Susie continued. "They haven't been right since Janie went missing."

Another couple joined the chat and introduced themselves before Alicia could ask Susie for more details after dropping that bomb. After another painful half hour of conversation and cookies, Alicia finally got a chance to pull Susie aside from the group.

Across the room, Samantha beamed at the two of them. Her wife, talking to an adult—her best friend's wife!— rather than getting sucked into the vortex of the girls' stories out of boredom and resistance to what was actually good and kind.

"What you said, about the girl who went missing."

"Janie?" Susie asked and then her face went dark. "Such a loss. Especially for the girls. The four of them were thick as thieves. It's been a couple years now."

"What happened?" Alicia asked.

"Nobody's really sure. The girls were hanging out after service, like always. They said Janie decided to stay outside while they came in. That's all we know. They were the last ones to see her." Susie smiled again. "It's nice that you've taken to them. I think maybe they needed a friend."

Out of the corner of Alicia's eye, she caught some movement.

The girls stood at the back door of the fellowship hall, smiling, watching her. Just as Alicia was about to make a heart with her hands to show them they were good, their smiles morphed into straight lines. They lifted their hands in unison, as always, and slowly slid their fingers across their throats.

Alicia laughed nervously, but their expressions didn't change.

It was a metaphor: She was dead to them now. But they'd come around. Like before.

Because it was a joke, Alicia thought. *They were joking. Right?*

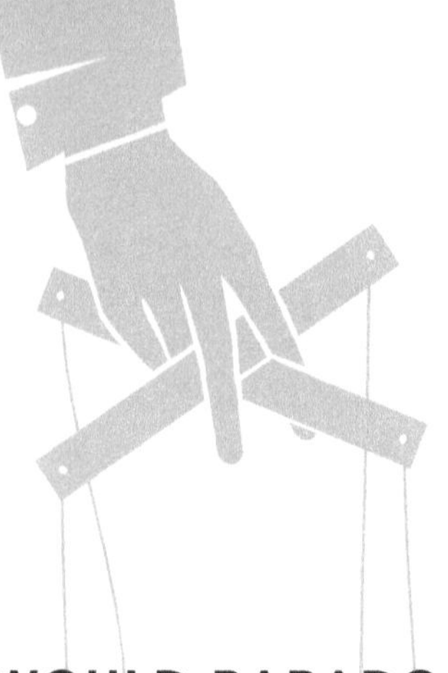

WHAT WOULD BABADOOK DO?

STEPHANIE GAYLE

"Tea? Coffee?" Sara asked Detective Wilkes. She tucked a strand of honey blond hair behind her ear with a trembling hand. He understood that cops made civilians nervous. He said, "Coffee would be great, Mrs. Hawthorne." She left to fetch it.

Wilkes appraised the room: modern, lots of light, a neutral palette. But the art was something else. An amateur Bless This Home embroidered sampler hung beside a Thomas Kincaid lighthouse painting. A terrifying oil of Jesus bleeding tears dominated the wall near the stairs. The far corner was taken over by plants, some with long twisting vines that reminded him of dark fairy tales. Above the plants was a sketch of a charcoal figure wearing a top hat, with spaghetti-long limbs, its open mouth showing rows of bared teeth. "What's that, Mr. Hawthorne?"

"Please, call me Jay." The man brushed at his starched Oxford shirt. "Our nephew likes scary movies. He drew that."

There was a wedding photo on the coffee table. Sara's dress was lace trimmed, and Jay wore a dove gray suit. Wilkes tugged at the bottom of his jacket. It was cheap, ill-fitting, and what every detective wore, bought during a two-for-one sale.

Wilkes cleared his throat. "As I said, there was a fire at Camp Cavalry. Destroyed most buildings. Worse, it left someone seriously injured."

Jay leaned forward. "Oh no! Are they okay?"

"In the ICU. Not clear if they'll survive."

"How terrible. Who was it?" His bright blue eyes were worried.

"The director, Mr. Philip Sands."

Jay bit his plump lip. "We'll pray for him."

"You and Sara attended Camp Cavalry."

He brightened. "Sure did. It's how we met."

"Ooh! Don't tell our meet cute without me!" Sara hurried in, carrying a tray with mugs. Jay jumped to take it from her and set it down beside homemaking magazines. She sat beside him, taking his hand. "We met seven years ago at the camp." Her smile was nearly as bright as the diamonds in her platinum wedding band.

"And you both enjoyed your time there?"

She said, "Not at first. Spending my summer at a Christian camp making friendship bracelets was not my idea of a good time."

"Did your parents suspect you liked girls? I understand the camp aimed to . . . correct certain behaviors."

She recoiled. "Oh no. The camp tried to bring everyone closer to Christ, but not everyone was fighting *that* sinful impulse. My parents had caught me drinking."

"But my parents," Jay said, his voice soft, "they thought I liked boys."

"Did you?" Wilkes watched him closely.

"No!"

She glared at Wilkes. "We're Christians. Besides, as his *wife*, I think I'm in the best position to say that my husband is very attracted to *women*." She giggled.

"Behave." Jay nudged her. She giggled again.

Dear God, Wilkes wouldn't need sugar for his coffee if this continued.

Jay explained, "My parents had strict ideas about what straight and gay behavior looked like. They found my music taste and refusal to play football worrying."

"More coffee?" She reached for Wilkes's mug. A flash of silver caught his eye.

"What's on your bracelet?"

"Oh." She rubbed it. "This old thing. WWJD. What Would Jesus Do? They gave them to us at camp. Jay has one." He wriggled his hand, and a matching bracelet fell to his wrist. "Camp gave us each other and a purpose."

"So, you stayed in touch after camp and married five years later. Awfully young."

She patted Jay's knee and smiled. "When you know, you know."

"But you finished college, after you wed?"

Her expression tightened. "I was one semester shy of graduating. My parents insisted."

He consulted his notebook. "And you went to a girl's school." He looked up in time to see another grimace. "Wellesley?" A nod. "You studied art? And you work in a museum . . ."

"No. Jay supports me." She leaned into him. "He's such a good provider."

He wondered how her fellow alumnae felt about that. Wellesley was a liberal school that churned out feminists. He doubted many of them aspired to be Christian homemakers. He cleared his throat. "Most kids who attended the camp didn't attend by choice. Right?"

Jay caught on. "You suspect a camper set fire to the buildings?"

"Accelerant was found on the scene. Is there anyone you can think of . . ."

"Mark," she interjected.

"Mark?"

"Sara, no." Jay set his hand on her arm, but she rushed on, "Mark Horne. Sent there because he was gay, and, let's face it, honey, he *was* gay. He's on Broadway now." She pumped her eyebrows at the detective.

"But Mark wasn't *violent*."

"Do you know where Mark Horne lives now?" They shook their heads. "Did you stay in touch with anyone from camp?"

"No," she said, but Jay contradicted her.

"Mae Larson came to our wedding. She was a camp counselor."

She nodded. "Of course. Mae. Lovely woman, very active in the church."

"One more question. Where were you Friday night?"

"You don't think—" she began, but Jay said, "At a charity auction. That's where we got that." He gestured to the Jesus painting. "Cost a pretty penny."

They'd paid for it? Yikes.

"That drawing your nephew did." They both turned to look at it. "I recognize it now. It's the Babadook." They shrugged in unison. "It's a famous queer icon."

"Really? A movie monster?" Jay looked doubtful.

Wilkes explained that a tweet about it had gone viral. Something about the creature being in a family that only recognized it as chaotic and terrible and mostly wanted to hide it away from everyone. The LGBTQ+ group saw themselves in that story.

Sara's face wrinkled with distaste. "Maybe we should take it down," she told her husband.

"Mr. Horne?" Detective Wiles prompted. "You were saying?" He watched Mark tap his mustache. He'd seen it applied by a pink-haired makeup artist earlier. Mark had insisted she use more glue, saying that last night it had nearly come off during the third act. Tucked along the mirror frame were pictures of Mark in his first two Broadway roles, at the beach with friends, and dressed as Dolly Parton for Halloween.

He met the cop's gaze in the mirror. "Right. Yes, I hated the camp. And, as you can see, despite their attempts to pray it away, this gay," he gestured to himself, "stayed."

"Yet you attended more than one summer."

He tugged at his red ringmaster's jacket. "My parents gave me a choice, go to camp or be kicked out. Camp sucked, but I thought being homeless would suck more."

A knock at the door and then a freckled woman peered around the frame and said, "Onstage in ten."

"Thanks, love." He gave her a little wave.

"How did you feel when you heard about the fire that destroyed the camp?"

"Delighted. But, as much as I'd love to claim credit, if the fire happened Friday, I couldn't have done it. I was on stage, and then winding down, with the cast."

"Right." He looked at Mark's discarded street clothes, laid out on a chaise lounge. "I don't suppose you were the only one who hated that camp?"

Mark spun on his chair. "More than half those kids would've burnt the place down."

"Remember their names?"

He tilted his head. "It's been a long time."

"And those you do?" Wilkes lifted his pen, ready to record names.

"I wouldn't rat out." He stood and grabbed his top hat and cane. "Not even for a starring role in *Hamilton*." He opened the door. "Of course, it wasn't only campers who hated that place, you had staff and parents." He stilled, and then, more loudly said, "*And* the folks who lived near the camp. Turns out tone deaf teens singing 'Still Feel the Nails' isn't a soundtrack for happiness."

"Parents?"

He turned away. "I'd focus on the neighbors. Now, if you'll excuse me."

"You might not care about the camp, but there was a man who was nearly killed in that fire."

"I know, and it's a real shame." He set the hat lightly atop his curls. "If God existed, he'd have let the fucker die. Have a great night!" He waved his cane and strode down the hall, toward the stage. The same stage he'd been on when Camp Cavalry burned. There was no way Mark Horne had done it. Unless he paid someone. He made good money, for an actor, but a look at his finances showed no large withdrawals to unknown vendors. Either he'd found the world's cheapest arsonist, or he hadn't paid someone to douse the cabins in lighter fluid and throw a box of lit matches at the director's building.

There were disgruntled parents. Some thought Camp Cavalry too expensive, some objected to the programming (too religious/not religious enough). But only Louise and Matthew Dalton had sent twelve emails, two threatening legal action. Odd, because they'd sent all four of their children to the camp, and had voiced no complaints until seven years ago, when their youngest, Rachel, returned from camp "a lesbian."

Louise Dalton's shellacked hair didn't move as she shook her head. "She came back that summer, obsessed with women's soccer. She refused to shave her body hair. Insisted we call her Ray."

Detective Wilkes frowned at the instant coffee they'd handed him. "Sounds like Ray was non-binary or trans."

"That's what she said. Non-binary!" She flapped her hands. "Wanted to wear basketball shorts all the time. Wanted to change her name."

"We told her she could change it when she got married." Matthew laughed at his own joke.

"What did you do?"

Louise thumped the chair's arm. "We wrote to the camp director and to the church, telling them that they needed to overhaul everything."

He scanned the room. There were photos of grown children, posed with their own families. Same Supercuts hairdos, same polo shirts and khakis, same grim smiles. On the wall was the God Bless This Home sampler the Hawthornes had.

"She lives in New Orleans now, doing palm readings and selling Satan's tools. Crystals, potions, dark magic stuff."

Dark magic? He'd bet none of their kids were allowed to read fantasy books growing up. "You heard of the Camp Cavalry fire?"

"Sure did. About time."

"Now, Louise," Matthew said, setting his palm atop her hand.

"No. That place needed a cleansing. You know it did."

Then he spotted it: the photo of all four of their children, at college/high school age. They held hands as if playing Red Rover. The one second from the left must've been Ray. They had short red hair. There was a dark smudge on their left wrist.

"Is that a tattoo?" He pointed.

Louise shivered. "She got it the summer after camp. She was only sixteen! I wanted to sue the tattoo parlor, but she wouldn't tell me where she got it."

The image was too small to see details, but was that a top hat?

"It had a funny name," Matthew said. "Bubba or–"

"Babadook?"

He snapped his fingers. "That's it!"

"I blame that camp. She never liked scary movies before she went there."

At the station, he discovered that the Daltons had attended a town hall meeting the night of the fire. Louise was recorded by local cable television articulating why *Captain Underpants* should be removed from the public library. Wilkes watched it on fast forward. Given the distance to the camp, and the meeting time, they couldn't have burnt Camp Cavalry down.

It took him days to find the person formally known as Rachel Dalton. They'd left New Orleans for San Francisco and had legally changed their name to Ray Vanek. They worked at an organic health store that did a sideline in fortune telling and dream interpretations. Ray didn't want to discuss the camp, or what had happened to it.

"Your parents claim it changed you."

Ray sighed into the phone. "My parents are idiots. I became who I truly am, and they hated it. They blamed the camp. But camp didn't make me who I am. Hell, most of the folks there tried their damndest to keep me from expressing myself."

"Most?"

"Not everyone sucked."

"Mind if I ask where you were on the evening of the 12th?"

"I went to the movies." They told him about the arthouse body horror film they'd seen, and about the vegan tacos they'd eaten after. "Want my ticket stub? The dinner receipt?"

"No, thank you. Do you keep in touch with anyone from camp?"

"Only Mae, though not lately."

"Mae Larson?"

"She was kind to me."

"I hear she's very active in the church."

"No one has perfect taste." He heard a tinkling bell. "I have to go. We're busy."

"One more thing. What were you up to last Thursday?"

"Last Thursday?" He heard her surprise. "Why?"

"Answer the question, please." He used the cop voice.

"I worked and came home."

"What'd you have for dinner?"

"I don't know. Why?"

"Thanks for your time." He ended the call.

The counselors at Camp Cavalry had been college-aged, and the axes they had to grind involved their living conditions (poor), wages (minimum), and supervision (none unless the director, Mr. Sands, disliked you and then it was excessive micromanagement). Most lasted two sessions. Mae Larson had worked there as a counselor for four long summers. She'd left when she'd moved to get her master's degree. She still volunteered at her local church. "Flower arrangements and helping out with the youth pastor's programming." She was almost thirty and wore a hoodie that read Childless Cat Lady. She caught him looking. "Not what you expected?"

"It's not that." But it was. From her résumé, he'd expected a middle-aged woman dressed in a sister-wives prairie dress with hair that fell to her waist. Mae's brown hair was chin length, streaked with deep purple strands. Around them, people sipped lattes and stared at their phones. "Your volunteer gigs have had some real bad endings," he said.

"Pardon?"

"Well, there's this fire, and two years ago, the church you volunteered at got shuttered. I heard the pastor was looking at," he lowered his voice, "child porn, on his work computer. Parishioners left in droves. Understandably."

"I had no idea. I helped them with their finances, not that they had much money to handle."

A barista shouted "Kate!" repeatedly. Detective Wilkes wondered where Kate had gone. Or had she slipped earbuds into her ears, and was deaf to the barista's cries?

He switched tracks. "Any idea who set fire to the camp?"

She blinked. "You're certain it wasn't an accident? It was a very dry summer."

"They splashed lighter fluid all over the place, and there were matchsticks everywhere."

She snorted. "Sorry. I'm not laughing about the fire. It's just that one skill the campers had to demonstrate was how to light one. They had to do it with a bow drill or flint and steel. It was excruciating. The director would assign it as a punishment."

"What for?"

"Not completing chores, being out after curfew, kissing another camper."

"Any camper or only those of the same sex?"

"The latter, though the former wasn't encouraged. Chastity pre-marriage and all that."

"And all that? Doesn't sound like you believed in it."

She shook a sugar packet. "They were hormonal teens. Of course they wanted to kiss."

"You think someone left the matches as a message. Any idea who? Maybe Ray Vanek?"

"Ray?" She scoffed. "No chance. Besides, they live thousands of miles away."

"Mark Horne?"

"He has the chutzpah. But he wouldn't risk his career."

"What about Jay and Sara Hawthorne?"

Her shocked laugh made a few patrons look their way. "They're a trad couple who fell in love at camp." She looked at him like he wasn't too bright. "Look, the camp wasn't fun. Lots of Bible study and being told you were a sinner. Plenty of kids were sent there against their will. I tried to make it as good an experience as I could, but I was hardly more than a kid myself. Many people hated the place and would be happy to hear it's a pile of ash. But would they burn it down? Doubtful. And Director Sands wasn't the nicest man. Isn't it possible someone went after him, and the camp was collateral damage?"

"You don't seem like the typical camp employee."

"Have you interviewed many of them?" She sipped her beverage.

"A few. They seem more . . . Christian."

She slammed her cup down, and liquid sloshed over the edge, puddling onto the table. "Fuck that. I'm plenty Christian. I believe in loving my fellow man and practicing charity and not throwing stones. I volunteer my time and donate money and try to make this shitty world slightly better for those in need."

"So why work at a camp that, forgive me, didn't seem to align with your beliefs?"

She mopped up the liquid from the table with thin brown napkins. "Because I grew up in a small town with limited options, and because I could make a difference in the lives of the kids sent there. They needed someone to accept them as they were, to tell them they weren't abhorrent or wrong or sinful. They were fearfully and wonderfully made. Psalm 139 verse 14." She grinned. "I don't suppose my ability to quote scripture proves I didn't set fire to the place."

"I know you didn't."

"I was—" She stopped speaking. "Wait. What?"

"You were volunteering at a shelter. I have witness statements."

"Oh."

"But I'd appreciate it if you could look at this photo. They found a drawing inside the director's cabin. Can I show it to you?" He slid his phone across the table. The wall was half gone, lost to the fire. But the non-charred bits had two long black vertical lines on it.

"Okayyyy. And?"

"Any idea who it is?"

"Who?" She squinted at the phone. "All I see are lines."

"Pretty sure it's the Babadook."

She blinked, then lifted her cup and drank deeply. Swallowed. "Babadook?"

"The horror movie figure."

"Not my preferred movie genre. I like romcoms."

"It's famous for being a queer icon."

"The Babadook?"

"It resists normal society. Doesn't accept being locked away as shameful. Sound familiar?"

She blinked at him. "Huh."

"You never encountered kids who had an affinity for it?"

"Maybe, but it's never come up. Most of the gay icons I know are a bit," she made spirit fingers, "more sparkly, louder."

"I think the term queer is considered more inclusive."

"Ooh. Someone paid attention during diversity training."

"May I have my phone back?"

"Of course. Sorry." She shoved it across the table. Her hoodie's sleeve rose to reveal the top hat inked inside her wrist. Unless she was a giant Mr. Peanut fan, he could guess what the rest of the tattoo looked like.

"Thanks for your time."

"Oh." She was surprised. "Is that all?"

"Unless you have something else you think I should know?"

"No, um, good luck."

He arrived on their doorstep when the autumn stars were white pin bursts in the inky blackness. He brushed at his cashmere sweater. Sara answered, hair in a messy bun, a streak of charcoal on her cheek. "Oh!" Her arms flew up to conceal her breasts, braless under a tank top. "Oh. Jay! It's the police."

"What?" His shout was lost as Chapelle Roan screamed about how her kink was karma. He wiped his hands on a dish towel, humming. When he spotted Detective Wilkes, he froze.

"May I come in?"

They looked at each other. "We're a bit busy at the moment," she said.

He nodded at the wall. "Princess Pamela?" The nude doll in the print was part of the famed queer artist's series. He stepped past her and saw that the embroidered sampler was gone. Where *Good Housekeeping* and *Real Simple* had been, there was a copy of *Alive at the End of the World* by Saeed Jones.

Chappelle Roan stopped singing. Jay held a remote in his hand. "I don't think we have to let you inside without a warrant."

"Sounds like you're not sure. Not wearing your ring." He pointed to Sara's hand.

"I don't wear it while I draw."

"What about when you go out to bars, like the Pink Taco. Wear it then?"

Jay said, "Don't talk to her like that."

"Like what? Like she's gay? Like this marriage is a ruse designed to persuade people that you're a straight couple who'd never be involved in burning down a Christian camp?"

She uncrossed her arms. "I'm bi, actually."

"Sara!"

"What?" She threw her hands up. "So, he knows I like women *and* men. Big deal."

Jay blinked. "We'd like you to leave."

"Before I tell you how you fucked up?"

"We didn't–"

He plowed on. "You did a good job. Most arsonists are dummies with a short temper, or insurance fraudsters who suck at covering their tracks. But a team banding together to destroy a camp they attended more than half a decade after the fact? That's inventive. Kudos."

"Oh, now we're part of a team? Some *Ocean's Eleven* bullshit?"

Detective Wilkes snorted. "If it was hella queer."

"Hey–" Jay said.

"No. Wait." She sat. After a few tense moments, Jay joined her. "Let's hear his story."

Wilkes sat across from them, leaned forward and said, "Seven years ago, during a summer spent being forced to wear 'appropriate' clothes and learn how to start fires using stones, a group of kids, led by a charming counselor, decided that enough was enough. But rather than destroy the camp immediately, they waited. The counselor worked there a few more years, protecting the most vulnerable campers. Then she went on to take down a priest via an online scandal. Used his computer to download child porn and then watched as his life fell apart."

"He deserved it." The words came out of Jay as if he couldn't stop them.

"One camping duo even took the extraordinary step of marrying, to present to the world–"

"And their families," she muttered.

"The picture of a happy, straight couple. That way, when Camp Cavalry went up in flames, they'd be the last people suspected."

"But you came to see us."

He stomped his foot. "Because six years ago, you ranted about Camp Cavalry all over your social media, and a magazine quoted it in a piece about gay conversion therapy. And that's why you don't post things online, Jay. Because they live forever."

"And you," he pointed to her. "Did you have to tag the wall with the Babadook?" He pointed toward the plant wall. "Your nephew didn't draw that. He's five. But you're an artist. That picture on the cabin wall was yours. What happened? Didn't burn like you'd planned?"

"We weren't at the cabin on the night of the fire." Jay looked smug.

"Riiiight. The fundraiser. Where you loudly bid on a terrible painting of White Jesus." He turned. "I see it's missing."

"Hideous thing is hidden in the garage," she said.

He shook his head. "There's a gas station on the road to the camp."

"The Sunoco," she whispered.

"I pulled tapes. A car with Kansas plates drove past that night, rented from California. Paid for by Mark Horne." Jay opened his mouth. "Don't. I know he didn't drive it. Your friend, Ray, did. You might let Ray know that when they're asked about alibis, they shouldn't have quite so many details. It's more suspicious than having none." He paused. "And they had company. You." He looked at Sara.

"She was at the auction with me."

"She snuck away early." Wilkes looked around. "You went a bit extra on the décor when I first visited. Name me one art grad with a Thomas Kincaid painting on her wall."

Sara said, "My aunt gave that to me when I was fourteen because I 'liked' art."

His sharp bark of laughter startled them both. "Nice bracelet. Can't help but notice it doesn't say WWJD."

She rotated her wrist. WWBD was now visible. "No one has ever noticed the letters before. They see WW and fill in the rest with what they expect to see."

"Why Babadook?"

"He's a chaos agent." She smiled.

"And he won't be destroyed." Jay glared at him. "You don't have enough to arrest us."

She rubbed her face, smearing the charcoal on her cheek. "That's not why he's here."

"What?"

"That's not why." She stood. Paced. "He knows who Greer Lankton is. He called Ray by their name, not their deadname. He recognized the Babadook. Mae said it was nothing, a few dark lines on scorched wood. *And* he knows what it means."

"What are you saying?"

"He's one of us."

Detective Wilkes gave a slow golf clap. "I'd hoped you noticed my haircut."

She had. As he detailed their errors, she'd noticed his shaggy hair had been cut and his facial hair sculpted. His outfit was stylish. And he smelled better. "So, why are you here?"

"I want in."

"What was the name of your camp?" she asked softly.

"Light of Christ."

"Hoo, boy," Jay said. "How long ago?"

"Twelve years."

"There's an oath," she said. "Might seem teenage, but you have to take it, and," she pulled up her tank a few inches to reveal a long-limbed, fiercely smiling creature wearing a top hat. "How do you feel about tattoos?"

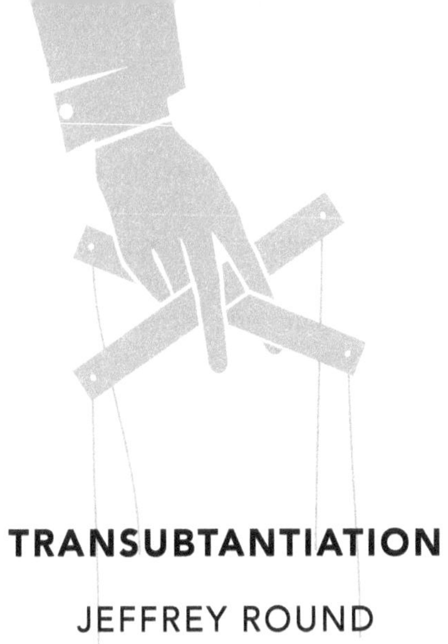

TRANSUBTANTIATION

JEFFREY ROUND

His first kill was unexpected. He'd had no choice, really. His body had started crumbling due to the genetic impurities imprinted on him at the time of his animation. This was before they'd perfected the process. Some New Form Humans had emerged from the tanks with extra limbs, others with tails and even gills. Luck of the draw. You took what you were given. What he was given were shitty longevity genes.

His current life expectancy was estimated at three hundred trillion neutron days—not a lot in the grand scheme of things. He'd taken the news in stride. The medicops could sample his DNA and reanimate him, but in all likelihood, he'd just end up with the same genes. He shrugged. He was sick of his history timeframe, and he was sick of his own kind.

On a whim, he applied for a license to become a Time Shadow. He'd always been curious about other timeframes. If nothing else, it might get him off this dirty asteroid. It wasn't that he hoped to avoid his fate, just escape it for a while. Like those trips to Disney-Moons they offered to terminally ill children.

It wasn't something given to everyone, so his expectations were low. When the holo-window appeared on the wall of his space cube, he was surprised. He was even more surprised to learn his request had been granted.

"Great," he said when they accepted him into the program. "And I'd like to visit Earth, if possible."

There was a hurried discussion by the committee, but in the end, he was given permission for that too. The committee, speaking in unison, said he simply had to choose the timeframe.

An image came to him: a photo-graphic of a snow-covered alpine village. It looked idyllic— cows, meadows, and an old church. The photo-graphic was not authentic. It had been retrieved by a Time Shadow who visited Earth eons after its real-time equivalent. They hadn't had the technology to record things back then. A bizarre concept, he could hardly imagine it, but apparently true.

Before the meeting ended, he'd asked a simple question: Was there a cure for what he had? The answer was just as simple: No. Here, the committee chair spoke solo, something else that seldom happened. There was a glimmer of hope, however. Another Time Shadow had gone to earth, conjoined temporarily with an Old Form Human, and survived beyond his expected disintegration date.

When the attraction between them was strong, the chairman explained, Old Form Humans experienced powerful emotions. New Form Humans only felt traces of such things, but early emotions had once been powerful indeed. Enzymes produced by the bodily secretions of Old Formers could add life to disintegrating genes. A battery boost, temporary but effective. If he conjoined with an Old Form Human while its emotions were at a fever pitch, he could rejuvenate his system, but the human would die. While not exactly forbidden, it was discouraged. At any rate, he must not interfere with human destiny. It could change the course of time.

This was curious news. He had conjoined with other New Form Humans of different genders for recreational purposes, but never with an Old Former. It had never occurred to him to cross boundaries. The segregation laws were strict.

"Does the emotion have a name?" he'd asked.

Love! the committee thundered in unison. The window closed on the session.

Not much chance of that, he told himself. His disintegration made him appear hideous, even to himself. He could barely stand to look in a reflector. His derma was cracking and flaking; violet light emanated from his pupils. These were the first signs of decay. He was repulsive even to his own kind. But the reality was he'd never experienced love and didn't know if he would even recognize it if he did.

In the end, he went to thirteenth-century Earth, where they weren't familiar with his kind, thinking it a good place to disintegrate. Alone, quietly.

The guise he'd chosen was that of a monk in a sect that hid their faces beneath hoods in the presence of other humans. The cloistered alpine village, not far from Lucerne, was called Heiligkreuz: *Holy Cross,* named for its church. On the altar, a splinter of wood was embedded in crystal at the center of a pewter cross. Legend held that it had been retrieved from a cross carried by a deity called Christ and brought to Switzerland, where it was venerated as a religious icon. He was vaguely familiar with such folk beliefs. They were considered primitive, like so much else declared obsolete in his timeframe.

No one questioned his arrival at the monastery. He was accepted as a wandering monk from another order and given a simple bunk in a small room not unlike his cube on the asteroid. He soon accepted that nothing in his environment was animated by nanotechnology and even grew used to lighting candles when the day waned. After all, he wasn't going to be there long.

He ate and prayed with the other monks three times a day. The food was plain but filling. Prayers were taken from a book called the Bible. They consisted of pre-written texts addressed to an unseen entity and murmured in unison. They were not unlike the requests sent to asteroid committees that responded from places unknown and unseen.

At mealtime, a young monk named Jonas often sat beside him. Jonas was simple and his conversation agreeable: Do you like the meal, brother? Yes, thank you, brother, I like it very much. Would you pass the bread please, brother? Yes, here you are, brother. Thank you, brother. And so on.

An evening mass was held in the church. Its dimensions resembled that of a space module, except the walls were painted and lacked technology. During the mass, something called a Host was shared by the monks. A small wafer was placed on the tongue to elevate the receiver to a higher level of existence in a symbolic conjoining with the Christ figure, who was said to love everyone indiscriminately. For a moment, he held a flicker of hope that this might be what the committee chair had discussed. He tried it but didn't feel any different afterward. Back in his room, the violet light still emanated from his eyes.

The days passed. He enjoyed walking the meadows. He'd never seen fields of grass growing naturally, and he enjoyed milking the cows each morning. It became an essential part of his day. It struck him that, despite the backward technology, life was pleasant on Earth. It dawned on him that he had not felt bored since his arrival and no longer looked on life as a drudgery. He found himself wondering what it would be like to stay indefinitely, but each time, he came up against the abrupt realization that this was not to be.

One evening, Jonas did not appear at supper. The other monks spoke in whispers. He had the dread disease that was spreading contagion and death in the cities: *plague*. No one was to enter his cell.

"Who will feed him?" he asked. "Who will bring him water?"

"No one," he was told. "Father Tobias has forbidden it."

He recalled an ugly old monk who scowled and frowned every time they crossed paths. "What will happen to him?"

"If the fever does not pass, he will die."

This was illogical. An afflicted entity needed nourishment. He secretly hid some rolls and cheese in his sleeves before the meal ended.

A feeble voice answered his knock. Jonas lay on a cot. The thin blanket each monk was given for warmth had been thrown aside. The young man's naked form glistened with sweat in the light of a single candle.

"I have brought you nourishment," he said, placing the bread and cheese on the table.

"That is very kind of you, brother. But you should not be here. It is not safe."

He was tempted to tell this simple Old Form Human that all viral and bacterial diseases had been eradicated in his time but decided against it.

"I am not afraid," he said instead. "God protects me."

"Yes, brother. Thank you. Forgive my nakedness. God bless you."

He withdrew back to his room.

Each night for the next two nights, he did the same thing, bringing not only food but water as well, in what Jonas called an act of mercy. To him, it was only sensible. Seeing the young man naked was also pleasant. He was lean and supple, his musculature attractive.

On the third day, Jonas emerged from his room, feeble but looking much more alive than he had. He was declared cured.

"It was God's love," one of the brothers declared at supper that evening. "Praise God!"

It was my nourishment, he thought, but no matter.

The following night, as he was preparing for sleep, a knock came at the door of his cell. When he opened it, Jonas was there. He held a wash basin and a cloth.

"Please, may I enter?"

"I do not need cleaning," he said, perplexed.

"Brother—you saved my life. I have come to bathe your feet." He allowed the boy in.

Jonas set the basin on the floor and instructed him to sit on the bed. He lifted a foot and began to wash it, speaking of his life as a boy in a small town. He had been an orphan since the age of twelve when the brothers had taken him in. He had lived at the monastery ever since. Father Tobias, in particular, had taken to him, letting him sleep in the same bed with him from time to time.

"The old man?" he asked. It was this same father who had forbidden them contact with Jonas while he was sick.

"Yes, that is him." Jonas smiled and lifted the other foot. "Tell me where you come from."

"Quite far away," he replied.

"Another country?"

"Yes, in a sense."

Jonas gave him a curious look.

"Your eyes are violet," he said. "I've never seen violet eyes before."

He reached a hand up to the hood. "May I . . . ?"

He offered no resistance as the boy removed his hood. Jonas did not gasp as he'd expected he would when he saw what lay beneath.

"You are disfigured," he said simply. "Was it a fire?"

"No—it was a sort of illness. Do you not find me repulsive?"

Jonas shook his head. "No—I find you beautiful inside and out."

"How is that possible?"

"You saved my life when no one else would come near. I would do anything for you. Do you understand?" the boy blurted out.

He felt a stirring and looked down where his foot was pressed against Jonas's crotch. The boy had an erection hidden beneath his robe.

"Forgive me," Jonas cried. "It's a sin!"

He leapt up and lurched from the room, leaving the door open.

Earth nights seemed unusually long, but this one seemed longer than most. Finally, morning dawned. So be it, he thought. The boy means nothing to me. I saved him. Why might I not just as easily kill him? If I can convince him to love me, he will die, and I will live. He is a poor orphan. Who would miss him?

The following night at supper, Jonas avoided him. He glanced over once as the meal ended but quickly averted his eyes. His discomfort was apparent. Clearly, he was feeling shame over what had happened between them the night before.

The monks went off to their cells. He waited in his room a while then made his way to Jonas's room, knocking softly. After a moment, the door opened. Jonas stood there with a fearful look.

"May I come in, brother?"

Jonas nodded. He entered and closed the door behind him.

"Come here," he said, taking the boy in his arms. "Let us lie down together like brethren."

Slowly, reluctantly, Jonas allowed him to strip off his cloak, and they lay naked on the bed. Stroking brought them both to life.

"Please don't hate me. I know it's a sin," the boy said feebly, making a futile effort to resist what was happening.

"Does the Bible not say we must love one another?"

Jonas looked up with a guileless expression.

"This old man who shares a bed with you. Father Tobias. Does he ...?"

"I don't love him!" Jonas cried. "Not like I love you. But it's still a sin."

"Shh! It's not a sin if you love me," he said.

The boy's erection slid inside him. Lying back with his legs raised, he watched with curiosity and a mounting sense of expectation as Jonas's facial expressions distorted.

The boy reached a feverish pitch, crying out, "I love you!" then slowly subsided in dying whimpers.

"There, there," he said, softly petting his head. "Don't struggle. Just let go."

In the morning, with the discovery of Jonas's body, a great cry went up around the monastery, Father Tobias not the least among them.

"It was the illness. He was not spared!" cried one.

"That God should have taken our beloved Jonas! The sweetest and purest among us!"

The lamentations went on till the crying became almost painful to hear. Skulking in a corner, he watched the others. Clearly, he had much to learn about Old Form behavior and this powerful thing called emotion.

The violet disappeared from his eyes almost immediately; his skin cleared up within a few days till he could look in a reflector and declare himself attractive, as he had been before the disintegration started. He stayed at the monastery for two Earth years. Whenever the violet light returned, he traveled to another village. Usually, once every six earth months was enough for him to select a donor, with the inevitable result.

On the asteroid back in the early days, he had not been strictly male or female. Hardly any New Former was. Learning to navigate the ways of gender was part of his growth process. It turned out to be useful the further he strayed in time, as some of his donors preferred females to males. So he simply appeared to them in that form. He was beginning to forget what he had originally looked like, having taken on numerous guises since his arrival on Earth.

It was during his third year that the holo-window opened during a stay in Nice, France. You couldn't disregard these things—they would always find you. They simply wanted an update, surprised that he had not disintegrated. He was truthful in his answers; they would have seen it in his aura if he had deceived them.

They said they were impressed at his survival—it held out hope for others like him, though they frowned on the taking of life. Still, it was only Old Formers who were expiring. The killing of New Formers was strictly forbidden.

Their sole note of caution was a simple warning to avoid jumping around too much in time. If he replicated too often, he could split his persona. There could be other versions of him running around.

"What if I meet myself in another timeframe?" he asked.

It could conceivably happen, the committee intoned in unison while assuring him the chances of meeting himself in another timeframe were low. Still, he needed to take care. *Don't rush around too much and visit too many places,* they advised

"Would we both be real?" he asked.

Again, the committee head spoke in solo voice. Technically, no, he was told. The other version of him would be a shell, a soulless monster wandering through eternity, just going through the motions century after century. *Don't let it happen,* he was told. *If you do, one of you will be canceled out permanently.*

"I won't," he assured them.

With time, he found it easier to attract Old Formers, or what he called donors. As the centuries sped past, the emotional state of humans had grown more malleable. People were yearning to love and be loved. He sensed glimmerings of such things inside himself now. He also sensed in the Old Formers something of a superior race in how they conducted themselves with one another. How could that be? he wondered. Was there something in them that died out when the New Formers became the dominant species? And was that thing *love?*

Still, love was not the only emotion ruling them. He'd spent time among them during what they referred to as World War One—the first of many, as it turned out. So perhaps they had spelled their own demise. During that time, he befriended an attractive young Englishman named Owen, a man with a poetic nature. Owen had felt so bad for his fellow soldiers that he turned himself inside out writing poems about their suffering.

Eventually, Owen conjoined with him beneath a bridge while a battle raged nearby. As always, he cradled him as he died. Only later did he learn that Owen was mourned not just as a good soldier but as the finest young poet of his generation.

The committee had taken him to task for this: he was warned yet again not to interfere in human life. Otherwise, he would subvert the course of history.

He was unrepentant. "What difference did it make? Owen was doomed. I saved him from sheer hell. Read the poetry. He would have died sooner or later."

The solo voice of the committee head intervened. They had

previously arranged for an armistice. Lieutenant Wilfred Owen would have made it another week and the war would have been over. He was to stop dabbling immediately in things he knew nothing of.

He shrugged. The malaise had set in again. He was bored. "I want to be free from this. I'm tired of it all."

You can be free if you learn to love, the voice boomed. The holo-window snapped shut.

The next time it happened was seen as an even more serious injunction. He had befriended a lonely, unstable young actor, made him fall in love, and coaxed him into conjoining. Neither feat had been difficult; the young man was so volatile. Only later did the committee inform him he had just terminated the best young actor of his generation—in a car crash, no less. The event spurred a wave of suicide among young people the world over upon learning of James Dean's death.

"Dean would have killed himself eventually. He had Death Wish written all over him," he sneered. "I faked the crash afterward to avoid answering difficult questions. There were always too many people around him."

He wasn't prepared for the vehemence of the committee's response.

Enough! they cried as one. *You were warned before!*

So what? he thought.

You ask us so what? came the reply.

He'd long suspected they could listen in on his thoughts: now he knew.

"Yes, so what?"

We will instigate proceedings to revoke your Time Shadow license. We order you to return home.

The holo-window snapped shut.

Not gonna happen, he thought. He could dodge around in time forever if he had to. He already knew the most obscure corners of history to hide in.

Not long after, he'd had a near shave while driving a shiny new Alfa Romeo along a seaside cliff in the Italian Riviera. He couldn't prove it was them, but he suspected it.

For a while, he turned to gambling. One of his donors had been rich. They'd met at a seaside resort. The unlucky man showed him his stash of cash right before they ended up in bed. He simply walked out of the hotel room with the money.

Now that he was rich, he discovered he could have anyone he wanted. His sexual proclivity had grown to the point where he was able to enjoy the conjoining act both passively and actively. He discovered he was a bit of a tease as well. Sexual games were right up his alley. He loved being a flirt. Someone labeled him a cock-tease. If you only knew, he thought. But then, who was he? Had he become that empty shell they warned him about—that unfeeling, soulless monster?

It came to him suddenly. The only one who had ever loved him for himself was Jonas: "I find you beautiful inside and out," he'd declared.

He sighed. He missed walking those rolling meadows, gazing up at the snow-covered mountains, and milking the cows at dawn. It had been his only meaningful existence off the asteroid. It made him sad to think of it.

He wasn't sure when it came to him, but one day, he realized he now loved Jonas as much as Jonas had once loved him. He thought of Jonas's gentle smile and considerate manner. What if I go back in time before he died? he wondered. I could be with him again.

Yes—he would do that!

He closed his eyes and waited until a vista opened before him. He could see the rolling meadows and hear the bells of the cows as they grazed. There was the church again and the monastery off in the distance. He made his way toward them.

A figure loomed up ahead. It was Father Tobias. He was even older and uglier than he remembered.

"Ah, the penitent has returned."

He hung his head. "Forgive me, Father."

"If you're staying with us, then you must take the Eucharist."

He followed Tobias inside the church and knelt before him.

"This is the body," Father Tobias murmured, placing the Host on his tongue.

Yes, but not the body I want, he thought, as the wafer dissolved on his tongue.

"Thank you, father. I have been wicked. I deserve to be punished."

"You will be, my son," Father Tobias said. "After the evening meal."

Then you can fuck me and die, you disgusting old pederast.

His heart leapt when he saw Jonas at supper that night. The timing was perfect. This was exactly the hour before he died. To his great joy, the boy welcomed his return. Once again, they met up after the meal,

Stripping off their cloaks, they fell on the cot and rejoiced in one another's arms.

"I love you!" Jonas exclaimed. "Let us make a pact to leave this place together."

He felt the boy's erection probing him, as it had the first time they were together.

"No—you mustn't!" he exclaimed.

"Why? Because it's a sin?" Jonas asked.

"Not that. You mustn't … ever do it to me again."

"*Again*? I don't understand," Jonas said.

"It's all right," he said, rolling the boy onto his back. "Let me pleasure you instead."

Jonas struggled at first, then let him in all the way. "It feels so good," he said as their rhythm picked up pace.

"I didn't realize it till now, but I love you more than anything."

"Do you not find me repulsive?" Jonas asked.

Why would Jonas ask that? He was one of the most beautiful Old Form Humans he had ever seen.

"You are not repulsive. I find you beautiful inside and out."

It occurred to him that they had switched roles somehow. No matter. This was the moment: he could subvert time and bring everything back to the way it was before Jonas's death.

"I love you!" he blurted out.

But it was no longer Jonas beneath him. A hideous, fierce-looking creature with cracking skin caught his body as it went limp. He fought briefly to hold onto consciousness.

"There, there. Don't struggle. Just let go."

The voice sounded as if it came from very far away. He barely recognized it as his own.

The last thing he saw was a glint of violet light.

For Felice Picano,
1944-2025
In memoriam.

NEVER MEET YOUR HEROES

MIA P. MANANSALA

Trans Filipina queen Geena Rocero starts her memoir with the iconic line, "I learned how to be trans in the Catholic church."

Despite being a queer Filipina and recovering Catholic, I don't hold the same reverence for the colonial institution that Ms. Geena Rocero does. No, for me, cosplay is my religion. And today, at Chicago ComiKon, I've come to worship.

"Excuse me! Mayari? Mayari! Can I get a picture?"

I haven't even picked up my badge yet when someone stops me for a photo. I grin and move off to the side, so we aren't blocking anyone's way, pulling out my kali sticks and getting into Mayari's signature stance. That attracts the attention of other con-goers who crowd around to take my picture as I move from pose to pose.

Finally, I straighten up and put my kali sticks away. "Sorry! I still need to pick up my badge and register for the cosplay contest."

"Ooh, you're joining the Bryan Sedgwick cosplay contest? Good luck!" A beautiful woman with pale skin and haunting gray eyes steps up to me, and I'm so absorbed by her lush red lips that it takes me a moment to clock her costume.

"Ohmigod, that is the BEST Athena cosplay I've ever seen!"

The woman is also dressed as a character from my favorite series ever: *Gods Are Monsters* by Bryan Sedgwick, art by Lillian Thompson. My older sister introduced me to the comic when I was twelve years old.

Soon, I'd devoured the entire series and sought out anything else

Bryan Sedgwick had written. And he'd written just about everything: comics, poems, science fiction novels, fantasy stories, TV shows. Books for kids and books for adults. His works were wonderfully different from each other, but they all carried the same magic: the feeling that someone, finally, understood me.

Gazing at the gorgeous goddess in front of me, I knew I'd found a kindred spirit. As I take in her intricate battle armor layered over her flowing robes, the contrast as stark as her raven black hair against her white skin, I have a sudden lightning bolt moment. "Holy shit, are you Sochi?"

At her nod, I start hyperventilating, and I know I should say something, but my brain cannot compute. Sochi is the handle for one of my favorite cosplayers *ever* and I've been following her for years. In my circle of fandom, she's basically a celebrity. She's also the first real-life woman I ever crushed on, so you know. You can forgive me for having a bit of a moment.

When I don't say anything else, she continues. "I don't think I've seen you around before. Is this your first con?"

"I—" My voice cracks and I rummage through my bag for my water bottle. After a quick swig, I've finally calmed down enough to interact like a normal human being. "I've gone to a couple of cosplay meetups, but this is the first time I've really put myself out there."

"As you know, I'm Sochi. And you are . . . ?"

I'm about to tell her my real name, then realize she referred to herself by her cosplay handle. Should I do the same? That's what most cosplayers do so it's easy to find them on socials while protecting their privacy. But I wasn't thinking of that when I chose my username at twelve years old, and now it's way too late to change it.

"My handle is 'themoongoddess,' but that's way too cringe to go by, so you can call me Mayari."

Mayari, the Filipino goddess of the moon, and my absolute favorite character from *Gods Are Monsters*. Tough and kind and beautiful and strong. All the many things I so desperately wanted to be, but knew I wasn't.

Sochi grins and it literally feels like she reached into my chest and squeezed my heart. "You got any plans, Mayari? Since this is your first time here, I can show you around."

I downloaded the con app and bookmarked the fifty million things I wanted to do since I could only afford to attend for one day, but I'm ready to throw those plans away and follow this woman anywhere.

"Once I'm done with registration, I'm down for whatever."

She looks deep into my eyes and another smile spreads across her face, this one sensuous and a touch mysterious. "That's what I like to hear. Time to take you under my wing, my lovely moon goddess."

She grasps my hand and tugs me forward. I'm not expecting the contact and stumble over my long robes.

"Sorry," Sochi laughs and straightens my costume. "Don't fall, *okay?*"

Too late.

For a few hours, Sochi introduced me to other cosplayers, taught me how to pose at photoshoots, and showed me around the con floor. Wandering the aisles of Artist Alley, I spot the OG artist for *Gods Are Monsters*. "Ooh, is that Lilian Thompson?" I got on my tiptoes to see past the crowded corridor, and sure enough, a familiar-looking older woman was sketching furiously on a pad, head tilted down, her signature wild gray curls making it easy to recognize her. Well, that and the giant banner above her that says, "Lilian Thompson Art." That helps.

I brought my entire collection of *Gods Are Monsters* and am eager to have Lilian sign them, but Sochi stops me.

"Why are you wasting your time? Bryan cut ties with her years ago. She's a jealous has-been that's been badmouthing him since he's successful, and she's not."

I knew about their creative split since it was all over fan sites when it happened, but I didn't realize it was hostile. I assumed they had creative differences and wanted to work on their own projects, which was the excuse they gave when they unexpectedly ended the series.

"I just want her to sign my comics. Her being bitter isn't going to change the way I feel about Bryan Sedgwick or his work."

Sochi nods, and I feel like I passed a test. "Just a warning, she's a real piece of work."

There's no line in front of Lilian's table, so I walk right up to her. "Hi, Ms. Thompson. I'm a huge fan of your work on *Gods Are Monsters*. Could you sign my comics?"

Lilian's hands still, and she finally looks up from whatever she's working on. Her eyes light up when she sees me and my costume, but then her gaze slides over to Sochi, and she scowls. "What do you want? Shouldn't you be following Sedgwick around like a puppy, kissing his flat British ass?"

Sochi's head whips toward me, and she gestures wordlessly like, *Can you believe this bitch?*

I clear my throat. "Sorry to bother you. We'll go now."

I start dragging Sochi away, but Lilian surprises me by calling out to stop me. "Wait! I'd love to sign your comics."

I reach into my backpack and pull out the entire stack, the books landing with a thud on her table. "I know there's a lot, so you don't have to sign them all. But at least the first volume? And my favorite issue, please."

I hold out the special one-shot comic starring my fave, and Lilian reaches out for it tentatively, almost reverently. "I created Mayari, did you know that? Her character, I mean. She was based on my best friend. She—"

"Co-created, you mean. Don't even try and take all the credit," Sochi interrupts.

Lilian's eyes, which were warm with nostalgia, suddenly harden. She quickly signs the comic in her hand and turns her attention to the stack of books in front of her, her silver Sharpie flashing as she silently finishes her task.

I thank her, and at the last minute, decide to buy a single issue of her latest comic to pay her back for her kindness and cut the tension that's building. After the transaction is over, Sochi walks away, but Lilian grabs my wrist to hold me back.

"You seem like a good kid, so let me warn you now: be careful around that girl. And don't be alone with Sedgwick."

Her intensity as well as the bony fingers forming a vice grip on my arm freak me the fuck out. I yank my wrist away and hurry after Sochi.

I catch up with her and am worried I pissed her off somehow, but she apologizes once she sees my face. "Sorry for running off like that. It's not you, it's her."

"You did warn me."

She shrugs. "I'm used to it. I'm just sad for Bryan, that's all. And for newbies like you who don't know what's up."

"I'm a quick learner."

She tucks a lock of my wavy black hair behind my ear, causing my heart to flutter again. "Good to know."

—〰— —〰— —〰—

Not sure what I thought a cosplay contest at Chicago's largest comic book convention would be like, but it sure wasn't this. I'm cowering offstage, trying not to look at the packed auditorium and praying I don't trip and humiliate myself in front of hundreds (thousands?) of people. On the stage is a table with the three judges: Bryan Sedgwick (of course), Vivi Valentine, a legendary cosplayer who won tons of contests all over the world and retired a few years ago, and last year's cosplay contest grand prize winner.

Each contestant heads onstage when their handle is called and walks down the runway as the announcer describes their costume and the amount of effort that went into crafting each item. There's a Crowd Favorite category, so the cheers and calls from the audience are super important and overwhelming.

I try to center myself by admiring the cosplayers, who are lined up in order of appearance, but the girl behind me is too distracting, muttering to herself and fussing over the bow and arrows of her Neith cosplay. My character uses Kali sticks, which I just purchased online. Short of me picking up whittling or constructing something cheap looking out of cardboard, I didn't see a point in making her weapon and focused all my attention on her intricate robes and accessories. I worry about that choice now that I see this Neith's impressive bow and arrow set.

Before I can think on it too much, my cosplay name is called, and I'm walking onstage and down the catwalk, taking care to show off the details of my costume and strike a few poses with and without my Kali sticks. I should be terrified since being perceived is the last thing I want in my everyday life. But cosplay is different. Clothed in the armor of my Mayari persona, I am confident. Fierce. The high I get from the roar of applause from the crowd hits me hard, and I wonder if it's possible to become addicted to this feeling.

I glance at the judge's table, and Bryan Sedgwick's intense stare hits me like a jolt of lightning, his gaze dragging slowly down the length of my body, taking in every detail. My skin tingles as if it were his fingers and not just his eyes surveying me. I meet his eyes, and the connection is so instantaneous; it's more than electric—it's like the red thread of fate. At this moment, on this stage, posing for my idol … I *am* Mayari.

All too quickly, my turn is up, and I make my way to the stage exit on the opposite side of where I entered, my blood still buzzing from the interaction. Maybe because I'm so hyper-aware of everything at that moment, I sense rather than see the sudden shift in energy onstage. My eyes cut toward the contestant after me, who just made it to the runway. After a quick turn to display her costume, she reaches behind herself to pull an arrow from her quiver, nocks it to the bow, then points her weapon at the judge's table. The movement is smooth, precise, the girl's face as calm and assured as her movements.

It's her eyes that give her away.

The announcer makes a joke, and everyone laughs, but my body reacts before my brain can stop me, and I sprint toward her. Her gaze meets mine, and I know I'm right: This girl means business.

Before she can let the arrow fly, I hurl one of my Kali sticks at her, breaking her concentration long enough for the announcer to realize what's going on, and he knocks the weapon out of her hand. Con security swarms the stage, restraining her, and one of them confirms what I suspected— the arrow is real.

"Stop! Let me go!" The woman, who doesn't look much older than me, is struggling against the security guard dragging her offstage. "Fuck you, Bryan! You deserve to die, you piece of shit! Don't let his act fool you, he's—"

"Okay! The cosplay contest is always the highlight of Chicago ComiKon, but this takes the cake!" the announcer says, drowning the screaming woman out. "Please give us a few minutes while I confer with the judges and security, and hopefully, we can continue the contest."

He switches off the mic and heads to the judges' table, where several official-looking people have gathered. After a quick conversation, he turns the microphone back on and informs everyone the event is shutting down early and to check the website for updates on the contest winners.

Security herds everyone out of the auditorium, but I'm stopped by an older white woman dressed in a pantsuit with a phone to her ear.

"Yeah, I've got her, hold on." She holds the phone away from her mouth. "I'm Paula, Bryan Sedgwick's personal assistant. He'd like you to come to his VIP room so he can thank you for saving his life."

Ohmigod WHAT.

"Um, I wouldn't say I saved his life. I just—"

"Yeah, yeah, you can do your modest act later. Come on, he's waiting for you." She murmurs something into the phone, something I can't quite catch, before hanging up and gesturing for me to follow her.

We wind down a bunch of random hallways until we reach a door with a sign that says, "Bryan Sedgwick VIP." I wait for her to open the door, but she suddenly turns to me.

"I forgot to ask. How old are you?"

"I'm eighteen. Is that a problem?" she grins. "No, that's perfect."

She knocks on the door and opens it without waiting for a response. The room is small, but everything about it screams VIP. There's a table laid out with lavish snacks, an ice bucket with champagne, a few bottles of wine, something called Lagavulin, canned beverages, and pitchers of water. There's also a plush couch tucked into the back of the room, and Bryan fucking Sedgwick rises from it to greet me. He's dressed in his trademark black, and despite the simplicity of his shirt and trousers, there's something undeniably luxe about them. I'm tempted to rub the fabric of his turtleneck between my fingers—something tells me it's sure as hell not polyester.

"Hello, dear. Lovely to meet you." He grasps my hand and raises it to his lips, the move devastatingly suave. "I wanted to thank you for stopping that attempt on my life. And commend you on your wonderful costume, of course."

God, he smells good, which may be a weird thought to have, but I focus on that rather than what he's saying because I'll straight up swoon otherwise.

Before I can embarrass myself by bursting into tears and/or fainting, there's another knock at the door, and Sochi lets herself in. Her eyes light up when she spots me.

"There's the hero of the night! Way to beat me here." Sochi makes her way over to the drinks and pours a generous amount of Lagavulin in a small glass along with a splash of water, which she hands to Bryan, and prepares a glass of red wine for herself. "Can I get you anything?"

"Just some water, thanks."

I discreetly wipe my sweaty hands on my robes and accept the bottle Sochi hands me, working up the courage to say, "Can I get a picture with you, Bryan?"

He, of course, kindly agrees and Sochi takes a few pictures of us with my phone, even convincing Bryan to do the heart fingers pose in a selfie with the three of us. I text my sister the photos, expecting her to reply immediately since she loves Bryan's work almost as much as I do, when I remember she's been cramming for her final exams.

"Bryan, sorry, one last favor. My sister is a huge fan of yours, but she couldn't come because she's studying for finals. Could I record a quick video of you cheering her on?"

I pull the small stand I use when taking cosplay pics and videos out of my purse and set up my phone. I am absolutely giddy at how wonderful and accommodating my hero is, so I figure I might as well livestream his greeting to my cosplay account so my followers can enjoy it, too. And let's be real, I also want to flex on them. Bryan gamely records a short message wishing my sister the best of luck on her exams, and right at the end, a loud ringtone makes me jump.

Paula, who I forgot was even here, answers her phone. "It's been handled? Good. Keep me updated if anything changes."

She hangs up and turns to Bryan. "Need anything else?

He shakes his head. "That should be all."

Paula nods and leaves the room. I hear her lock it from the outside. Before I can wonder about that, Bryan, who's gotten comfy on the couch with Sochi, calls out to me.

"Come join us," he says, patting the seat next to him. "No need to stand on ceremony, love."

Despite his gesture, sitting so close to him feels presumptuous, so I awkwardly drag one of the chairs from the snack table toward them and perch on that.

Bryan smiles at me. "There's no need to be so nervous. I'm just a writer of silly little stories, nothing to—"

"They're not silly!" The words burst out of my mouth before I can stop myself. "Your stories are everything to me. I don't know what I'd do without them. So please don't talk about them like that."

There's an awkward silence after my outburst and I debate making a run for it before I embarrass myself in front of my idol more than I already have, when Sochi speaks up.

"What did I tell you, Bryan? Isn't she the absolute sweetest?" She gets up to refill her wineglass and returns with the bottle as well as a canned cocktail for me. "No pressure, but I think you'll like this."

Not wanting to be rude, I accept the drink, the condensation from the ice bucket chilling my fingers. I pop the top and take a sip. It's my first time trying alcohol, and I choke a little as it burns its way down my throat. She's right, though; I do like it.

Bryan smiles at me. "Your passion for my writing means the world to me, love. And I absolutely adore your costume. Mayari was always one of my favorites."

"Her attention to detail is amazing, isn't it?" Sochi adds. "Look how she …"

And the two go back and forth, taking turns complimenting me and my cosplay, pointing out what they love so much about my outfit. The attention feels good, almost too good, so I chug down most of my drink and shift the conversation to the character of Mayari and what makes her special to me.

Bryan and Sochi are so kind and not only put up with my rambling but encourage me by asking questions that show that they're actually listening, not just nodding politely like most people in my life. By the time I crack the top on my third drink, I've loosened up enough to share more about myself, somehow comfortable telling them things so intensely personal I haven't even dared to write these thoughts in my diary. Yet here I am, spilling them to my hero and my first crush.

"—and so yeah, it was a really rough time. My grandma kept trying to pray the gay away, and I thought my parents were gonna kick me out. They didn't, though. We just … never talked about it again. They love me, of course," I add, though I'm not sure who I'm trying to convince. "They just don't get me, that's all. Which is why your books mean so much. My parents don't understand me, but you do."

Bryan takes my hand. "Of course I do, love. Thank you for sharing that with me. An unfortunate thing I've learned is that blood doesn't make someone family. Sometimes you have to create your own. Isn't that right, Sochi?"

Sochi takes Bryan's other hand and kisses it before pressing it to her cheek. "Thank you for making me part of your family."

Just like when I was onstage, I feel the energy in the room shift. A very different kind of danger, but danger all the same.

Bryan caresses Sochi, dropping kisses along her bare throat but never taking his eyes off me, never letting go of my hand. Sochi beckons me to join them but I'm rooted to the chair. This can't be happening. This isn't who he is. It can't be.

I snatch my hand away. "I thought you invited me here to thank me for saving your life?"

"I can't think of a better way to show my appreciation. Can you?" Bryan drops the soft-spoken gentleman act and leers at me. "I'm all about giving the fans what they want."

"And if we don't want it?"

"In the end, you all want it. Whether you know it or not."

A sick feeling settles in my stomach as the events from the cosplay contest suddenly make a whole lot more sense. "That girl earlier. Was she one of the ones who…?"

"Just another misguided soul. Those types are so volatile, you never know how they'll react when you break up with them. Thanks again for stopping her."

Sochi nuzzles against him. "It's already circulating how that girl's a crazy bitch who wanted revenge after you ended your very consensual relationship."

"That's my girl." He drops a kiss on her temple.

"Don't look at me like that, Mayari. I've told you not to listen to that poison people say about him. I'm just protecting him."

I close my eyes as if not seeing her beauty would make her betrayal hurt less. "Maybe he's not the one that needs protecting."

Sochi glares. "Don't you start. Bryan is the kindest, most genuine, and talented person I've ever met in my life. We started talking when I was fifteen, and not once did he put his hands on me, even when I made a move on him. He waited until I was eighteen because he wanted to show he was serious. He loves me and takes care of me in a way that nobody ever has. Getting to share him is the highest honor I can think of."

Since she was fifteen? Bryan Sedgwick is almost fifty, and Sochi is only a few years older than me. Does she not see how fucked up that is? I don't know shit about love, but I do know it's not whatever this is. And I want no part of it.

Bryan suddenly tosses back the whiskey in his glass and gets up to pour another drink. "This is all rather tiresome, love. You said you found me the perfect toy, but now I'm starting to wonder if you've lost your touch."

Sochi clutches at him, her face so desperate I have to look away. He knows exactly how to play her. "Bryan, no, please. I can fix this."

He sets his glass and the liquor bottle on the low coffee table in front of the couch and sits back down. "Then fix it."

I don't know what they mean by "fix it" and I don't wanna find out. I race to the door, forgetting that Paula locked it from the outside. I pound on it, hoping someone in the hallway can hear me, but Sochi puts her hand over my mouth and drags me to the couch, where she shoves me onto Bryan.

I'm kicking and screaming, and Sochi is doing her best to hold me down. "Stop fighting! This is a dream come true for any real fan!"

Her voice shakes like she's trying to convince herself.

I change tactics. "Sochi, you know this is wrong. Maybe he's shown you some kindness, but what about the others? There has to be more like that girl from the contest. There can't be so many whispers about him without some truth mixed in."

She shakes her head, not because she doesn't agree but because she can't. Because agreeing would make her complicit in all that he's done. And because it would mean the love that she poured everything into was a lie. She doesn't have to say it for me to understand.

She still has me pinned down, so I soften my voice, hoping that I wasn't imagining it earlier, that we shared a connection. "He can't keep doing this. He's hurting people."

Maybe we did have something. Or at least, we could've. But we just met. That tiny spark isn't enough to overcome years of grooming and manipulation.

"You're wrong. He loves me. No one cares more about his fans than Bryan does!"

Bryan Sedgwick has been sitting beside us the whole time, watching us in amusement. "Are you done yet? With whatever this is? Love, you have to know this is ridiculous. Who's going to believe you? Those people out there? They worship me as a god. Your words mean nothing. You're nothing without me, Mayari."

I fight back tears. This is the man who pulled me from the deepest depths of depression, who gave my life meaning again. The person who I thought looked deep into my soul and saw a person who was worthwhile. The one who saw *me*. And it was all a lie.

But then I notice something. Something that fills me with the strength, the confidence, I've always wished for. And I think, *FUCK HIM.*

"First of all, my name is Tala. You're the one who taught me the power of words, Bryan. And you're right, fans do see you as a god. Which is fitting, because if there's one thing I've learned from your writing, it's that gods are monsters. But do you know what else you taught me?" I ask, eyes trained on my phone in its stand, which had been streaming this whole time.

"Monsters can be slain."

INVISIBLE

ROBYN GIGL

She held the .44 Magnum Ruger Redhawk in her right hand, opened her mouth, tilted her head back, and pointed the barrel up toward the roof of her mouth. The intended trajectory would result in a quick and painless death. She paused momentarily, wondering what they'd think when they found the framed, autographed, front page of the *New York Daily News* from December 1, 1952, hanging on the wall across from where she was sitting. But let them wonder what it meant. She was dressed as they'd expect and had purged all the other evidence of her true identity. The newspaper would be a cipher.

The cellphone on the night table next to her began to ring. *Don't look. Just squeeze the trigger.* But some primal conditioning overruled the screaming in her head, and she glanced at the phone's display. She sighed, laid the gun on the bed, and picked up the phone.

"Yeah," she mumbled.

"Whata we got?" Homicide Detective Sergeant Max Kirby asked as he walked into the house, already buzzing with the forensic team.

Clay County Detective George Mace cocked his head in the direction of the unmistakable rasp of his immediate supervisor and watched the others in the room part to allow Kirby to pass. Kirby might not have maintained the muscle tone from when he played linebacker at State, but he still possessed the girth.

"Officer Christine Madison, Brunswick PD," Mace responded. "Looks like a suicide," he added.

"I don't want speculation. I want to know what we have," Kirby chided.

Mace looked down at his notepad. "Single gunshot wound to the right temple. Her Smith & Wesson 9mm service weapon was lying on the couch next to her. A neighbor across the street heard a noise—could've been a gunshot—around 11 p.m. The neighbor looked out her window, saw the lights go out, but didn't see anyone leave. Madison was scheduled for a swing shift tonight, midnight to ten. When she didn't show up for roll call or answer her phone, the shift commander sent a unit over to check. After getting no response, they broke in and found her around 1:30 a.m."

Kirby walked over and looked at Officer Madison's body. He owed her that respect. Then he took a few minutes to look around the room, taking in the details. "Who's here from Brunswick?"

"Captain Cage," Mace answered, nodding toward a man wearing a blue Brunswick Police Department windbreaker.

Kirby crossed the room to where Cage was standing. "Paul," Kirby said, extending his hand to Cage. "Sorry, man. I know this one has to be tough. I didn't know Officer Madison well, but she worked the crime scene on a few of my cases. Seemed like a good cop."

"Thanks," Cage replied, shaking Kirby's hand. "And she was a good cop, Max. She was about to make sergeant."

"Did she know that?" Kirby asked.

"I'm sure she had a pretty good idea. She was number one on the sergeant's list and had a great interview. Her killing herself just doesn't make sense."

"I'm not sure she did," Kirby replied.

"Wait? Are you saying she was murdered?" Cage asked.

Kirby nodded. "Look around, Paul. See the guitar in the stand? It's strung for someone who plays left-handed. Check out her gun belt on the back of the kitchen chair. Her holster's on the left side. She was left-handed. Not sure what your dominant hand is, but I'm right-handed. If I were going to put a gun to my head, I'd use my dominant hand."

Cage's eyes locked onto Kirby's. "Whatever you need, you got it. If you're right, we need to find out who did this—and fast."

"We'll grab her cell and laptop to see what's there," Kirby said.

"But let's start with the usual suspects. Did she have a boyfriend? Girlfriend? Significant other?"

"Rumor was she was dating Carter Braxton."

"Wait. Carter Braxton? As in Senator Clayton Braxton and—" He managed to stop himself before he said, "Catherine the Great,"a derisive moniker sometimes used for Senator Braxton's wife because of her haughty demeanor. "Catherine Braxton's son?" he finished.

"The one and only."

Fuck, Kirby thought. Senator Braxton was not only a U.S. Senator but rumored to have Presidential ambitions. Sniffing around his kid had the potential to end careers fast. "You know anything about him—the kid, not the father? Everyone knows the father—and the mother," he added.

"Just what was on the news when the kid was growing up. The parents paraded him around all over the place—baseball games, political events—the kid looked like he was a prop in his father's political career. Haven't seen much of him in five years or so. You going to pay him a visit?"

Kirby gave him an are-you-shitting-me? look.

"I don't envy you that one," Cage said.

"Nice neighborhood," Mace offered as Kirby rolled up in front of Braxton's townhouse in the trendy Riverview section of Brunswick.

"Yep. You can live here too; all you need is a couple million bucks," Kirby replied. "Anything from the ME?"

Mace glanced at his phone. "She's heading in to start the autopsy."

"Okay. Let's go," Kirby said, looking at his watch to record the time for his report—7:15 hours.

They climbed the five steps to the solid mahogany door, took out their credentials, rang the doorbell, and waited.

The door swung open, and there, framed in the doorway, was Carter Braxton. If you looked up "preppy" in the dictionary, his picture would be there. He was about six foot with sandy hair. His face was ruggedly handsome, and he looked like he could still play lacrosse at Georgetown, where he had starred as an undergraduate. He was dressed in a white button-down shirt, khaki pants, and brown dress loafers.

"Can I help you?" he asked.

"Mr. Braxton, I'm Detective Sergeant Max Kirby, and this is Detective George Mace from the Clay County District Attorney's Office. May we have a word with you?"

"What's this about, Detective?"

"May we come in, Mr. Braxton?"

"Not until you tell me what this is about."

Kirby allowed his face to morph into an are-we-really-going-to-play-this-game? expression but had little choice except to play along. "Do you know Police Officer Christine Madison?"

Braxton looked puzzled. "Sure. I know Christine. Why? Is she okay?"

"No sir, she's not. That's why we'd like to come in and talk to you."

Braxton hesitated, then stepped aside to allow Kirby and Mace into the foyer. As soon as they did, Kirby noticed a suitcase in the hallway.

"What do you mean Christine isn't okay? What happened? Where is she?"

"When was the last time you saw her?" Kirby asked.

"Yesterday. We had dinner together." Braxton's tone shifted. "Detective, what the hell is going on? Is she hurt?"

Kirby inhaled. He didn't know yet if Braxton had anything to do with Madison's murder, but if he didn't, this was going to be a gut punch. "Mr. Braxton, I'm sorry to have to tell you this, but Christine is dead," he said, consciously avoiding how she died.

Braxton's eyes went wide. "What? Dead? No! No, that can't be." He staggered backward a few steps; his face suddenly ashen. "I . . ."

Kirby watched him, well aware that some of the best murderers were also the best actors. "Would you like to sit down, Mr. Braxton?"

Braxton moved a few steps down the hallway and turned to his right, passing through the open French doors into the living room, making his way to a black leather sofa, and dropped onto it.

"I noticed your suitcase in the hallway, are you leaving town?" Kirby asked, not trying to mask the implications in his question.

When Braxton looked up, Kirby saw anger in his eyes, barely shrouded by the moisture welling in the corners. "Yes, Detective. I'm flying to L.A. at 10 a.m. for a business trip. But that isn't important right now. What's important is Christine." He sighed. "What happened? How did she . . ." He stopped, seemingly unable to utter the word "die."

"Where and when did you have dinner together?" Kirby asked, ignoring Braxton's question.

Braxton's shoulders slumped. "Her house—around 5:30 p.m. We ate early because she was working the overnight last night."

"What time did you leave?"

"Around 7:30 p.m."

"How was she when you left?"

Braxton hesitated, and it appeared to Kirby that he was trying to gauge what they already knew. "She was pretty upset," Braxton finally got out.

"Why?"

Braxton squeezed his eyes shut as if trying to block out a painful image. "Because we had an argument and broke up last night."

"I'm sorry," Kirby said reflexively, his years in Homicide having robbed him of any real empathy for murder suspects.

"How long have you and Christine been together?" Kirby asked.

"About two years," Braxton replied.

Before Kirby could move on, Mace nudged him and handed him his phone, an email from the ME open on the display: "Doing the autopsy now. No gunshot residue on decedent's hands, indicating that the shot may not have been self-inflicted. Also thought you should know that the preliminary findings indicate decedent was likely transgender. Will update when I have more—Kaufman."

Kirby reread the email, processing the information. He had already figured out Madison had been murdered, but her being transgender was a surprise. Even though he knew being trans could get you killed, it didn't generally happen to someone like Madison—white, a cop and, from what Kirby could tell, not out to anyone. *Even being invisible hadn't saved her*, he thought ruefully.

Kirby waited a beat making sure he showed no reaction, before handing the phone back to Mace, giving him a slight nod, hoping the gesture would keep Braxton guessing as to what they knew. "Why'd you end the relationship?" Kirby asked, now wondering if Madison being trans was the reason.

Braxton's glare foreshadowed his response. "That's personal."

"Mr. Braxton, not to be rude, but Christine is dead. There's nothing personal anymore." *Especially not now*, he thought.

Braxton's stare remained defiant. "You never answered my question, Detective. How did Christine die?"

"Probably suicide," Kirby lied.

"Ah, fuck," Braxton muttered to himself, leaning forward and burying his face in his hands.

Kirby watched, taking in Braxton's reaction. He waited a while before asking, "Where'd you go after you left her place last night?"

Braxton slowly lifted his head from his cupped hands. "What?"

"Where were you around eleven last night?"

"Here. Packing. Why? You just told me she killed herself."

"I said it was probably suicide."

"Wait. Are you saying there's a possibility someone killed her?" Braxton rose from the sofa, his eyes wide. "What's going on, Detective? What happened to Christine?"

"It's under investigation," Kirby replied. "Based on that, I'd suggest you not leave town," he added.

Braxton's eyes narrowed. "It's time for you to go, Detective. As much as I don't want to, I have a flight to catch. When I get back, maybe you'll be honest with me about what happened to Christine."

"When will that be, Mr. Braxton?" Kirby asked.

"Friday," Braxton snapped.

"See you then," Kirby said, turning toward the door, before stopping and facing Braxton. "By the way, do you have contact information for her next of kin?"

"No."

"You know if she has any family?"

Kirby watched as Braxton's scowl faded a bit. "She told me she was from Illinois, and her parents had divorced when she was twelve. She and her mom had been close, but her mom died shortly after Christine graduated high school. She said she hadn't seen or talked to her family since she moved here about fifteen years ago."

"You know why she had no contact with her family?" Kirby asked.

"No," Braxton said, walking around them. "Have a nice day, Detective," he added, opening the front door.

When they were back in the car, Kirby glanced at the BMW sitting in the driveway. "Run the plates on the Beemer," he said to Mace. "See if it shows up on any surveillance videos near Madison's house. Also, find out what flight Braxton's on and ask LAPD to keep tabs on him. Given who his father is, I don't think he's a runner. But if I'm wrong, I want him stopped before he disappears."

—m— —m— —m—

Dr. Leena Kaufman flipped the file on the table and slipped into a chair opposite Kirby and Mace. "What do you have for us, Doc?" Kirby asked.

"We've only had the case for three days, but it's certainly suspicious. No GSR on her hands or arms. According to forensics, there's some back spatter, but not as much as they'd expect from a contact gunshot wound to the head."

"Meaning someone holding a gun to her head may have been hit with the blood and tissue?"

"Exactly. There's one other piece," Kaufman continued. "It's too early to make a definitive conclusion, but based on a quick urine analysis, the GHB in her system is higher than I'd expect to find based on endogenous concentrations."

Kirby's head snapped back. "Are you saying she was drugged?"

"Like I said, Max. I can't say for certain until I get the full toxicological screening back, but based on what I've seen so far, yeah, I'd say that's the likely result."

"Fuck," Kirby mumbled. "If she was, Carter Braxton has a lot of explaining to do."

"What about the fact that you think she was a dude?" Mace asked.

Kirby shot him an exasperated look. "Jesus, Mace, get your head out of your ass. She wasn't a fucking dude." *No wonder she wasn't out,* Kirby thought. *This is the stupidity she would've had to deal with every day.*

Kaufman nodded. "Max is right. She was a transgender woman."

"Would someone dating her have known she was transgender?" Kirby asked.

"Not necessarily. The autopsy revealed evidence of gender-affirming surgeries," Kaufman replied. "In her case, that included a vaginoplasty."

"Vaginoplasty?" Mace repeated, the scrunch of his face betraying his confusion.

"Yes," Kaufman replied. "It's a procedure that some transgender women undergo to create a vulva and vagina from the scrotum and penis."

Mace winced. "Ah, fuck," he muttered.

Kirby sighed. "For crying out loud, Mace. Stop the bullshit. You're not in middle school anymore."

"Any signs of sexual assault?" Kirby asked, changing the subject.

"No. Also, no evidence of any physical assault."

"How long before you have the tox report?" Kirby inquired.

"I can put a rush on it, but it'll still take around four weeks."

"Thanks, Doc," Kirby said, rising from the table. "Let's go," he said to Mace.

"Where?"

"Madison's house. And call the office. I want a crime scene team to meet us there ASAP. The easiest way to administer GHB is in a drink. We need to do another search of her place to see what we can find."

Kirby and Mace hovered in the background as the Investigative Unit dusted the sink, dishwasher, and the two cups and saucers in the dish-drying rack for prints.

"Anything?" Kirby asked impatiently.

"Sorry, Sarge," Detective Simmons said. "The dishwasher had been run. The dishes in the rack were clean, and nothing on the sink or faucet. The place is clean. Actually, looks like it was scrubbed."

"Shit," Kirby muttered to himself. He crouched down and opened the cabinet under the sink with his gloved hand and peered inside, unsure what he was looking for. There was a sponge, dish detergent, and soap pods for the dishwasher. The only other item was a pair of dishwashing rubber gloves hung over the *U* in the sink drainpipe.

"Hey Simmons," he suddenly called out.

"Yeah."

"Is it possible to get fingerprints from the inside of rubber gloves?"

"What are you talking about, Sarge?"

"There," Kirby said, pointing to the rubber gloves. "Suppose someone put those on to wash those cups and saucers in the dish rack and clean up—maybe even hold a gun. Could they have left their fingerprints inside the gloves, or even on the outside?"

Simmons crouched down next to Kirby to get a look at the gloves. "Yeah. It might be possible."

"Good. Take some photos, bag 'em, and let's see if you can find some prints either in or on them," Kirby said.

—⁂— —⁂— —⁂—

A week later, Mace sat across the desk from Kirby. "We ran diagnostics on Madison's phone, which shows two weeks before she was murdered, she received a text from a number that comes back to a prepaid phone. The text attached a DNA report from a company called Heritage.com, showing her sex as male, with a message, 'we need to talk mr madison.' I was able to get Assistant DA Brennan to authorize a subpoena to Heritage, and the answer to who ordered the report is C. Braxton. Paid for with a gift card."

"Continue," Kirby said, his curiosity piqued.

"Based on the Heritage report, his fingerprints being in her apartment and his description of them having an argument, we were able to secure a warrant for Braxton's cell phone records," Mace offered. "Cell tower information is consistent with him leaving her place around 7:30 p.m. Then, at 8:30, he sends a text to his parents saying, 'well, you should be happy just broke up with Christine.'"

"Sounds like mom and dad weren't fans of Christine. Anything else?" Kirby prompted.

"He tried to call her twice and then sent a text to her at 9:42 p.m. saying he loved her and was sorry. She replied, 'we need to talk but not tonight.' The cell tower shows his phone stationary the rest of the night. The diagnostics on Madison's phone confirm the two missed calls and the text exchange, but there's also a call at 9:46 that lasted two minutes from the same prepaid phone as the message with the DNA report."

Kirby stroked his chin. "Shit. Based on what Simmons came up with on the gloves, everything fits."

"Yeah, but . . ."

"I know," Kirby interrupted, well aware that, based on what they had, the DA would never authorize moving forward against a member of the Braxton family. "We need more," he said, drawing in a deep breath. "Let's go pay Mr. Braxton a visit and see if we can get what we need."

"Thanks for agreeing to see us," Kirby said as he and Mace followed Braxton into his living room. "I'm sure it's been a tough week since you got back from L.A., what with the wake and funeral."

Braxton nodded. "It has. But you said you have some leads. What can you tell me?"

"Actually, Mr. Braxton, we'd like to ask you a few questions first," Kirby said.

"Like what?" Braxton asked, the reluctance evident in his tone.

"Did you know that Christine was transgender?" Kirby asked.

Braxton's eyes narrowed. "Transgender? What are you talking about? She never said anything about wanting to be a guy."

"Umm, that's not exactly what I mean, Mr. Braxton," Kirby said before explaining the ME's findings concerning Christine's transition and gender-affirming surgeries, leaving Braxton staring at the floor, avoiding Kirby's probing gaze.

"When we spoke to you two weeks ago, you said you and Christine argued the night she was murdered. We need to know what you argued about."

Braxton looked up at Kirby, cupped his hands, and covered his mouth. "Kids," he whispered.

"Kids?" Kirby repeated, sounding surprised.

"Yeah, a family. We had talked several times about getting married, but we had a fundamental disagreement over having children—I wanted a family; she didn't. Over dinner that night, I raised the fact that we were both thirty-five and that we should get married and start a family. I ... I didn't know ... you know, the transgender thing. I said something about her biological clock ticking, and she got really upset, telling me if that's why I wanted to marry her—to have kids—we should just end it. So, I did." He looked up, tears streaming down his cheeks. "I wish she had told me."

"You said you left around 7:30 p.m. Did you talk to her afterward?" Kirby asked, knowing what he hoped to hear.

Braxton wiped away a tear. "Talk? No. But we did text."

"When?" Kirby inquired.

"Around 9:30. I felt bad—I mean the way I had left. I tried to call her, but she didn't answer, so I texted her and told her I loved her and was sorry." He looked up at Kirby. "She texted back that we needed to talk, but not then. Those were her last words to me."

"Did your parents know you were thinking about marrying Christine?"

"Yeah. I had talked to them about it," Braxton replied.

"How'd your parents feel about Christine?"

Braxton grimaced. "They didn't like her."

"Why?"

"They thought she was beneath me—you know, me being Georgetown and in finance and her being a cop with only a high school education. The last time Christine and I had dinner at my parents' house, my mother was so condescending toward her that it got really awkward."

"When was that dinner?"

"About a month ago."

"You told us that you didn't know anything about her family. Do I have that right?" Kirby said.

"Yeah."

"You ever check her background on Heritage.com or any of those sites?"

"No. Why would I do that?"

"I don't know. Maybe because you were thinking of getting married and wanted to know more about her—especially if you wanted a family with her," Kirby suggested.

"No, Detective. I loved her. Her family didn't matter."

"What about the fact that she was transgender? Did that matter?"

Braxton glared at Kirby, his face showing a mixture of anger and pain. "Listen, Detective. I didn't know Christine was transgender until you told me five minutes ago. Would it have made a difference? I hope not. But who knows? Just like everybody else, I can be an asshole sometimes and swayed by what other people think. But I'll never know, will I?" He paused. "Because someone fucking killed her," he said, emphasizing each word.

Kirby waited, giving Braxton time for his rage to cool. "One last thing," he finally said, laying two pictures on the coffee table. "Do you recognize these?"

Braxton leaned over and studied the photos. "They look like the rubber gloves that Christine used when she washed the dishes."

"Does your mother have gloves similar to these?"

"My mother?" Braxton snorted. "Detective, you obviously don't know my mother. I'm not sure she's ever washed a dish in her life. So, I think it's a safe bet that she doesn't own any rubber dish gloves."

—⁓— —⁓— —⁓—

Three weeks later, as Kirby testified at the probable cause hearing, he kept one eye on Assistant DA Brennan and the other on Braxton, watching Braxton's reaction.

"And did any surveillance tapes from the night of the murder show any vehicles parked near Christine Madison's home around 11 p.m.?" Brennan asked.

"Yes, sir. A 2023 black BMW, similar to one registered to the suspect."

"And did the search of the suspect's residence uncover any evidence?"

"Yes, sir. A prepaid disposable phone was recovered, along with a copy of a Heritage.com DNA report run on Ms. Madison."

"Does the report show who ordered it?"

"Yes, sir. C. Braxton," Kirby answered.

"And were there any fingerprints belonging to the suspect discovered in Ms. Madison's home?"

"Yes, sir. Inside a pair of rubber gloves used to wash dishes."

"And where were those gloves located?"

"In a cabinet under the kitchen sink in Ms. Madison's home."

"And all this has led you to conclude there is probable cause to believe that after discovering what was in the Heritage report, the suspect, Catherine Braxton, went to Ms. Madison's home, placed GHB in a cup of coffee, incapacitating the victim, and then shot the victim with her service weapon to make it look like a suicide. Do I have that correct?"

"You do," Kirby replied, shifting his gaze to Catherine Braxton, sitting beside her lawyer.

After Kirby's testimony, Brennan placed everything Kirby had described into evidence. Judge Gibney quickly ruled there was probable cause to charge Catherine Braxton with murder and set bail at a million dollars.

Kirby watched as two corrections officers handcuffed her and led her out of the courtroom. *She'll be bailed out before I get home for dinner,* he thought. Kirby shook his head. In this political climate, no trans person was safe. Just as troubling was the possibility that she'd walk by claiming temporary insanity. Based on her lawyer's cross-examination,

Kirby could already see that her defense would be that she'd panicked when she learned the woman her son was dating was transgender, convinced that if the truth came out, it would ruin her son's life, even if Kirby suspected it had more to do with protecting her husband's political reputation.

When Kirby walked outside the courtroom, a gaggle of reporters had microphones shoved in Carter's face. Kirby paused to listen and was heartened when Carter told them that it didn't matter to him that Christine was trans; he loved her. *Interesting. Maybe there was still reason to hope*, Kirby thought, heading for home, and the Ruger locked in the gun case.

Maxine stood in front of the mirror, adjusting her wig and smoothing her dress, unimpressed by the image reflected back at her. Like many women, she longed to be more attractive, but try as she might, she still looked like a guy in drag. There weren't any foundation garments that could disguise her former linebacker's body or makeup that would soften her rough facial features. But despite that, Maxine Kirby knew she was just as much a woman as Christine Madison had been. Looks couldn't change that. Max had discovered long ago that looks were ephemeral; being trans was not.

She walked over to the framed, autographed front page of the *New York Daily News* from December 1, 1952—"Ex-GI Becomes Blonde Beauty,"—the headline proclaimed. *You were a beautiful woman,* Maxine thought, looking at the photos of Christine Jorgensen underneath the headline. *And you were accepted. How times have changed.* Then Maxine remembered something they had discovered during the investigation—a journal recovered from Madison's bedroom. In it, Madison disclosed she had chosen the name Christine in honor of Christine Jorgensen because, when Madison was twelve, she had found a copy of Jorgensen's autobiography in the library. Madison had taken the book home to her mom to read, and that helped convince her mother to take Christine for the gender-affirming care she desperately wanted.

Maxine returned to the mirror, gazing at her image. Ironic, she thought, how Madison had remained invisible because she blended into cisgender society, while she had stayed invisible for the opposite reason—she didn't blend in. No, she wasn't like Jorgensen. She'd probably never come out of the closet. But for now, surviving would be her own act of defiance against a world that increasingly seemed to hate her, and all trans folks, simply for existing. Somehow, solving Madison's murder had given her time to pull herself back from the abyss. She brushed a strand of hair from the wig out of her eye. *Just do the best you can—live!*

BUY THAT WOMAN A BEER

BAXTER CLARE TRAUTMAN

"Frank."

"Gomez."

The two women smiled and shook hands. In unison they stared out over the dry wash at the man dangling from a lone valley oak.

"You're sure he's dead?" Gomez asked.

Frank nodded. "Plenty dead. Looks like he's been there since last night. Cup a coffee?"

She pulled a Thermos from the truck cab.

Gomez stepped away from her squad car. "If you have extra."

Frank poured into the Thermos cup and splashed some into her own travel mug. The women leaned against the Tacoma, eyes back on the motionless body.

"What brings you out here? Not your jurisdiction, is it?"

"Nah, but Monterey Sheriff's got some rookies on the loose. I've met two males so far that didn't leave a great impression. And one female. She seemed smart enough, but gosh, pretty soft. We should place bets on how long she'll last. Anyway, she's responding—soft, but I've heard good things about her—never met her. I figured with it quiet this morning I'd come out and see for myself and offer a hand if she needs it. Heard she's part Latina, part Native American from one of the tribes around here." Gomez waved a hand at the sharp peaks looming west, the mountain bulwark that kept the Pacific Ocean from drowning the Salinas Valley.

"Damn. Monterey County Sheriff's all over their DEI program."

"From what I hear she wasn't a DEI hire as much as head of her class. Her name's D'Red, and of course 'cause she's part Native American they're already calling her The Red."

Frank smiled. "Back in the day I was the only female street cop in my division. Queer to boot. They called me Le Freak, after the Chic song. Remember?"

Badly off-key Gomez sang, "Le Freak, c'est chic."

"That's it. But I did my job, did it damn well, and always gave as good as I got. They keep trying to legislate respect but out on the street the only way to get it is to earn it. You know that."

"*Orale*, sister. I hear ya."

They sipped their coffee and stared at the half-naked body.

"What about you?" Gomez asked. "What brings you down off the mountain so early?"

"Grocery day. Library run. Got a stack of overdue books." Frank indicated the pile on the passenger seat. Gomez glanced at it.

"Anything good?"

"Oh, wow, lots. I was so focused on work my whole life I never took time to read any of the gay lit pioneers. People like Katherine Forrest. Lee Lynch. Joseph Hansen. May Sarton. Forster. Rita Mae Brown. So many gutsy writers. It was all such pivotal stuff. They were out there, getting beat up and locked up. They were plenty brave, back when it wasn't nearly as acceptable to be queer. They paved the way for people like me."

"Huh." Gomez squirmed and changed the subject. Tilting her chin at the sedan parked on the opposite shoulder of the country road, she asked, "That his?"

A Monterey County Sheriff patrol vehicle pulled up behind Gomez's car.

"Yeah. His wallet's sitting out in plain view and the car looks tossed. But the funny thing is, his license, all his cards, they're still neatly in the wallet."

"You looked," Gomez scolded.

Frank made a helpless gesture as they turned to watch an angular, honey-skinned young woman in a tan uniform unfold herself from behind the wheel of the patrol car. She adjusted her ball cap, locked up, and strode toward them.

Gomez extended her hand and introduced herself. Then said, "This is Lieu—er, Frank. She's the one called it in."

She'd lost an inch or so since her prime, but Frank was still used to looking down at most females and it was awkward to be looking up into the taller woman's dark gaze.

"Ma'am," D'Red said in a low, barely audible voice. Letting Frank's hand go she swept her gaze over the cars on the shoulder of the quiet country road, the wide sandy wash, the body beyond. Pulling her duty pad from a pocket she ascertained, as Gomez had, that the man was indeed dead, then thoroughly questioned Frank.

When she asked how Frank had happened to find him, Frank motioned her into the empty roadway.

"I stopped next to the car to see if someone needed help. Reception's pretty spotty out here. I looked through the window and if you take a look, you can see the body from here."

The cop did just that, bending and peering through the driver's window. Apparently satisfied she straightened and made a note. Then she glanced at her cell phone, stuck it back in her pocket, and made another entry. Probably verifying there was reception, Frank thought, impressed.

She bent and looked through the window again.

"You have good eyesight," she told Frank.

Frank shrugged. She'd gotten used to taking in the landscape; the crows and ravens on the fenceposts as she drove down from the ranch, the hawks and vultures waiting on oak limbs to ride the thermals. She almost always spotted deer browsing in the scrubby chaparral and this morning she'd rounded a bend to see three coyotes running across a lower pasture. An adult male dangling from a tree was definitely something she'd notice.

Finished with Frank, D'Red slowly turned her attention to the gray sedan. The kid was quiet and calm, but if she was anything like Frank had been at her first homicide, her mind was scrambling, frantically pouring through procedurals, manuals, protocols, in a desperate effort to not make mistakes that would compromise the investigation.

She asked Gomez hopefully, "Any idea who this is? A local?"

"No one I know."

D'Red nodded stoically. She walked back to her car to return with a clipboard and roll of crime scene tape.

Gomez asked, "Did the coroner give an ETA?"

"They're finishing another call. They said they'd be here next."

D'Red led the way across the empty road and glanced inside the car, hands on her knees. She asked Frank if she'd touched anything.

She raised her hands, palms up. "Nope."

She and Gomez shared a grin while D'Red slid into a pair of gloves. Gingerly pulling the license from the wallet she muttered the name, glancing again at Gomez, who shook her head. She studied the interior of the car a long silent minute while until Gomez asked if she could help her stretch out the tape.

Frank lounged back against the Tacoma, happy to gaze at the dark peaks brooding beyond the road, her cabin somewhere up in there. She'd thought when she'd moved into the wild heart of the Big Sur mountains that she'd be done with death but apparently it wasn't done with her. At least she didn't have to clean up after it anymore.

"Okay," D'Red said. "Let's go have a look. Which way did you go in?" she asked Frank.

Giving the kid credit for wanting to minimize impact to the scene, Frank swallowed the dregs of her coffee and pointed up the road a little.

"Ma'am," she told Frank. "You're free to go. I have your contact information if I need to get ahold of you."

"Are you kidding? I wouldn't miss this for the world."

The sheriff started to protest but Gomez said, "It's okay, Deputy. She's with me. She's old LE."

D'Red looked doubtful but deferred to Gomez.

As they walked single file down the bank, D'Red carefully leading the way over Frank's prints, Frank complained to Gomez, "You didn't have to say *old* law enforcement."

"I call 'em the way I see 'em."

"Thanks," Frank grumbled.

Gomez chuckled and behind her Frank grinned. She'd always liked Gomez exactly for that reason. No bullshit, and though the cop went pretty much by the book, she would occasionally bend the rules for common sense. D'Red followed Frank's circuitous route to the oak tree. Frank and Gomez maintained a respectful distance.

The morning was still, the sun freshly risen. Soon the day would be hot. Already flies had found the easy meal on the man's carved chest. One bumped lazily into Frank's forehead, and she waved it away, equally languid. The three women considered the body.

"Gonna be a bitch to get him down," Gomez said.

Frank nodded cheerful agreement, glad to be a spectator.

Gomez spelled out the smeared letters cut across his breasts. "S? Looks like a V. And . . . L. SVL?"

"Soledad Vatos Locos?" Frank guessed.

"I guess you're not so isolated up in the boonies after all."

"Well, you know, *old* LE and all that."

Gomez's grin turned into a frown as she looked back at the corpse. "What's a white guy done to get strung up by the SVL?"

As she asked that another Sheriff's car came down the road and parked behind the sedan. Frank thought it might be the coroner, but Gomez, said, "Uh, oh," quietly enough that D'Red didn't hear. "I think that's one of the numbskulls I was telling you about."

When D'Red saw who it was she stiffened, getting even taller than she already was. The newcomer started down the bank straight toward them, but D'Red startled Frank, shouting, "Hey! You're contaminating the scene!"

She waved her hand to the right and yelled, "Follow our prints!"

"Where are they?" he yelled back.

"Jesus," Frank murmured. "I see what you mean."

D'Red waved again. "That little coyote bush! To your left!"

"What? What the hell's a coyote bush?"

They could hear D'Red grind her teeth. "It's the only bush there! To your left."

He spotted the plant and started to clamber down in a rush of rocks and loose dirt. D'Red turned back to the body, jaw jumping, fists knotted.

The beefy meat-and-potatoes young deputy joined them, not bothering to introduce himself to the two older women.

"What you got, Big Red? I heard you got a body," he answered himself. "I came to help you."

"I'm good," she said through clenched teeth. "I got it."

"You sure? Looks like the poor son of a bitch pissed off the wrong people."

He started to brush past D'Red, but she shot out an arm.

"Greaves," she growled, "back up. You're contaminating the scene. Again."

"Oh. Yeah." Greaves took a step back. "Well, whatever happened to the poor bastard, he must have fought back before they taped his hands together. See? He's got a bruise there on his forehead, and it looks like defense cuts on his arms." The young sheriff pointed to the sand beneath the tree. "You can see where it's disturbed there, where he would have struggled."

Frank couldn't say definitively from where she was standing, but it appeared there were only her footprints and one type of smooth footprint, which looked like it might match the victim's dangling loafers. The soles were worn almost through. The vic was thin but not muscled. He showed none of the portliness of your average fifty-year-old white guy. She noticed that even though his car had been tossed, he wore a gold wedding band. She considered a couple of other things, then let her gaze return to the mountains.

Greaves was still yammering, pointing things out to D'Red who ignored him. Frank shook her head. It didn't seem like much had changed in forty years, what with some man still needing to man-splain things to a woman who probably understood them far better than he did.

D'Red stepped carefully around the scene, writing notes. Gomez moved back next to Frank, shaking her head at the mutilated body. She murmured, "You thinking what I'm thinking about this?"

"Probably."

Greaves heckled, "I'm not sure why you're making such a big deal outta this, Red. I mean, look around, man. It seems pretty obvious. I don't know why you're wasting so much time on a guy who clearly got lifted by some bangers."

Frank muttered, "How'd this kid even get out of the Academy?"

"I think this is the one who's daddy's a congressman up in Lassen County."

"Hm. Daddy probably had the good sense to ship him out of his district."

Gomez nodded. "Probably knew someone somewhere."

"Alright, you know what? Daylight's wasting and I want to get into town before it gets too hot. You gotta maintain cordial relations with these kids but I don't."

Frank called, "Deputy D'Red. What are you seeing here?"

"Ma'am?"

"Your colleague here seems to think this is a slam dunk murder and all you've got to do is find the bangers that did this."

Greaves nodded and crossed his arms triumphantly. "Yep. Seems pretty obvious."

"What do you think, Deputy D'Red? Is it obvious to you?"

D'Red squinted up into the oak. "For starters, that knot bothers me. Someone climbed up there and made it."

"And why's that bother you?"

"If I was struggling to hold a man against his will, I wouldn't bother climbing up a tree to tie a knot. I'd throw the rope over and make a slip knot so I wouldn't have to let him go."

"Hell, Red, he's all trussed up like a Christmas turkey. Where's he gonna go?" Greaves smirked and rolled his eyes. "Besides, there was probably plenty of guys holding him and one of the little beaners just shimmied up the tree and tied it off. Simple as a dimple."

Out of the corner of her eye Frank saw Gomez bite the inside of her lip, glaring at the beaner remark.

"Kid," Frank said. "What's your name?"

"Greaves." He pointed proudly at his name tag. "Says so right there."

"Greaves, how many different sets of prints you see around this tree?"

"Well, there's leaves and such, so I'd have to get closer to be sure, but this is D'Red's scene, and I don't want to interfere with it."

"Commendable," Frank said. "Gomez, how many you see around here?"

"Who me?" she asked innocently. "This little old beaner?"

It was Frank's turn to smirk.

Gomez stepped to where D'Red stood. "I'm seeing your prints here." She pointed out Frank's. "And what I'm assuming look like the vics smooth soled shoes. But other than that, it doesn't look like there were a whole lot of men here."

"D'Red what else?"

"Working my way down the tree, I'd like to see if there would be any fibers that match his pant material. See there?" She pointed to his khaki clad rump. It looks like bark. I wonder if that'd match the tree or not. If it did, it might mean he was sitting up there." She indicated the stout limb that held the rope. "He might have jumped."

"What?" Greaves jeered. "You're thinking he's a suicide?"

Playing Devil's advocate, Frank argued maybe they forced him up there. "Maybe they held a gun on him, made him climb up and jump."

D'Red nodded grudgingly. "Maybe."

The oak was still bare from winter, just starting to sprout new green leaves. Indicating the dry yellow grasses and carpet of old oak leaves, she explained, "Some of the grass stalks are broken, but a lot aren't. There are places where the leaves are scuffed around, but looking at the sand around where it's bare, I'm not seeing any other prints. A better search might turn some up but I'm not seeing any in the immediate vicinity so who are all these people, other bangers or even one banger, that forced him up there?"

Greaves interjected. "You can see where he tried to fight. He's got a knot on his forehead."

D'Red agreed, peering closer at the bruise. "But it looks like there's …" she leaned in, trying to stay as far back from the immediate scene as she could. Frank silently applauded her caution.

"What is it?" Gomez asked.

"It looks like bark."

"See? He hit his head on the tree while he was struggling," Greaves said.

"But he doesn't have any scratches or scrapes," D'Red observed. "How'd he fall hard enough against the tree to get a bump like that on his head but not leave any other marks?" Then it dawned on her, "Almost like he deliberately hit his head, to make it look —"

"Aw come on, man, it's—"

Frank held up a hand. "Hold on, kid. What was your name again?"

"Greaves." He pounded under his tag with two fingers. "See? Right here. It says Greaves."

"Greaves," Frank agreed. "Greaves, indeed, sorry. I don't have my glasses on. Anyway, what else, D'Red?"

"Other than the ligature marks, it doesn't look like there's any trauma or defensive injuries to his neck. I think it would be hard to hang a grown man without a lot of struggle. Unless he was drugged, maybe. But then I'd expect more shuffling, more scuff marks. I guess it's possible they could have brought him down here with the rope already around his neck, maybe drugged up, but again, I'm not seeing the prints or disturbed ground to support that."

Greaves countered, "What about those cuts on his arm? They look like defense wounds to me."

"Maybe," D'Red allowed. "But they're very shallow. It doesn't look like they bled much. And they're all on his left hand but none on his right."

"What's that say to you?" Frank pushed.

D'Red thought. "His attacker was on his left and he lifted that arm to shield himself, or—"

"—or maybe he was right-handed and cut himself," Greaves interrupted proudly.

Frank grinned. "What can you tell me about the cuts on his chest?" Both Greaves and D'Red leaned in for a better view.

Greaves noticed first. "They're deeper on the left side than the right."

"What's that tell you?"

Greaves guessed, "The cutter was left-handed?"

"Not likely. Ninety percent of the population is right-handed."

D'Red supplied, "If he was right-handed, he'd probably cut on his left side first. But it hurt so the letters get shallower as he cut to the right?"

Frank nodded. "Possible. And see how his left wrist is taped really tight? The right one not as much, and both together aren't tight at all."

Again, Greaves earned brownie points, asking, "Why would someone trying to subdue him tape his hands individually? That doesn't make sense."

"It doesn't," Frank agreed. "You might find tape residue on his mouth where he tore it from the roll."

Gomez chimed in, "What about his car?"

They all looked across the wash toward the sedan.

D'Red mused, "If I was going to hang someone, I'd bring them in my own car, where I'd feel more comfortable securing them, and driving. And I'd know what was in my own car, where everything was, what it did and didn't have in it that I might need. Why would anyone bring him here in his own car?"

"Maybe his wife did it," Greaves exclaimed. "It was a murder *staged* to look like a suicide." The women ignored him as D'Red continued musing aloud.

"His car was tossed but he still had all his credit cards, his license, all still in his wallet. And he still has his wedding ring on," she said, spinning to check the gold band. "So maybe he wanted it to look like a robbery gone bad? But why would anyone randomly pull him over to rob him, not take anything, then drag him all the way down here to hang him?"

"The wife," Greaves said again. "She lures him down here, says there's going to be a little hanky-panky under a romantic full moon, then she gets him up the tree at gunpoint, makes him jump, then messes up the car."

"Goddamn, Greaves. If I hadn't been at the Academy with you, I'd have sworn you'd never been."

"What? It's possible."

"Occam's razor. Remember, the simplest answer is usually the right answer."

"Yeah, okay." Greaves shrugged. "But if someone had a beef with him, they'd have grabbed him somewhere else, bundled him into their own ride, like you said, and brought him here. But why here? Out in the middle of nowhere but right on a road where anyone could have seen them? You're right," he told D'Red. "That dog don't hunt."

Gomez and Frank shared a smile.

Frank pointed above the body, where the thick limb met the trunk. "I'll bet my pension you find a roll of duct tape up there."

"Huh," Greaves marveled. "So, he staged his own suicide."

"You don't know that yet but it's certainly plausible." She advised D'Red, "Look into his financials, his life insurance, state of mind. All that good stuff. See if you can't figure out where the rope came from, the tape when you find it. See if it ties back to him or not."

D'Red nodded, scratching in her notebook.

Greaves was looking up into the tree. "The closest branch is way over my head. I don't know if I could reach it even if I jumped. And I'm in way better shape than that guy was. How the hell did he get up there?"

Frank grinned. "Aw, come on now, I gotta let you have some of the fun."

"And where's the knife?" Greaves scanned the ground but D'Red had turned to look back at the sedan.

Smiling behind her hand, Gomez mumbled, "That boy's a piece of work. Just goes to show, it ain't what you know it's who you know."

"Did you know anyone, Gomez?"

"No ma'am. You?"

"Nope. Had a helluva rabbi, though."

Watching Greaves circle the tree like a hound dog, Frank remembered her mentor, the guardian angel who'd taken her under his wing. She wondered how far she'd have gotten without him.

Frank sighed. "I reckon we were both pretty stupid a long time ago, yeah?"

Eyeing Greaves, Gomez shook her head. "Not that stupid."

Frank smiled. Taking pity on the kid, she called him over, beckoning with two fingers. He trotted to her.

"Son, why do you want to be a cop?"

"Well, duh. To catch bad guys."

Frank nodded. "You want to get better at doing that or just collect a paycheck and a bigger badge?"

He narrowed his eyes. "What's it to you?"

"Nothing. But your answer's gonna be everything to you."

He twitched a shoulder. "Both, I guess. I wouldn't mind being a chief someday, but I reckon I gotta be good enough to get there."

And good enough to go through D'Red, Frank thought.

"Why would you want to be a chief? They just manage the guys that find the bad guys. You wanna be a manager or a cop?"

"Well," he scratched the back of his neck. "A cop, I guess. I don't think I'd like sitting behind a desk all day. I like being here. Outside."

"Good. That's good. Now, you didn't ask for it but I'm gonna give you a piece of advice anyway. All that stuff you learned in school is great background, but what you really got to do, the most important thing you have to do to be a good cop, is open your eyes. You've gotta learn to see what's *really* in front of you, not what you want to be in front of you. Seeing what you want to see, or expect to see, ain't gonna help you catch the bad guys. It might even get you killed. See D'Red's like you but she keeps her mouth shut and her eyes open. You do the same, kid, and you'll be alright." She cuffed his arm. "Take a page outta her book."

D'Red turned to Frank. "His shirt's in the car. It's balled up in the passenger seat. If someone was forcing him down here, they wouldn't have made him take his shirt off. They wouldn't have cared about his shirt. They probably would have just ripped it off him. He took it off before he came down here."

Frank said quietly to Gomez, "If I were you, I'd poach her ASAP." Then louder, "Always a pleasure, Sergeant."

She lifted a hand at the kids and started back to her truck.

"Hey, wait a minute," Greaves said behind her, and D'Red asked Gomez, "Who the hell is that?"

Gomez chuckled. "That, kids, is Lieutenant LA Franco. Los Angeles Police Department, retired. And you have just had a master class in homicide investigation. If I were you two, I'd buy that woman a beer someday."

NOTES ON HOW TO BE ICONIC

MARCO CAROCARI

Flat on her back on the musty ground and blinking up at the moonless sky, Angelique could already picture the headlines: *Beloved Celebrity's Near-Death Experience*, right next to Sally Ride's trip to space.

Dizzy and sick to her stomach, she could barely process that she was still breathing after her monumental fall from the terrace above. She blinked at lights glimmering from the mansion uphill through a row of trees as sounds of chirping cicadas mixed with distant laughter and music from the party. Elton John proclaimed, "I'm Still Standing"—and so would she, once she caught her breath that the impact had knocked from her lungs.

But for an instant, she forgot about everything: her money troubles, that humiliating party, her extremely dead nemesis whose nosedive from that same terrace had taken a decidedly less ideal turn ...

That old saying about life flashing before your eyes during a brush with death? Totally true.

Like, not while she was flipping through the air like a ragdoll (her mind registered little other than, *oh shit*), but *after* the tree trunk downslope brutally stopped her epic tumble, thinking of people and incidents she'd done her best to bury on her path to fame.

Like the spring of '65, when she was ten and still Chrissie, and her aunt and uncle with their two daughters in Queens took her in after her parents—

Her eyes stung even now, the memory still bitter all these years later.

How many times had she told that story—how they'd dropped her off two days before the tragic news of their fiery car crash broke? How previous, short visits with her relatives had mostly passed without major incidents, but how living under one tight roof 24/7 was an entirely different story?

Suddenly, there had been *sharing* and *being considerate of others* and having to vie for affection that had once come freely. No more clothes from Neiman Marcus but hand-me-downs from her older cousins, Martina and Blythe. Her unsolicited opinions were no longer required or appreciated and frequently resulted in punitive chores like Cinderella's by her evil stepmother.

That's when she decided she'd one day be famous like all those iconic celebrities her mother admired. Someone who mattered. Someone her parents would have been proud of.

Growing up, Chrissie's mother instilled five golden rules in her, handwritten in beautiful, cursive letters on parchment paper she kept on an ivory Tudor desk, titled *"How To Be Iconic."* These rules were pieces of wisdom she'd acquired by emulating her idols Audrey Hepburn, Coco Chanel, and Brigitte Bardot.

She wanted to raise a strong, independent woman, and even at five years old, Chrissie did not disappoint, commanding a room full of people with her wild stories and little performances.

She could still hear her always perfectly coiffed and exquisitely dressed mother's voice stage-whisper, tilting her head with a faraway look as if performing for captive audiences, "No matter what the world throws at you, find your inner strength and *rise above it all.*"

Technically, the last of her rules, Chrissie always said it became the most important during her formative years with the relatives because:

> —*Make Them See You* generally got her accused of grabbing the limelight to overshadow her cousins.
> —*Speak With the Voice of a Rebel* was considered talking out of turn or being petulant, frequently backfiring into her getting grounded.
> —*Create Myths That Influence Culture* got her chided for daydreaming or outright lying (and grounded).
> —And, *Defy Convention* was viewed as being rebellious and ungrateful (and, yep, you get the gist), by which time,

believe you her, it became increasingly damn taxing to *Rise Above Anything*.

She had to toughen up quickly because it was her against the world. Some comfort she found in the tattered old covers of her mother's favorite historical romance novels by Anne Golon about the beautiful heroine Angélique. They were in French, so she couldn't read them, but she remembered her mother, who'd spent two years in France as a young woman, reading to her.

The day she turned nineteen, Chrissie hit the road, hightailing it back to the Big Apple. She'd grown into a fairly pretty young woman despite a bulbous nose and weak lips in desperate need of all that modern makeup could provide.

She'd saved up a few hundred bucks and hocked a pair of diamond earrings, the only heirloom left by her mother, that covered a few months' rent for a small apartment in SoHo.

But little happened in the fame department. With money running out fast, she found herself waiting tables at a diner all day before diving into bellbottoms and flower power shirts and sneaking into CBGB in the Bowery, a grungy Rock bar featuring up-and-coming bands and singers.

And lying on the mossy ground in the darkness, she also remembered fair-skinned, doe-eyed Michael, whom she'd met in January of '76 after he and a few rambunctious but expensively dressed buddies stumbled into the diner one evening. By shift's end, trust fund baby Michael asked for her number, and after a short whirlwind romance—and under stern objections of his conservative parents— they were married in March.

Bliss lasted less than a year on account of his infidelities and her lack of a penis as her beautiful new husband realized—a skosh late— he preferred heavy aftershave on hairy leather bikers to her feminine wiles. Because he wasn't out to his family, Michael agreed to a quick divorce with a hefty settlement that paid for a cute one-bedroom in the Village and allowed her to procure the talents of Dr. Harold Lichtenstein, who retrofitted her with a slim button nose, lush lips, and tits that put Jane Mansfield's to shame.

And her transformation didn't stop there—Chrissie started moving more slowly and seductively, talking in a suggestive, breathy voice, and dyed her mousy brown hair a lush red mane reminiscent of Ann-Margret's.

Voila—Angelique was born, and her new name felt poetically full circle.

Freshly minted back at CBGB (where few people recognized her, which suited her just fine), her anamorphic appearance finally got her the attention she'd craved. She teamed up with a few B- level musicians and even got to belt out a few ditties during off-*off* hours, but her only brush with actual fame came by orbiting Patti Smith or Debby Harry, who performed there over the years.

She realized she had to shoot for bigger and bigger meant Studio 54, the hottest new disco in town, swarming with stars from screen and stage.

Nipples to the wind in outrageous spandex and leotards, she soon rubbed shoulders with fashion designer Halston, Bianca Jagger, Liza Minnelli, Grace Jones, Cher, and Warhol, expertly inserting herself into any available photo-op. Invited or not.

Once, she even ended up on Studio's infamous balcony, where guests eagerly partook in drugs or sex, and she frequently let it slip that she'd serviced Gene Simmons from Kiss there while the crowd below danced to "Love to Love You Baby."

Putting herself front and center and following all her rules got her noticed, sure. But despite becoming a fixture in party culture, nothing translated into money, a career, or anything remotely iconic.

Worse: one pesky suitor whose advances she'd successfully thwarted while using him for all his connections finally kicked her out of his VIP section one night while blaring, "No more freeloading for nobodies" over the thumping disco bass.

Turning on her heel as if she didn't care, she barreled through a sea of half-naked party guests gyrating to hypnotic beats under pulsating neon lights, her eyes burning sharply.

She rushed upstairs and elbowed her way through the crowded burgundy lounge, but she found no refuge in the co-ed bathrooms full of lipstick-wielding, Quaalude-popping starlets and wannabes.

Stumbling back out to the lounge, she caught her reflection in a floor-to-ceiling mirror and was horrified at the upset, out-of-breath raccoon staring back at her. The night was a disaster.

"You're so pretty," a bright, girlish voice behind her yelled over the music, and Angelique tensed—who dared make fun of her?

Jaw tight, she spun around to a young, busty bleach-blonde

holding up a calming hand. "I am so sorry. I didn't mean to scare you," she stammered, her brows crinkling apologetically. Made up like a modern-day Monroe in a tight, sequined silver dress, she seemed genuinely concerned.

But Angelique hated being vulnerable. Especially in front of strangers.

She turned back to fix the warzone on her face only to realize she'd left her clutch behind.

"Here," the blonde said, handing her a tissue from a purse that matched her dress. "You want, I can fix that for you in no time."

Angelique *didn't* want. "Listen—"

"Tanja," the blonde smiled brightly, extending a slim hand. "Tanja Lavonya, and your biggest fan. Gee…this is something," she gushed. "You're my idol. I . . . I have seen you so many times, but I never had the courage to come talk to you. You're just always so . . . so stunningly sexy and . . . graceful."

Well, since she put it that way, Angelique forced a smile as one does for fans and said, "Thank you." Not that she'd ever noticed the girl before.

"Please." Tanja took a tentative step forward, fishing eyeliner and several tiny bottles from her purse. "I swear I'm really quite good at this."

Angelique's instinct was an emphatic no, but Tanja pleaded with hopeful puppy eyes. "Fine, but careful, I have very sensitive—"

She could barely feel Tanja's fingers as they softly and swiftly cleaned the mess before she, with just a few strokes under crappy lighting, made Angelique's eyes pop more dramatically than she'd ever managed herself.

A new alliance was formed, and Angelique felt benevolent for taking a young naive chick under her wings. They laughed, drank, and danced the night away until Studio's mechanical Man in the Moon descended from the ceiling, "snorting" blow from a sparkling silver spoon under its nose.

But trouble soon loomed on the party horizon: within a few months, Tanja more than once dropped Angelique's name to get favors or access to parties where she got drunk, behaved poorly, *and* screwed half the guys there.

Angelique was furious. Sure, she'd flirted, seduced, and dated on both sides of the aisle, but despite her outrageous appearance, she just sold the illusion of sex and, mostly, just promised carnal favors for financial gains (without ever following through). It was called having standards.

The final straw was Tanja giving Angelique—on purpose, she was certain—the wrong time and date for a backup singer audition. Tanja got the job, and their friendship morphed into an icy rivalry that found them at parties circling each other like orcas hunting seals.

Angelique's luck finally changed in early '79. Paul Blaser, a short, stout, and flamboyant Swiss banker, started following her around like a puppy. He made no secret that despite the thin black mustache and snazzy men's attire, he was technically still Paula, born some fifty years earlier in Zurich.

Angelique didn't care. Paul treated her like royalty and even moved her to a swanky penthouse on Park Avenue. Friendly and jovial, he wasn't much to look at, but she grew to care about him deeply, grateful he didn't ask much in return.

Around the same time, Bernie Feldbaum, a paunchy, unassuming man who resembled Truman Capote and knew virtually everyone, became her agent. It was his idea to buy billboards across town asking, "Who is Angelique?" above her half-naked, lounging figure on massive ads south of Times Square.

To the many who wanted to know, he'd say, "Book her for your gala or private party at ten grand a pop and find out."

And it worked. Finally, the masses saw her—were literally at her stilettoed feet, ready to revere and emulate her. Within a year, she was raking it in by just showing up, drinking bubbly, and making a splash, being her brassy, colorful, story-telling self.

But being Angelique had its drawbacks, and it became harder to separate herself from her fictional persona. Most people saw her as a kooky character, not an influential artist, and her nightlife friendships were superficial. Paul's work often kept him abroad for months, and whenever loneliness hit or she felt uneasy, she had to remind herself that iconic fame was just around the corner.

A corner that felt more imminent when a Hollywood Studio invited her to audition for a tiny part in a low-budget horror flick. Unfortunately, so was Tanja.

When the casting director and one of the male co-stars soon after came down with a nasty case of the clap, Angelique started the rumor that Tanja was the culpable petri dish, getting her booted from the project.

Part in hand, Angelique soon realized she wasn't taken seriously and cast only as a one-line novelty.

Five years in, people had grown tired of her shtick and lack of real talent in any given department. Worse: the uptight Swiss gave Paul ten years for embezzlement, and with the penthouse and cash influx suddenly gone, her life was disintegrating.

Then, two weeks ago, she was offered a measly three grand to appear at music mogul Randy Riker's birthday bash at his rural mansion in upstate New York. She was gravely insulted (but also broke), and Bernie told her he'd have to drop her if she didn't take the job.

But even a hemorrhaging ego recognizes a silver lining: this was her chance to charm Riker into a recording session that would secure her glorious comeback (to what—if she was completely honest—wasn't entirely clear to her either, but hopefully, after that weekend, no one would give a damn).

Riker's sprawling concrete bunker of a mansion was a twenty-minute drive from the last stronghold of civilization, surrounded by acres of wilderness. Driving up the winding road in the dusk, she saw it sit atop a low, dark hill, shining like the sole beacon of hope. Or depravity, because she'd heard about the sex parties and Riker's passion for hunting weekends, to which he frequently invited guests up to shoot deer, birds, or whatever poor critters roamed his land.

It gave her the willies, and she slowed down her rattling orange Thunderbird with the failing paint job, so she didn't accidentally increase the body count if nearby wildlife was feeling erratic.

But if hunting turned the man on, she was game—and would turn the tables.

Pulling up before the mansion, the attendants greeted her with looks reserved for pilgrims arriving on donkeys.

Unfazed, she tossed them the key and strutted up the wide concrete stairs like a Paris fashion runway. She'd show them.

The party was already in full swing: women in fashionable, revealing gowns and sequined dresses, men in tight slacks and colorful shirts unbuttoned down to the crotch. Troves of sparkling jewelry on both sexes while Giorgio Beverly Hills and Drakkar Noir polluted the air.

David Bowie's "Let's Dance" pounded from speakers, and she slapped on a smile, struck a pose, and belted, "Never fear, Angelique is here."

But only a handful of guests paid her any attention. Some snickered, and two women rolled their eyes before returning to the person they'd been conversing with.

Whatever, Angelique thought, *I've faced tougher crowds than this.*

Taking a deep breath, her short, black, season-before-last Calvin Klein number painfully cut into her back and armpits, bringing her dangerously close to a wardrobe malfunction, and she quickly exhaled again.

Chin up, she floated into the sprawling living room and made her rounds, playfully touching arms and cocktail-wielding hands, cooing, "Hello, dahlings, happy to see you again," even if she'd never met them before, bouncing from one cluster of guests to the next like a pollinating bee. Some smiled, but most ignored her, and someone loudly whispered, "Who is that?" to which another replied, "Literally, no one."

Worse, Randy Riker was nowhere in sight, and the photographer snapping pictures of virtually everyone else had successfully pirouetted out of reach every time she got within four feet of a frame. *What in hell was going on?*

Finally, an excited murmur spread across the room, and everyone broke out in cheers and applause.

And there he was, the sexagenarian birthday boy with the tragic dye job and meaty, black sideburns that went out of fashion the day the King of Rock & Roll died. Donning revealing white slacks and an open blue satin shirt that exposed a shag carpet of a chest and an unfortunate purple appendix scar (which Angelique would fake craving every inch of if it got her back in the game), Randy Riker descended from a curved staircase on the arm of a voluptuous blonde in a revealing, sage-colored gown.

Tanja-Goddamn-Lavonya.

Adrenaline jabbed Angelique's neck and curdled her smile like sour milk. Quickly retracting several steps, she snatched a glass of bubbly from a passing tray and downed it in a gulp.

That wretched bitch here was definitely *not* how she'd pictured the evening. Still, that viper would have to detach herself from Riker's arm sooner or later. Angelique just had to be ready to pounce.

Except, the sad cow never left his side, skillfully keeping him at opposite corners of whatever part of the mansion Angelique circled like a lioness stalking her prey. Worse, she'd overheard several guests whisper insults at her back.

And she almost faltered, surrounded by these painted and powdered animals with their fake grins and ugly personalities. Almost.

After all, Riker had invited her here. Time she showed them who was boss. Time this cunning feline went for the kill.

Bulldozing her way through the crowd like a heat-seeking missile, she marched out to the pool, where Riker stood with Tanja and some guests. Noticing the crack in Tanja's smile upon realizing she'd underestimated her timing to whisk him out of reach comforted Angelique immensely.

"*Dahling*," she purred at Riker, holding out her hand to be kissed, "thank you so much for the invitation, this is the most ... *dahling* party I've been to in years."

He turned with a faint smile and empty gaze, briefly squeezed her fingers, and said, "You're welcome, honey, think nothing of it," before returning his attention to the group.

Confused, Angelique's stomach churned with a bad feeling as Tanja's acid smile deepened. She opened her mouth, but a tall, conservatively dressed man appeared and whispered in Riker's ear. He excused himself, and before Angelique could say anything more, the whole group walked off and left her standing there.

Dumbfounded, she stared after Tanja, who rushed up the stairs.

Michael Jackson's "Beat It" started playing, and Angelique seriously considered it. But she hadn't been paid yet.

Angelique set her jaw. She'd get to the bottom of this and, more importantly, her damn money.

Glancing over her shoulder to see if anyone was watching—they weren't—she followed Tanja upstairs to what she suspected were Riker's private quarters. The top floor gallery featured two massive doors on her right, and one stood slightly ajar.

She advanced and peeked inside an enormous bedroom suite that was as lavish as it was gawdy: shimmering, black velvet walls, red satin sheets on a king-size bed drowning in pillows, and golden statues of busty, naked women everywhere.

At the far end, a glass slider opened to a large terrace, where Tanja stood with her back to Angelique in a cloud of smoke.

With the downstairs noise drowning out her movements, Angelique swiftly crossed the space to where Tanja stood against a modern, waist-high glass railing overlooking a wooded area. A sharp, pungent scent filled the air.

"Finally found a lucrative ride to hitch your wagon on?" Angelique said coldly.

Tanja flung around, startled. "Shit. Who let you up here?" She flicked ashes off the fat joint in her hand.

"How insecure you must feel, shielding me from Randy like that," Angelique purred like scolding a five-year-old. "I'm here on his request, you know."

Tanja snorted a harsh laugh that shook her bony shoulders. "God, you're an idiot. He doesn't even know you exist."

"Of course he does. He even said it was wonderful to see me."

Tanja rolled her eyes. "He said, 'You're welcome, think nothing of it,' like to dozens of other unimportant morons he couldn't give two shits about, half of which were invited by his publicist for a good photo op. No, dear—I 'invited' you because I thought it would make for a good laugh to watch the talentless discount bottom-feeder spend the entire night trying to cozy up to people only to realize all of them are my friends and know what you did to me."

She paused for effect with a malicious smile. "You know, for once, everyone *is* talking about you—about how ridiculous you look and what a joke you are. And that, dear, is my gift to me. Well, Riker's, not that he knows or cares . . . I'd sooner croak before ever spending a single cent on you."

Angelique curled her fingers into fists. "I don't have to stand for this!"

Tanja smiled. "Actually, you do if you ever expect a dime of your bargain basement rate. Stay or get sued for breach of contract."

"You dumb whore," Angelique snapped, trembling. "You think I give a shit about your money? I'll make ten times that anywhere else. I *am* someone with talent you can only dream of. All you know is how to spread diseases with that worn-out Venus fly trap you call a—"

The sharp slap sent Angelique staggering back. With burning rage, she blindly charged forward and shoved her nemesis hard in the chest.

Tanja slammed against the glass banister with a yelp. It broke with a loud, sickening crack before she soundlessly tumbled over the edge, eyes wide and arms flailing.

Angelique's hand flew to her mouth. Her heart racing, she stumbled forward and stared over the edge at a faintly illuminated woodsy area below where, some twenty feet down near a bush and the base of a large oak tree, Tanja's body lay twisted, a glint in her open eyes.

But open eyes meant she was okay, right? A broken leg or arm, but fine and dandy? She sure hoped so but had to admit: the jagged, bloody tree branch protruding from her abdomen lowered those chances drastically.

Sweet Jesus, what had she done?

Terrified, she stumbled back into the bedroom and ran for the door.

And froze . . . her throat tight.

Had anyone seen her come up?

She opened the door and peeked out to the gallery, looking for an exit, but her only escape was down the stairs.

She unclenched her fists and took deep, shaky breaths. *Don't panic; it was an accident.* She tried calming herself. *If no one saw you, everyone would think the stoner had an unfortunate accident.*

But for a moment, overcome with guilt, she nearly crumbled.

Then she heard her mother's voice . . . and found her strength.

True, no one would ever know the magnitude of her thespian bravado, but she'd *make* them see her—when she was ready and only how she wanted them to—and *speak* with a rebel's voice, spinning her tale her way, shrouding the events in *myth* so no one questioned her presence up there. And yes, she was totally defying convention here, ignoring the part of her brain screaming to get the hell out before it was too late. No, she'd work this tragedy to her advantage and finally rise above it all like a goddamn phoenix.

Pushing out her chest, she took a step forward. But Riker's baritone stopped her in her tracks.

Standing halfway up the stairs with his back to her, he was calling to someone in the party below. He started turning her way, and courage left her as quickly as she'd found it.

She had no business being up here. And what if he was looking for Tanja?

Beside herself, she bolted back into the bedroom and stumbled out to the terrace, realizing her mistake too late. Hiding behind the wall, she strained her ears, but the downstairs ruckus and her hammering heart made it impossible to know for sure if he'd entered the bedroom.

Angelique carefully peeked around the corner, but the room was empty.

Maybe Riker was in the can? Okay, *that* she could work with.

She'd sneak back in, attach herself to him the moment he came out, and drag him away from here—or into bed if necessary— to do what she'd come here to do: talk her way into a recording session.

Hell, if anyone asked, she was with him the entire time after following him up here to talk business. The perfect alibi. But first, she had to get off that damn balcony.

She stepped forward . . . and her eyes snagged on the broken glass banister. A chill shot down her spine, and everything around her slowed to a trickle. Guilt twisted her insides, making her dizzy. Invisible hooks steadily dragged her forward to the scene of the crime.

She hadn't meant to hurt Tanja, truly—it was an accident. Was there *any* chance she was still alive?

Carefully avoiding chunks of broken glass, Angelique looked over the edge on wobbly legs. Nope, she was screwed—royally.

"What are you doing?" an unfamiliar voice behind her thundered.

Angelique jerked and turned sharply. She took a hasty step back but found no solid ground— just a troubling weightlessness that replaced the beefy security guard's stern mug with the dark night sky.

Tree branches punched her body and slashed her skin before the bushes below assaulted her, miraculously breaking her fall. She slammed on the dirt with a sharp cry and briefly glimpsed Tanja's impaled body before bouncing downhill on musty soil, grass, and broken twigs.

A tree stump put a full stop to her swan dive. She felt like throwing up, and shrill ringing in her ears distorted the sounds around her.

But she had survived—a living, breathing miracle.

Iconic, really. People would flock to her like that Lady in Lourdes.

Her life flashed before her eyes for less than a minute until she realized that the security guard had to have discovered Tanja's body by now. Angelique needed a cover story. Fast.

How about she followed Riker upstairs and unwittingly discovered the crime—uhm, tragic accident? No, wait—she'd literally just survived the same fall that killed Tanja. Yes—a divine premonition about someone's distress sent her rushing up to the terrace in grave concern. Much better.

Elton was still carrying on, his uplifting song giving her hope.

Except, she couldn't actually feel her legs or hands. Surely, she was just numb or something. But panic crept up on her as another thought struck: if the cops fingered her for Tanja's death and looked into her past—like *really* looked—everything would unravel.

All that she'd worked so hard for all these years, dissolving like Fizzies.

Because lies had legs of their own, didn't they? Shit, most she'd spread for so long she believed them herself. Others—well—she'd needed those to cope with life.

After all, who wants to admit to having narcissistic parents who dumped her at her relatives before vanishing into thin air because they couldn't take it—no, *her*—anymore? A mother and father who once doted on her and granted her every wish and had unwittingly created a little monster that just kept taking and demanding until they were at their wit's end? That, shortly before their disappearing act, Chrissie had become so difficult that her mother broke down, crying, "My God, you suck the life from every living thing!"

The truth was that her relatives had bent over backward to make her feel at home. And she'd milked it for all it was worth and treated them like shit, resenting them for pitying her because their pity suggested that there was something wrong with her.

Of course, she wanted people to see her as a victim of a tragedy, not the root of it.

Sure, some of her stories were absolutely true—about Michael and rubbing elbows with celebrities at Studio 54—except few A-listers paid her much attention because her talent, what little there was, couldn't back up the illusion.

That thing with Gene Simmons? Never happened. The guy looked more like—but still wasn't—*Richard* Simmons (it was dark, all right?), but Gene had passed her earlier that night, so it'd be his word against hers if it ever came to that.

Good god, if the cops got her for Tanja, she'd rot in jail. A loser who'd spent her entire life accomplishing absolutely nothing. All because she wanted to be someone and prove her parents wrong.

No, to spite the bastards.

That saying about selling your soul to the devil to get ahead? Also, totally true.

A growl filled the air.

She smelled the rancid newcomer before she saw it—a big, mangy, dark-snouted creature with glistening eyes. A mountain lion. *In Upstate New York? What the—?* It cautiously approached on large furry paws.

She inhaled sharply, not making a single peep.

The menacing cat looked like it hadn't eaten for days. It also seemed damned determined. The beast swiped at her feet with a claw. Angelique whimpered but felt nothing.

She watched horrified as the mountain lion opened its jaw and sank its teeth into her flesh, and yet she still felt nothing.

But she finally found her voice. And screamed.

True, the massive ugly creature dragging her into the underbrush was the primary motivator, but so was realizing that despite all her sacrifices, the sweat and tears, and her mother's goddamn rules, *this* would be all anyone would remember her for.

And that wasn't iconic . . . just criminally ironic.

WILDE ABOUT MURDER

DAVID S. PEDERSON

Detective Brunswick Shields parked his Jeep Compass in front of the small Casita Hotel, noting a rainbow flag hanging above the entrance, and turned off his light and siren. He grabbed his coffee from the cup holder and got out with a sigh, slamming the door shut. A dead man is *not* how he wanted to start his weekend. He had a date that evening with a furry librarian he'd met on Scruff, and he'd made plans to attend the Arizona Book Festival on Sunday, possibly with the librarian, depending on how things went. He glanced at his watch and hoped this wouldn't go late, interrupting his evening plans.

Ignoring a few reporters and nosy citizens, Brunswick followed the police tape around to the back of the hotel to a collection of EMTs, police officers, and a couple of rather attractive firefighters. He took it all in, then forced his blue eyes away from the tight rear end of a handsome policeman to Sergeant Sikov, who was standing over the corpse, his brow furrowed. Sikov was slightly older than Brunswick, in his early fifties, and married to a great cook. Brunswick was a frequent guest at their house for dinner.

"What ya' got for me, Billy?" Brunswick said, walking over to him.

"Another body," Billy Sikov said, glancing up at the tall detective.

Brunswick bent down and took a closer look. "His head is split open. Awful lot of blood. What's with the cape?"

Billy stared down at the corpse, who was wearing only a red cape, twisted about his shoulders, and a pair of black Andrew Christian briefs. "He and a few other guys were here for some sort of reunion of a LGBTQ+ Oscar Wilde group they had in college. Apparently, they all dress like him."

Brunswick arched a dark brow as he got to his feet. "Somehow, I don't think Oscar Wilde ever wore Andrew Christian briefs. I've read all his works, and a couple biographies, but black briefs were never mentioned."

Sikov laughed loudly, causing a few bystanders to stare curiously. "I'm sure they weren't."

"So, what happened?" Brunswick said, taking a sip of his now lukewarm coffee.

"I'm told he went up to his room for a cigarette. He must have stripped down to his underwear for some reason, put the cape on, and went out onto the balcony to smoke. From there, it's anybody's guess."

"Where did he fall from?"

Billy Sikov craned his neck and pointed. "The balcony on the top floor. That's his room apparently. I've got an officer stationed at the door."

"Anyone see him fall?"

"One of the fellows in the group was in his own room, which is below this man's. He said he saw the body go past his window. He's the one who found the guy."

"And who is the body? I doubt he had I.D. tucked in his underwear, but I assume someone in his group identified him."

"Right." Billy took out his notebook and flipped it open. "Richard A. Tyrell, goes by, went by, Rick. Thirty-two years old, from Sacramento."

"Any sign of foul play?"

"Nothing obvious. He was still holding a cigarette in his right hand, though. His fingers were actually wrapped around it, and it burned his palm."

Brunswick pursed his full lips. "Interesting. What's the name of the man who saw the body go past his window?"

"Vance Davenport. He's one of the Wilde aficionados." Billy pointed again. "He's over there."

The detective looked at a motley collection of four men huddled behind the police tape, each wearing a Victorian cape, an oversized hat, a bow tie, a flouncy shirt, and baggy pants. "Okay, let's look at this man's room and see if we can't determine why he fell. Do you have a passkey?"

"Yes, I got it from one of the owners. Mr. Tyrell was in 5C, third floor. There's no elevator."

Brunswick took the keycard from him and slipped it in his pocket. "Okay. Stairs are good for my glutes, anyway."

"And bad for my knees."

"I keep telling you to have those replaced, Billy. And come with me to the gym once in a while. It'll do you good."

"Yeah, yeah, you sound like my wife. We can't all be six two and built, you know."

Brunswick smiled and followed Sikov inside. The two men climbed the stairs to the third floor and down the hall to 5C, where a police officer was standing.

"Has anything been touched inside?" the detective said, stopping at the door and fetching the keycard from his pocket.

"No, sir," the officer said.

"Okay." Brunswick put on a pair of latex gloves from his coat pocket, unlocked the door, and stepped in as Sikov followed. The uniformed policeman stayed in the hall.

The room was sparsely decorated. A bed, two nightstands that doubled as dressers, a couple of lamps, and a desk and chair by the doors to the balcony. A photograph of Camelback Mountain hung on the wall.

"Mr. Tyrell seems rather tidy. Nothing out of place, everything picked up," Brunswick said, walking around. "It appears the pants and shirt he'd been wearing have been neatly folded and placed on the bed, his shoes and socks on the floor. His hat is hanging on the back of the door." He checked out the bathroom and then crossed to the balcony doors. He swung them open and stepped out, peering over the railing at the body below. "That's quite a drop."

"Yes," Sikov said, joining him. "The building slopes down the embankment at the back, so even though this is the third floor, it's a good four stories down."

Brunswick shuddered involuntarily and stepped back inside, stopping at the desk. On it, he found a handwritten note which read, "Forgive me, I can't go on living."

The detective whistled. "Take a look at this, Billy."

Sikov peered over his shoulder at the piece of hotel stationary. "Suicide note?"

"Appears to be. There's a postcard here, too, written to someone named Dale, but not stamped or addressed yet. Same handwriting, with the dots over the I's like little O's." Brunswick noted the desk held nothing but the postcard, the note, stationary, and a lamp. "Hmm, no drawers in the desk, and the chair has been pushed back."

"So, he sat down here to write the note, then jumped to his death," Sikov said.

The detective didn't respond but instead surveyed the room again. The floor around the desk, as elsewhere, was spotless. The garbage can contained nothing but a used tissue. The nightstands, one with his wallet, keycard, and iPhone atop it, each had a lamp but nothing else. The drawers in the nightstands held his clothing, all neatly folded, and the closet contained just a couple of shirts, an extra blanket, and a pair of tennis shoes. There was nothing under the bed except for a small suitcase.

"At least we now know it was suicide," Sikov said.

Brunswick stroked his cleft chin slowly. "I wonder."

"Huh? Pretty cut and dried to me. We can both get home tonight in time for dinner. It looks like suicide, pure and simple."

"But the truth, as our Mr. Oscar Wilde said, is rarely pure and never simple."

"You and your Wilde quotes," Sikov said. "This case was made for you."

Brunswick smiled softly. "Mr. Wilde was a brilliant playwright and clever and witty. I've often wished I could be more like him."

"He was also a flamboyant homosexual. You may be gay, but you're not flamboyant."

"You haven't seen me at a Palm Springs all-male resort, my friend. Come on, let's chat with our Wilde group," the detective said, removing the gloves and leading the way back downstairs.

When they reached the ground floor, Brunswick turned to Sikov. "Let's start with the man who found the body. What was his name again?"

"Vance Davenport."

"Okay. Is there a room we can use?"

"Yes, the guy wearing the green cape is the owner that gave me the passkey. He said we could use the hotel office if necessary."

"Fine. Show me where that is and then go get Mr. Davenport."

—✺— —✺— —✺—

Sikov left the detective in the small office, returning shortly with Vance Davenport, who looked nervous and rather pale. Like all the men in the group, Mr. Davenport was in his early thirties, though he had developed a paunch, and he stood slightly stooped.

"I'm Detective Shields of the Phoenix Police, and this is Sergeant Sikov."

"Hello, Detective," the man said. "The sergeant and I met earlier. I'm Vance Davenport, from Rancho Mirage. Do I need a lawyer?" His left eye twitched from beneath the wide brim of his oversized hat.

"Only if you want. This is just routine questioning," Brunswick said, finishing the last of his coffee and tossing the paper cup in the trash can next to the desk.

"Okay," Vance said, biting his lower lip. He took off his hat and black cape and set them on one of the chairs opposite the desk, smoothing out his prematurely thinning blond hair as he sat down in the other.

"Sergeant Sikov here tells me you saw Mr. Tyrell fall."

"Yes, that's right. I saw his body go by the window of my room." His eye was twitching fervently now.

"A falling body would take less than one second to pass the average-sized window. Were you able to identify it as Mr. Tyrell immediately?"

"Well, no. I mean, I saw a flash of red and what looked like a body. My room is on two, and Rick's was on the third floor, right above me. After it happened, I tried to look out, but the windows don't open far enough, and my room doesn't have a balcony like his does. So, I went downstairs, outside, and around to the back. That's when I found him. I stood there in shock for several minutes and nearly vomited. Finally, I decided I'd better alert someone else. I didn't bring my phone with me, and the back door was locked, so I had to walk up the embankment and around to the front, but I eventually found George."

"Okay. Do you know why Mr. Tyrell was wearing only his underwear and a cape?"

"Not really. We were all in the bar and breakfast area just beforehand, reminiscing. Rick was being kind of a jerk."

"In what way?"

"This was the ten-year reunion of our college Oscar Wilde club.

We called ourselves Wild about Wilde." He paused and eyed the detective warily. "It was an LGBTQ+ club."

"Yes, the sergeant informed me of that. You can speak freely here, though, Mr. Davenport. I'm gay and a Wilde aficionado."

"Oh, you are? That's good, then. Not all cops are welcoming of us. Of gay people, I mean." His eyes flicked to Sikov.

"The sergeant is an ally. You can trust him, too."

Davenport looked slightly relieved, but his eye still twitched nervously. "Well, anyway, this is the first time we've seen each other since graduation. There's a lot of history between all of us, some of it not pleasant."

"Would you be more specific, Mr. Davenport?" Brunswick said.

Vance took a breath, held it a minute, and let it out slowly. "I can't believe he's dead. Just like that. I feel bad talking about him, you know?"

"That's understandable. There were just five of you in the group, is that right? In the club?"

"Yes. Myself, Howard Shelly, George Jenkins, Tony Sanford, and Rick. All gay. I guess it was more of a G club rather than LGBTQ+," Davenport said with a nervous giggle. "Anyway, Howard used to be involved with Rick until Rick dumped him for me."

"You and this Howard both dated Mr. Tyrell?"

"Yes, in college. At the time, I thought I was lucky, though Howie was royally pissed. Rick was pretty hot back then. He wore the tightest jeans and button-downs that were unbuttoned practically to his waist. He had a great build, high cheekbones, bright blue eyes, jet-black hair, and a perfect smile. Everyone seemed drawn to him, like the proverbial moth to a flame. And then they got burned."

"In what way?"

"When Rick broke it off with Howard, he told everyone, and I mean *everyone*, that Howie had E.D. That means he couldn't get it up."

"Yes, thank you, Mr. Davenport, I'm familiar with the term."

"Well, anyway, Howard was furious. He denied it and threatened to beat the crap out of Rick, but he never did. Then, when Rick dumped *me*, he told the guys I have a small dick. I mean miniscule." Vance's face flushed. "It wasn't true, it's *not* true, and I can prove it, if you like."

"That won't be necessary, Mr. Davenport." Brunswick's gaze traveled down to Vance's crotch, but he could determine nothing through the baggy trousers. "You said others got burned by Mr. Tyrell as well?"

"Yeah. Richard Alexander Tyrell. R.A.T., and he lived up to it. Tony and George were a couple, even back then. They're the ones who own this hotel. Tony was one of the few who didn't put up with Rick's shit, and he frequently told him off. Somehow, Rick managed to seduce George behind Tony's back, just to get even with Tony, I think, after he'd dumped me and Howie."

"Did Tony find out?"

"Yeah. Rick told us all afterward, including Tony, that George had given him genital herpes. George insisted that it was Rick who had given *him* herpes. Tony was hurt, of course, but he eventually forgave George and put the blame on Rick."

"Okay, so Mr. Tyrell sounds like he was a real pain in the ass ten years ago."

"Yeah, and he still is, or was. In the bar earlier, he taunted me again for having a small dick in front of everybody, daring me to take down my pants and prove I didn't. George came to my defense and told Rick to shut up. Rick then told us that George only graduated from college because he'd been sleeping with two of his professors, and *that's* where he first got herpes. Howard went to punch Rick in the face, but Tony stopped him. Rick said Howard always used violence to compensate for his E.D. Tony told Rick to go to hell, and Rick said something about seeing us all there. He then stormed out of the room, saying he needed a cigarette."

Brunswick shook his head slowly. "Damn. I'm surprised any of you even wanted him here for the reunion."

"Well, besides the fact that we were all rather hoping he'd lost his looks, which he hadn't, there was something else, another reason. I suppose I should mention it, but don't tell the others I said anything, please."

"What?"

"Well, we all talked, all of us except Rick, beforehand. We thought it would be fun to play a trick on Rick, to humiliate him, get some revenge, you know? We'd planned to get him here, then get him really, really high. Rick's always liked weed, and it's legal in Arizona. We'd all go to a leather bar called the Anvil; only Rick wouldn't know where we were going. Once inside, we planned to get a ball gag in his mouth, strip him naked, lock him in the cage, and sit back and watch, taking pictures as the night wore on. He's a total top and has always bragged he's never been a bottom."

"Just so you know, a joke like that would be considered illegal, Mr. Davenport."

"Yeah, well, it never happened because he fell to his death. It wouldn't have happened anyway, because Rick somehow got wind of it, which is probably why he was so nasty in the bar. Just before he left, Rick told us he knew what we were planning, and we could go screw ourselves."

"Okay. So, what transpired after that?"

"We were all in a rather foul mood. I went up to my room; I'm not sure about the others. As I said, mine is directly beneath Rick's, and as soon as I got inside, I could hear him blasting his music, which pissed me off even more. I considered calling George and Tony and complaining but decided to wait a few minutes to see if he'd turn it down. Next thing I knew I saw his body go by the window." Davenport's eyes opened wide, and his thin brows shot up. "Hey, I just remembered something. After he fell, it stopped."

"What stopped?" Brunswick said.

"The music. He'd been playing Wham. Then, suddenly, in the middle of 'Wake Me Up Before You Go-Go,' it stopped. After he went, went."

"Funny. So, the music stopped after you saw his body go by? You're sure?"

"Pretty sure. I mean, it was a bit of a shock. I might have gotten things mixed up."

"Hmm. By the way, was he right-handed?"

"Rick? Yeah, why? The only leftie in the group is Howard."

"All right, thank you for your time. You're free to go, but please stick around the hotel for the time being."

Vance got to his feet and collected his hat and cape, wiping sweat from his brow. "Sure, I'll be in the bar." He left, leaving the door ajar.

"Interesting fellow," Sikov said.

"Indeed. What would our friend Oscar make about this little gathering of friends?"

"You'd know more than me, Bruns. I'm a George Bernard Shaw fan myself."

"And I don't hold that against you. But there's an Oscar quote about friends that seems applicable here if I could only just recall it."

"You will, I'm sure."

"Probably. Oh, well, might as well send in Howard Shelly next."

"Right," Sikov said, going out.

Brunswick paced about, his mind racing as he mulled over the note on the desk, the strangely clothed corpse, Oscar Wilde, and the cigarette burn on the victim's right palm. In just a few minutes, the sergeant was back with Mr. Shelly, his hat in hand, and they went through the standard introductions before Howard took a seat in the chair Vance had vacated. Shelly was attractive and in better shape than Davenport, with a full head of chestnut hair, which matched the mustache on his upper lip.

"So, Mr. Shelly, I understand Tony stopped you from punching Mr. Tyrell earlier," Brunswick said.

"That's right. I was pissed. He brought up some rather personal stuff again, just because he's an asshole. A lot of it wasn't even true, at least what he said about me."

"Okay. What happened after Rick left?"

"Vance went to his room, and I went to mine. I was scrolling through emails when Vance knocked, saying the jerk had fallen off his balcony. We went down and joined the others."

"You were the last one to get to the body?"

"Yeah. Vance found him, and he went in and got George, who told Tony, and then Vance came and got me."

"All right. And are you right-handed or left-handed?"

"Left, why?"

"Just curious. Thank you, Mr. Shelly. Please don't leave the hotel for the time being."

"Sure," Howard said. "I saw Vance heading to the bar, think I'll join him." He got to his feet and left without another word.

"Who's left?" Brunswick said.

"Just Tony Sanford and George Jenkins, the owners of this place. They're waiting in their apartment."

"Okay, let's start with Mr. Sanford."

Once more introductions were dispensed and the preliminary facts laid out before Brunswick, now perched on the edge of the desk, said, "When Mr. Tyrell left the bar and breakfast room, what did everyone else do?"

"Well, Vance left shortly after Rick. Then Howard. I believe they went to their rooms. I had a splitting headache, and George told me to go relax, so I went to our apartment downstairs in the basement. George remained in the bar to clean up."

"So, at the time of Rick's death, everyone was alone. Interesting and convenient."

Tony shrugged. "I guess so. A little while later, George came to get me, saying Rick had fallen."

Brunswick cocked his head. "But how did he manage to fall?"

"Beats me. Rick was tall, six foot four, and probably only weighed 175 pounds. He and I were both in track in college, and I still run. He probably did, too."

"And?"

"And, perhaps he leaned over to have a look at something below, and that was it. Or maybe he jumped."

"Suicide?" Brunswick said, arching his dark brow again.

"Maybe," Tony said. "I think he found out today how much we hated him. We uh, had a little surprise planned for him that he overheard us talking about, you see."

Brunswick scowled. "Yes, pretty mean trick."

"Would have served him right. He's relied on his looks to get him things, walking all over people. Maybe he went up to his room, took a hard look in the mirror, and decided to end it, once and for all. Listening to Wham, and especially 'Wake Me Up Before You Go Go,' would certainly drive *me* to kill myself, no offense if you're a George Michael fan."

"I am," Brunswick said, "But no offense taken. Why do you think it was suicide versus an accident?"

Tony shrugged. "Might have been an accident, though if it was, it wasn't our fault. This hotel has passed all safety inspections, trust me. The railing on his balcony is secure and regulation height."

"I'm sure. By the way, how many rooms are there?"

"Guest rooms? Nine, why?"

"And how many are currently occupied?"

"Just Rick's, Vance's, and Howard's."

"That's a lot of vacancies."

"Well, it's a slow time of year, and I wanted to keep it just the five of us for tonight, so to be honest, I turned away a couple of bookings. George wasn't too happy."

Brunswick cleared his throat. "Yes, well, that's everything for now, Mr. Sanford. Wait in the bar with the others for the time being, please."

"Okay." Tony stood up and went out, Sergeant Sikov following behind. In short order, Sikov was back, this time with George Jenkins,

Tony's husband. Like Tony, he was in decent shape, a bit taller, and a ginger with creamy white skin.

"I understand there was a bit of unpleasantness in the bar earlier and that Mr. Tyrell left abruptly," Brunswick said after introductions had been made.

George frowned. "You can say that again. He said some pretty shitty stuff and stormed out. Everyone was quite upset."

"Including you?"

"Of course. It was a mistake having him come here for the reunion. He's just as big an ass as he always was. He seduced me one night, you know, and then he gave me herpes and told everyone it was *me* who gave it to *him*. He also blabbed a secret about me and two of my professors."

"That had to make you angry."

"We were *all* angry, for various reasons. Anyway, sometime after everyone else left the bar area, Vance came and told me Rick had fallen from his balcony. I called 911, and told Vance to let Howard know. I went downstairs to our apartment, got Tony, and together we went outside. The sight was quite a shock."

"I can imagine. Any idea why he was wearing only underwear and a cape?"

"I suppose he just wanted to get comfortable, so he undressed. Since it's unseasonably chilly outside, he probably draped the cape over his shoulders to go out for a smoke."

"Makes sense. Do the room doors lock automatically?"

"Yes, as soon as they're closed."

"And who all has access to the rooms?"

"Tony and I both have master keycards we carry for housekeeping and what not. There's no one else."

"No outside staff?"

"We bring in help during the busy season but otherwise manage everything ourselves."

"All right, thank you, Mr. Jenkins. If you'd be so kind as to wait in the bar with the others."

After George left, Brunswick turned to Sikov. "Well, Billy, what do you think?"

"It was suicide, Bruns. And just between you and me, I think it's too bad they didn't get to play that joke on Tyrell."

"As for the latter, that will definitely stay between you and me.

And as for the former, I don't think it was."

Sikov screwed up his face. "But if it wasn't suicide, if he fell by accident, why the note?"

"Because I'm pretty sure it wasn't an accident but murder, made to look like suicide. Let's go have a chat with them all, shall we?"

The two men walked down the hall to the bar and breakfast room, where the four Wilde aficionados had gathered, each nursing a drink.

"Ah, gentlemen, glad you're all here," the detective said as he and Sikov entered.

"Well, if it isn't the gay detective. What do you want now?" Tony said.

Brunswick glanced at Mr. Davenport, whose face turned an interesting shade of red.

"I, uh, mentioned that to them. I hope you don't mind."

"I'm out and proud, doesn't matter, though you'd be wise to keep confidences unless you're certain the other person doesn't object, Mr. Davenport. And as to what I want, Mr. Sanford, just some further clarification. When I was in Mr. Tyrell's room earlier, I found a suicide note on the desk."

"You're joking," Howard said. "Rick killed himself?"

"That's how it appears, but I noticed no pen on the desk, floor, or anywhere else in the room. Where did the pen go that was used to write that note? And the balcony doors were closed. Why? Did he go out there, light a cigarette, close the doors, and then jump, clutching the pen?"

"Seems unlikely," Sikov said.

"Very. And why carry the pen? Why not just leave it on the desk?"

"True," Sikov said. "And there was no pen found on the ground around him or nearby and nothing on his person except the cigarette."

"And that was in his right hand. If he *were* holding the pen when he jumped, logically, it would have been in his right hand also, as he was right-handed." Brunswick turned to Vance again. "Do you recall saying that shortly after you got to your room, you could hear Mr. Tyrell blasting Wham above you?"

"Yes, it was annoying."

"There's no radio in the room, not even a television, so he must have been streaming it off his phone," Brunswick said. "And later, Mr. Sanford, *you* mentioned the music, too. Specifically, the song 'Wake Me Up Before You Go-Go,' which Mr. Davenport said had abruptly stopped just after the body went by the window. You said that you went to your basement apartment after Tyrell left the bar, and that's where you were a short time later when George came to get you after the body had been found. So, how would you know what music was playing in Tyrell's room? Surely the volume from his phone wasn't so loud that it carried all the way down to the basement."

"That's curious," Sikov said.

"Yes, indeed," Brunswick said. "I believe that instead of going to the basement, you went to see Tyrell, Mr. Sanford. You were angry over Rick seducing George behind your back ten years ago and then giving him herpes on top of it, which, perhaps, he passed on to you. All that anger resurfaced earlier today when Rick brought everything up again, and he also told everyone that George had been sleeping with two of his professors. *And* your revenge plot fell apart. So, you went to give him a piece of your mind. I'm told you're the only one that ever did that. You knocked, but there was no answer. You could hear the music blaring, so you entered with your passkey. You noticed Rick on the balcony, his back turned. Seeing an opportunity, you slipped out and pushed him over. Panicked and thinking quickly, you came in, closed the balcony doors out of habit, and wrote the note with a pen on the desk, using the postcard to copy Rick's handwriting so it would look like suicide, though in hindsight, you would have been better off making it appear an accident."

"I don't know what you're talking about," Tony said.

"Don't you? Wham was still playing loudly, irritating you, so you shut his phone off. Then you absentmindedly put the pen in your pocket and rushed back down the stairs to the basement, an easy task for a runner."

"You've no proof," Tony said.

"No? I'm willing to bet there's a pen in your pocket, forgotten, and I expect the lab will determine it was used to write the suicide note. I bet they'll also find Rick's and your prints on it. And I'm sure yours are on Rick's phone from where you turned it off. Come to think of it, your prints will be on the back of Rick's cape, too."

Tony's face went pale. "I just wanted to talk to him, like you said. I was in a rage, not thinking. Then suddenly, he went over. I panicked."

"And you didn't wear gloves because you hadn't planned to kill him."

"That's right, it wasn't premeditated. That's not as bad, is it?"

"Bad enough."

"But he deserved it. He stabbed me in the back. He stabbed all of us in the back, right guys?"

"Oh, Tony," George said. The other three just stared at him, their eyes wide.

"He may have stabbed you in the back, Mr. Sanford, but you did far worse. Read him his rights, sergeant, and take him downtown," Brunswick said, then snapped his fingers, his blue eyes lighting up. "The quote just came back to me, Billy."

"Oscar's quote?"

"Yes, quite fitting in these circumstances. Mr. Wilde said, 'True friends stab you in the front.'"

THE FOURTH MONKEY

PENNY MICKELBURY

"Wake up, Y'all! Wake up and come quick!" Loud pounding on the door accompanied the shouts and Esther Adams rolled out of bed and into overalls and a tee shirt as quickly as if she still was a battlefield nurse in Korea instead of a charge nurse at Harlem Hospital . . . and still as much soldier as nurse, she grabbed her pistol from the nightstand and dropped it into the deep pocket of her pants. Then she gently poked the bundle buried under the covers.

"I'm coming," Mame Tolliver muttered sleepily, and she threw off the covers and sprang from the bed as if she heard the reveille horn. She caught the shirt and skirt Essie tossed to her and, donning her clothes and pulling the scarf off her head, she followed Essie into the living room and to the front door.

"Who's out there?" Essie called out, even as she flung open the door where four people huddled in a bunch—two women and two men. A big, strong-looking man stepped forward, removed his cap, and saluted Essie.

"Sorry to bother y'all, Captain, but we got a problem," he said, but a woman who held his arm interrupted him.

"There's a little girl out yonder in the alley, skinny as a stick and real dirty—" she said, sounding a mixture of angry and frightened and sad.

"Her clothes is nothin' but rags and her hair is all matted—" said the other woman.

"And don't none of us know her, ain't never seen her before tonight," said the other man, "and we don't know what we oughta do—"

"But we know we cain't leave her out there in the alley. It's 'sposed to turn cold tonight—"

"So we thought y'all might know what to do."

Mame turned quickly and, without a word, ran into the kitchen. A drawer opened and closed and a knife cut fast and sure, and then Mame was back with the crowd at the front door.

She reached around Essie, opened the front hall closet door and snatched their jackets from the hangers. "We'll help whatever way we can," she said, and they all followed the Army man down the hallway toward the rear of the apartment building and down the steps to the always locked heavy door that exited to the alley. They heard the mewling before they saw the child.

"Oh, my dear Lord!" Essie whispered, the words as much prayer as curse as she took slow, short steps toward the child. By dint of training and experience she knew better than to touch her, but she bent low. "Can we help you, Little Girl? If you don't want to be cold and hungry and scared anymore, and if you want to get out of this filthy alley, we can help you," Essie said, and waited, still crouched low. "Can you tell us your name?"

The child looked at Essie, looked behind Essie at the other strangers who were looking down at her, then she looked back at Essie, but she did not speak or acknowledge Essie's words. Mame leaned down and whispered to Essie who nodded, smiled thanks, and reached into her pocket.

Inside the folded napkin were slices of orange. She held them out to the girl who did not respond. Essie put an orange slice into her mouth and muttered sounds of pleasure as she devoured the fruit. She removed the naked orange rind from her mouth and showed the girl who was watching closely. "Now your turn," Essie said, and proffered the slice of orange. The girl reached out slowly. Her eyes darted from Essie to the orange slice and back until it was in her hand and then in her mouth. Her eyes widened and she smiled and chewed and reached for another slice of orange until the napkin was empty. Essie stood up and nodded at the Army sergeant who nodded to his wife, who bent low toward the child.

"What's your name, Sweetheart? And why are you out here? Don't you want to go inside where it's warm?" She extended her hand toward the girl, and they all watched the expressions that roamed across the child's face, fear being the most prominent, followed by confusion. After the briefest hesitation the child took the woman's hand and stood up on spindly, wobbly legs. Legs that didn't support her and she stumbled and fell. Arms and hands hurried to help her stand and to offer assistance, but the child now tried to back away from them on her weak stick-legs.

"What's your name, Child, and where do you live?"

"Why are you out here in this dirty alley?"

"And where's your mama!" A demand for information rather than a query.

"I could eat some grits and eggs," Sarge said rather too loudly. "Anybody else hungry?"

And the heretofore silent man turned to walk away, his right arm extended behind him, palm up. A tiny hand grabbed it and six adults and one little girl filed into the rear door of the five-story apartment building on 134th Street. It was a clean, well-lit area thanks to a janitor everyone in the building remembered generously at Christmas. The women already had decided to bathe the child in the deep wash sink so soap and towels and cloths awaited them, as did scissors to cut hair that was too matted for comb and brush. The girl didn't shrink away from the hands that removed the rags she wore, and she sighed deeply as warm water cascaded over her. She closed her eyes and welcomed the kind of attention she'd never before enjoyed from adults. Essie expertly cut the matted hair almost to the scalp and the other women took turns washing and scrubbing, from the top of her head to the bottoms of her little feet.

"I'm going upstairs and get a bed ready for her," Mame said to Essie.

"And if you don't mind, I'll go with her, maybe put some ice in the bucket and put some water on to boil for the grits," the Army man said, adding that his wife could vouch for his usefulness around the house. "And I know not to get in the way," he said with a sideways grin at his wife.

Half an hour later they all gathered around the dining room table, the adults neglecting their drinks as they watched the little girl eat grits and eggs as if it had been a long time since she'd eaten, but Mame had to feed her because the girl had no proficiency with fork or spoon, and she gulped milk so fast she choked on it. As a unit the adults stood to pat her on the back and wipe her face and hold the glass so she could drink. Slowly. And when she finished the milk she looked all around and said, "Molly. My name Molly." And she started to cry. Hard, bitter, choking and gulping tears and sobs. "I kilt him and then I run fast as I could 'way from there and I ain't never goin' back and cain't nobody make me!"

"You say you . . . killed him?" Essie asked, willing her voice into the controlled calm needed to calm and control patients. "Who did you kill, Child? And how do you know he's dead?"

"Can you tell us where he is so we can help him if—"

She cut Sarge off with a sharp, piercing scream. "You cain't help him 'cause he's dead! I tol' you! I kilt him just like Lolly told me to: I stuck a knife in his neck right here." She made a stabbing gesture at the right side of her throat with her index finger where the carotid artery led down from the brain to the heart and Essie shuddered. If the child had in fact stabbed someone in this place with any force the person indeed would be dead.

"Who is Lolly?" Mame asked softly, and the little girl smiled through her tears.

"She my big sister." Pride, love, and longing filled her face and her voice, "and we look just alike 'cept she the tallest." Then the strong, positive tone collapsed. "But she gone. She promised she wouldn't never leave me, but she did, after she kilt the first white man." The girl swiped at the tears and stared into the six pairs of eyes that were staring at her. "If Lolly don't come get me I ain't got nowhere to go!"

"Where is your Mama?" Mame asked gently. She still sat close to the girl at the table.

"I don't know and I don't care! I hope she dead! I hope somebody done kilt her, so I don't never have to see her no more!" And suddenly the torrent of words halted, and fear replaced anger in the girl's face and body. "'Cause if she ain't dead she'll kill me for sure 'cause I kilt that white man she sold me to."

Not one of the adults had a response to this. Mame got up like a two-ton weight sat on her back. Of all the ugly realities she imagined could have befallen such a young girl, what she just heard was not one of them. It was nothing she could have imagined. "Let's get you ready for bed, all right, Molly?"

"I ain't never slept in a bed," the girl said, and jumped to her feet as if she'd received an electrical charge, and she settled into the surplus Army cot as if it were a luxurious bed in a luxurious hotel. She nestled her head into the pillow and pulled the sheets and blankets up to her chin. She was deeply asleep in less than a minute. It was another minute before anyone spoke.

"Does anyone think she's not telling the truth?" Essie asked, and all heads shook. "Then what do we do? If we believe she's telling the truth, we can't ignore her."

"But what can we do about it, even if she is telling the truth?" And they all knew the answer: If two Colored girls had, in fact, killed two white men, regardless of the reason, they could do nothing about it.

"Sarge and me are letter carriers," Cal said. "We can ask around. People know us, trust us, might tell us something . . ."

"But if people know a woman is selling her girls to men for sex—" Essie began and said no more because it wasn't necessary to say more.

"Ain't nobody gonna admit to knowing that," Sarge said darkly, "but they won't be able to stop talking about dead white men with knives in their necks." And he stood up and reached out a hand for his wife.

"Sergeant," Essie said, "you seem to know me, but I don't think I know you."

"And I'll never forget you, Captain. I'm alive and standing here on two legs because of you." And everyone watched him look back into his memory of serving in the Korean War. "I was bleeding out from a wound right here," and he gave a pat to his right thigh several inches above the knee. "The orderlies dropped my stretcher on your table and the blood gushed up from my leg like a geyser. And you whipped off your tee shirt, grabbed the scissors from your belt, and cut it into strips. You wrapped the longest one around my thigh and pulled it so tight I almost passed out from the pain. Then you packed that hole with those other strips an' told the orderlies to get me into a surgical suite on the double—"

"But before they carried you away you sat up and whipped off your tee shirt and tossed it to me. Then you passed out and I was able to restore what was left of my modesty," Essie smiled and extended her hand. "A pleasure to meet you officially, Sergeant."

Everyone clapped and cheered except Mame who ran out of the room, was gone just seconds, and ran back in waving an olive-green tee shirt, which she gave to Sarge.

"Is this . . . it can't be . . ."

"Your tee shirt, the one that saved my modesty," Essie said.

"Definitely cleaner and better smelling than the last time I saw it," Sarge said.

"Would it help if I took care of Miss Hansberry this morning?" Mame asked her boss, the Senior Librarian at the 135th Street Branch of the New York City Library.

"Oh, indeed it would, Mame, thank you!" Dorothy Homer exclaimed. "I've accepted that my budget will never support hiring additional librarians—or any staff for that matter."

During the artistic, cultural, and social explosion of Negro life that occurred in Harlem, beginning in the 1920s and growing exponentially in the years since, the Harlem Branch of the New York City Public Library, at 135th Street and Broadway, was the de facto center of learning for Negroes.

Lorraine Hansberry arrived exactly on time. Mame met her at the front door, introduced herself, and led the way to a meeting room which she unlocked and relocked when they were inside.

"I am here to assist you, Miss Hansberry. But first, may I be so bold as to ask you a question, and share some important information with you?"

"Of course." The woman's visage changed from smiling to serious.

"My neighbors and I found—and rescued—a little girl in the alley behind our building . . ."

"Found!" Hansberry exclaimed, jumping to her feet. "Was she lost? Was she injured? Did you locate her parents?"

Mame calmed her guest and related the bare bones of the story: "We bathed and clothed and fed her and eventually persuaded her to talk to us. None of us were prepared for what we heard: two little girls were sold to white men by their mother. To protect themselves, the girls killed the men and ran away. We are searching for the other girl—"

Lorraine Hansberry made a sound that caused Mame to stop talking and look with concern at her guest. "Miss Hansberry?"

"I've heard some terrible things in my life. I know terrible things happen. But I've never heard anything like this! What do you want from me? I don't know what I can do! I am speechless and I have no idea how I can help."

"Some of the neighbors are working to build a factual story from a horror story, and if we're successful I hope you would consider how the newspaper you're a part of could tell this story without sending two little Negro girls to prison." Mame inhaled deeply as she considered her next words. "I don't know a lot about the newspaper you're a part of—I've seen it a few times—and I will honestly tell you that I don't care very much about Communism or the struggle of Colored people in Africa. I care about the struggles of Colored people right here, especially the plight of two little Negro girls in Harlem."

The writer dipped her head slightly, acknowledging and accepting the criticism of the Pan African newspaper, *Freedom.* Then she said quietly, "Any published story about the plight of these little girls will bring the force of the New York City Police Department down upon them—and you—and there will be no stopping it. They will be seen as murderers of the worst kind: those who kill white people, and there will be no salvation for them. I'm sorry I cannot be of more help, Miss Tolliver."

"If we can find decent homes for the girls—"

"I pledge whatever financial support I can gather," Lorraine Hansberry said.

"That's better than nothing, isn't it?" Essie asked later that night, after her midnight shift at the hospital.

Mame shrugged, then nodded. "I suppose. Truth be told nobody can help those children if the police find out."

"Then we must figure out a way to help them," Essie said. "But we can't let anyone know what those children have done!"

"Then what do you want to do, Mame?"

"Find that pitiful excuse of a mother and—"

"And have you sharing a cell with that pitiful excuse of a mother? No thank you. I plan to grow old and gray with you, Miss Tolliver."

"We must do something, Essie—"

Rapid knocks on the door interrupted and, with a quick one-armed hug, Essie hurried to open the door.

"We have news!" Sarge barreled in, pulling June in behind him, followed closely by Cal and Sandra. Both men still wore their postal service uniforms.

"We know who the dead white men are!" Cal exclaimed.

"And we know who the Mama is—and where she is," Clara said darkly.

"Not half a block from them two stores," Sandy said between

clenched, angry teeth, "and they're the raggediest places in the block."

"They been there more'n twenty years, both of 'em, and they always been raggedy and half- assed—just like them two who own 'em," Sarge said.

It took a while with four people telling the story but the details finally emerged: the men and their businesses were neighborhood fixtures but neither was profitable or popular. A run-down market that sold cigarettes, rotgut liquor, beer, soda pop, stale chips and staler candy, and next door to it a shoe repair shop that almost nobody used since a bigger, better, and more professional operation opened a block away six months earlier.

"The important thing to know," Sarge said, "the businesses share a basement."

"And there's a way into the basement from the alley at the rear," Cal said, "and nobody would ever see those girls go in or out."

"How in hell did the Mama—" Essie began.

"She offered to sell herself, but she was too old, being a grown woman," Cal said. "However, her daughters—"

"All right, all right!" Mame snapped, not needing to hear the rest. She jumped up and began to pace.

Essie watched her for a few seconds, then said, "Whoever knows so much about the mother also knows where she is." It was a statement, not a question, and a demand, and Sarge took a piece of notepaper from his shirt pocket and passed it to her. "We need to find Lolly fast. And maybe we need to talk about how to deal with the mother?"

"I'd like to drop her in the East River," Mame said. "A burlap bag filled with every child-rearing book we have in the library tied around her waist." The look on her face and the tone of her voice said she meant every word.

Essie stood and headed for the door. "I'd like to talk to her first. If any part of her right mind is left, I want to get the girls' birth certificates."

"Suppose they weren't born in a hospital?" Clara asked.

"That might work in our favor," Essie said, and she was gone.

Polly Giles lived in a one room basement apartment in a decrepit building around the corner and two blocks East of the shoe repair and snack shops. The basement was dark and dirty and the door to Polly's apartment looked like a good, solid kick would fling it open but Essie knocked with the bottle in her right hand. No response. She knocked again, louder, again to no response. Finally, she pounded, hoping she wouldn't break the bottle. The door swung open, and a bleary-eyed mess glared at her. "The fuck you want? Them others been here an' gone long time ago." Essie took the cigarettes and the bottle of rotgut vodka out of the bag, showed it to Polly, and immediately felt sorry. The need and greed that almost brightened the woman's eyes was one of the most painful things Essie had ever seen, and the nurse had seen more than enough pain. "If you can give me the girls' birth certificates, I will say thanks with this," and she held up the bottle.

"The whats?"

"Birth certificates. A piece of paper that says when and where they were born."

Polly was shaking her head back and forth. She was wobbling back and forth. She began to whimper. Essie wanted to just give her the booze because that would be kinder than what she was doing. "Only papers I got is from the church when they got baptized—"

Essie wasn't much on praying but she could change her mind if Polly Giles had baptismal certificates. "May I please see them, Polly?"

Polly eyed the bottle. "I can still have that?" And when Essie nodded, she crossed the room to a chest of drawers that once had been a fine piece of furniture. She flung open and slammed shut drawer after drawer, rooting around until she found a fat folder. She flipped through pages, triumphantly grasping several documents which she thrust at Essie. They said "St. Peter's Claver Catholic Church, Shreveport, Louisiana." Lolly's name on one document, Molly's on the other, and the dates. "And these ones—I had forgot about them—is about some shots they got at the hospital when they was babies." Essie gave her the vodka and the cigarettes, thanked her, and turned to leave. "I want them papers back, you hear me?!"

"It's a good thing you did, Polly, getting the girls baptized," Essie said kindly.

"I'm from Loo-sianna and we all got baptized so we wouldn't go to hell. But them priests the ones oughta went to hell for what they done to us chil'ren."

Essie ran up the steps from the basement and out the front door and would have kept running away from that basement but for the half dozen police cars on the block. Her stomach dropped.

Were they looking for Polly Giles? Essie changed direction but what she saw next answered several of her questions: the morgue van was parked next to the crime scene collection truck. How long before fingers pointed at Polly? Essie stepped into the street and flagged a cab. She couldn't get home fast enough, but the police activity slowed traffic to a crawl which was a good thing because otherwise she would never have seen Lolly stumbling down the sidewalk. Molly was right—they could've been twins except for Lolly's height.

"Stop!" she yelled at the driver. Unnecessarily because they weren't moving. She tossed money up to him, opened her door, and scrambled out, missing the front bumper of the car in the next lane by barely a foot. She ran to the sidewalk and stopped a few feet from Lolly, who looked even more filthy than her sister had been, but who also was beyond exhausted and on the brink of collapse.

"Lolly," Essie said gently and quietly. "I'm a friend of Molly's and she's very worried about you." And she stood still and allowed Lolly to observe her.

"Where she at?"

"My home, where my friends are taking care of her."

"Taking care of her, how?"

"A hot bath, clean clothes, good food, a warm bed."

Lolly scrutinized her closely and carefully for several long seconds. "What she had to do to get all that?"

"Not one thing, Lolly, I promise you."

"A bed by herself?"

"Yes, and you will, too."

Lolly began to cry. "I wanna go where Molly is."

"Oh dear Lord! That poor woman was just doing to her children what was done to her!" Clara sobbed and Cal held her tightly. They spoke in near whispers because Lolly and Molly were asleep in the next room, sharing a bed. Lolly was bathed in the big basement sink with Molly telling her sister everything that would happen, and she asked Sarge to please fix grits and eggs. Lolly drank two glasses of milk and fell asleep, the glass still at her mouth. And because Sandy and Clara had gone shopping for Molly, Lolly had pajamas to sleep in instead of a tee shirt-as-nightgown.

Though an explosion probably wouldn't have awakened the girls, the adults spoke quietly as they perused the documents Essie brought from Polly's, marveling at the timing: If she had been five minutes later leaving . . .

"Don't even think it!" Mame cautioned, even as she thought of nothing else. She touched the papers spread out on the table almost reverently. "The woman wanted to do the right thing . . . tried to do the right thing . . . but she never had a snowball's chance in hell."

"Does that mean Molly and Lolly are doomed?" Sandy asked, "'Cause we want to adopt those girls, give 'em a good home and an education—"

"They are not doomed," Essie said, "though they will have a stony path to trod, and you will need strength and courage to help them forward."

They all knew the words to the song but had never thought to apply them to children. And yet . . . these two little girls . . . none of the adults could imagine their trauma, not even those who had experienced the Southern United States and a foreign war. Clara touched the papers. "Will this be enough to let us adopt them? Without birth certificates?"

"Enough to keep them out of jail?" Sandy asked.

"It's enough to move carefully forward: a documented midwife delivery along with a record of shots at the hospital—that's a very good start," Essie said.

"On the other hand," Mame said quietly, "if there are no school records . . . we do have work to do. And to start, you will have to move out of this neighborhood."

Sarge said what four pairs of shocked eyes thought: "We can't afford that."

"I might know somebody who can help with that," Mame said, almost certain that Lorraine Hansberry and whoever her friends were would rise to the occasion.

"Are we criminals if we adopt the girls?" Cal asked.

"Do you think you are?" Mame asked, making eye contact with the four of them, people who in less than a week had become friends, and four heads shook in unison.

"I am not a criminal for saving a child's life," Sandra said.

"Me, neither," said Clara, and their husbands verbally followed suit.

"The criminals are all those people in that block who had to know what was going on and did nothing!" Sandy said.

"What could they do?" Clara challenged. "Tell the police?" And since that never was an option, they sat silently until Clara said, "And we are *not* criminals!"

"I might be, though, because I intend to create records at Harlem Hospital that do not currently exist," Essie said, and Mame fanned herself and feigned a swoon.

Lorraine Hansberry kept her promise to help, pointing the way to apartments for the two families five blocks away and part-time jobs for Sandy and Clara at a daycare center on the corner. The neighborhood elementary school enrolled Lolly and Molly and accepted their Louisiana documents and Essie's claim of little access to regular formal schooling.

Cal and Sarge got transferred to a new route that was further from home, but which almost guaranteed they would not be recognized. The four adults were happy and the children seemed to be thriving. "Except at night," Clara said sadly. "They have bad dreams. Of course they do! So they sleep together—they alternate apartments. And they call us Mama and Papa—both of them call all of us Mama or Papa."

After a dinner of chicken, collard greens, and black-eyed peas— "They won't eat anything else—except eggs and grits!" Sandy wailed before calming herself. "But at least they eat."

"Y'all know 'bout them three monkeys, right?" Lolly said one evening after dinner. "The people in the Chinese laundry where I work sometimes told me 'bout 'em: See No Evil, Hear No Evil, and Speak No Evil. That's their names." Lolly put her hands over her eyes, her ears, and her mouth as she spoke of the monkeys. "Well, I'm making myself the Fourth Monkey." And she raised her left arm straight up, palm facing out, like a Broadway traffic warden. Her right was pulled close to her chest, the fist balled tight and ready to strike hard and fast.

"And what's your name, monkey number four?" Mame asked.

"Take No Evil," the girl said between clenched teeth. "Take no shit from no evil-doer."

HEARTBREAK ALLEY

ANN APTAKER

I must be getting old. Nights at the dyke bar give me a headache. The dancefloor is too crowded, the music's too loud. Sure, the bad old days of police raids are over, our love lives are no longer criminal—though that could change, and we all live a little scared because we know it could change tomorrow. Anyway, music-wise I'm more Billy Strayhorn than—well, I don't know who the hell they are, especially the way the DJ mixes it all up. My torch-song-loving ears can't make out who's who in the tangle of tunes and thumps.

So I don't drop by the bar as much as I used to, only now and then on nights like tonight when my studio apartment feels cramped. Even filled as they are with art and knickknacks I like, the four walls fail to keep up their end of the conversation.

It's the same story tonight at the dyke club unless you call shouting over the music conversation.

Still, it's fun to watch the young ones drape all over each other, everyone of every race mixing easily—butches, femmes, transwomen, and all the recently proclaimed genders—while I lean against the bar and drink too many beers. I guess you could say I'm living my unglamourous version of that "Lush Life" Strayhorn's dark and beautiful melody extolled. Too bad he drowned in it, using alcohol to soothe his closeted gay pain. It didn't, any more than it soothes my aching nostalgia for the days when I was a daring young dyke with a series of delicious dames on my arm, police raids be damned.

Time to get outta here before I cry in my beer.

I leave by the alley door. It's closer to the bus stop down the block.

Glare from the single lightbulb above the door makes navigation difficult for the uninitiated, but I know the alley's shadows and its slippery beer-stained cobblestones underfoot well enough to make my way. And besides, I may be past my best-by date for the hip-and-cool crowd in the dyke bar, but I'm still sure-footed, my knees still hold me up, and my hair's still brown; well, more or less.

All the beer I'd swilled complicates matters a little. The shadows in the alley aren't as stable as they should be, the light above the door and the glow from the street are a bit watery, casting a wiggly luminescence on a woman who's walking into the alley. I guess she's on her way to the bar.

She's familiar. Her shape is familiar; curvy, substantial, feminine for the ages. Her walk is familiar, each step claiming the cobblestones and the whole earth under them as her own.

I know her. She broke my heart. It took a lot of emotional stitches to bind my heart up again.

A loud blast and a flash of light crack through the alley. The noise ricochets against the walls, echoes in my ears, threatens to shatter my skull. I see a shadow, a silhouette, blur and disappear from the street.

I see the woman fall to the ground.

Her name slides through my lips: "Alexandra."

I rush to her. I see her face in the streetlight creeping into the alley. I see her open, terrified eyes. She tries to speak when her eyes find me. A bloody gurgle flows from her mouth before she can finish the word she tries to say: Josie. My name.

I hear a woman's voice shout through the bar's door, "What's that noise? Sounded like a firecracker." I look over my shoulder, see the bartender—Dani's her name, a tee-shirt-and-jeans type we used to describe as androgynous but nowadays goes by non-binary, which is a pretty good description of Dani, and me, too, truth be told. Several bar patrons are behind Dani, rubbernecking in the doorway, pushing their way through, silhouetted by the light behind.

Someone shouts, "What happened? What's going on?"

I shout back, "She's been shot!" and pull my cell phone from my pocket. That scary word, shot, stops the crowd in its tracks.

Only Dani comes over. She puts her strong hand under my arm and hauls me up from my crouch over Alexandra. "Who're you calling?"

"911," I say. "She needs an ambulance."

Dani's eyes flash a combination of panic and disgust. "Are you nuts?" she says. "An ambulance call for a gunshot wound will bring the cops, and there are women in this bar whose relationship with the police is iffy at best, even fucking dangerous."

I escape Dani's grip. "Don't you understand? I have to get her to a hospital!" I say.

"Not from this alley, you're not."

A calmer voice says, "Don't bother." The voice belongs to a twenty-something femme in a pale green cocktail dress who I just now notice is crouched over Alexandra, two fingers pressed against the side of Alexandra's throat. "She's gone," she says and stands up.

"No," I say and grab the twenty-something by her arm. "No. You're wrong. Who are you to decide Alexandra's dead?"

"I'm a doctor. Well, almost," she says. "I finish medical school this year, but yeah, they taught us to know when someone's dead. Now, let go of my arm."

The bar patrons scatter, some back into the bar to collect their things, some just make it fast down the alley and out to the street. Death at their doorstep and the specter of cops wasn't exactly the sexy night of drinking, dancing, and flirting they'd planned. Only Dani and the young almost-doctor hang around.

The almost-doctor says, "Let her call the damn ambulance, Dani. They'll take the body to the morgue. After that, it's a police problem. But don't worry, there's nobody here now for the cops to question or push around."

Dani rushes back to the empty bar. She pulls out her ring of keys, presumably to lock the place up, inside and out, turning it into a closed establishment where no one was ever here, so there was no one to see or hear a thing.

The almost-doctor says, "I'm gone, too. Sorry about your girlfriend, if that's what she was."

"She—wasn't."

"Well, whatever. But if I were you, I wouldn't be here when the ambulance arrives." With nothing more to offer than a sympathetic shrug, she walks out of the alley and into the street.

I'm alone again with the woman who broke my heart. Only now she's dead at my feet, breaking my heart again.

I call 911, tell the operator to send an ambulance.

I kneel down to Alexandra, slide bloodied strands of her black hair from her cheek. "Damn, I loved you," I say.

Standing up again, I slip my phone back into my pants pocket: my dyke-y pants pocket under my dyke-y leather belt and my dyke-y tailored men's white oxford shirt and my dyke-y leather jacket. I take the almost-doctor's advice and get dyke-y me the hell out of the alley.

I hear a siren.

There's a knock on my apartment door. It disrupts my communion with a bottle of beer, my memories of my steamy affair with Alexandra, and the tears I'm in a losing battle to prevent.

The knock becomes insistent, forcing me up from the couch. I lumber over to the door, look through the peephole, catch my breath. A middle-aged, brown-haired guy is at my door. He's wearing a lightweight tan jacket, the zipper open to a gray T-shirt. He holds up a badge.

"Open up," the cop says.

I've got two lousy options: open the door or go out the window and down the fire escape to the street. A quick analysis of the situation tells me that though the first option has absolutely no appeal, the second option turns me into a fugitive, which would put me on the sort of police department list it's not a good idea to be on.

I wipe my eyes and open the door.

The cop comes inside, shows me his badge and ID. He's Sergeant Thomas Sloan. I bet everyone calls him Tommy.

He looks around the room, at the pictures and knickknacks on my walls, at the well-worn purple couch, the white enamel-top table that serves as a dining table and desk. I can't tell if he likes what he sees or thinks I'm weird. "You Josephine McGraw?" he finally says with no expression at all.

"Yeah, I'm Josie McGraw," I say, uneasy as hell that he knows my name. "What can I do for you, sergeant?"

"You can tell me about the dead woman in the alley."

I say nothing, just swallow hard to keep my heart in my chest and my beer in my belly.

"Oh, come on," Sloan says with a know-it-all sneer. "You should've used a pay phone if you didn't want us to trace the 911 call back to you, but, hey, where can you find a pay phone these days?" He seems to find that funny.

I find it another reminder that, yeah, maybe I'm past my best-by date.

"So, about the dead woman," Sloan says, all business now. "The driver's license in her wallet ID'd her as Alexandra Zervas. Did you know her?" The casual way he says it scares me.

My beer-filled stomach tightens, my throat feels raw, but I manage, "I haven't seen her in a few years." I don't offer any more. If all those cop shows on TV are correct, the less I say the better, and never volunteer anything.

"Uh-huh," Sloan says, still all business. "But you knew her."

"Well, yeah, sure, I knew her."

"How well did you know her?"

"Why?"

"Look, Miss McGraw," he says, annoyed. "I'm not here to inspect your bed, okay? None of my business. Not anymore." The way he says "not anymore," as sort of an afterthought, I'm not sure if he misses those old days of raids and arrests or is relieved he doesn't have to bother with dirty sheets work. "Just fill me in on Miss Zervas," he says. "I've got a dozen other homicide files on my desk, and I'd like to clear this one fast and easy. So if you knew her well, maybe you also know anybody who wasn't too crazy about her."

Crazy about her. I wish he hadn't used that expression, because that's what I was, crazy about her. Crazy about her despite the darkness that surrounded her like a seductive mist. Despite the sketchy women who showed up at her door. Maybe one of them followed her to the alley tonight, with a gun.

I didn't know their names. I didn't want to know. And even if I knew, the idea of snitching on other women, especially other dykes, turns my stomach.

Either way, I have nothing to tell Sergeant Sloan.

The way he looks at me now gives me a creepy feeling, like he's looking so deep into my eyes he sees all the way down to my childhood. By the time he comes back up, it's like he's dragged up my whole life story with him. "Well, did you see the shooter?"

I shake my head, say, "Just a blur in the street, then they were gone."

"Uh-huh. And you have no idea who it might have been?"

He gets another headshake.

"All right," he says, "looks like I'll have to jog your memory. Let's go."

"Go where?"

"The police station, sixth precinct."

"Why? Am I in trouble?"

"Not yet."

The detective squad room isn't like on TV. It's not noisy with ringing phones, or shouting cops, handcuffed petty criminals, or sequined streetwalkers. It's just a fairly quiet and shadowy room. The most prominent noise is the click and clatter of computer keyboards attended by shirt-sleeved guys and casually dressed women. Some speak quietly into cell or desk phones. Almost everyone is taking notes, either written on a pad or typed into their computers. Everyone's face looks otherworldly or sickly in the false light of their computer screens.

It's all too eerie for my taste. I'd rather it was a roomful of cops smoking cigarettes and yelling into big black desk phones. At least the place would have a human touch. Instead, I feel like I'm in a low-budget dystopian sci-fi movie.

I was right, though, about Sloan's name. A couple of detectives nod or wave with, "Hi, Tommy."

"Sit down," Sloan says and indicates the chair beside his desk. He sits down in his own chair, boots up his computer, and types something on the keyboard. "Well, lookie here," he says and turns the screen enough for me to see.

There's a photo of Alexandra, a mugshot dated five years ago. Next to the photo is her description—age: thirty; height: five-foot-three inches; hair: black; eyes: dark brown—followed by an arrest record that lists only a single charge of unlawful use of a credit card and sentenced her to three months prison time.

Sloan types: *Known associates.* Mugshot photos of four women come up on the screen. "You know any of these people, Miss McGraw?"

I say nothing, just look at the photos, but I feel my face tighten.

Sloan's smile is a knowing smile, a cop's smile. "You recognize one of them, don't you? Or maybe more than one."

I still say nothing and try my damnedest not to fidget in my seat.

Sloan says, "Okay. I get it. No one wants to be a snitch. And I guess that goes double for your crowd."

"My crowd?"

"You know very well what I mean, Miss McGraw, so don't jerk me around. And if you think I don't understand the spot you're in, you're wrong. But I'm trying to catch a murderer. I don't know exactly what Alexandra Zervas was to you, but I can guess, so help me out here. Which one of these lovely ladies," he says, pointing at the screen, "do you recognize?"

I could beat myself up for what I'm about to do, but I'm stuck with a lousy choice. And I really don't want to know any more dirty dealings Alexandra, my Alexandra, might have been involved in.

I have only one way to slip out from under Sloan's grip, so I buck up, tighten my insides, and point to the photo of a red-haired woman.

"Martha Brennan," he says. "How do you know her?"

"I didn't say I know her. I only recognize her."

"You telling me you've never met her?"

"That's right."

"Then how do you recognize her?"

I swallow what tastes like a throat full of bile.

Sloan notices. "Come on, McGraw. Let's have it."

I take a deep breath, take the breath in slowly, then let it out slowly, too, before I'm finally able to say, "When Alexandra and I—when we were together, Brennan once dropped by Alexandra's place."

"What did she want?"

"I don't know. They went into the kitchen for a few minutes, and then Brennan left."

"Well, weren't you curious?"

"Listen, sergeant," I say, my throat tight, "Alexandra and I—well, it wasn't the sort of relationship that was going to end with a picket fence, a puppy, and an adopted kid or two. It was more heat than homey. I didn't ask questions about what Alexandra did with her life. I was only interested in her time with me. Whatever was between Alexandra and this Brennan woman was none of my business, and I wanted it that way."

"And you never saw Martha Brennan again after that?"

"No. And like I told you, I haven't seen Alexandra in a while. Three years, actually."

Sloan turns back to his computer, clicks on the photo of Martha Brennan. "Huh. Nice company your girlfriend kept. Brennan's got an interesting sheet. Seems she was a con artist, cheated tourists with phony theater tickets, among other scams. At the time of her arrest, she was carrying an unlicensed weapon, a .38."

That's the first helpful news all night. "You think she might be Alexandra's killer?"

"Not unless they allow long-range weaponry in the women's state pen. She's currently near the end of her first year of a one-to-four stretch."

"Oh."

"That's just where we want her," Sloan says. "She's what you might call a captive audience, or just a captive, at any rate, meaning I won't have to search for her to question her. She might have a lot to say about Zervas's life and activities. And her parole hearing is likely coming up, too, so she'll be in a very cooperative mood."

"I thought you said nobody likes a snitch, sergeant."

"Unless it means a get-out-of-jail card," he says with a grin.

"Okay," I say, "let's go talk to her."

He turns the computer screen back to him, out of my view. "You're not going anywhere, McGraw. You're going to stay out of police business." Then he types something on his keyboard. "Well, this is interesting, though not surprising. Must've been tough, McGraw."

"What are you talking about?"

He turns the screen back to me. There's an old black-and-white mug shot of me as a young, scared dyke almost forty years ago after one of the last police raids of the gay bars. I was grabbed along with about fifty other women. We spent a hard night in the city jail, where the guards and police matrons made no secret of their contempt for us. A few even spit on us.

"Must've been tough," Sloan says again.

"I survived it," is all I say, feeling again the chill of that hellish night. "Am I free to go, Sergeant Sloan?"

"Go home, McGraw."

"But don't leave town, right?" I joke, trying to make this nightmare more TV show than real life.

I get up from the chair, start to walk away, but turn back for one last confrontation with Sloan. "Do me a favor, sergeant. When you catch Alexandra's killer, don't make me hear about it on the TV news or the internet. Tell me about it yourself."

—◇— —◇— —◇—

Whoever's banging on my door at five o'clock in the morning should be arrested, their hands lopped off at the wrists. I holler at the door, "What the hell, motherfucker?" while I pull myself out of bed and throw on a shirt and a pair of chinos I find next to a few of last night's empty beer bottles on the floor. I'm not about to answer the door naked.

I'm also not about to lop off the hands of this pre-dawn barbarian when I look through the peephole and then open the door. It's not smart to assault a cop.

"Good morning, McGraw," says a red-eyed, unshaven but unnaturally alert Sergeant Sloan. He walks in without being invited, looks around, and gives me a questioning look after spotting the empty beer bottles. Then he ignores them. "I'm here to do you that favor," he says.

It takes me a minute to tune into what he's talking about. It's been a week since I last saw him. I finally blurt, "You found Alexandra's killer?"

"I just came from booking him."

Him? Not one of Alexandra's sketchy female associates? What was this? A random street crime?

"You got any coffee around here?" Sloan says. He eyes the beer bottles again. "You look like you could use some. I know I can."

I'm in no mood for the time it takes to make coffee, and in no mood for sharing a couple of cups with Sloan. "Sergeant Sloan," I say, more hiss than words, "please drop the social crap and tell me who killed Alexandra."

He gives that an okay-whatever shrug and sits down at my enamel-top table. He unzips his jacket, exposing the butt of his gun nestled in his shoulder rig. "All right," he says. "First of all, just as I suspected, Martha Brennan's parole hearing comes up next week, which made her plenty cooperative. She's a pro, so she knows the drill. She knows that one negative report from me could deny her parole and keep her locked up for the full stretch. So even though she acted tough, she spilled her guts on her friend Alexandra. Oh, and she was very sorry to hear about Alexandra's death. Sorry, but not surprised."

My grief for Alexandra just got deeper, deeper than even the hell of this past week that all that beer couldn't soothe.

I really don't want to hear whatever ugly story Sloan came here to tell me, but I have to hear it. I have to know who killed Alexandra, and I have to know why. Maybe then that lush life I've been drowning in won't rot me.

I steel myself for the rest of Sloan's tale. "Brennan told me all about the scams she and Alexandra set up and some of the crew they worked with. This led me to one Henry Reiss," Sloan says. "Seems Reiss aspired to High Society. He certainly had the money. Inherited some, made the rest himself; some real estate, some import-export. But he was kicked to the curb by the snooty crowd because his money was so new the ink on it was barely dry. It didn't have the pedigree to get him into the finer clubs. So he was drowning his sorrows in a bar one night, and that's where Reiss met Brennan. When he was drunk enough and spilled his guts about his humiliation among the monied, it was easy for Martha to recruit him to spot big-time, big-money marks for her and Alexandra to fleece. It was a way for Reiss to avenge his resentments, and he jumped at it."

"You saying this Reiss guy killed her?"

"He even confessed. He was too scared, or too stupid, to call for a lawyer. He even peed in his pants." There's a vicious undertone in Sloan's chuckle. There's also a hint of pity.

"But why would he kill Alexandra?" I say. "She wasn't a member of the society crowd. She'd have no reason to humiliate him."

"Oh, but she did humiliate him. I guess you don't know men very well, McGraw."

I'm tempted to tell him that I know men well enough to count them among my pals, but they can't compare to a woman's embrace, a woman's kiss, a woman's body in my bed. I let it pass, though. Maybe Sloan would appreciate it, maybe not. This isn't the moment to take the chance. So I just give him a sly smile.

He says, "Some men don't like it when women say no, McGraw. And your Alexandra said no every time he tried to romance her. He let it slide until he stopped by her apartment one night last week and found her with a woman. For a guy who'd been humiliated by the society crowd, I guess this was the one humiliation too far. He went home, bought a gun the next morning, waited outside Alexandra's place until she came out, then followed her all day and into the evening. He found his moment when she stepped off the street and into that alley."

All the fears of every dyke, every gay man, every trans, everyone in the whole LGBTQ alphabet, are in the story Sloan just told. The reality of those fears showed up in the alley that night, knocked on my door this morning, and came inside with Sergeant Sloan.

My foot kicks one of the empty beer bottles on the floor as I stumble my way to the couch. I know I'm gonna land on my ass and cry for Alexandra, cry loud and long for her and for every bruised, beaten, and dead woman who's said no to some guy who couldn't take it.

My foot kicks another beer bottle as I crash down on the couch. The bottle rolls around, making a sad music, a torch song for Billy Strayhorn, and me.

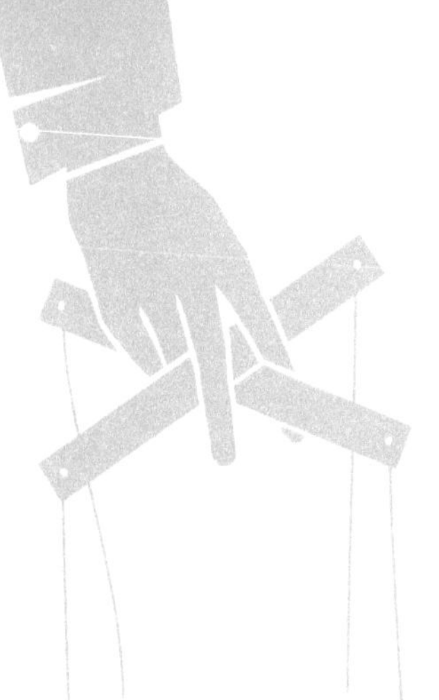

LIPSTICK, GRENADINE, OR BLOOD

KRISTEN LEPIONKA

I've spent most of my adult life behind the bar at the Blue Angel, which should tell you something about either my admirable work ethic or my questionable life choices. Or both. But after almost two decades, the place is a second home to me—and to a lot of people here in town. It's a queer bar that's been open since the early '90s and has managed to outlast a lot of its neighbors, which are increasingly being spirited away by developers in favor of yet another stack of overpriced condos and niche storefronts like float spas or artisanal breakfast taco stands.

The space is narrow and lit low by a smattering of patinaed pendant lamps, with a heavy oak bar top running along one side and a row of ripped vinyl booths on the other. Between the two, a sticky dance floor, just large enough for the small but loyal group who meets for line-dancing on Tuesdays. We've also got karaoke on Wednesdays, a burlesque act on Fridays, and drag king bingo on Saturdays, which gives way to the rowdiest crowds of the week as the night goes on. The wall opposite the bar is adorned by a series of large, framed photos of Marlene Dietrich, the bar's adopted patron saint. We had nearly all of her iconic roles depicted on our walls, smirking through cigarette smoke like she knows your secrets.

Usually, the biggest problems we face are bad tips and worse dancing. That is, until the body on the floor.

—m— —m— —m—

Thursdays in bar life are caught between the post hump day slump and the pre-weekend buildup— just enough customers to keep the bartenders busy but not so packed that we'd need crowd-control measures. Nell, our best bartender, was slinging drinks with her usual flair. She's the star behind the bar, always remembering special requests: a splash of pineapple juice for one patron, an extra lime for another. She's tall enough to reach the top-shelf liquors, not that most patrons can afford it. Her tip jar is perpetually fuller than anyone else's, though she claims it's just luck.

Around midnight, I was in the back office, elbow-deep in spreadsheets, when everything suddenly went quiet. The silence hit me like a slap. No DJ spinning Chappell Roan or Debby Friday, no hum of conversation or trill of laughter—just the muted hush of something very wrong.

I nearly tripped over a stray box of cocktail napkins in the hallway as I headed out front. The lights in the main bar were still pulsing neon, but the crowd had parted in a tight circle near the corner booth, which now had a figure sprawled on the floor before it.

The person on the ground was Jana Newman—a petite woman who liked gin gimlets and soft butches. Her eyes were open, but unfocused. A gash on her temple crested an angry, quick-forming bruise.

Nell knelt beside Jana, hands hovering near her neck, as though she'd been about to check for a pulse but lost her nerve. The crowd pressed closer, collectively holding its breath. I dropped to my knees beside Nell. The floor was damp under my jeans.

"She's not breathing," Nell whispered, her face pale.

"Call 911," I said as calmly as I could, checking Jana's wrist for a pulse. My own heart hammered, each beat echoing in my ears. Jana's veins were still. Someone behind me was speaking to an emergency dispatcher in low, urgent tones.

I felt for Jana's lower ribs through her shirt. You don't work in nightlife this long without a passing familiarity with CPR. By the time the paramedics arrived, my arms were shaking. They took her away on a stretcher, lights flashing in the blackness of the street.

The police arrived soon after. Detective Stevens, wiry with sharp brown eyes, asked the usual questions: *When was the last time you saw Jana conscious? How well did you know her? Any history of health problems? Alcohol or drug abuse? Signs of a struggle?*

I told the detective everything I knew about Jana Newman, which wasn't much. She was fairly new in town, had started to come to the Blue Angel about three months ago. She asked me, once, where she could score some coke, her eyes flicking towards the restroom, and I told her that my bar wasn't nice enough to be a cocaine bar. About a week ago, she'd come in with a resume and wanted to apply for a job. I'd told her we weren't hiring, which was true, but in truth, it was the coke question and a general vibe of shiftiness that I got from her that made me toss her resume in the trash.

"What does that mean, a cocaine bar?"

"Our patrons don't have the disposable income," I said. "Try Route 36, downtown, for that."

Stevens frowned at me. I wondered if she had ever been in a lesbian bar before and assumed no—not because she was straight, but because she was no fun. She was scribbling in a small notebook as I talked. The notebook made me nervous. "What can you tell me about the time leading up to the incident?"

I tried to recall Jana's last hour. She'd come in around ten, alone, as usual, and ordered a drink. I remembered seeing Jana engaged in animated conversation with Nell at the bar shortly after she arrived. I hadn't thought much of it at the time—the bar is a place for passionate chats, sometimes borderline arguments, but they usually blow over in seconds.

Still, the detective latched onto that detail. "So your bartender was the last person seen with her?"

I winced. "No, there were dozens of people here."

"But they were arguing."

We were standing on the sticky dance floor, near the booth where Jana had fallen. The wall above the booth featured a picture of Dietrich as Amy Jolly in *Morocco*, the classic top hat and tails in the scene where she kisses a female club patron full on the mouth, before the Hollywood code made such things impossible for decades. This picture was my favorite, but Dietrich's eyes seemed to be watching me now, suspicious. I said, "Maybe Jana was complaining about the price of Hendricks."

Stevens raised an eyebrow, making notes in a small notepad. That notepad made me nervous. "We'll need to talk to Nell."

I shouldn't have said anything about the conversation. Nell was a lot of things—snarky, charismatic, occasionally reckless—but not violent. "I think you have the wrong idea here."

"We talk to everyone who interacted with the victim," Stevens said with a noncommittal shrug. "Hopefully, Jana wakes up and can tell us about what happened."

Spoiler alert: she didn't.

News travels fast in the queer scene—faster if it's bad news and faster still if it's dripping with gossip. Jana was dead, and the police were asking a lot of questions about Nell. By midday Friday, every dyke in the city had heard about it and was texting me for deets:

WHAT HAPPENED?!?!?!?!
Is it true??
I knew she was secretly a psycho
OMG does this mean you guys are hiring?

Stevens called to ask about the bar's security cameras. I explained we had two: one near the front entrance and one behind the bar, both nearly as old as my tenure at the Blue Angel.

I pulled the footage for them, but it wasn't very revealing—just a bunch of grainy figures grinding together. The floor in front of the corner booth area was just out of frame, but the bottom of the footage captured Amy Jolly's smoky eyes. I started at the beginning of the evening and tried to watch Jana's every move, but she moved in and out of the frame a lot, ordering no fewer than four drinks and disappearing towards the restrooms twice as many times. She moved with the increasingly unsteady gait of someone trying to obliterate her consciousness. Other than the bartenders and a brief stop at the DJ booth, she didn't appear to speak to much of anyone.

Nell didn't come in that night. I couldn't blame her. When I texted, she responded: *Need time to process.* She'd told the detective everything she knew, so there was no reason for me to doubt her. Right?

Our resident burlesque act, Tassels of Fury, canceled their show, citing a contagion of sprained ankles, but luckily, I got Casey to sub in for entertainment at the last minute. She offered me a half-smile when she arrived, and I snapped the lids off two bottles of Stella, one for her and one for me.

"I watched the security cam footage today," I said, "and noticed that Jana briefly talked to you while you were in the DJ booth. Remember anything about the conversation?"

Casey drank deeply for a minute before she said: "It was kind of strange, actually. She mentioned Nell. Indirectly."

"Indirectly?"

"Well, I had witnessed them talking in the alley about a week or so ago. Things got a bit heated. Jana told her something like, 'It'll be on you,' and Nell said to back off. So then last night, Jana said, 'Just remember what you saw.'"

A chill ran down my spine. Nell hadn't mentioned these specifics. Detective Stevens would love this. "So Jana knew that you had seen them talking?"

"Apparently so." Over her shoulder, a portrait of Dietrich as Altar Keane in *Rancho Notorious* watched us, tying her lace-up booties in silent judgment.

"And she just walked up to you last night and mentioned it, out of the blue."

Casey nodded. "I've been thinking. How well do we really know Nell?"

"Well enough," I said, but how well could you know anyone?

On Saturday night, our drag king bingo host—Justin Boober—bailed on their gig, citing sudden onset laryngitis, and I thought about not opening up at all. But a single evening of zero income could be the beginning of the end for a bar. People still came in but the crowd was thinner than usual, the chatter laced with worry.

Around midnight, Nell walked in. She paused just inside the door, scanning the room as if she expected torches and pitchforks.

I waved her over. She approached; shoulders tense. "Sorry about yesterday. And, well, tonight. I've been fielding calls all day." Nell's voice shook. "Jana's friends are convinced I had something to do with what happened."

I started fixing her an old-fashioned, Dietrich's favorite drink, served just the way she liked them: Canadian whisky, orange curacao, Angostura. "Tell me about your convo with her."

Her eyes flickered with something. "She ordered a tequila sunrise, so I grabbed a highball and started to make it. Then she flipped out and insisted that she had ordered a gimlet. I know that's her usual order, but she definitely ordered a tequila sunrise that night."

"And that's all."

Nell nodded unconvincingly.

I slid the rocks glass across the bar to her. "You don't have to confide in me like a friend," I said, "but please, at least tell me the truth about what happened in my bar. Casey said she heard her threatening you last week, out back. So I think there's more to all of this."

"Okay, but listen—last night, that really was all to the conversation."

"I'm listening."

Nell sighed. "We used to live together, Jana and me. Roommates. This was years ago, in Chicago. She wanted there to be more between us, but there wasn't. I moved out. But she couldn't let it go."

"How so?"

"First she kept inventing emergencies that she begged me to help with, like she was locked out of our old place, or then she was worried about her cat—I did love that cat—but she kept coming up with ways to get me to respond to her. And when I finally said no to that kind of thing, she started, like, doing shit such as showing up at my girlfriend's yoga studio to take a class."

"To what end?"

"I have no idea. Eventually, I moved back home, here. It all stopped. But then Jana moved here too, and she turned up in the bar—and she acted like she didn't even recognize me. Honestly, it was fucking weird." Nell dropped her head to her hands for a while.

"Why didn't you tell me?"

"Tell you what? That someone I used to know was frequenting the bar and ignoring me? What would you have said to that?"

She had a point. I motioned for her to continue.

"Then I saw her talking to you, applying for a job. I'd been trying just to ignore her, but I couldn't go through this again. At that point, I should've come to you; I see that now. So I followed her outside, and we really got into it. She kept saying that I abandoned her, that we were meant to be together. That if I refused to see it, she was going to make things very, very unpleasant for me. I told her to leave me the fuck alone, or I would call the police."

I nodded. That fit with what Casey had overheard. "Then what?"

"That was the last time I saw her, until Thursday night, when she showed up acting like she didn't know who I was, and she ordered the tequila sunrise. Em, that's the absolute truth."

I studied her. "You realize how bad this looks—your argument, the threat, then Jana turning up dead."

She closed her eyes briefly. "I sure do. But nothing else happened between us, I swear."

"What exactly was Jana going to do to make things unpleasant for you?"

Before Nell could answer, the detective arrived—Stevens, wearing the same tired expression as two nights before. She locked on to Nell immediately. "Mind coming down to the station for more questions?"

By Sunday morning, the rumor mill was in warp drive. Some claimed Nell confessed; others said Jana was an undercover cop. One person insisted Jana was part of a secret ring of diamond thieves.

Nell texted me: *Can we talk?*

I texted her the name of a local diner.

She arrived in a hoodie, baseball cap pulled low like a fugitive. We slid into a booth, and the waitress took our coffee order without a word, shooting Nell a wary glance.

"The detective insisted they found evidence of a struggle," Nell said quietly. "Apparently, her wrist was broken and bruised, like someone could have grabbed her. They asked me for a DNA sample."

"No, don't do it."

"I already did," Nell said.

I sipped coffee, black, wishing it was something stronger. "Why would you do that?"

"They're saying something under her fingernails contained DNA." She grimaced. "My DNA will not be under her fingernails. But they found my fingerprints on a piece of glass near the booth. I felt like I needed to do something to show I have nothing to hide."

I thought of the chaos around the bar on a busy night. Easy for anyone's prints to end up anywhere. But the police wouldn't see it that way. "You need to get a lawyer, Nell."

"Like I can afford a lawyer."

My mind was spinning through our regulars at the bar as I tried to remember if any were defense lawyers.

Nell stared into her cup. "I'm telling you, Em, I didn't do this. Sure, we had history, but I wouldn't—the coroner said she was struck on the head with a blunt object."

The words sank in. "Could her injuries be accidental somehow?"

"Stevens said there wasn't proof that they were intentional, but that there is a lot of circumstantial evidence pointing my way," Nell said, bleak. "I've heard about circumstantial evidence before, obviously, but it never really hit me what it means—a theory that can't be disproven by direct evidence."

The waitress returned with a plate of toast we hadn't ordered. She set it in front of Nell as if in apology for eavesdropping. We both stared down at it. Finally, Nell stood. "I hope you believe me, but even if you don't, I'm going to figure out a way to prove it."

I nodded, but the sliver of doubt in the back of my mind refused to fade.

Our Sunday night trivia host—Facts Fatale—canceled with a text that just said, *Sorry, too much weirdness.* I rolled my eyes, but I did appreciate the honesty. So I left the "CLOSED" up and flicked on the overhead lights. Marlene Dietrich stared at me from half a dozen frames— smoky eyes perpetually aloof. I dropped my coat at a table below the image of Dietrich as Orson Welles' dark-haired fortune-teller in *Touch of Evil*, windswept by the water in the final scene, when she uttered the film's devastating final line: "What does it matter, what you say about people?"

"It seems to matter a lot these days," I said to her.

I retraced Jana's final steps. She'd come in, chatted with a few patrons, argued with Nell. Then, she must have walked over to the corner booth. Jana's half-empty coupe glass had still been on the table when paramedics arrived.

I studied the booth. The dark blue vinyl upholstery was scratched. There were scuff marks on the floor. But the vinyl in every booth was scratched, and every tile on the floor was scuffed. I half-regretted turning the lights on.

Next, I opened the supply closet, rummaging for any sign of something that could have struck Jana. The mop handles, a few battered brooms, boxes of napkins. Could a box of napkins be a murder weapon? I remembered tripping on one when the music had abruptly stopped on Thursday, and now I studied its placement in front of the shelving, almost like someone had been using it as a step stool. I stepped on it carefully and spotted a broken highball on the top shelf. Why would we stash a broken glass there? We usually toss them straight into the trash bin. I used a paper towel to pull it down. The bottom half of the glass was intact, but a jagged triangle was missing from the top. The heavy base of the glass had a smear of something dark on it. Could be anything—lipstick, grenadine.

Or blood.

Nell arrived mid-evening. Hair a messy tumble around her face. She looked more amped up than before, as though her desperation had metabolized into caffeine.

I locked the front door behind her. "I found something," I said, brandishing the plastic bag that held the cracked highball. "But this wouldn't have been Jana's—" I stopped as I suddenly realized what it all meant. The napkin box-step stool. Jana making a show of switching glasses. The threat to make Nell's life unpleasant. Randomly mentioning it to Casey the way she had. "Nell, I think Jana was trying to frame you."

But then we heard footsteps outside. A brisk knock. Detective Stevens strolled in, hands resting casually on her gun belt. "Evening," she said, eyeing the sign on the door. "You always closed on a Sunday night?"

"Inventory," I lied. I set the bag containing the glass down in the ice machine. I wanted to discuss it more with Nell before looping in the detective, so I willed her to leave.

Instead, she nodded at Nell. "Semi-good news for you. The coroner found no conclusive evidence that you directly caused Jana's injury. Doesn't mean you're off the hook, but it buys you time."

Nell looked visibly relieved. "You believe me?"

Stevens didn't confirm or deny but turned her attention to me.

"Em, mind if I take another look around?" Without waiting for an answer, Stevens did a lap about the bar, scanning up and down. Her gaze landed on a photo of Dietrich in a flowy, stripy shirt and white trousers, face half-shaded from the Riviera sun by a white hat—a photo taken by her lover Mercedes de Acosta in the mid-'30s. "You a big fan?"

I tried to muster a grin. "She's kind of our patron saint. The Blue Angel was named after the film."

"What film?"

I couldn't tell if she was being serious. "Um, *The Blue Angel.*"

Stevens scowled as she continued her circuit, eventually joining me behind the bar. Nell had barely breathed since the detective walked in, and now her eyes flicked ever so slightly down to the ice machine—a subtle movement that Stevens did not miss.

She peered into the cold depths of the ice machine. "What's this?" Nell and I exchanged glances.

Stevens reached in with a gloved hand and lifted the bag out, her eyebrows inching together. "This looks like—"

"Listen," I said quickly. "I think I know what happened."

"Really, now," Stevens said, still focused on the glass.

"Hear me out. I think if you test that, you're going to find Nell's prints, Jana's DNA, and some grenadine," I said. "From a tequila sunrise that Jana ordered when she first came in. The broken glass shard you found near the corner booth is probably a perfect match for the missing piece on this."

Stevens frowned. "What are you saying?"

"I think Jana's intention was to fake an injury and blame it on Nell—to punish her for turning Jana down over and over. We already know that she was obsessed and capable of going to extremes, based on her behavior towards Nell over the last few years. She made a cryptic comment to our DJ, Casey, to plant a seed of doubt. Nell, after Jana started making a fuss about the tequila sunrise, what happened to the glass you were going to use?"

Nell's eyes widened. "Oh my God. I don't know—I turned away to prep her gimlet instead, and I'm honestly not sure what happened to the glass. Why?"

"I think Jana grabbed it. Broke it. And then she stashed it just inside the office on the top of the shelving unit. Jana is—was—fairly short, so she used a box of cocktail napkins as a step stool."

Stevens frowned. "Where'd you get that idea?"

"Because I almost tripped on it that night when I ran out of the office to see what was happening. The glass was on the top shelf right above that. I have a feeling that Jana's fingerprints could be up there."

The detective looked interested now. "Okay, Miss Marple, what happened next?"

"Well," I said, feeling more confident in my theory the more I spoke it aloud, "I think she took that shard of glass over to the corner booth and was going to, I don't know, use it to give herself a minor injury, a cut on the arm or something, then insist that Nell had done it. But then I think she was more drunk than she realized, and she slipped on the floor. On the way down, she grabbed for something, anything, to regain her balance—the vinyl booth. There are scratches that look like fingernail marks. I bet that whatever's under her nails will be a match. But she couldn't catch herself and ended up hitting her head on the table. This was never supposed to happen."

"That's quite a story," Stevens said. "Conveniently, one that can't be proven."

"Well, I can't prove what was in her mind," I said, "but I think that if you look at the evidence, all the pieces that don't seem to add up, it all makes sense."

Nell's face was stony, but a tear rolled slowly down her cheek. The detective took the bag containing the broken highball and left without another word.

The details came to light gradually. The final report from the coroner suggested a blow to the head consistent with a fall. Her blood-alcohol level was sky high, and the only thing under her fingernails was a waxy dirt that matched the film on the ripped vinyl booth. Most convincingly, her fingerprints were found on the top of the shelving unit in the hallway leading to the back office where the broken highball had been found. We'll never know exactly what she intended, but the police consider the matter closed.

A week later, I was elbow-deep in spreadsheets again, marveling at the numbers I was seeing. After the initial slump after Jana's death, we suddenly got busier than ever—it turned out that Detective Stevens had written down everything I'd said in her little notebook, including the mention of Route 36. She looked into the place, finding evidence of a lot more illicit activity than just a dusting of cocaine, and shut the place down.

Nell popped into my doorway and knocked lightly. She looked less haunted. "Got a minute, Em?"

"Sure."

She held out a small, flat package wrapped in tissue paper. "This is for you."

Curiously, I took it from her. "Too thick to be a letter of resignation," I said.

Nell laughed. "No, you're stuck with me. I just—I wanted to thank you. For not assuming the worst about me. And for putting the pieces together the way you did. *Miss Marple.* And I realized that your office is the only place in the bar where you don't have a Marlene picture. Open it."

I tore open the end of the package and slid out a five-by-seven silver frame featuring a photo of Dietrich cozied up in a corner with Edith Piaf, a lifelong friend and one of her rumored lovers. Edith was grinning while Marlene tenderly held a palm to one cheek and kissed her on the other.

"Nell, I love it. Thank you so much." I pushed a few small, messy stacks of paper into one larger, messier stack to make space for it on my desk.

"I really like the way they're looking at each other," Nell said. "Affection, obviously, but more than that, it's trust. It's important to have someone like that. You know?" She cleared her throat. "That's all I wanted to say."

The intimacy in the photo stirred something in me—like Nell said, affection was part of it, but it was mostly trust. It wasn't easy to find that in this world. I flipped my computer closed. "Have a drink with me?" I said, and Nell smiled.

SNOW JOB

J.M. REDMANN

Bad, so bad.

It sounded easy, so easy when I took the job.

I'm from New Orleans. I'm looking at white frozen stuff falling from the sky. When I got on the plane, it had been sixty-eight degrees. Here, in Minneapolis, it was—I didn't want to know. What I did know was I was not properly dressed, even wearing the clothes that got me through the coldest of New Orleans weather—colder than that, and we didn't go out.

But I was being well paid to look into a long-ago murder. The police called it solved. Gay man hit on a straight man. Straight man protected himself. Gay man killed. As my client noted, "With twenty-three stab wounds." It had happened in the early '90s, the height of AIDS paranoia. Straight people were worried eating popcorn in a gay bar might infect them.

My client was his niece, Marielle Darden. She wanted justice for her uncle. I told her it was unlikely I would find much, with old age or a grave likely making justice impossible. She agreed but said, "I know. But he was my favorite uncle, always kind and generous to a nerdy girl. He made me feel special, not weird. My software company just got bought out; I'm richer than anyone should be. I want to do what I can for him."

She was wealthy, the case sounded interesting, and I forgot to check the weather.

I made the rookie mistake of stopping to stare at the snow. A woman who had not stopped bumped into me.

"Could be worse. At least it's not too cold to snow," she said.

I turned to see who had spoken—and keep the horror off my face that it could be too cold to snow.

A woman in my age range, middle of middle age. A face that balanced kind and shrewd. "You have checked luggage, right?" she asked. "With a real coat in it?"

I glanced down at my carry-on bag, my only bag. I managed to mumble, "Um, no, but this is a short trip."

She eyed my leather jacket, lined, mind you, barely making it to the top of my hips.

"Yeah, I know," I said, admitting the obvious. "Not quite prepared for it."

She shook her head, but it was bemused and kind.

"I'm Micky Knight," I said. "From New Orleans."

"Jane Lawless. From here."

"For real? One of my favorite mystery series is set here. Ellen Hart, the writer. You have the same name as her main character."

"Maybe this is a book," she answered.

"If it were a book, I could write in a warm coat."

"Maybe my writer is more prepared than yours is," she countered.

"Ask her to make a coat appear," I grumbled. "Between here and the rental car counter."

"I'll walk with you. Where are you headed?"

I told her a B&B near Once Upon a Crime, the bookstore. Books and crime-solving go together.

"I live not that far away. Lend you a coat for a ride." She motioned to follow her. "See, my writer figured it out for you."

I hurried after her. She wasn't quite my height of five-ten, but she walked with a purpose. "Ask if Ellen can help solve a thirty-year-old murder for me."

"If it's a book murder, probably. If it's a real one, well, life isn't always fair or kind."

As we walked, I told her about my case. Frederick Darden, Uncle Freddie, had moved up here for graduate school, and Marielle suspected, to get away from a family that wanted him to hide being gay—or pray it away. She visited one summer, and he took her to all the sites, lakes too cold for a Louisiana girl to swim in but fun to sunbathe and watch the people. "I have so many great memories of him," she said. She'd given me the few names she could find, friends who sent flowers to his funeral, one she could remember from that trip.

I had to cease talking to her to deal with the rental car desk. I had to argue against a "great upgrade" to a large SUV and insist on something smaller, maneuverable, and easy to park.

Jane gave me directions, more helpful than navigation, which seemed to think that suicidal left-hand turns were easy-peasy. As we drove, I told her my plan was to get the police record and talk to anyone I could locate. At best, I would find memories of Marielle's uncle and a few people who still knew him from back then. Maybe give her the name of the man who had killed him and what happened to the murderer, hoping for jail or some other karmic end.

The ride wasn't long; between me telling her about the case and her giving me directions, we were at her house in good speed.

"Come in," she said.

"You're inviting a stranger into your house?"

"You're Micky Knight from New Orleans. All the lesbian PIs know you. Have to honor the code and take care of you."

"Oh, right. I think I let my membership lapse."

She didn't answer, instead she motioned me inside. It was a cozy bungalow, wood floors that creaked with age. She pulled three coats from a hall closet. "Late fall, early winter, mid-winter," she said as she handed each of them to me. Pointing to the closet, she added, "also freezing rain, below zero, shoveling snow," for coats still hanging up.

I quickly settled in the gray early winter one.

She walked me back to the car.

"I might have a police contact," she said. "I'll call her and see if she can help." We exchanged our professional PI cards. Getting the police report would be a big help.

With a wave, she went back inside. I managed the five blocks to the B&B without getting lost. I checked in with the two way-too-cheery gay men who ran it. "Blueberry pancakes! Do you like blueberry pancakes? We have a stack every morning."

Professing my extreme love of blueberry pancakes got me past the chitchat and taken to my room.

It was late enough that people might be off work. Call from here? Or drive? If I were in New Orleans, I would do it in person. Phones lack body language and facial expression. But I was a stranger in a frozen city, and the room was warm. I waffled, then decided to call the name Marielle had given me: the man she remembered from that summer, Aaron Green.

"No, I don't want to buy anything," he answered.

"I'm not selling anything. Marielle Darden hired me to look into her Uncle Freddie's death. I'm a PI from New Orleans, Micky Knight."

Silence. I didn't fill it. He might have been Uncle Freddie's partner, and I was dredging up painful memories.

Finally, "Marielle. How is she?"

"Good. Happily married, two girls. Doing what she loves. Sold a software company she founded."

"She was such a fun kid. So smart. We had . . . hoped to have her up here every summer."

"You and Freddie were partners?" I asked, then added, "I'm a lesbian."

"Yes, we were. What the cops said happened, didn't happen," he said bitterly.

I made a decision. The snow seemed to have stopped. "Would you like to talk in person?" I suggested a coffee shop of his choice, but he asked me to his house.

The winter gods smiled on me. It was about twenty blocks from here. "Thank you for inviting me here," I said as he opened the door.

"If Marielle hired you, that's good enough for me," he said, ushering me in. He was in his mid-sixties, hair full silver, a trim man that time had been easy on. He offered coffee and freshly baked cookies, which I happily accepted. Lunch had been a not-great sandwich in the Nashville airport.

He placed a scrapbook beside my coffee.

"Freddie and I met over oranges at the supermarket. Friends, then more. He was compassionate, smart and had a wicked sense of humor. Handsome, with a great smile and a hint of the New Orleans accent."

I just nodded; no need to go into the dozens of New Orleans accents.

He and Freddie had been together about four years when Marielle visited. Aaron was introduced as a "close friend." He flipped through pages, pictures of them at Lake Harriet, downtown, eating ice cream, an ideal summer with the gay uncles.

Aaron closed those pages. "No way Freddie would have tried to pick up a straight man. Before treatment for HIV. We were both negative and wanted to keep it that way. Four other gay men were also killed, beaten, or stabbed. Like Freddie. Months between, so the cops never connected them."

"You think they were?"

"Lot of hate then. Gay men had brought the plague. Maybe the same people attacked Freddie, a group that acted out their anger and fear. But … the cops jumped to the usual assumptions, rough trade, or propositioned the wrong straight man."

"The man who killed Freddie? He claimed self-defense. His name must be in the record."

Aaron got up and paced across the room. "Smug bastard. He told the cops what they wanted to hear. They ruled it self-defense."

"Be nice if women could defend themselves that way."

He gave me a grim smile. "I will never forget the look on his face, full of himself, knowing he'd gotten away with murder."

"Do you know what happened to him?"

"No. Freddie was gone; he would get no justice. I had to close the door." Hearts break in so many ways, even the years can't repair the pain. The sorrow showed on Aaron's face.

I reached out and covered his hand with mine. "I think Marielle would love to hear from you. To know that Freddie was loved."

He blinked tears. "I'd like that."

He gave me a generous bag of cookies and asked me to let him know what I found.

I headed back to the B&B. It was dark, and lazy white flakes were again drifting down. I picked up a hamburger at a bar and grill nearby. Then on to internet searching.

Frederick Darden had been killed on September 21, 1991. The mainstream news parroted the police version, self-defense. The queer news told the real story—who Freddie was, a graduate student, in a relationship, gentle and kind. Everyone who knew him said he wouldn't pick up strange men and certainly not fight if they said no. He worked part-time at a bar near campus and was walking home late. The gay papers said it was likely he was attacked by gay bashers. A group heard the fight and rushed to help. Too late to save Freddie; he lost too much blood. They saw one man next to Freddie with the knife in his hand and several others running, but they couldn't say for sure they were involved. The man tried to run but tripped, and they caught him. When the police arrived, he told his story of a predatory gay man.

He claimed he was so scared that he didn't know how many times he had stabbed Freddie.

I stared at the screen and felt sadness for Marielle and Aaron.

The killer's name wasn't mentioned in the news articles; he was innocent, after all. But one of the gay papers had it, George Goren.

A fine upstanding citizen. Not. Jail time for a DUI about a year after Freddie's murder.

I then looked up the other killings of gay men around then. Same MO. Late at night, robbed, but the attacks were far more brutal than needed for a robbery. Likely, the attack was the point, the robbery to blur the motive.

They stopped around the time George went to jail.

But it was late; I was tired. I closed the computer and went to bed.

The next day, after the required pancakes, my next move was to get the police report. More to be thorough than that it would add anything except anger at how easily queer people's lives were thrown away.

I found the card from Jane Lawless. Call her? Or just go my own way? I'm a lone wolf. But she lent me her early winter coat, far better than me buying one I'd never wear again.

My phone rang. "Lawless. My contact is Songa Olofsson."

I wrote down the number. She blew off my thanks with a "stay warm."

I called, rehearsing the message I'd undoubtedly have to leave. Instead, I reached a real person. I got out my name before she cut me off.

"Yeah. Jane explained. I owe her a big favor. Can you be here in an hour? You have to look at the file here; I can't let you take it."

I agreed and found out where she was.

The police station was not close to the B&B, so it took me most of the hour to get lost a few times on my way there.

Songa was, as her name implied, a tall Nordic woman, strawberry blond hair in a hasty bun, shoulders that could push a plow or cuff a perp.

"You look cold," she said, motioning me to follow her.

Good detective work. I *was* cold. I followed her to a small interview room, the temperature of which did not inspire me to take off my coat.

She put a file on the table. "I'll check on you in a half hour. It's not long."

I nodded and thanked her, telling myself I had a stack of blueberry pancakes in my stomach to keep me warm.

It was a thin file for a murder. One man said it was self-defense; the other one was dead. Case closed. Despite the witnesses seeing other people running, the autopsy noted defensive wounds on Freddie and George himself admitting he hated gay people.

Songa was right on time, back in twenty-nine minutes.

"Any chance I could look at the arrest file of George Goren?" I asked. "The man that killed Freddie." Her expression was skeptical. To sway her, I added, "Several other gay men were killed around the same time. It stopped when he went to jail for a DUI."

Skepticism changed to interest. She motioned to follow her to her desk. She pulled up his file on her computer, letting me look over her shoulder. Brushes with the law of the libertarian variety—driving rules and public behavior, like where to urinate—didn't apply to him. The DUI he went to jail for was his third; he put two people in the hospital.

She scrolled down. "Last address we have. Be careful if you approach him."

I scribbled it down. "Oh, I'll be careful, all right." I thanked her and headed out into the brutal cold. A woman passed me wearing shorts. Heavy coat, but shorts.

I found a coffee shop and a quiet corner to warm up with a triple mocha latte.

Social media time. George liked to spew his vitriol online. He railed against health insurance companies, the socialist/fascist government, the police for not coming fast enough when someone sideswiped his car (was that slow socialist or corrupt fascism?), and, of course, everyone who wasn't straight, white, and male.

I had to fortify myself with a caramel chocolate latte halfway through, adding a toasted cheese sandwich to make it lunch. Disheartening to know people are void of facts and empathy and that they fill that void with hate and bigotry. But it told me who he was and what kind of careful I'd have to be.

Next stop was to acquire a few props on my way back to the B&B.

I texted Jane while waiting at the checkout, asking if she had any fun PI gadgets.

She responded while I was sitting in my car, staring at the map, trying to figure out how to get where I was going.

She said to come by her place and gave me directions.

At least it wasn't snowing. Only two wrong turns, and I was at her house.

I told her my plan. She cocked an eyebrow.

"I'll use a Southern accent; that should work."

The eyebrow remained cocked. "I'll go with you. Call 911 if it goes further south than your accent."

I ignored that. "Do you know someone named Cordelia?" In the books Jane Lawless had a best friend named Cordelia Thorn. I needed to reread them; they were so good.

"I do. Don't you?"

Yes, but I said, "I'm not in a book, even a good one by Ellen Hart."

"How can you be sure? Characters can be real, you know. The writer creates them, and the readers animate them. In some form, we are real. Come on, book or actual life, we need to catch a murderer."

Jane lent me her spare bathroom to put on my disguise. Pink and a little makeup would have to do.

It was late enough that George should be home.

Jame again raised an eyebrow at me when I appeared with a sparkly pink scarf wrapped around my neck. The coat would cover my pink sweater, and I needed to appear like a pink kind of girl at first glance. That included pink lipstick, which I last wore at Halloween two decades ago.

"We should take your rental because my Subaru has a rainbow sticker on it."

I agreed since I could depend on her for directions.

George lived out in the conservative suburbs; the kind of place I don't feel safe. His house was easy to spot, with leftover political signs showing his allegiance to being lied to.

We parked a few houses away. "Safe word?" Jane asked.

"New Orleans, of course," I answered.

"My hand will be on the phone." I nodded and got out.

George had more security than his modest house merited. Paranoid? Hiding something?

After a few moments of standing in front of his video doorbell, the door was flung open.

"Not buying nothing. What do you want?" he barked.

A much older man than the one I saw in the mugshot stood before me. The years hadn't been kind to George. I knew he was in his late fifties, but he looked ten years older. Scraggly white hair, thin on top and in need of a cut, eyes that wrinkled from squinting and frowning, no smile hidden in them, a stomach that stretched his stained Vikings sweatshirt, a clash of purple and ketchup.

"Not selling anything," I chirped in a higher-than-normal voice. "I'm Michele Winter," I said, handing him a card from a stack I kept for times like this. It was bland, listing me as a consultant. "I'm with the Patriot's Patriot People, and we've noticed you online. You seem to be doing some mighty fine work."

His face went from belligerent to confused to a half-smile. "You're what?" he said.

"Michele, from the Patriot's Patriot People. You were nominated in the Upper Midwest division for your online promotion of our cause."

Confused and belligerent warred with interest on his face.

"Never heard of you."

"We are only a few years old, to be honest. We're doing our part to promote patriot messaging, like yours, to keep the country safe from filthy immigrants, the dirty gays, man-hating feminists and—" I paused because this is not my natural language.

"Yeah, all of them! Plus, idiot wokes, Jew globalists, all the trans trash—"

I interrupted, "May I come in? It's kind of cold out here," I said. "I love your lawn signs," I added. "And as a present, I brought this." I pulled out a bottle of bourbon. I remembered to give him a pink lip-sticked smile just in time.

That got a smirk from him. The kind little children would run from. Dental work had been neglected.

He gave me a once-over. I wasn't a cute blond but a woman with sparkly pink on and a hint of a Southern accent. I stooped my shoulders enough that I wasn't taller than him.

"Who nominated me?" he asked, still keeping me out in the cold.

"Can't say; wouldn't be fair. Just know you've really impressed some people."

Another one of those smiles you don't want to see on a dark street at night. He stepped aside to let me in. I unzipped my coat but kept it on, though the house was overheated. In case I had to leave in a hurry. I pulled out a recorder and asked if I could tape our talk, claiming it was for our podcast, adding that if he was the winner, he would get five thousand dollars.

As I had suspected, George liked flattery. Most people do, but he fell for it: hook, line, whole fishing rod, and boat. I told him I liked his "Don't Tread on Me" rattlesnake biting the gay-woke flag poster. (Had to remind myself not to call it the Pride flag.) I politely listened to his views on people like me—"shoot all the queers"—along with his take on science—"vaccines kill you"—and all the things he was expert on, despite only barely graduating high school.

George also liked bourbon. He had opened the bottle immediately and politely offered me some. I turned it down like a lady should. He kept refilling his glass.

The bourbon loosened his inhibitions, both verbally and nonverbally.

He put his hand on my knee. I playfully swatted it away like a good Southern girl. "I got to get through this interview, or my bosses will be mad."

He took another swig of bourbon and launched into another rant about immigrants.

When he finished, he scooted closer to me on the couch. "I've done a whole lot to make the world a better place," he bragged. After another gulp of bourbon, he said, "Turn that thing off, and I'll tell you what I've really done."

I did as he asked, edging away from him.

"Got rid of some fags." Said with a smile that made his previous ones look happy-clappy.

"Really? That was brave of you." So hard to keep my face neutral.

"We were real brave. Got away with it mostly. Caught once but told the cops I had to defend myself. They let me off. Took pictures of all but that one." He got up before I could stop him. He went to a closet under the staircase and, after a bit of digging, came out with an old cookie tin. He set it on the coffee table, almost knocking over the bourbon. Sitting closer to me.

"Thank you, sir. I agree it was a virtuous thing. But I'm not good at looking at those kinds of pictures." I stood up. "It's been fascinating to talk to you! I really appreciate it. You were so interesting; time has flown, and I must report back to my bosses."

He grabbed my sparkly pink scarf and yanked me back down.

"I don't show this to anyone," he said, the bargain clear in his voice.

"I'm working," I said. "This is Minneapolis, not New Orleans."

He tightened his grip on the scarf. "We can be quick."

I tried to pull away, but moving back only tightened the scarf. Bad, so bad, worse than the falling frozen stuff. I could smell the bourbon and the need for dental work on his breath.

A pounding on the door, with an authoritative, "Open up. FBI."

He stared at me.

From outside, "We know you're in there, Michele Winter! Open up now, or we break the door down."

He glared at me, then the door.

I managed to yank the scarf out of his hands and ran for the door. "Don't open it!" he yelled.

I ignored him.

Jane was standing there, wearing aviator sunglasses, even though it was dark. She waved something that could be a badge—probably her PI license. I knew the tricks.

"Michele Winter, you are being extradited back to New Orleans," she said in an ominous tone. "Harvesting alligators out of season is illegal. Come with me."

Jane grabbed me roughly by the arms and pretended to drag me down the stairs. She didn't need to; I was moving as fast as I could, trying to not gag. For once, the cold air helped.

Jane hustled me to the car and jumped in the driver's seat. "I was worried about you; that took a long time," she said as I got in.

"I was worried about me, too," I said. "Get us out of here."

She pulled away.

I snatched the scarf off. "You got it all on tape, right?"

"Loud and clear, so much easier to wear a wire in the winter." She had some pretty sweet PI gear. If George managed to grope me, he would have found the wire. If this was a story, Jane clearly had the better author; mine left me being strangled by a smelly drunk.

I called Songa. She asked us to come to the station.

When we arrived, she listened to the recording from the wire. "Legal enough for us to get a search warrant. Photos would be major evidence."

I described the cookie tin, "Bright red, big square, snowflakes on it, a dent on one side." Songa told us she'd be in touch, and we left.

After dropping Jane off, the only thing I did before crawling into bed was book my plane back to New Orleans. I could wait for the results in warmth.

Songa called in the morning. They had found the pictures. George was arrested.

I swung back by Jane's place to return her coat. It had probably saved my life—at least my fingers from freezing and falling off.

"Which author gets credit for this?" I asked as I handed it to her.

She laughed. "Let the reader decide." Then added, "Maybe this is real life, and if you don't hurry, you'll miss your plane. A blizzard is coming."

I gave her a hug and glanced at my watch. She was right. If I had an author, she wasn't great about making sure things like getting through security lines weren't a slow pain.

I turned for one final wave, a last view of her kind and shrewd smile.

I made it with minutes to spare, only to find my plane was delayed. If this was a book, I wanted to fire my author. With two extra hours to kill, I downloaded several Ellen Hart books. Time to reread them. See if her description of Jane matched the woman I'd met.

AFTERWORD

KATHERINE V. FORREST

These tributes to LGBTQ icons, brought to us by many of today's mystery writing icons, vary so widely in theme and life experience, with settings ranging from the repressive darkness of 1929 to our present day, that the question suggests itself: what contrasts in the genre between back then and now?

Woven into the mystery heart of these stories is greater visibility and affirmation of our lives, and positivity. Since gay marriage has not, as prophesied, visited Armageddon on the civilized world, and the behavioral sciences continue to consign to the garbage heap any categorization of LGBTQ people as unnatural, perverted, or child molesters, generalized prejudice against LGBTQ people has lost some traction and momentum in recent decades—a huge benefit of our coming out and our expanding LGBTQ visibility through the arts and on social media.

But, as shown in the stories, we have by no means achieved equality. Still, not equality. The quicksand of prejudice lies unchanged under the entire span of decades. The stories confirm the unrelenting denial of the legitimacy of our existence, expressed in the same bullying and brutal behaviors, the same physical and emotional persecution. What's also negatively, poisonously new in this day and age is that the advances in technology bringing us closer together as a community have added their own opportunities to spread disinformation, distortion, propaganda and false news around every aspect of our existence.

The stories surely illuminate a fundamental driver behind the resistance to any sexual and gender divergence, much less transition or gender neutrality. In today's mainstream culture, a woman may have "advanced" to where she can flaunt suits and ties, our transgression into traditional male attire tolerated with scant or muted murmurs of protest. But if a male dons a dress? Revulsion, ridicule, hostility, and a rage that far too often extends to the homicidal. Why? *WHY* so visceral and specific a response to a gender variation that harms no one?

That answer is conclusive, as vividly demonstrated by our transgender authors. The rabid determination to render these lives invalid exposes the very root of homophobia: misogyny and toxic masculinity. The pervasive, culturally ingrained, set-in-concrete male view of the feminine as inferior, limited, lesser in every way. Reinforced by paternalistic religious doctrine and with allies in white supremacy.

Transgender visibility is today's target of convenience under a false flag, the true goal being, as ever, the demolishing of an ideal of a democratic society: aspiration to diversity, equality and inclusion.

Our books are especially dangerous, having raised alarm bells with their capacity to open minds and expose prejudice with their revealing, authentic depictions of LGBTQ lives. An array of weaponry has been brought to bear on us: censorship and scare tactics over any manifestation of difference, along with gender cant, religious cant, and all the distortions, slurs and catch phrases too familiar to us all.

Crime Ink: Iconic, in its honoring of those who blazed trails for us, is a significant and signal achievement. This tribute to our LGBTQ icons is in itself a continuation of the mystery fiction which has always been at the forefront of our path to visibility. From its very origins—M.F. Beale's 1977 classic *Angel Dance*, the pioneering, classic 1970s Dave Brandstetter mysteries of the great Joseph Hansen, Barbara Wilson's 1984 *Murder in the Collective*, the decades-ranging mystery fiction of Sandra Scoppettone, the 1980s Valentine and Lovelace novels of Nathan Aldyne—these pioneering, groundbreaking mysteries and authors brought us our first images of lesbians and gays who defied stereotypes, exposed the irrationalities and injustice of the dominant culture. Their early depictions of lesbians and gay men of principle and agency pushing back against a lethally unwelcome world bequeathed to us the example of their courage, their idealism in calling for fairness and justice—a justice to be always fought for, even if not always won.

Our books, our stories, have elbowed their way into mainstream American literature with nationally known and acclaimed authors.

Our mystery novels lay claim to the worth and rightness and dignity of our lives, and this historic collection of writing icons honoring cultural icons will now take its place among the LGBTQ books on the front lines, soldiers arrayed against censorship and prejudice.

We're here. Living our lives in every permutation of gender. Defiantly visible and united, in our lives and in our books. In all our diversity, equality, and inclusion under the radiance of our rainbow flag.

CONTRIBUTORS

CHRISTA FAUST writes original novels, as well as comics, novelizations, and media tie-ins. Faust won the 2009 Crimespree Award (Best Original Paperback) for *Money Shot*. *Money Shot* also received nominations for Best Paperback Original from the Edgar Awards, Anthony Awards, and Barry Awards. She has worked in the Times Square peep booths, as a professional dominatrix, and in the adult film industry both behind and in front of the cameras.

Why James Whale?

"Bride of Frankenstein is one of my all-time favorite classic monster movies and its sly, deliciously queer subtext felt like a secret message from filmmaker James Whale to the little teenage monster that I was. Whale lived openly as a gay man in an era when few others could and died by suicide just as the House Un-American Activities Committee (HUAC), the Blacklist, and other powerful cultural forces started cracking down on anyone who didn't fit in. Sound familiar? It did to me too, which is why I chose him as my icon and why I needed to write this story right now."

ANNE LAUGHLIN'S novels have won four Goldie Awards and been nominated three times for Lambda Literary Awards. She is the 2022 recipient of the Alice B Medal for her body of work and is a two-time Lambda Fellow. Anne is currently a board member of Mystery Writers of America and a member of the Queer Crime Writers Association. She reviews books for the *Gay & Lesbian Review*. After seven contemporary crime novels, Anne is finishing work on a historical thriller set in pre-war Germany. In her spare time, she teaches adults to read at Literacy Chicago.

Why Vita Sackville-West

"I have long been fascinated by the life of Vita Sackville-West, the aristocratic author, master gardener, diplomatic wife, raconteur, lover of Virginia Woolf and many, many other women. For me, she represents boldness and supreme self-confidence. She chose to live as her authentic self in the early part of the twentieth century, when that was virtually unheard of for queer people. She dressed as a man and would go away for weekends with her lover, pretending to be husband and wife. She was an inspiration."

CHERYL A. HEAD'S writing always includes diverse characters and explores themes of racism, human rights, and justice. Her award-winning Charlie Mack Motown Mysteries, whose female PI protagonist is queer and Black, was featured this year on the game show *Jeopardy!* Head's 2023 crime fiction novel, *Time's Undoing*, was shortlisted for the *Los Angeles Times* Book Award, the Hurston Wright Legacy Award, and the Anthony Award. Head was named to the Saints & Sinners LGBTQ+ Literary Festival Hall of Fame in 2019 and is a 2022 recipient of the Alice B Award for her body of work.

Why James Baldwin?

"James Baldwin is one of the most enduring intellects of the twentieth century. Black, gay, complex and brilliant, one cannot consider queer icons without his inclusion. In my story I wanted to explore Baldwin's acuity in navigating the competing challenges of his blackness, queerness, and literary celebrity. I wish he were alive today to help us make sense of America's renewed chaos."

CHRISTOPHER BOLLEN is the author of six literary thriller novels, including *Havoc, The Lost Americans,* and *A Beautiful Crime.* He writes for a number of publications including the *New York Times, Vanity Fair,* and *Interview Magazine.* He lives in New York City.

Why Elton John?

"I wanted to write a story about unexpected visitors set in Venice, and several years back I visited Elton John's apartment on the tip of Giudecca when a friend was staying there as a guest. Although Elton John was not at home, I was still the unexpected and perhaps unwanted visitor. I may not be a big fan in Elton John's taste in art, but I loved his music from a very young age. He may well have been the first openly gay musician to find my ears, and certainly he was one of the few figures at that time whose queer flamboyance was so happily embraced by the mainstream. I also wanted to sneak in a tribute to the song 'Daniel,' which played on the radio when I was on my way, at 15, to my friend's funeral (he'd killed himself). Songs become emotional portals to the dead, and whenever I hear 'Daniel,' I instantly think of Mike."

RENEE JAMES' novels and screenplays have been honored in a variety of competitions as finalists and medal winners. Her short stories have appeared in four anthologies, including the 2022 Mystery Writers Association collection, *Crime Hits Home*. She has also edited several developmental anthologies for Off Campus Writers Workshop, including the 2023 release, *Meaningful Conflicts*. Her novels include the Bobbi Logan trilogy and the Publishing Triangle Ferro-Grumley finalist, *BeatNikki's Café*—all of which depict the life and times of a transgender women in Chicago.

Why Laverne Cox?

"Laverne Cox was the inspiration for the heroine in my story, 'These Truths,' because I wanted Sydney to be a modern transgender woman, someone poised, intelligent and successful, someone who came of age in that moment of American history when trans people were sometimes encouraged to become whole people."

KATHERINE V. FORREST'S awards and honors include five Lambda Literary Awards and the Pioneer Award from Lambda Literary, the Lifetime Achievement Award from the Publishing Triangle, the Trailblazer Award from the lesbian community's Golden Crown Literary Society. Her seventeen works of fiction include the enduring lesbian classic *Curious Wine*, and the celebrated Kate Delafield mystery series which features the first lesbian police professional to appear in American literature.

Why Dickinson, Whitman, and Bannon?

"Emily Dickinson, Walt Whitman, Ann Bannon—iconic indeed. Lines from Dickinson's timeless, heart-piercing poetry provide lyrical counterpoint for my story of first discovery in the novel that launched my writing career, *Curious Wine*. *Leaves of Grass* by Walt Whitman was an oasis in the desert for many generations of us, especially my gay brothers. And Ann Bannon—her books saved my life. Those five pioneering novels of hers, set mainly in Greenwich Village in the late 1950, were life-giving and essential to countless numbers of us, and will always remain concrete-foundational in lesbian literature."

MEREDITH DOENCH is the award-winning author of the Luce Hansen Thriller series. Doench's works of short fiction and nonfiction have appeared in literary journals such as *Hayden's Ferry Review*, *Women's Studies Quarterly*, and *The Tahoma Literary Review*. She currently serves on the board of Mystery Writers of America, Midwest Chapter. She is a senior lecturer of creative writing, literature, and composition at the University of Dayton in Ohio.

Why WNBA stars?

"In a parallel universe, I'm a starter on a WNBA team alongside some of the league's original players: Sue Bird, Sheryl Swoopes, Rebecca Lobo, and Diana Taurasi. This level of ball is all about rivalry, athleticism, and whole-hearted devotion to the game, and my story explores what happens to elite players after they've given every ounce of themselves to the sport and still it's not enough."

JEFFREY MARKS is a freelance writer and interviewer whose work has been published in *The Armchair Detective*, *Mystery Scene*, *Mystery Readers Journal*, and other magazines devoted to crime fiction. His own short stories have appeared in *Kracked Mirror Mysteries* and other periodicals. He is a member of Mystery Writers of America and Sisters in Crime.

Why C. Auguste Dupin and Ellery Queen?

"The Great Detectives of Mystery, like Poe's C. Auguste Dupin, have always been queer-coded. Indeed, Dashiell Hammett once asked the two men who conceived Ellery Queen to explain their character's sex life. When I look back at all the mysteries I read as a teen, they were my icons."

MARGOT DOUAIHY is the author of the Sister Holiday Mysteries published by Gillian Flynn Books/Zando. She is the recipient the Publishing Triangle's Joseph Hansen LGBTQ Crime Writing Award, the Saints & Sinners Emerging Artist Award, The Pinckley Prize for Crime Fiction, and *Boston Magazine's* 2023 Best Author Award.

Why Radclyffe Hall?

"'High Hit Area' is a lyrical Maine noir about the dangerous allure of traps. Influenced by the tensile and trenchant novel *The Unlit Lamp* by Radclyffe Hall, I wanted to write a lesbian crime story that triangulates unmet potential, lust, (dis)trust, set in an isolated place where desperation and desire leave the same tracks in the snow."

DIANA DIGANGI is the author of the award-winning novel, *Last Chance Chicago*. She holds both bachelor's and master's in journalism from Virginia Commonwealth University, where she started her journalism career in television news, then returned to the D.C. area to pursue her career as an investigative journalist.

Why Sally Ride?

"While brainstorming, I asked my girlfriend—an astronomer at Hubble—to name a queer icon, and she suggested Sally Ride. Once she did, the idea of an all-female space voyage named in her honor occurred to me, and the themes of treachery, frontierism, and runaway technology (all already on my mind) quickly helped flesh out the concept."

KATRINA CARRASCO is the author of *The Best Bad Things*, which won a Shamus Award and was a finalist for a Washington State Book

Award and a Lambda Literary Award. Her short fiction and essays have appeared in journals and outlets including *Witness, Post Road,* and *Literary Hub.* She was a Yaddo fellow and has received support from Jentel Arts, Blue Mountain Center, Lighthouse Works, Artist Trust, and other residencies and foundations. She lives in Seattle.

Why George Michael?

"I adore George Michael and his music. My story called for a recognizable sound (that would also add humor in the moment), and the saxophone riff from 'Careless Whisper' was a perfect fit. It brings a little light to the dark world of the story. Love you, George."

JOHN COPENHAVER is an award-winning author whose latest novel, *Hall of Mirrors,* was named a *New York Times* Crime Novel of the Year. His debut, *Dodging and Burning,* won the Macavity Award, and *The Savage Kind* earned the Lambda Literary Award. A founding member of Queer Crime Writers, he teaches at Virginia Commonwealth University, mentors in the University of Nebraska MFA program, and lives in Richmond, VA, with his husband, artist Jeffery Paul Herrity.

Why Truman Capote?

"Truman Capote has long been an inspiration to me, and *In Cold Blood* is one of my favorite books—not just for its true crime narrative, but for its deeper exploration of how men can incite violence in one another and the fragility of masculinity, which Capote perceived so clearly. In my story, I wanted to explore a similar dynamic: how patriarchal institutions render male friendships fraught, painful, and potentially violent."

ANN MCMAN is the two-time Lambda Literary Award-winning author of fourteen novels and two short story collections. She has won numerous Independent Publisher (IPPY), *Foreword Reviews* INDIES, and Golden Crown Literary Society medals and awards, and she is a laureate of the Alice B Foundation for her outstanding body of work. She divides her time between Winston-Salem, North Carolina, and Grand Isle, Vermont.

Why Dolly Parton?

"During a visit to the legendary Jugtown Pottery in rural North Carolina, I discovered a beautiful hand-thrown grave marker that bore the inscription, 'Find out who you are, then do it on purpose.' It was a perfect summation of my own life's journey to self-understanding and self-acceptance. The words had been spoken by Dolly Parton, who has always been an ally and advocate for the LGBTQ+ community. Dolly also never forgot her humble roots—and she set upon a path to use her considerable means to inspire a love of reading in *all* young children, including the queer ones. Dolly's Imagination Library delivers, for free, more than 28 million books a year. She is, in one word, *iconic.*"

GREG HERREN is a writer and editor, who publishes work in a variety of genres, including mystery novels, young adult literature, and erotica. He publishes work both as Greg Herren and under the pseudonym Todd Gregory. He lives in New Orleans, where he also works as an HIV/AIDS counselor and educator. He is also a co-founder of the Saints and Sinners Literary Festival.

Why Tennessee Williams?

"Tennessee Williams is indirectly responsible for my career. The Tennessee Williams and the New Orleans Literary Festival exposed me to great writers, master classes, and eventual publication. The table is there, too."

KELLY J. FORD is the Anthony-nominated author of *Real Bad Things*, *Cottonmouths*, a *Los Angeles Review* Best Book of 2017, and *The Hunt*. An Arkansas native, Kelly writes crime fiction set in the Ozarks and Arkansas River Valley.

Why Langston Hughes?

"The price of admission for having childhood friends in the Bible Belt was that I had to get saved because many parents believed I was going to Hell—not for my sexuality but because I was a feral girl who lacked parental guidance. Despite fan-girling Jesus before the age of five, the first time I felt any type of belonging related to spirituality was not in church but through a Langston Hughes poem. This story is an ode to those feelings, filtered through my heathen heart."

STEPHANIE GAYLE is the Pushcart Prize-nominated author of *Idyll Threats*, *Idyll Fears*, and *Idyll Hands*. Her first novel, *My Summer of Southern Discomfort*, was chosen as one of *Redbook's* Top Ten Summer Reads and was a *Book Sense* monthly pick. She's a former president of Sisters in Crime and a member of Queer Crime Writers.

Why Babadook?

"The horror movie monster, the Babadook, began its tenure as queer icon as an online joke (Babadook created a popup book just to create drama!) but queer folk also saw themselves in the maligned monster, consigned to a basement for not conforming. And truly, what's more queer than claiming a misunderstood being and celebrating it, and adopting it as a symbol of the LGBTQIA+ community?"

JEFFREY ROUND'S seven-volume Dan Sharp mysteries won a Lambda Literary Award. *Bon Ton Roulet*, the fourth volume in his other queer mystery series, Bradford Fairfax, got him invited to read at the 300th anniversary of the founding of New Orleans alongside then-mayor Mitch Landrieu. He is also an award-winning filmmaker and songwriter. His latest book is *The English Tutor* from Rebel Satori Press.

Why James Dean and Wilfred Owen?

"I became obsessed with James Dean on seeing *Rebel Without a Cause* when I was seventeen. I have travelled to his birthplace, death site, and other locations associated with him, and wrote a series of poems about him published in my collection *Threads*. The World War I war poet Wilfred Owen haunts me for the same reason, as the personification of talented youth cut down too soon."

MIA P. MANANSALA is a writer from Chicago who loves books, baking, and bad-ass women. She is the author of the multi-award-winning Tita Rosie's Kitchen Mystery series and the YA novel *Death* *in the Cards*. She uses humor (and murder) to explore aspects of the Filipino diaspora, queerness, and her millennial love for pop culture.

Why Geena Rocero?

"Filipina queen Geena Rocero is a trans activist, model, beauty pageant winner, and so much more, and I think the world needs to know about her. Her memoir, *Horse Barbie*, was such an entertaining and enlightening read that I knew I had to create a story around chapter one's opening line."

ROBYN GIGL is the author of four novels featuring Erin McCabe, a transgender criminal defense attorney. *Time* magazine selected her novel, *Survivor's Guilt*, as one of the 100 best Mystery/Thriller books of All Time. It was also named as one of the best crime novels of 2022 by the *New York Times*, received a starred review from *Publishers Weekly*, and won the Publishing Triangle's Joseph Hansen Award for LGBTQ+ Crime Writing. Her fourth novel, *Nothing But the Truth*, was selected by the *New York Times* as one of the best crime novels of 2024.

Why Christine Jorgensen?

"When I was growing up in the 1950s and '60s, Christine Jorgensen was one of the few out and open trans people. At a time when information on being transgender was impossible to find, her visibility let me know that I was not the only person who felt the way I did. She was a beacon of hope to a generation of trans people."

BAXTER CLARE TRAUTMAN is the author of the Lambda Literary finalist L.A. Franco mystery series. She also wrote the award-winning *The River Within*, and *Spirit of the Valley*, a natural history of California oak woodlands. A practicing wildlife biologist, she lives in central California with her wife.

Why Queer Literary Giants?

"Katherine V. Forrest. Lee Lynch. Joseph Hansen. May Sarton. Forster. Rita Mae Brown. Aside from being my personal favorites, what stands out to me, as with so many other queer writers, is their sheer gutsiness.

In a time when being anything other than straight was considered deviant, satanic, criminal, these writers had the guts and audacity to speak for all of us. They brought hope and comfort into dark closets, boldly giving us the courage to speak, to fight for our love. And eventually, to be brave enough to continue in their giant footsteps."

MARCO CAROCARI grew up in Switzerland, where he worked in a hardware store, traveled the globe working for the airlines and later as an internationally published photographer, and frequently jobbed as a waiter, hotel receptionist, or manager of a professional photo studio. In 2016 he swapped snow-capped mountains, lakes, and lush, green pastures for the charm of the dry California desert, where he lives. His debut novel, *Blackout*, was nominated for a Lefty and won The NYC Big Book Award and Independent Press Award for Best LGBTQ Novel. His short stories appeared in *Malice Domestic: Mystery Most Diabolical* and the Saints and Sinners New Fiction from the Festival anthologies.

Why the Queer Icons of NYC in the '70s and '80s?

"When prompted with a clear, single task, my mind usually bursts into a million directions simultaneously—which is likely how we ended up with my contribution (and it sounds much better than saying I couldn't make up my mind). Loosely inspired by *All About Eve* and the pitfalls of fame at any cost, I approached the theme more broadly, mixing iconic eras (the '70s and '80's in New York City) with iconic characters and the iconic places they frequented (Studio 54 and CBGB)."

DAVID S. PEDERSON has written multiple mysteries, all featuring LGBTQ+ characters. He's a two-time finalist for the Lambda Literary Award for Gay Mysteries. His second book, *Death Goes Overboard*, was selected by the GLBT Round Table of the American Library Association for the 2018 Over the Rainbow book list. Two of his poems, "My Candle" and "I Never Knew," were used in the 2024 OCTC stage production of "Love Notes Cabaret of Words & Music." He's passionate about mysteries, old movies, ocean liners, and reading.

Why Oscar Wilde?

"Oscar Wilde was ahead of his time: flamboyant, witty, and quite clever. In my short mystery, as in many of my novels, I strive to remind people of his brilliance as a poet, author, and playwright, and to show how pertinent his quotes are, even today, by weaving them into my narratives."

PENNY MICKELBURY is an African American playwright, short story writer, mystery series writer, and historical novelist who worked as a print and television journalist before retiring to focus on her creative writing. As a member of the *Washington Post* Metro Seven, she was inducted into the National Association of Black Journalists' Hall of Fame. She is the recipient of the Alice B Medal for lifetime achievement. In 2025 she was awarded the Golden Crown Literary Society's Trailblazer Award for her contributions to the advancement of lesbian literature.

Why Lorainne Hansberry?

"My mother was the librarian at Spelman College, and I got to hang out on campus growing up. Naturally my favorite refuge was the library, but the Drama Department was a close second. I loved watching rehearsals, but I lived for the magic of opening nights. When I later learned about Lorraine Hansberry and her magnificent accomplishments I set my feet upon that path. And when I learned she liked girls? Well, writing novels became my life's work, but Ms. Hansberry set my heart's dreams on having a play produced."

ANN APTAKER'S Cantor Gold Crime series has been the recipient of Lambda Literary and Golden Crown Literary Society's Goldie Awards. Her short stories have appeared in the anthologies *Fedora, Mickey Finn: 21st Century Noir, Private Dicks & Disco Balls, Scattered, Smothered, Covered & Chunked, Our Happy Hours: LGBT Voices from the Gay Bars, Switchblade Magazine, Black Cat Mystery Magazine*, the *Guns & Tacos* novella series, and the online zine *Punk Soul Poet*.

Why Billy Strayhorn?

"The first time I heard composer/lyricist Billy Strayhorn's 'Lush Life' years ago, I'd just emerged from a broken love affair. Strayhorn's haunting, plaintive tune and wistful lyrics, full of barely disguised queer hurt, has stayed in my heart and soul ever since, as has the memory of the woman I lost."

KRISTEN LEPIONKA is the author of the award-winning Roxane Weary mystery series. The first installment, *The Last Place You Look*, won a Shamus Award and was nominated for Anthony and Macavity Awards. Its follow-up, *What You Want to See*, won Shamus and Goldie Awards. Kristen's work has been selected twice for *Best American Mystery & Suspense*. She lives in Columbus, Ohio with her wife and two cats.

Why Marlene Dietrich?

"I chose Marlene Dietrich as my icon in 'Lipstick, Grenadine, or Blood' because she embodied mystery and defiance—glamorous, sharp-witted, and unapologetically herself in a time when women, especially queer women, weren't allowed that freedom. Her gender fluidity, command of the screen, and refusal to conform have captivated me forever, and when I was invited to write something for this anthology, I knew right away who my muse would be. Marlene was iconic, subversive, and always in control of the room, whether she's the one being watched or the one doing the watching (as she is on the walls of the bar in my story)."

J.M. REDMANN has published twelve novels featuring New Orleans PI Micky Knight. Her first was published in 1990, one of the early hard-boiled lesbian detectives. Her books have won multiple awards, including three Lambda Literary awards, two Golden Crown Literary Society awards, and the Publishing Triangle's Joseph Hansen Award for LGBTQ Crime Writing. Her third book, *The Intersection of Law and Desire*, originally published by W. W. Norton, was an Editor's Choice of the *San Francisco Chronicle* and a recommended book of NPR's *Fresh Air*.

Why Ellen Hart?

"Once we were outlaws. Two women having sex? Illegal. Equal rights for queers? Forget the back burner, not even in the kitchen. Despite, or perhaps because of, being an outlaw, Ellen Hart decided to write a mystery, one where the protagonist was a lesbian—the outlaw deciding what was justice. She, along with Katherine V. Forest, Barbara Wilson, and others, dared to claim space not ceded to us—to be the hero, to be the ones who decide right and wrong, innocence and guilt. Ellen Hart inspired me to start putting words on a page, as she has inspired, taught, listened to, and supported so many of us."

ELLEN HART is the award-winning author of the Jane Lawless and Sophie Greenway series. She is an inductee of the Saints and Sinners Hall of Fame and was awarded the Golden Crown Literary Society's Trailblazer Award. She is the recipient of six Lambda Literary Awards, and was named Grandmaster by the Mystery Writers of America.

Why This Anthology?

"I've always known that being awarded certain honors came because I was a token, that I was helping those groups redress years of ignoring lots of fine writers. Still, it was something. Not that it opened every door for everyone, but hopefully it cracked a few in the mainstream world—whatever that is today. There are still lots of monoliths out there that need their doors cracked, if not outright kicked in. This anthology is doing that."

SALEM WEST is the publisher and executive editor of Bywater Books and its Amble Press imprint. She was a Lambda Literary Award finalist in 2014 and later became a trustee of Lambda Literary. A vocal opponent of book bans and censorship of LGBTQ+ and BIPOC literature, she continues to use her voice to champion First Amendment rights.

Why These Crime Writers?

"Every single writer in this collection is essential and at the top of their game—some have just risen, and some have been holding strong for the span of their careers. It's a lifetime opportunity to work with them on this volume that stands in defiance to the prejudice and status quo of the crime-writing world."

ACKNOWLEDGMENTS

We would like to express our heartfelt gratitude to the authors and supporters of this anthology.

Special thanks are due to Ann McMan for her stunning cover art, and to Carleen Spry and Paula Martinac for their invaluable editorial support.

A deep appreciation is also extended to the membership of Queer Crime Writers, and to Marianne K. Martin, and Christel Cogneau for their unwavering support of the project through Bywater Books.

Also, our sincere thanks go out to the early readers and endorsers whose feedback and encouragement helped bring this anthology to life.

**The 2024 Foreword INDIES Publisher of the Year award
was presented to Bywater Books for its twenty years
of ushering in the "coming of age of queer literature."**

"In a year when LGBTQ+ communities faced renewed attacks and the names of DEI efforts were sullied by those in power, Bywater remained firm in its commitment to publishing titles that celebrate queer existence and that embrace diversity. Their world-widening books make us laugh, make us cry, and stand as enduring testaments to the breadth of love and the human experience."

—*Foreword Reviews*

Bywater Books believes that all people have the right to read or not read what they want—and that we are all entitled to make those choices ourselves. But to ensure these freedoms, books and information must remain accessible. Any effort to eliminate or restrict these rights stands in opposition to freedom of choice.

Please join us by opposing book bans and censorship of the LGBTQ+ and BIPOC communities.

At Bywater Books, we are all stories.

For more information about Bywater Books, our publishing mission, authors, and our titles, please visit our website.

https://bywaterbooks.com